FATAL WHISPERS

A Megan Scott/Michael Elliott Mystery

SANDRA NIKOLAI

Vemcort Publishing
ISBN: 978-0-9880389-3-6

Layout and design by Carolyn Nikolai
www.carolynnikolai.com

This novel is dedicated to my sister Norma who laughed, cried, and shared a lifetime of memories with me.

CHAPTER 1

There were times when I wished I could change the future. This was one of them. The cheerful family atmosphere around the kitchen table obscured the sequence of ominous events about to unfold, and I couldn't do a thing about it.

"Who's ready for a second serving?" My cousin Bianca smiled with pride as she carried a plate of pancakes to the table.

"Me." Four-year-old Alex held a fork tightly in his little hand.

"Son, don't forget to say please," Victor whispered to the toddler sitting beside him.

"Please," Alex said, giggling.

"How about you, Michael?" Bianca asked the new man in my life.

"Please," he said, prompting Alex to giggle. "Please, please." More giggles from Alex.

While Bianca distributed the pancakes, I glanced around the kitchen. Stainless steel appliances punctuated mahogany cabinets and granite counters. A mixing bowl, measuring cup, and large spoon that Bianca had used to make the batch from scratch lay on the counter by the stove. The aroma of fresh drip coffee was making its way to me from its niche on an adjacent counter. Alex's drawings of stick people were pinned to a corkboard above that counter, as was a short list of grocery items. On my right, sunlight reflected on the dark wood floor. I traced its path to French double doors that led outside to a stone patio and a backyard bordered by a tall hedge.

"Megan, remember how our mothers took turns making

pancakes on the weekend when we were kids?" Bianca asked me.

"Yes," I said. "Except when we misbehaved."

"I can't picture you ever misbehaving." Michael grinned at me.

"I did once—when I was five years old," I said, teasing him. "I snuck a bag of chocolate marshmallow cookies into the bedroom one night when Bianca slept over."

"Oh, I remember that." Bianca laughed. "I ate the marshmallow tops. You ate the biscuit parts. We woke up the next morning with dirty faces and sore stomachs. Our mothers grounded us for a month." She laughed again.

I smiled at her. I'd have bet there weren't any marshmallow cookies in *her* pantry.

Looking at us today, no one would guess that Bianca and I were first cousins. I stood two inches shorter than her five-foot-eight frame. My auburn hair, hazel eyes, and pale complexion— let alone my name, Megan Scott—were in constant denial of the Mediterranean half of my Irish-Italian heritage. In contrast, Bianca's dark hair, medium skin tone, and classic features mirrored her parents' dual Italian legacy. We were about the same age—thirty-one. While Montreal, Québec, was still my hometown, Bianca's marriage to financial advisor Victor Hobbs had meant relocating to Portland, Maine. Victor had proved to be as shrewd in business as he was in caring for his family, and Bianca hadn't had any regrets about the move.

"There's one pancake left," she said. "Since Michael offered to cook dinner for us tonight, he gets it." She caught the surprised look on his face and laughed. "Just kidding. Ever since you two arrived last night, Megan hasn't stopped raving about what a good cook you are. You're like me—you appreciate healthy homemade meals. Right?" She placed the remaining pancake in his plate before he could protest.

"I'm up for cooking dinner," Michael said. "No problem. It's the least I can do to thank you for your hospitality."

She waved a hand in the air. "Oh, no need for that. I'm glad Megan finally accepted my invitation to come visit us and brought you along." She sat down next to Alex.

"Actually, Michael brought *me* along," I said.

"That's right." Victor looked at Michael. "You did mention you were here on business. I'm assuming it has to do with your writing." The coffee maker beeped. Victor went over to get the pot.

"I'm working on a newspaper article," Michael said, reaching for the maple syrup on the table. "Jeff Avery—a reporter at *The Portland Press Herald*—is an old friend from university. He's going out of town on assignment and asked me to finish up an investigative piece for him. It's about a homeless woman who passed away here last week."

"Glad rags Gladys. That's the name she went by." Bianca's eyes reflected compassion. "They found her in the alley behind my shop last week. I'd often seen her panhandling on nearby streets. Poor woman."

"I don't mean to pry," Victor said as he poured coffee into our cups, "but wouldn't the *Herald* have other reporters on staff who could cover the story?" He glanced at Michael. "Why ask you to come three hundred miles from Montreal?"

"There's a shortage of experienced investigative reporters here," Michael said. "The papers have to rely on freelance guys like me to bridge the gaps. Jeff and I have helped each other out on occasion. In fact, Megan and I are having lunch with him today."

Victor smiled. "It always comes down to who we know, doesn't it?" He placed the pot back in the coffee maker, then sat down. "By the way, I read your latest true crime novel. I'm fascinated by your extensive investigation into the drug trade in Canada. It must have been a job and a half to consolidate years of information into one book."

"I had lots of help from a reputable ghostwriter." Michael put his arm around my shoulder and hugged me. "Megan organized my zany adventures so they made sense."

I felt a slight blush. "You deserve all the credit, Michael. You risked your life getting the inside scoop for every article in that book."

"Sounds like you two work well together." Victor chuckled. "Is there another crime novel in the works?"

"Yes," Michael said. "I'll be working on it when we get back home."

"I hope you'll make time to visit the sites while you're here," Victor said. "Portland's waterfront area is fabulous. There's Cape Elizabeth's Head Light, the oldest lighthouse in Maine. From ships to shops, there's a lot to see. Lots to eat too. Nothing beats a fresh lobster dinner."

Michael smiled, no doubt already planning outings to local seafood restaurants.

"We'll definitely have to take you both shopping at LL Bean and Ralph Lauren in Freeport," Bianca said, her eyes lighting up. "Lots of artsy shops and museums in town to browse through too. Which reminds me. I'm heading out to Bianca's Gardens in about an hour. Would you and Michael like to drop in after your lunch with Jeff?"

"I'd love to see your new place," I said.

Michael shrugged. "I have a meeting at the *Herald* afterwards. Can I take a rain check?"

"I'll hold you to it." Bianca jokingly waved a finger at him. "Megan, I've been thinking about creating a monthly newsletter for the shop. Maybe you could give me a few pointers later." She took a sip of coffee.

"I don't know very much about the retail flower business," I said.

"One of my girls could give you a crash course."

"Bianca, are you sure you need a newsletter?" Victor asked. "Your sales have been booming ever since you moved to the larger location last year." He looked at Michael and me. "A lot of commercial groups in town order their flowers and plants from Bianca's shop. Organizers trust her to make all the decisions about arrangements for their social events. She's developed an excellent reputation for quality and personal service."

Bianca smiled. "We were so busy on Mother's Day, we had to re-direct customers to competitors. Imagine?" She laughed. "I owe a lot to my girls. Wait till you meet them. They're wonderful with customers and like a second family to me." She glanced at Victor. "Getting back to the newsletter, I think it would add prestige to the business...keep the channels of communication open between the shop and customers."

Victor shrugged. "But everyone in town already knows who you are."

"I'm not so sure about that," Bianca said. "People still introduce me as Mrs. Hobbs whenever we go to an event." She gazed at Michael and me. "One of Victor's business clients is a multi-millionaire named George Gray. His parents live on an estate the size of twenty football fields. George and his father sit on a handful of Portland's corporate committees between them. George is president of a refrigeration company that his father set up decades ago. He runs in elite circles, though we bump into him at a fund-raising event once in a while. He operates a huge warehouse out of town and his business offices take up two floors in a building across the street from my shop. He sends a lot of customers my way. Why am I telling you this? Because Victor happens to be George's financial advisor." She swung her gaze to Victor. "Thus the *Mrs. Hobbs.*"

"Don't shortchange yourself." Victor reached behind Alex to squeeze Bianca's shoulder, then looked back at us. "George's wife, Tiffany, was a huge factor in boosting sales at Bianca's shop. She was heavily involved with charity work around town and ordered flowers and plants regularly for corporate and fund-raising events, cocktail parties...that sort of thing."

"That's true," Bianca said. "But I can't count on her anymore."

"Why not?" I asked her.

"I'll explain in a bit." She turned to Alex. "Sweetie, you're all done? Why don't you go upstairs and play in your room for a while? Daddy will take you to the park later. Okay?"

"Okay, mommy." Alex slid out of his chair and scooted across the floor.

"Don't forget to brush your teeth," she called after him. She stood up and reached for a folded newspaper on the counter. "Tiffany Gray died yesterday." She handed me the paper.

I glanced at the Saturday morning headline of the *Herald*. It read: *Local Heiress Found Dead.*

My eyes darted to the photo beneath it. A woman in a black

evening dress, her blonde hair cascading over bare shoulders, smiled easily for the camera. A man in a tuxedo stood next to her. Slim, gray hair at the temples. His face radiated pride, though no one had bothered to tell him his bow tie was crooked. The caption read: "George Gray, president of Gray Climate Care, and wife Tiffany raise money for Children's Hospital at charity gala."

I scanned the first paragraph: "Tiffany Gray...twenty-nine years old...discovered Friday, October 5...mansion on Prospector's Drive in Falmouth...autopsy to determine the cause of death."

"Oh...they live in Falmouth too," I said to Bianca. "Nearby?"

"About fifteen minutes from us," she said.

I glanced at the photo. "She was so young."

"I know. I still can't believe she's gone. George must be taking it hard." Bianca's expression turned glum.

"Any children?"

"No, but a customer who belongs to the same women's lunch group as Tiffany once told me she heard they'd been trying."

"There was a considerable age difference between George and Tiffany," Victor said. "But on the surface, they appeared to be happily married, despite being childless."

"Between George's business and Tiffany's charitable events, I doubt either of them would have had time to raise a family." Bianca paused. "I'm sure my girls have heard about Tiffany's death by now. I should be there for them when the store opens." She started to clear the table.

"It's okay, I'll clean up," I said to her. "You go get ready."

Victor stood up. "I'll get Alex dressed for the park."

After Bianca and Victor had gone upstairs, my thoughts drifted back to the mansion on Prospector's Drive, where a woman two years younger than me had collapsed and died. "Weird."

"What's weird?" Michael asked, stacking the dirty dishes in the sink.

"Tiffany Gray's death."

His blue eyes locked on mine for a moment before he turned away and began to place the dishes in the dishwasher.

"Come on, Michael. Say something."

6

"She wasn't murdered, if that's what you're getting at."

He was toying with me, playing down the similarity between this unexplained death and my husband's. I couldn't blame him. That I hadn't yet come to terms with Tom's murder was nobody's fault but mine.

Bianca had given Michael and me an extra set of house keys each, so we locked up before heading to town. An interlocking stone path led from the Hobbs' colonial-style house to a circular driveway where their BMWs were usually parked. My leased Nissan Altima emphasized that I was Bianca's less wealthy relative.

It was a fifteen-minute drive south along the I-295 to downtown Portland. Home to about seventy thousand people, this friendly town offered an eclectic mix of art, fashion, and culinary scenes, and I was eager to experience it all. As Michael drove, I relaxed and enjoyed the blend of past and present architecture that was so characteristic of Portland. I read off the names of streets along the way: Marginal Way...Franklin...Congress... I couldn't help wondering if they'd been chosen from a government handbook.

We parked the car on Congress Street and walked down to Dave's Bar and Grill. The restaurant buzzed with lunchtime patrons—mostly shoppers, judging from their casual attire. Any memory of the pancakes I'd eaten this morning was soon forgotten as the aroma of grilled food wafted my way and stirred my appetite.

A man stood up at a table about twenty feet away and waved us over. Another man was sitting at the same table.

Michael introduced me to Jeff Avery, a slender man with warm brown eyes and a boyish grin. His sports shirt and jeans reinforced his youthful appearance.

"It's comforting to know there's more to your life than chasing bad guys down dark alleys," Jeff said to Michael, then smiled at me. "Great to meet you, Megan."

He introduced us to Drew Calloway, the assistant editor at the *Herald*. Drew's shaved head accentuated blue eyes and an engaging smile. I placed him in his late forties. Like Jeff, he wore a sports shirt and jeans.

"So this is the infamous Michael Elliott," Drew said. "Jeff has been talking my ear off about you."

"All good, I hope." Michael smiled.

"Nothing but," Drew said as we sat down.

A waitress arrived to take our orders moments later. We all followed Jeff's lead and ordered cheeseburgers and soft drinks.

After she'd left, Jeff said to Michael, "I was telling Drew earlier how you and I go back to our university days at Ryerson in Toronto and how we worked together after we graduated." He turned to Drew. "You wouldn't believe the leads this guy dug up during our initial street-level investigations. Since then, he's won a stash of journalism awards to boot. What I'm saying is that I wouldn't trust anyone else to cover for me while I'm out of town."

"Thanks. It works both ways." Michael gave him an appreciative nod.

"I have no qualms about you replacing Jeff," Drew said to Michael. "I've read your work. In a way, I had no choice. Jeff shoved every article you wrote in front of my face."

"Well...not *every* article," Jeff said, eliciting laughter from the rest of us.

Drew leaned forward. "We have an excellent relationship with the police community here. They contact us regarding breaking stories. They know they can rely on us to tell it the way it is and not screw up their investigation. In return, we help them when we can. I've added your name to the roster of reporters they can contact. Jeff will brief you later."

"Right." Jeff looked at Michael. "We'll head over to the *Herald* after lunch, and I'll fill you in on the assignment details. Shouldn't take too long." He glanced at me. "Megan, do you need a lift back home afterward or—"

"I have a car," I said. "I'll be staying in town until late afternoon, but Michael—"

"No sweat," Jeff said. "I'll drive you back home, Michael. It'll give us a chance to talk about old times."

After the waitress served our meals, the conversation turned to more familiar topics, like sports, technology, and travel. Before we knew it, lunch was over. The men headed to their meeting at the *Herald*, and I drove off to see Bianca.

I swung onto Middle Street and steered past a string of red brick commercial blocks, then turned onto Exchange Street. When New England-style shops and galleries peeked out at me from under arches, I knew I wasn't far from my destination. I veered into an alley and parked the car in one of the spaces reserved for staff behind a row of retail outlets. I stuck the employee pass Bianca had given me in the windshield and stepped out. It was a short walk back to the street.

The sun's rays felt strong on my face, but the cool October breeze that swirled the autumn leaves along the sidewalk hinted at an approaching change in season—a time when frosty windowpanes, glistening icicles, and spiraling gusts of snow would bestow a postcard quality upon the city.

The four-story brownstone that George Gray's offices occupied loomed ahead—a structure perhaps as daunting as George himself. I had to admit that Bianca and Victor had aroused my curiosity.

I detoured to pick up two coffees at Starbucks, then walked back along Exchange Street toward the dark green awnings of Bianca's Gardens. I tucked one cup inside my elbow and opened the door with my free hand.

The door chimes announced my arrival. A spicy floral scent reached me, but I couldn't pinpoint the exact source of the heady fragrance from the dozens of potted flowers on display.

Bianca was standing by the checkout counter. She nodded my way, then continued to speak with a short, stocky man whose green T-shirt bore the shop name in white letters on the back. A chubby blond-haired female wearing the same kind of T-shirt stood next to him. Both seemed so engrossed in the conversation with Bianca that they didn't turn around to see who had walked in.

"But Mrs. Spencer said she never received the flowers, Henry." Bianca's voice broke the flow of Pachelbel's *Canon* playing throughout the high-ceilinged structure.

"Maybe the delivery address was wrong," he said with a shrug.

"I entered the order in the computer myself," the female employee said. "I'm positive it was Mrs. Spencer's address, but I could be wrong."

Henry ran a hand through thinning gray hair. "I can't explain it, Bianca. It's wicked confusin', it is."

I felt as if I'd intruded upon a family spat. I shifted my view to two female employees in green aprons who were setting up pumpkins, corn stalks, and clay turtles on bales of straw stacked in the center of the floor. A scarecrow stood its ground in the midst of it all, a crooked red smile painted on its face.

"The error could have been caused by a computer glitch," Bianca said. "I don't want either of you to worry about it anymore. Henry, go ahead with the rest of the deliveries. Okay?"

"Okay, Bianca." Henry plodded, head bent, toward the exit at the rear like a child who'd been told to go to his room.

"I'm sorry, Bianca," Doreen said. "I don't want to make any trouble for Henry. He's a good guy. Maybe I got sloppy and entered the wrong address. It's probably my fault."

"Don't worry about it," Bianca said. "It's over. Done with. Okay?" She gave her a little smile. "Now scoot." She waved a hand in the air.

"I'll go finish unloading the new inventory." Doreen walked toward the back of the floor and exited the same door as Henry.

I offered Bianca a coffee. "I thought you might want one."

"Super." She accepted it. "Thanks."

I glanced around. I didn't wonder why Bianca's upscale shop had been featured in several wedding magazines. Stylish flower arrangements in groups of deep yellows, oranges, and purples tempted me to go over and touch them, smell them. Suspended foliage and small trees in terracotta pots bordered the floor-to-ceiling windows. Potted plants in more varieties than I could imagine filled the space at the floor level. A cooler at the back of the store contained roses, tulips, and other delicate species of flowers. Off to the side, dried and silk flower arrangements in artsy ceramic vases graced glass tables.

"The place looks terrific," I said to Bianca.

"Thanks. The renovations took forever, but it was worth

moving to a bigger location."

"Excuse me, Bianca." A female employee came up to where we were standing. Blue eyes protruded beneath sun-tinted bangs, and freckles sprinkled her cheeks. She had that fresh-faced look that promoters love to use in teen skin care commercials. "George Gray's personal assistant is on the phone. She wants to know if you'll be here Friday."

"Tell her yes."

The employee nodded and walked away.

Bianca whispered, "Let's go to my office. It's more private."

I followed her toward the back of the floor and up a flight of wood stairs bordered with wrought iron railing.

Upstairs, the first door on the right led to her office. The lingering odor of the indigo wall-to-wall carpet was a tip-off to its recent installation. A computer, a white ceramic cup with MOM painted on it in pink, and a framed picture of Bianca, Victor, and Alex sat on an oak desk. A burgundy leather couch and filing cabinets lined the opposite wall.

Bianca shut the door behind us, then crossed the floor and pulled open the horizontal blinds. Blue slats parted to reveal a window. "Things run more smoothly when my girls know I'm keeping an eye on them." She smiled.

The view offered a semi-circle span of activities on the main floor, with a focus on the checkout counter where staff handled transactions on the point-of-sale, or POS system, and wrapped purchases. It also provided a clear view of anyone walking in or out the front door.

Bianca sat down at her desk. "You can store your purse in my desk drawer if you want." She slid it open.

"Thanks." I stuffed my oversized handbag into it beside her smaller, daintier purse, then took a seat opposite her.

"I had a pep talk with my staff this morning. I didn't want them getting down in the dumps about Tiffany's death. You know how it is. People feel sorry for anyone who dies before their time." She caught herself. "Oh, I'm sorry. I didn't mean to offend you. About Tom, I mean."

"You didn't."

She flipped open the lid of her cup. The aroma of brewed coffee flowed between us. "It's hard to believe Tiffany was in here a week ago Friday lodging a complaint."

"A complaint? About what?" I removed the lid from my cup.

Bianca glanced away as if she were recalling the incident. "I had errands to run that day, so I wasn't here when Tiffany came in. My girls told me she had returned a box of long-stemmed roses and said the flowers weren't fresh. Sarah arranged to send out a replacement order the same day. Tiffany was okay with that as long as we didn't send that *sneaky little driver* to her place again." She raised her fingers to form air quotes.

"Who was the driver?"

"Henry Glover. The man I was talking to when you came in. Tiffany told Sarah he'd loitered in her driveway after making a delivery and she didn't like it."

"He seems shy. Not exactly what you'd call sneaky."

"You're right about that. When I asked him about the incident, he said he'd dropped a delivery card in the van while he was parked in her driveway and he was looking for it."

"Do you think he was lying?"

She shook her head. "No, his reasoning is too basic for that. He suffered a nervous breakdown twenty years ago. He can only handle simple tasks. Nothing stressful." Her expression softened. "When he applied for a job here this summer, he was desperate. He's fifty-five years old and couldn't find work. I hired him on the spot. I don't regret it. He's such a sweet man. Very easygoing."

"So the problem with Tiffany's flowers was resolved?"

"Not quite. Tiffany insisted I call her back as soon as I returned from my trip."

"Did you?" I drank some coffee.

"Yes, it was important that I smooth things over with her. She'd never complained about the roses before, and I didn't want George to think less of my services because of it."

"Why would he?"

"After they were married a year ago, George set up a standing

12

order at my shop for delivery of a dozen long-stemmed roses to Tiffany every Friday. We've honored that delivery every week since then. But now..." She chewed on her lip.

"What's wrong?"

"I feel guilty and have to tell someone. You're the only one I can trust." She leaned forward and spoke in a low voice. "When I saw this morning's paper, I was stunned by Tiffany's death. After Victor mentioned how she'd helped generate sales at my shop, I got to thinking how badly her death might affect future sales...and the welfare of my staff." Her expression turned somber. "You must think I'm a horrid person."

"You're protecting your interests like any other business owner would."

"I suppose so." She shrugged. "Thank goodness I can still count on George for referrals."

The thought that Bianca and Victor owed George a lot crossed my mind. It flitted away when Bianca changed the conversation.

"I'm going ahead with the newsletter for Bianca's Gardens," she said, tucking a strand of hair behind each ear. "I'll ask one of my girls to give you a crash course. I'll even put you on the payroll. What do you say? Will you help me?"

"Michael and I are driving back home next week."

"Even one week would be a big help."

Nothing ever came that easy with Bianca. "What's the catch?"

"No catch. Kathy LeBreton, my part-time girl, is away on a course for two weeks. With Halloween and Thanksgiving coming up, I could use an extra hand. Keep it in the family, so to speak. How about working half a day on the newsletter, half a day with my girls in the shop? Please say yes."

I gave it some thought. I had no ghostwriting projects lined up and welcomed any chance to increase my cash flow. I'd brought along my laptop, so I had everything I needed. "Okay. Sounds like fun."

"Super. Let's go back downstairs. I'll introduce you to the staff."

Employee Joyce Sutton's voice was as soft as the cloud of gray hair framing her face. "So happy to meet you, Megan. Bianca has spoken so much about you. I feel as if I already know you." She smiled at me.

"Joyce was the first girl I hired to work in my shop," Bianca said. "She has decades of experience and taught me everything I know."

"Hush now, Bianca." Joyce chuckled and adjusted her rimless glasses. "You were a fast learner, that's all."

Next Bianca introduced me to Sarah Robinson, the freckle-faced employee I'd seen earlier. "Sarah is studying to become a floral designer. She'll give you a quick tour of the shop and introduce you to the main species of plants and flowers we sell here."

Before I could reply, the chimes rang and two men in suits walked in. Short haircuts, eyes that scanned the premises, and a sense of purpose in their stride. I knew they were police detectives before they'd dug out their badges.

The taller one approached Bianca. "Mrs. Hobbs?" he asked, even though it was obvious he already knew who she was. "I'm Detective Sergeant Wayne Flanagan. This is Detective Ed Gordon." He tucked his badge away. "We'd like you to come to the station with us to answer a few questions."

"To the station?" Bianca's eyes went wide. "What's this about?"

"Tiffany Gray's death."

"What does it have to do with me?"

"Please, Ma'am, we're just following procedure."

Bianca paused. "Can I go upstairs to get my purse?"

Detective Flanagan nodded. "Yes."

In the meantime, the two men walked around and casually looked at the flowers and plants. Now and then, they'd check the little tags attached to them.

Bianca returned, purse in hand. "I'll be back soon," she said to me and followed the detectives out the door.

Sarah stood by the window next to Joyce and me. We watched Bianca get into the unmarked sedan. After the car had sped away, Sarah asked Joyce, "Do you think she's going to be okay?"

"Of course, dear." The serenity in Joyce's voice was reassuring. "Why don't you give Megan a tour of the shop? I'll finish up the display." She gestured toward the bales of straw.

"Okay," Sarah said.

"I have to use the washroom first," I said. "Be back in a sec." I hurried upstairs.

I closed the door to Bianca's office and dug my smartphone out of the handbag I'd stored in her desk drawer. I called Michael, hoping he'd be done with his meeting.

I was in luck. Jeff had already dropped him off at the house. I told him about the police visit.

"I know," he said. "Bianca phoned here and spoke to Victor minutes ago. He called his lawyer and went to meet her at the police station. I'm watching over Alex."

"I can't help wondering why the police would want to question Bianca about Tiffany."

"Yeah, it's plain crazy." A pause. "What you said about Tiffany this morning, I think you're right. Sounds like the cops suspect foul play in her death."

CHAPTER 2

A seven-foot-high divider cut off the workroom from the rest of the main floor in Bianca's Gardens. A rectangular wood table sat in the center of the area, its varnished surface making it water-resistant. Sarah and I were working on an order for a flower basket when a rattling sound grew closer.

Doreen wheeled a cart into the workroom, huffing as she maneuvered it around the corner. I had a better look now at the employee I'd seen standing next to Henry when I first arrived. She was about thirty years old. She had a ruddy complexion—probably a result of the load she was heaving. Her straight blonde hair was cropped to below her ears and hugged her head like a helmet. She grunted as she gave the cart a final thrust. "The wheels on this damn thing have to be adjusted." She looked up, gave me a rapid once-over. "Oh...Bianca didn't say anything about hiring new staff."

Sarah introduced me to Doreen Dale. "Doreen, don't you remember? Bianca told us her cousin would be visiting today."

"Oh...yeah," Doreen said. "The cousin from Canada." She paused. "You get snow all year up there, don't you? Must be tough getting around."

"Not really," I said. "We have four seasons like you do here."

"Really?" A flicker of skepticism registered in her eyes.

"I'm giving Megan a crash course on Flora 101," Sarah said.

Doreen grimaced. "Bet you won't remember a damn thing by tomorrow," she said to me. She wiped the perspiration from her forehead with a hand large enough to clutch a football. "If you want to learn the trade inside out, it takes more than a crash course or a fancy diploma like the one Sarah's studying for."

I glanced at Sarah, expecting a reaction to Doreen's comment.

She met my gaze with a smile. "I'll take this basket to the front and go print out the customer's bill. Be right back."

With nothing else to do, I watched Doreen grab two twenty-pound bags of potting soil from the cart. She heaved them under the worktable, making short work of the remaining four bags. I couldn't help but wonder if she'd missed her vocation as a weight lifter. Or a garbage collector.

Doreen had moved the cart out of the way when another one made its noisy arrival. A dark-haired woman wheeled in a load of four bags of potting soil, her ponytail swinging from side to side as she maneuvered the cart up to the table. "This is the last of it," she said to Doreen. Looking lost in a pair of oversized green overalls and mud boots, she adjusted a shoulder strap and smiled at me. "You must be Megan. Bianca told us to expect you today. I'm Gail Parker."

We had a brief chat during which Gail told me she was a flower design graduate whom Bianca had recruited in the spring.

"How do you like working here?" I asked her.

"I love it," she said, enthusiasm lighting up her face. "There's so much to learn. I'm glad I studied the technical aspects of the trade at school first. It helped a lot."

Out of the corner of my eye, I detected a tiny smirk on Doreen's face.

Joyce hurried in waving a stack of papers. "Girls, these phone orders have to be filled ASAP." She handed them out and kept one for herself.

I tagged along with Sarah while the other girls fetched the supplies they needed to fill the orders. One by one, they returned to the workroom and began to assemble their flower arrangements.

"I can't get over what's been happening in our little town lately," Joyce said, her voice low. "First, a homeless woman dies in the alley behind our shop. Then Friday, Tiffany Gray drops dead."

"Two deaths in one week," Sarah said. "It's pretty creepy."

"The homeless woman probably died of old age or malnutrition," Gail said. "Living on the street is a death penalty." She wedged a pink carnation into a block of wet green foam at the base of a wicker basket.

"What about Tiffany?" Joyce shook her head. "Who would have thought such a beautiful young woman could drop dead for no reason, the poor dear?" She reached for a glass vase on a shelf by the wall.

"Yeah, Joyce. She was a gen-u-ine Miss Congeniality." Doreen dumped a bag of soil into a terra cotta pot the size of a large pumpkin.

"Well, she did a lot of work for charities," Joyce said, returning to her spot adjacent to Doreen. "You have to give credit where credit is due."

Doreen looked at her. "She's no better than the rest of us, you know. She might have been rich and famous and had the means to do all those fancy things, but she ended up in the same place we all will. Six feet under." She clutched a small spade and jabbed it into the soil, making a hole in the center.

"No one deserves to die young," Joyce said in a low voice.

"Bitches do. Admit it. She was a total bitch—especially to us. Right, girls?"

Heads nodded among murmurs of agreement.

"She was a difficult customer at times," Joyce said, adjusting her eyeglasses. "But still..."

"Get real, Joyce. The woman was bad news all over town." Doreen positioned a large fern into the pot and added more soil. "I know some of the staff who served at her fancy events. She drove them nuts with the preparations, fussing over this and that and whatever. Martha Stewart, look out." Doreen snickered, then broke into a loud chortle, her plump frame quivering.

Her guffaw—reminiscent of the motorized fat lady with the deep-bellied laugh in an amusement park—made me uneasy. The other women chuckled along, no doubt used to it.

From the other end of the worktable, Gail said, "Hey, Sarah, too bad you were on cash the last time she came in. You were way too kind to her—especially after she practically threw those roses at you."

"I guess she was having a bad day," Sarah said with a shrug. She took hold of the silver balloon I handed her and fastened it to a birthday basket of purple asters, yellow daisies, and white spider mums.

"I wish I'd been there," Doreen said to Sarah. "I'd never have let her talk to you like that—or to any of us. You guys are like family to me, you know that." Her gaze flitted around the table.

"We know that, Doreen," Joyce said, smiling at her. "How else can we get through bad days without joking and teasing one another?" Then she whispered, "Or gossiping about customers?"

"You want gossip?" Doreen picked up the conversation. "Remember that day in July when that blonde Barbie darted in here and insisted she get served ahead of other customers? I was working the cash. Lucky for her, another customer put her in her place, so I didn't have to cool her down over there." She nodded toward a pair of deep stainless steel sinks in a counter along the back wall.

More laughter.

"Nothing beats the time she complained about the rubber plant she'd ordered," Gail said. "Remember how disappointed she was when she found out it didn't have blossoms?"

"Yeah," Doreen said. "That bitch complained all the time. She ordered miniature carnations once and called us to say they were too small. As if we could grow them to size or something. Give me a friggin' break, lady!"

More giggles and laughter.

The girls' amusement abated when Bianca poked her head inside the workroom. "Girls, please, keep it down. I walked in and could hear you clear across the floor. Good thing there weren't any customers in the shop."

Doreen turned to face her. "Did you hear us mention anyone's name?"

"It doesn't matter. What if her husband happened to walk in and overheard you. Don't you think he'd have guessed who you were talking about?"

"Whatever." Doreen shrugged, then reached for a roll of cellophane and began to wrap the plant.

"We need to maintain a professional image," Bianca said, her gaze encompassing everyone. "We don't want customers thinking we're a bunch of gossips, now do we?"

Doreen glanced at her. "Sorry, Bianca," she said, prompting the others to do the same.

"How did it go at the police station, Bianca?" Joyce asked.

"Fine. Everything's fine," Bianca said. "After you girls finish up here, figure out whose turn it is to make customer appreciation calls. Okay?"

The girls uttered their affirmative responses.

Bianca looked at me. "Megan, can you come to my office after you're done?"

"Sure," I said.

She nodded and ducked out.

"Hush now, all of you," Joyce said to us. "Bianca is right. We need to show compassion for you-know-who's husband. He lost the love of his life." She inserted a purple liatris into the vase.

"Love is blind," Doreen said. "If he'd been in our shoes, he'd have seen her true character—the one she showed us."

Joyce kept her voice low. "She's dead. We need to show some respect."

"Respect?" Doreen let out a scratchy whisper. "The whole town knows what a tramp she was, hitting on anything that wore pants, including their live-in personal trainer."

Gail giggled. "I don't know about you guys, but that Tyler Wilson sure is hot stuff."

Doreen went on. "Serves her husband right. That's what you get for robbing the cradle."

"Oh, I don't believe she cheated on her husband for a minute," Joyce said. "He would have divorced her if he knew she were having an affair."

"With the price of alimony these days?" Doreen grimaced. "A divorce would have cost him a fortune. All in all, he got off damn easy. I'm going to bring this order out back." She clasped the pot and walked out.

After the rest of the orders were completed, I helped Sarah carry them out back to the loading dock where she introduced me to Henry Glover. He gave me a shy hello and continued to load deliveries onto the truck. She also introduced me to Lee Chen, the driver. We exchanged greetings—if you could call Lee's mumble a form of salutation. He was tall and lean, though strong biceps protruded from the sleeves of his T-shirt. He had deep ridges along his cheeks, narrow eyes, and thin lips. I placed him in his mid-forties. A musty odor emanated from him, like the scent of snuffed candles. He wore black thick-soled boots, the sort you'd expect to find on the feet of a tactical squad. His appearance might explain why Bianca had hired him as a driver and not a delivery person.

On our way back inside, Sarah whispered to me, "By the way, Lee is Doreen's husband."

I did the math. Lee was at least ten years older than Doreen. I wondered why she'd derided George for having married a much younger woman.

"He handles two part-time jobs," Sarah said, as if I needed to know more about Lee. "When he's not working here, he's working for George Gray."

I had a hard time visualizing Lee doing any job that involved customer service or office duties. "Doing what?"

"He loads inventory in George's warehouse."

If the shoe—or boot—fits, I supposed.

I went upstairs to find Bianca sitting at her desk and staring into space. "Bianca?"

She waved me in. "Shut the door behind you."

I did and took a seat opposite her.

"Thank goodness Victor met me at the police station." Her voice was unsteady.

"What happened?"

"They questioned me about Tiffany Gray." She took in a deep breath.

"What did they want to know?"

"You won't believe this." She stared at me. "They asked if my shop dealt in toxic flora."

I felt my knees go weak and was glad to be sitting down. "What did you say?"

"That some species could be considered dangerous, but we usually don't encourage our customers to eat their purchases."

I laughed. "You actually said that?"

She nodded, let out a nervous laugh. "They questioned Victor too. They made us feel like common criminals...like we were dealing in illegal drugs or worse. They even asked for a list of flora we imported from exotic locations. I'm not stupid. I can see where this is heading. They suspect Tiffany died from a toxic flower or plant, and they're looking for a scapegoat. Victor and I can't afford a scandal. It would ruin our lives." Tears welled in her eyes.

Something nagged at me. "They couldn't possibly have completed the autopsy yet. Even if they suspect that Tiffany was poisoned, why would they link her death to your shop?"

"Victor asked the police the same question."

"What did they say?"

"That they were following the only lead they had so far."

The tension hanging over Bianca's dining room table that evening was heavier than the platter of cheese tortellini making the rounds. Even the abstract painting in vivid oranges, yellows, and reds hanging on the wall didn't do much to lighten the mood in the room.

Bianca had gone to buy groceries after closing the shop at five. It was eight o'clock by the time we all sat down to dinner. Victor had fed Alex and put him to bed earlier.

"If you ask me," Victor said, his forehead lined with worry, "the fact the police interrogated us without legal representation was completely unwarranted. I called our lawyer afterward and brought him up to date. He agreed to represent us if the police drag us further into their investigation."

"I don't understand why they interrogated you too," Bianca

said. "What would they have done if you hadn't met me at the station?"

"They would have caught up with me eventually." He took a sip of wine. "All they wanted was general information anyway. They asked if George was my client, how long I'd known him...routine questions."

"I can't believe this is happening." Bianca looked at him. "Why would they interrogate us? We're not murderers, for heaven's sake."

"They're going to question other people that George dealt with too," he said. "It'll take the focus off us for a while."

"For a while? Let's hope it's forever." She ate some tortellini.

"They're just following protocol," I said, having learned more about murder investigations than I'd cared to after my husband had been killed. "If they think Tiffany's death is suspicious, they'll want to retrace the events of her last days. Like they did with Tom."

An awkward silence followed.

"Well...some good news came out of my meeting at the *Herald*," Michael said, easing the mood. "Drew—he's the assistant editor there—asked me to write a background piece on Tiffany." He took a scoop of cucumber salad sprinkled with chives and basil and passed me the bowl.

Victor raised an eyebrow. "About her life?"

"More like a tribute to her life," Michael said. "He wants me to write about the charities and other institutions she helped out."

"It's one way to sell more newspapers," Bianca said with a shrug.

"Readership," Michael said. "That's what it's all about. Give the public what they want and they'll lap it up."

"Showing Tiffany in a humanitarian light will definitely add value to the Gray family reputation," Victor said. "They're well-known philanthropists."

"Lately," Bianca said.

"True," Victor said. Opting for an explanation to Michael and me, he went on. "The Gray family donated to a number of causes in Portland over the years. I have to admit they never invested in charitable endeavors to the extent they did until Tiffany came on board. She raised their status on the benevolent scale."

"Can you name any of these charities?" Michael asked. "I could use them as sources."

"Oh, there were many. She held fund-raising events for the Children's Hospital, the food bank, and homeless shelters in town. She helped raise awareness about LostNMissing, a group that supports the families of missing people. Most of the events she organized were gala dinners where she and George rubbed elbows with Portland's elite who donated hefty sums to their causes."

"It doesn't change anything." Bianca took a sip of wine.

"What do you mean?" I asked her.

"Hanging around people with money only buys artificial smiles and handshakes." Bianca shrugged. "Maybe even enemies."

A wry smile crept up on Victor's lips. "When you're one of the richest men in Portland, you can expect to have a few enemies. It's part and parcel of their family reputation."

"Family reputation?" Bianca raised an eyebrow. "Everyone knows how George refused to take on his father's business. The feuding between them went on for years until George gave in. Even today, there are rumors that not everything is okay between them."

"From what I know, their business hasn't suffered from it," Victor said, then looked at Michael and me. "To fill you in, Gray Climate Care is located on prime land in an industrial sector on the outskirts of town. George's father, Stanley, originally bought the 20,000-foot warehouse for storing freezers and coolers. He'd hoped his son would join him in managing the company, but George wasn't interested at first. When he finally took over operations ten years ago, he added a 40,000-foot cold storage wing to the facilities for housing frozen food. It strengthened his role as a middleman between manufacturers and retailers. He's an extremely busy man, but he took time out to build a mansion in Falmouth for his new bride."

"Speaking of George," Michael said, "Apparently he ran a full-page ad in the *Herald* right after his wedding. It was a public vow to send Tiffany long-stemmed roses every week for the rest of their lives. Did he order the roses from your shop, Bianca?"

"Yes," she said, smiling. "My girls thought it was such a romantic gesture."

"While we're on the topic of George and Tiffany Gray..." Victor leaned forward. "There's something I'd like to share with all of you." He grew pensive. "Michael, I want your assurance that what I'm about to say will stay within these walls."

"No problem," Michael said. "Journalistic privilege."

Victor switched his gaze to Bianca and me. "This confidentiality agreement applies to both of you too."

"We're family," Bianca said to him. "You can trust us. You know that." She glanced at me.

"Of course," I said.

Victor took in a breath. "I mentioned how I called my lawyer earlier. When I told him my firm was handling George Gray's investment portfolio, he said it might present a problem in the future."

"How?" Bianca asked.

"If Tiffany's death wasn't an accident and George becomes a murder suspect, my firm might be asked to testify in court."

"That's ridiculous." Bianca waved a hand in the air. "George isn't a murderer."

Victor went on. "The police would be entitled to seize all documents pertaining to George's investments for investigation purposes—maybe even freeze his assets. George's accounts make up a fair share of my firm's capital investments. Depending on the outcome of the investigation, the loss of revenue to the firm—not to mention the damage to its reputation—could be significant."

A hush fell over the table.

"We have the flower shop," Bianca said. "We can always sell it."

"I could never let you do that." Victor smiled at her, then said to us, "There's something else you should know. George dropped by the office last week. He gave me a revised copy of his last will and testament days before Tiffany died. I can't divulge the contents. I can merely say I wouldn't want to be in his shoes right now if my life depended on it."

By the time Michael and I turned in for the night, an uneasy feeling had flared up inside me, and it wasn't from eating too much tortellini either. Sure, I was concerned about the police investigation zooming in on Bianca, but it was Tiffany's unexplained death that lingered in my thoughts. Anyone might argue that morbid curiosity or misplaced anxiety was at the root of my obsession, but I knew better.

My mind kept comparing the similarities between Tiffany's death and Tom's. Was I stretching the bounds of my imagination by trying to find a common link between them, or was I heeding my intuition—that tiny voice I often ignored and later wished I hadn't?

To begin with, both were young and healthy and had led active lives. If the rumors about Tiffany were correct, she'd cheated on George just like Tom had cheated on me—though it was anyone's guess if her flings were as extensive as Tom's. Both had collapsed to the floor and suffered a premature death from an initially unknown cause. Tom had died from cyanide poisoning. As for Tiffany, it sounded as if the police were considering the possibility she might have been poisoned from a toxic plant or flower. Had it been accidental?

Logic told me not to jump to conclusions. The investigation was far from over. Yet the churning in my stomach told me Tiffany had been murdered too.

CHAPTER 3

Over a light breakfast on Sunday, Bianca and Victor announced they were taking Alex to his friend's birthday party later that morning. The invited kids and their parents would visit the Children's Museum afterward. Bianca suggested that Michael and I visit the shops in town in the meantime and have lunch at Portland Lobster Company.

In spite of the dark clouds that threatened the New England town, Michael and I thought the trip was a good idea and looked forward to it. I was thankful I'd packed a wool coat and scarf. The dampness in the air alone was enough to make me shiver.

As Michael backed the car out of the driveway, I said to him, "The next time we drive five hours to come visit Bianca, it'll be in the summer." I stuck my hands in my pockets.

Michael turned on the car heater to ward off the humidity. "This should make you all toasty again." He smiled at me.

"Thanks." I smiled back. "Do you realize this is our first outing here as tourists? There's so much to see. Oh…did you remember to bring your camera?"

He nodded. "It's on the back seat." He paused. "I need to make another stop before we head over to the Old Port area. Check something out before I send my article to the *Herald* this afternoon."

"Oh? Where are we going?" I was eager for any tidbits he was ready to dole out from his meeting yesterday at the newspaper. With the conversation focused on Bianca and Victor's police interrogation yesterday evening, we hadn't had time to talk about his assignment.

"You'll see," he said.

Minutes later, we were cruising along Middle Street past the sporadic but overwhelming presence of massive red brick buildings I'd noticed yesterday. I was curious about their origin and retrieved a pamphlet from the glove compartment. It described these red blocks as "imposing commercial buildings distinguished by the Italianate, Romanesque Revival, Queen Anne, or Mansard style architecture of the latter part of the 1800s." It stated how Portland had suffered severe devastation from war and fire throughout the course of its history, and how it had managed to rebuild and recover from its losses each time. The result was the construction of these resilient red brick structures in diverse architectural styles—a symbol of the city's lasting power.

Michael steered the Nissan off Exchange Street into the alley behind Bianca's Gardens. "Care to join me?" He turned off the ignition and stepped out.

I put the pamphlet back into the glove compartment and got out. "Why are we here? What's the big mystery?"

"No mystery. I want to get a feel for the article I'm writing about glad rags Gladys." He reached into the pocket of his leather jacket and retrieved his smartphone. He opened an app and tapped the screen. "This is the picture of Gladys that Jeff took at the scene." The image was too small to see the details, but I could tell it was a woman positioned on her back. "I'd say they found her body about here." He took ten steps to the left and pointed to an area on the ground.

I followed his gaze. Purple wildflowers grew between the cracks in the asphalt. "So?"

Michael shifted his attention to the row of commercial buildings on both sides of the alley, their rear doors facing us. "Question is: What was she doing here?"

"Maybe she was taking a shortcut through the alley to get to the next street." I looked around. Aside from the buildings that bordered opposite sides of the alley, a chain-link fence that measured about ten feet high closed off a third side leading to a street. There was no other way out except the way we'd come in. "On second thought, forget it."

Michael studied the neighboring buildings and held his gaze there. "The rear exit of Bianca's shop faces this alley. It's close to where Gladys's body was found."

"Are you saying you think there's a connection?"

"I don't know." He tucked his phone away. "Okay. I'm done here. Let's go visit the Old Port." He gave me a sunny smile.

I didn't budge. He'd planted a seed of apprehension in my mind. "The police think Bianca's shop might have a connection to Tiffany's death. Now you're insinuating the same thing about Gladys's death."

He shrugged. "I'm merely saying it's a coincidence."

"You mean a potential lead for the police."

"It's a long shot." He looked at me. "Come on. Let's go visit Portland."

We drove to the Old Port District and left the car in a parking lot. A downpour seemed imminent, so I grabbed my umbrella from the back seat. I'd been caught once too often in the rain without one. Ending up with frizzy hair resembling cotton candy was something I tried to avoid at any cost—even if it meant lugging an umbrella around long after the sun had returned. Michael grabbed his camera from the back seat and off we went.

The New England style clothing stores and quaint craft shops along Fore Street were familiar from the photos Bianca had sent me over the years. The cobblestoned street added an old-fashioned charm to the area, and I almost expected to hear a horse-drawn carriage approach.

Since we'd only had toast and orange juice for breakfast, it didn't take more than the mouth-watering treats in the window of the Old Port Candy Co. to lure us inside. The aroma of chocolate, maple, coconut, and other divine scents filled the shop. After ten minutes of browsing, I chose a bag of their famous chocolate-covered blueberries. Michael selected gourmet truffles. We shared our goodies and promised not to tell Bianca we'd eaten such rich sweets at ten in the morning.

We turned up Exchange Street and visited arts and crafts outlets, an art gallery, and trendy clothing shops. The Italianate structure and mauve trim on the façade of Serendipity drew me inside. Michael bought me a stylish wool jacket—a little over my budget but he insisted on paying for it—and two long-sleeved sweaters to keep me "toasty" over the next while. Then we went into a children's toy store and bought a Lego set of racing cars for Alex called The Pit Stop. Michael was so excited about the purchase that I thought he'd end up buying a set for himself too.

He surprised me later when he lingered in front of a jewelry store. "What do you think about tying the knot one day?" He pointed to the engagement and wedding ring sets perched on small satin pillars in the window.

I froze.

He put an arm around my shoulder. "We've talked about this before. I won't rush you into anything, you know that." He bent over and kissed me.

"I know. It's just that...well..." My thoughts scattered as the same old fears and uncertainties swept over me.

"We can't keep on living in the past if we want to build a new life together."

He was right. Not all married men cheated on their wives like Tom had cheated on me. Yet I held back. "I need more time."

"No problem. However long it takes." He looked away and tiny muscles pulsated along his jaw line. I'd come to recognize it as an involuntary reaction whenever something bothered him.

We strolled down cobblestoned Moulton Street and crossed Commercial Street to the waterfront, where ferries and colorful pleasure boats dotted the world-renowned port. I took a deep breath of the refreshing sea air and made a mental note of its soothing scent. I wished I could bottle a sample to take home with me.

Michael captured Portland in his own way by taking photos of seagulls and sailboats, and ferries boarding passengers for cruises into Casco Bay. After he'd snapped shots of seafood eateries that caught his interest, the next words out of his mouth were, "How about going to that restaurant Bianca mentioned?"

With cold hands and a renewed appetite, we headed for Portland Lobster Company on Commercial Street. Bianca had often raved about the excellent choice of restaurants here, especially along the waterfront. Rumor had it that Portland boasted more eateries per capita than any other city in the USA. This factor made it a bonus trip for Michael—his appetite peaked all day long.

We ordered lobster stew with chunks of fresh Maine lobster meat, followed by a fresh lobster roll with crispy fries and coleslaw. We were handed a plastic light-up lobster that blinked when our order was ready. Whether it was the seaside air or the fact we'd walked around for hours, I didn't know, but we finished our meals in record time.

We were enjoying our coffee when Michael's phone rang. "Hi, Drew. No problem... You're kidding... Yes, it's about ready to go... Okay. Bye." He looked at me and said, "Drew received the preliminary results of the autopsy performed on Gladys. It revealed an anomaly in her lungs."

"An anomaly? What kind of anomaly?"

"Liz doesn't know. They're still running tests."

"Who is Liz?"

"One of our contacts. She's a forensics trainee who happens to be Jeff's girlfriend." He grinned.

"She works on Sunday?"

"Yes. For a private forensic pathology practice. They have no set working hours or days." He paused. "About Gladys, let's keep it between us. I don't want to alarm Bianca and Victor until we're a hundred percent sure about the origin of the anomaly. Okay?"

"Sure."

He checked his watch. "Maybe we should head back home. I'd like to start working on that new tribute article to Tiffany. Something tells me it's going to be a crazy week."

His instincts were usually right.

Monday morning, Michael's article on Gladys appeared in the

Herald. I sat down with a cup of fresh-perked coffee and read the first paragraph:

"Gladys Lindstrom was laid to rest in St. Andrew's cemetery on the weekend. Patrons who paused on the street to donate their spare change to one of Portland's most recognizable senior citizens will remember her as glad rags Gladys—a nickname she used when thanking her benefactors."

I'd looked over Michael's article before he'd sent it in, but I read it again now. Even on the second read, it had the ability to arouse empathy from anyone with half a heart. By writing about a citizen whom readers could identify with, he'd raised social awareness about the dilemma of homeless people in this city and maybe other cities around the world.

Accompanying the article was the same photograph of Gladys that Michael had showed me but enlarged for print. A gray-haired woman was stretched out on the pavement with her eyes shut. She wore layers of frayed brown skirts over dark stockings. A red handkerchief was wrapped around her head. Her joined hands held a wispy bunch of wildflowers—the same ones I'd noticed growing in the alley where her body had been found. Flanking her side was a handbag; its contents, though indiscernible, had fallen out. In the background were the rear doors of shops and several garbage bins.

I put down the paper and gazed at Michael across the kitchen table. "Glad rags Gladys. How tragic is that?"

"Tell me about it," he said, gazing at me over his laptop.

"She died days before Tiffany, and the *Herald* only ran the article now?" I took a sip of coffee.

He shrugged. "Jeff had fallen behind in his work—including the article on Gladys. I guess Tiffany Gray's death took priority in the newsroom as soon as they heard about it."

I studied the photo. "There's something odd about the way Gladys is holding the flowers, don't you think? It almost looks staged."

He nodded. "As if she knew she was about to die."

"Any idea what was in her handbag?"

"Coins, a small bottle of whiskey, red ribbon, two plastic tubes, a broken pencil, paper...other odds and ends."

"That's even sadder. Wait...you said plastic tubes. Like the ones florists put on flower stems?"

"I think so."

"She probably got them out of the garbage cans in the alley." I checked my watch. It was eight o'clock. "I heard Victor leave earlier. Bianca is going to drop Alex off at day care on her way to work."

"Aren't you riding into town with her?"

I smiled at him. "Are you trying to get rid of me so you could have the house all to yourself?"

"If you put it that way." Michael chuckled. "I'm still thinking about how much Alex loved our Lego gift last night."

"Almost as much as you did. I knew I should have bought you a set."

"Christmas is only two months away." He grinned.

"Cute. How's the tribute to Tiffany coming along?"

"Drew sent me testimonials from some of the charities she helped through fund-raising events. I'll be contacting other groups for more testimonials."

"Sounds interesting." I walked to the sink and rinsed my cup. "I'd better go get ready before Bianca drives off without me. I need to talk to her about the newsletter she wants for the shop." I went over to him, wrapped my arms around him, and planted a kiss on the top of his head. I tousled his thick brown hair and ran off laughing, barely missing his grasp.

After I'd changed my clothes and applied a bit of makeup, I made the bed and tidied up the room as I'd done every morning since we arrived. I didn't want our hosts to think we were sloppy houseguests.

When I went back downstairs, Michael was still hunched over his laptop, his eyes focused on the screen as if he were waiting for a starter's pistol to go off. The tiny scar on his cheekbone, evidence of the blows he'd encountered during one of his investigative quests for justice, seemed to strengthen his resolve.

I remembered the first time I'd seen that look of determination.

A year earlier, Bradford Publishing in Montreal had assigned me to help ghostwrite a crime novel for an investigative reporter named Michael Elliott. We'd become inseparable ever since.

I grabbed a bag of chocolate almonds that Bianca had stocked in the pantry—she'd remembered my passion—and put it in my handbag. "Okay, Michael. I'm leaving now."

He walked over, put his arms around me, and kissed me, releasing a flurry of butterflies inside me the way his kisses always did. "See you later."

"Later."

I heard Bianca and Alex coming down the stairs and met them in the foyer. After another round of goodbyes to Michael, we left the house.

On our ride into Portland, I didn't have the chance to raise the topic of Bianca's newsletter. Normally a quiet boy at home, Alex spoke to his mother all the way to town, asking over and over why he couldn't bring his Legos to day care and a gazillion other questions. The kid was so cute that I didn't mind the competition.

Once we arrived at the shop, I had every intention of pursuing my discussion with Bianca. I followed her upstairs and into her office.

We'd just sat down at her desk when the phone rang. From the gist of the conversation and Bianca's rapid note taking, I assumed a client was at the other end of the line. A minute later, Bianca looked at me and shrugged, signaling it could take a while longer.

I slipped out and quietly closed the door behind me. I was about to go downstairs when I heard muted voices coming from the kitchen. I tiptoed closer.

"Why the hell that old hag decided to go shopping there of all places, I'll never know," Doreen said in a brassy whisper.

"Stop making such a big deal about it." Lee's voice was low and nasal. "Who gives a rat's ass about her anyway?"

"That's not the point."

"Look, it's not over yet."

"What the hell are you talking about?"

"I got that dude to dish out ten grand, didn't I? He owes me ten times that much now. He'll pay up or regret it." A shuffle of feet. "Gotta go unload stuff."

I ducked into the bathroom and quietly shut the door. I waited until Doreen and Lee had walked by. Then I exhaled.

I wanted to call Michael but remembered I'd left my handbag by the chair in Bianca's office. I opened the door to her office and peeked inside.

Bianca glanced my way and smiled. "Come in, Megan. Wait till you hear this."

I sat down across from her. My foot hit my handbag—a reminder that I needed to call Michael.

Bianca's smile widened. "I got a request to provide flower arrangements to The Birchwood Club."

"Oh...that's good," I said, clueless.

"It's a private club in Falmouth with a world-class golf course and other elite recreational facilities. It also hosts special occasions. That's where I come in. They want me to visit the premises and discuss the flower décor requirements for a lavish charity gala they're hosting on behalf of the Women's Sponsorship Committee." She stopped to breathe. "Isn't that super?"

"It's terrific. When will you be driving out there?"

"We—you and I—will be driving there in an hour."

"We?"

She nodded. "While I'm meeting with Hillary Ward—she's the event planner at the club—you can take photos of the premises...note areas where they might want to position flower arrangements...you know, all the details that are essential to the success of a mega project like this."

"Right." Bianca had a talent for making anyone feel important, even if they didn't know what they were doing. "How long will we be there?"

"A couple of hours for sure," she said. "Keep your fingers crossed that the Women's Sponsorship Committee orders their flowers from my shop too. They're planning that gala event at Birchwood. It would mean a double project for me."

When Bianca went downstairs to check on one thing or another,

I retreated to the kitchen and made sure no one was around. I tried to call Michael but he didn't pick up. Just my luck.

CHAPTER 4

Bianca steered her BMW X1 along the circular driveway and stopped in front of the vaulted entrance to The Birchwood Club. She reached for the Canon PowerShot camera in her purse and handed it to me. "Here, Megan. Take as many shots of the club as you can. Okay?"

"Sure." I placed it in my handbag.

An attendant clad in a black vest and pants hurried over to the driver's side. "Park your SUV, ma'am?"

"Thank you." Bianca handed him the keys and we stepped out.

I looked around. Nestled within lush green woods sprinkled with bursts of red and gold maple trees, the pristine landscape of The Birchwood Club rivaled some of the posh country resorts I'd seen on television and in travel magazines. As expected, it acquired its name from the birch trees common to the area. Although the club was located minutes from Portland, its sprawling grounds gave one the feeling of being in another country. The serenity of the landscape was sprinkled with the chirping of birds—sounds that city dwellers like me don't often hear.

I took a breath of fresh air and caught a whiff of an earthy fragrance. I traced it to bright orange mums in ceramic pots flanking the walkway to the front door.

We entered the club and crossed the lobby to the reception desk. While Bianca spoke to the clerk and stated the nature of her visit, I glanced around. Comfy sofas and armchairs. Oversized ceramic tiles on the floor. An incredible view of the landscape through tall windows bordering three sides of the lobby.

A fifty-something woman wearing a navy blue jacket and matching skirt approached us, her ID card clipped to a side pocket. "Hello. I'm Hillary Ward. You must be Bianca. A pleasure to meet you." She shook her hand and then mine after Bianca introduced me as her project assistant. "Please come with me. I'll show you the reception room."

We followed Hillary around a corner and down a wide corridor.

"Did you know that our club offers year-round recreational facilities and services?" Hillary asked over her shoulder. "We have golf, tennis, fitness, and swimming facilities, not to mention that we're one of the premier spots in Maine for events like weddings."

"Yes, I know," Bianca said. "One of my corporate clients is a member. He invited my husband and me to a Christmas party here last year."

"It was a lovely event, wasn't it?" Hillary gave her a quick smile.

We entered a reception room filled with a dozen round tables that seated ten each. Sunlight poured in from tall windows here too and reflected off the silverware that a server was placing on the tables. The young girl in a white long-sleeved shirt and navy blue skirt glanced our way and smiled, then continued with her task.

"This is where the charity gala will be held," Hillary said, waving a hand to encompass the room. "The women's committee is expecting a decent turnout."

We followed Hillary further into the room. A wall-to-wall carpet in a muted beige and brown print felt soft underfoot.

"When is the event scheduled?" Bianca asked her.

"In a month. Oh, I realize it's short notice, but George Gray did say you were the best."

"George Gray?" Bianca's eyes went wide.

Hillary nodded. "He's been a member at our club for years. His wife Tiffany was on the women's committee that's planning an upcoming gala here. She passed away before we could finalize certain details. Surely you've heard about her untimely death."

"Yes...of course. My husband and I know the family well. You mentioned that Tiffany was working on a gala event here."

"Yes, it's the same one you and I are discussing today. Oh...I gather she hadn't had the chance to talk to you about the floral arrangements before she... Well, I'm sure the Women's Sponsorship Committee will contact you and bring you up to date." Hillary glanced at the server and lowered her voice. "I mean no disrespect when I say this. To be frank, Tiffany was a perfectionist when it came to organizing events. I remember how she and the other women on the committee had planned a fund-raising event for the food bank here last spring. Tiffany kept in touch with me and dedicated an enormous amount of time to overseeing the fine details. Despite the odds, the event turned out to be a big success." She smiled.

"Despite the odds?" Bianca asked.

Hillary leaned in closer. "Days before the event, Tiffany discovered a problem with the specially crafted candles she'd ordered for the tables. They didn't light properly. With no help from the other women on the committee, she called all over the state to find a suitable substitute. I don't know how she did it, but she had a supply delivered here at the last minute."

Out of the corner of my eye, I noticed the server glancing in our direction.

Hillary went on. "Last week, she was having a problem with the printer regarding the invitations to the gala here next month. I heard that George has since confirmed they were printed and sent out to the intended audience." She glanced around at the sound of silverware clinking. "Speaking of which...I suppose we should sit down and discuss the club's flower arrangements for that gala. We like to fancy things up around the club when special events are held here. We can talk in my office across the hall."

Bianca looked at me. "Megan, would you take photos of the reception room and other areas in the meantime?"

"Sure." I retrieved the camera from my handbag but waited until she'd left with Hillary. I wanted to talk to the young server. I sensed she had something on her mind. I walked up to her. "Hi. The table settings look beautiful."

She smiled. "Thank you. After you do the same thing over and over, it becomes second nature." She placed another setting of silverware on the table.

"My boss wants me to take photos of the room for an upcoming gala event. I imagine you've probably served at those events here."

"Too many to count." She rolled her eyes, then whispered, "I couldn't help hearing what Hillary was saying about Tiffany Gray's problem."

I took a guess. "About the candles?"

She nodded. "I was one of the table servers assigned to her fund-raising event last spring. I know why the first batch of candles she ordered didn't work." She glanced around, then back at me. "I was serving coffee here to the women's committee while they were discussing plans for that spring event. When Tiffany stepped out for a minute, the other women began to talk bad about her."

"What did they say?"

"That she came from a lower-class family...that she married into money...that she couldn't compete on their level. I swear, some people treat table servers as if they're invisible." She shook her head, placed more silverware on the table. "Anyway, one committee woman said she would bring Tiffany down a notch or two by making sure the event would be a disaster."

"You think it had something to do with the candles?"

"Maybe."

"How?"

"The original boxes of candles had arrived a week before the event. Management kept them in a storage room here. Days later, Tiffany wanted us to set a table serving with the candles to see what it would look like with the lights dimmed low. When we went to get them, we noticed the boxes were wet. I mean, really soaked."

"That's why the wicks wouldn't light."

She nodded. "The floor was wet too, but the other things in the room were on shelves, so they were okay."

"Did anyone ever find out how water got into that room?"

She shrugged. "I don't know, but I felt sorry for Tiffany, in spite of what she put us through."

"What do you mean?"

"She was so picky." Another roll of the eyes.

"Perfectionists are known to be picky."

"Not like her. She fussed over the table settings like you wouldn't believe. She had us change things five times before she made a final choice." She gave the tables a cursory glance. "I'm done here. I have another room to prepare. Good luck with the photos." She smiled and left.

I spent the next hour taking photos of the reception room from every imaginable angle and the outer corridor leading to it as well. I extended my subject matter to other accessible areas of the club, indoors and outdoors. My job over, I wandered back inside and sat down in the lobby, hoping that Bianca's meeting would end soon. My stomach was growling.

Then I remembered the chocolate almonds I'd stashed in my handbag earlier. I discreetly popped one into my mouth, savoring it. Then I chewed on a couple more while I watched people come and go through the lobby.

Half an hour later, Bianca resurfaced. She smiled but didn't say a word until we were safely inside her SUV.

"Guess what," she said as we drove away. "I suggested that the club should have flowers on the receiving table, flowers at the base of a podium announcing the event, flowers in the lobby..." She caught her breath. "Hillary said yes to everything."

"Terrific," I said.

"That's not all. Hillary called the Women's Sponsorship Committee to speed things along at their end. They confirmed I had the contract for the gala too. We'll be meeting with them tomorrow afternoon. Double good news." She laughed.

"I'm not surprised. Your reputation speaks for itself."

"Well, George Gray did have a hand in it. Just once, I would have liked to earn a project of this size on my own."

"Oh, I'm sure you'll find a way to forgive him," I said, making her laugh again.

Bianca was so excited about the double project she'd landed at The Birchwood Club that she couldn't think about having lunch. She opted to head back to the shop instead but would drop me off at the house first. "You can work the rest of the day on the newsletter," she reminded me.

It couldn't have worked out better. Michael was home and had cooked a pot of spaghetti. Meatballs were simmering in a tomato sauce and a delicious aroma filled the kitchen.

"Oh, you saved my life." I hugged and kissed him. "I'm starving."

"How was your visit to Birchwood?"

"Good. Bianca landed a major contract for a gala next month."

"Way to go." He smiled.

"Thanks to George Gray. He's one of the club's elite members."

Michael shrugged. "A referral from the inner circle. All the better."

"Made any progress on your tribute to Tiffany?"

"Almost done. You can look it over after we eat." He filled our plates and set them on the kitchen table. "I made more than enough for everyone's dinner tonight too, so dig in." He sat in the chair adjacent to mine.

I ate a few mouthfuls before I remembered what I'd wanted to tell him. "I overheard Doreen and Lee whispering this morning in the kitchen at Bianca's shop. They were talking about an old woman who had gone shopping in a strange place. It seemed to upset Doreen."

"Yeah, shopping in a strange place would upset me too." Michael grinned.

"Cute." I gave him *the look*—a stare that women use instead of words because it drives the point home better. "Here's the interesting part. I think Doreen and Lee are blackmailing someone. Lee said 'dude,' so it's probably a man."

"What makes you think it's blackmail?"

"Lee said the man had already paid him ten thousand dollars and would pay a hundred grand more or regret it if he didn't."

"Could be idle talk."

"I doubt it."

He eyed me with concern. "Be careful, Megan."

After we'd finished our meals and cleared the dishes, I sat down and reviewed the tribute that Michael had drawn up for Tiffany:

"The citizens of Portland mourn the passing of Tiffany Gray, a passionate and generous woman who made a significant contribution to the community through her tireless fund-raising efforts. She served on numerous committees and was instrumental in raising awareness about the underprivileged in our city."

Michael's tender words moved me. By the time I'd finished reading the rest of the tribute, I felt genuinely sorry for the kind-hearted woman whose life had ended too soon.

Short testimonials followed the tribute—simple words of appreciation from charities and committee members alike. I read two of the eight testimonials:

"Special people like Tiffany Gray made it possible for our charity to support less fortunate members of the community." *The Food Bank*

"The Women's Sponsorship Committee recognizes the generosity of Tiffany Gray who graciously devoted her time and energy to our fund-raising events." *Christina Reed - Chairperson, WSC*

I read the other six testimonials, then said to Michael, "Too bad Tiffany isn't around to see how much her work meant to so many people. These tributes are wonderful and so is your article on her."

He looked up from his laptop at the other end of the kitchen table and smiled. "Thanks. It's running in Tuesday's paper. I'll send it to Drew in a bit. I want to check my email first. Waiting for confirmation for another interview." He gazed back at the screen.

I had things to take care of too. "I'll go work in the guest bedroom. See you later."

He nodded. "Later."

Upstairs, I took Bianca's camera out of my handbag and uploaded the photos I'd taken at The Birchwood Club to my laptop. Unaware of it at the time, I'd zoomed in to take a photo of the entrance and captured a familiar face—that of George Gray. He was leaving the club. A younger, more muscular man with short blonde-tipped hair accompanied him. I didn't give it a second thought.

I worked on Bianca's newsletter the rest of the afternoon. A search on the Internet gave me general ideas for articles but nothing that I considered groundbreaking. I needed a more viable source of information. Time was running out.

At dinner that evening, Bianca lifted everyone's spirits when she recapped the news about her contract at The Birchwood Club. "Talk about a stroke of good luck." She smiled.

"You see?" Victor said to her. "Things are taking a turn for the better." He poured more wine into our glasses.

"Plus Michael prepared this fabulous pasta dinner for us," she said. "Thanks, Michael."

"My pleasure," he said.

"When will they choose the flowers for the gala at Birchwood?" Victor asked Bianca.

"Tomorrow. Megan and I will be meeting with the women's committee there." She looked at me. "I usually provide clients with a short list of seasonal options so they don't start asking for the moon. Then I make a presentation based on my recommendations. If they have any questions, they'll ask me."

"And my purpose at that meeting?"

"I want you there because you add credibility to my business. You're creating my newsletter, right?"

Before I could say a word, Michael's phone rang. He glanced at the screen. "It's the *Herald*. It could be important. Excuse me." He answered. "Hi, Drew. No problem. Yes." A short pause. "Can you hold on a sec?" He put Drew on hold and gazed at me. "Jeff is still away on assignment. Drew is asking if I can stay in town until the cause of Tiffany Gray's death is determined. Depending on the results of the autopsy, he might need me to write a series of investigative pieces."

Bianca touched my arm. "Oh, Megan, please say yes."

I noticed the expression on Michael's face—excited and hopeful about the new assignment. I couldn't refuse. "Okay...yes."

He relayed the message to Drew, then thanked him and ended the call.

"One tiny question," I said to Michael. "How much longer will we be staying in town?"

He shrugged. "It depends on when the final autopsy report becomes available."

"It could be another week," I said. "We'd better check into a hotel."

"We wouldn't hear of it." Bianca waved a hand in the air.

"That's right," Victor said. "We insist you remain our houseguests for as long as you want. Michael, you're free to use my home office. It has a computer, printer, phone, and fax. I rarely work here anyway."

"The main benefit of working in Victor's office is that it's close to the kitchen," Bianca pointed out to Michael with a wink.

Despite the change in our plans, things seemed to have settled down.

Or so I thought.

CHAPTER 5

My schedule hit its first snag at eight o'clock Tuesday morning. If it hadn't been for the sound of the fax machine echoing from downstairs, I'd have slept in. I nestled under the cozy blankets, hoping that my efforts at cocooning would return me to my former dormant state. After another fax transmission, I knew I'd lost the battle for good. I dragged myself out of bed, showered, and got dressed. The empty bedrooms upstairs confirmed that the Hobbs had already left the house.

I found Michael standing by the coffee maker in the kitchen.

He smiled at me. "Hi, gorgeous. Want some coffee? It's fresh—and strong."

"Yes, please. It's exactly what I need." I glanced at the table and noticed sheets of paper with the heading FAX. "Did you find out anything more about Tiffany this morning?"

"You know I can't discuss information from my sources with you. Journalistic privilege."

"Oh, come on, Michael. You swore me to secrecy on other assignments you covered. I didn't let you down, did I?"

"Well..." He frowned, pretended to weigh the matter.

"You big tease." I poked him.

He chuckled. "Okay. Drew sent me some preliminary info while we wait for Tiffany's autopsy results to arrive. Sources reveal that she was the athletic type. She and George hired a live-in personal trainer...played golf on the weekends...had a lifestyle everyone dreams of. She often accompanied George on business trips to the Bahamas, South America, Florida...you name it." He already sounded like an expert on the Gray family.

"Anything about her side of the family?" I sat down at the table.

He placed a cup of coffee in front of me. "Nothing so far. In fact, nobody seems to know much about her background."

"Ah...a mystery woman." I drank some coffee and hoped the caffeine would take effect soon to make up for the sleep I'd lost.

"There's more. Rumor has it she had a fling with their personal trainer, Tyler Wilson."

"Old news. The girls at the shop are already gossiping about it." I took another sip of coffee. "You mentioned Tiffany's autopsy. What if it reveals something weird?"

"If it conflicts with the results of a physical examination she requested in June—"

"A physical? How did you get that information?"

"Through Liz in forensics. She has university buddies who work in the medical field."

"You said Tiffany requested the physical? Why?"

Michael hesitated. "She was trying to get pregnant."

"Oh." Another familiar cord struck home. I'd been trying to conceive while my husband was sleeping around with other women.

"Something else," Michael said. "Tiffany asked for a lab test to check for STDs."

"Do you know why?"

He shrugged. "Either the rumors about her are true or George is enjoying a little hanky-panky on the side."

"Anything else?"

"To answer your other question, if her autopsy reveals even the slightest discrepancy, her death will be ruled as suspicious."

"I thought it was already considered suspicious."

"Not in the formal sense. If it becomes formal, the police will launch an inquiry and request an official autopsy for their own purposes."

The doorbell rang—a melodious tune that seemed to go on forever. Michael went to answer it. He returned moments later with a UPS envelope. He opened it and pulled out a stack of sheets.

My suspicions were confirmed when Michael fingered the first sheet and said, "Drew sent me a copy of the preliminary autopsy for Tiffany. It revealed an anomaly in her lungs—a contrast to the clean bill of health noted on her annual checkup. He confirms the police will mount an official investigation into her death, along with a request for a comprehensive autopsy."

"An anomaly? How odd. Gladys had an anomaly too."

"Plain crazy, isn't it?" Michael's gaze grew intense. "Additional testing will tell us more."

"Does the preliminary autopsy on Tiffany state which tests were performed?"

He skimmed the sheet. "They've written off street drugs, medications, and industrial poisons because of the side effects that they would have had on her body. They're running tests for plant poisons now."

"Plant poisons?"

He nodded. "I'm guessing it's routine in this type of investigation. Some species are known to be dangerous when ingested."

"Are you saying she ate plants?"

"Not necessarily, but the flowers—"

"I doubt that anyone who wasn't a connoisseur would risk eating flowers."

"That's the general consensus but—"

"From what I've heard," I cut him off again, feeling the caffeine finally kick in, "Tiffany doesn't strike me as the type of person who had the panache to pick out edible petals."

Michael chuckled. "That's probably true, but we're talking gourmet delicacies here, not field daisies."

I stood my ground. "Wouldn't a blood test or an examination of her stomach reveal a poisonous substance?"

"It might—if she had swallowed it."

"You lost me."

"It's a long shot. Tiffany might have been allergic to one of the flowers or plants she purchased. She could have touched a spike or petal and had a bad reaction to it. Even taking a whiff of a poisonous plant could have had a fatal effect."

"Wouldn't anyone else who had handled the flowers be dead too?"

"Not if they wore protective gear—like gloves and a mask."

"Which would suggest that her death was premeditated."

He shrugged. "Anything's possible." He laid out the other papers on the table. They were photos.

I squinted. "These pictures are all grainy. How can you see anything?"

"That's the best I could get."

"Where were they taken?"

"From inside the Gray mansion."

"How did you manage that?"

"Not me. Jeff has a contact named Craig who works as an independent crime scene photographer. When he's not taking photos of victims and crime scenes, he works as a lighting assistant in a theater."

"Jeff sure has lots of friends in the right places."

Michael grinned. "It's who you know that counts."

I sipped my coffee. "You're not going to publish these photos, are you?"

"Of course not. They're for my eyes only. Make that *our* eyes." He lifted a photo from the pile and turned it over.

I held out my hand. "Give. I'm a big girl." The photo was hazy like the others, but I could distinguish a woman with blonde hair collapsed on a dark wood floor next to a row of white cabinets. "They found Tiffany in the kitchen?"

"Yes. Why?" He pulled up a chair next to me.

"They found Tom's body in the kitchen area of the cottage he'd rented." I shuddered.

Michael put a hand on my shoulder. "Want to talk about it?"

"No."

The tiny muscles along his jaw line twitched. "Don't shut me out, Megan. You know I'm a good listener."

"I'm okay. Honest." I smiled at him, then peered at the photos. I noticed an empty vase on a pillar in the center of a spacious area.

The thought that it didn't contain flowers crossed my mind. "Is this the foyer?"

He leaned over to get a closer look. "Yes."

"It's the size of a bowling alley."

"If you think that's something, check out the dining room and the living room."

I followed his gaze to two other photos. "We could fit our entire condo in either one of those rooms." I studied the other photos. While the rooms in the Gray home didn't reveal more than a foggy reproduction of sofas, lamps, tables, and chairs, I noticed a recurring element in every room: flowers or plants. Even the bathrooms had vases of flowers in them. "It's a creepy theory, but you're saying that one of the plants or flowers in her home could have killed her."

He shrugged. "Don't know yet. Forensic investigators sent them out for analysis. I don't expect the tests will produce much."

"Aren't you contradicting yourself?"

"No. Records indicate they're the type of flowers and plants commonly found in retail shops—roses, daisies, ferns—"

"The detectives who visited Bianca's shop checked out the little information tags on some of the plants. They didn't take notes. Maybe they had a specific name in mind."

"Could be."

"No wonder they questioned Bianca about toxic species." I gave it more thought. "On the other hand, if I were the killer, I would have discarded whatever flower or plant had killed Tiffany. If it were possible, that is."

"True."

My optimism waned. "If the evidence is long gone, it's a dead end."

"Not yet. I'm hoping the final comprehensive autopsy will tell us more about the cause of the anomaly."

"What if it doesn't?"

He grinned. "Megan, you should know me better by now."

There it was again—that undeniable look of determination in his eyes. It was the same look he'd given me when he'd pledged to find my husband's killer and risked his life to make it happen.

Bianca picked me up at home after lunch and we drove out to The Birchwood Club. The sun had broken through the clouds and cast a warm glow over an autumn landscape that still exhibited a fair amount of greenery. Bianca didn't talk much. I figured she might be a tad nervous about her presentation.

Minutes later, Christina Reed welcomed us to the Women's Sponsorship Committee meeting about to take place in one of the boardrooms at the club. I recognized her name from a testimonial Michael had included with his article on Tiffany. Christina's stature, the grey highlights in her hair, and serious brown eyes commanded respect and added credence to the take-charge attitude she conveyed. I noticed her astuteness when, in one rapid pass, she seemed to assess the cost of my wool jacket right down to my high-heeled leather pumps. I made a mental note to thank Michael again for the trendy jacket he'd bought me on the weekend.

Christina drew the attention of the other five members with a tap of her pen on the table. "Ladies, please be seated." She began the meeting by introducing the committee members to Bianca. "Most of you are already familiar with the lovely assortment of plants and flowers at Bianca's Garden. Also joining us today is Megan Scott, who is launching a newsletter for the shop and welcomes any suggestions for articles that you ladies might have."

Bianca handed out the paperwork she'd prepared for the meeting. It included color photos of the flower choices and accessories she recommended for the gala event the committee was planning. She asked the women to tick off their preferences on the sheet as she went through her presentation so as to narrow down their selection. She paused now and then during the hour-long talk to answer any questions.

After Bianca had finished, Christina spoke on behalf of the group. "Thank you for sharing your expertise, Bianca. We certainly have an excellent collection to choose from, don't we, ladies?" The members murmured in agreement. "Let's take a fifteen-minute break and continue our discussion afterward."

I caught Christina's eye as we both stood up. She gave me a polite smile before turning to chat with another member.

I walked out of the room and headed for the bathroom. I didn't know what the staff had put in the coffee they served at the women's meeting, but I couldn't wait another minute.

A committee member named Ida caught up to me. "These sit-down meetings are so hard on the you-know-what." She laughed. "Especially at my age."

"I thought it was the coffee."

"That too." Ida laughed again. "So you're writing a newsletter for Bianca's Gardens. I think that's such a clever idea. I have dozens of indoor plants. It would be wonderful to learn about the different varieties and how to care for them."

"Do you have a specific plant in mind?"

"Heck, no. Start with A and go straight to Z." The laugh lines around her eyes deepened. "I don't have a green thumb. Instructions would have to be simple so I could follow them."

"Thanks for the suggestion," I said to her and meant it. I was already envisioning future newsletter articles based on her idea.

I held open the door to the washroom as Ida continued the conversation. "I'm so happy the committee is going ahead with the fund-raising event next month. I was worried Tiffany Gray's death might put a damper on things."

"Oh?"

She glanced at the floor beneath the bathroom stalls to make sure we were alone. "I helped her as much as I could, but she was handling most of the event details herself. She was quite the perfectionist, you know. She had to be, considering the way the other women picked her apart."

"What women?"

"Some of the women on our committee. Tiffany went through hell trying to earn brownie points from them, but they never complimented her or said as much as a thank you. Heck, they never lifted a finger to help her either. I won't mention names, but I will say that no matter how much money you have, you can't take it with you when you die."

She entered a nearby stall. I chose one at the far end.

I was still dwelling on Ida's words when two more women entered the washroom.

"That bitch wanted—"

"Shhh!" the second woman said to the other.

Ida walked out of the stall and washed her hands. "That was a lovely presentation, wasn't it?"

"I would have preferred to take a tour of the shop to see the real flowers and plants," the first woman said in an annoying nasal voice.

"Why? Your three-story mansion is overflowing with them," the second one said. "When you had Brian and me over last weekend, I thought I was walking through the Hanging Gardens of Babylon."

"The *what*?" the first woman squeaked.

There was a shuffle of feet, the sound of a door opening and closing, then a brief silence.

The second woman spoke. "Okay, we're alone now. What were you saying about Tiffany?"

"That bitch wanted me to call the printer last week and take care of the gala invitations. I told her I was too busy. I had appointments for my hair, nails...the works. You know how hectic it gets when you're a doctor's wife. Jason and I get invited all over town. Well, she said that if I was too busy, I should let someone else take my place on the committee. Imagine the nerve of that wannabe?" The first woman's voice reached a high-pitched squeal.

"Wannabe is right. What did you say to her?"

"That I don't have time to deal with people like printers. Besides, I raise a lot of money for these events through Jason's contacts."

"Yeah, a lot of good George's money did her. She croaked before she could spend it."

I surfaced from the bathroom stall and smiled knowingly at the gaping mouths staring at me in the mirror. I washed my hands and left.

As soon as everyone had returned to the meeting room,

discussion resumed about the choice of centerpiece for the tables at the gala event. The group offered a short list of choices for fresh flowers, preferred color schemes, and types of vases. Pros and cons were tossed about, but the women couldn't reach a consensus.

The two women who had gossiped about Tiffany in the washroom checked their watches often and didn't participate much in the discussions. I discovered that the high-pitched nasal voice belonged to Val, a stylish woman in her late thirties who wore a leopard top and a diamond ring the size of a large pea. Her friend was Stacy—mid-thirties, a hot pink jacket over a black skirt, ankle leather boots with spike heels.

During a lull in the discussion, Ida surprised me when she quietly said, "It's unfortunate that Tiffany Gray is no longer with us. She'd have no problem choosing the arrangements."

Val and Stacy exchanged side-glances, then Val spoke up. "What makes you think she was any better than us, Ida? Stacy and I brought in a quarter of the donations at the last event."

"Any of us can call up friends and business contacts and ask for donations, and we did," Ida said. "But Tiffany made most of the decisions and organized things to get the events up and going. She did the hard labor."

"Hard labor." Val grimaced. "The only hard labor she ever did was between the—"

"Does anyone have any more questions for Bianca?" Christina cut her off. When no one replied, she said, "You've been very generous with your time, Bianca. If you wouldn't mind giving us a few more minutes, I'd like to make the final decision and call it a day. The committee has other events on the agenda and we need to move on."

"Of course," Bianca said.

Christina studied her list. "I'll go with the carved white pumpkin shell as the vase. It's a seasonal piece and it'll add drama to each table. I loved your suggestion for an arrangement of fresh roses, tiger lilies, sunflowers, and berries. The yellows, peaches, and shades of orange will look spectacular on the tables. As fillers for the tables, the orange tinted glass holders with votive candles will do fine." She looked at Bianca.

"Excellent choices," Bianca said, smiling. "They'll add warmth and ambiance to the room."

"Thank you." Christina addressed the committee members. "Ladies, please submit any suggestions for Bianca's newsletter to me by this evening. I'll make sure there's no repetition before I pass the information on to Megan. I'll be seeing some of you again tonight at the book-club meeting, so there are no excuses." She adjourned the meeting.

Val and Stacy grabbed their handbags and left the room in a huff.

As for me, I was still processing the conflicting comments I'd heard about Tiffany Gray and trying to decipher what was true and what wasn't.

CHAPTER 6

With the Birchwood meetings over, I fell back into my old routine on Wednesday: mornings working on the newsletter at home and afternoons working at Bianca's Gardens. Since Michael had moved his work setup to Victor's home office, the kitchen table was once again serving its intended purpose. I was having breakfast with Michael when my phone rang.

Christina Reed was the last person I expected to hear from at nine o'clock. "I have several newsletter suggestions to forward to you by email, but some of our committee members have cut out pages from decorating magazines and provided hand-written notes for you as well. I could send them to you by courier, or if you happen to be in town this morning, you could pass by my office." She gave me the address on High Street.

I took the hint. "I'll drop in. What time is good for you?"

"I have another meeting at eleven. How does eleven-thirty sound?"

"Perfect. I'll see you then." I ended the call. "Things are finally coming together for Bianca's newsletter," I said to Michael. "The women's committee has a bunch of suggestions for me. I'm meeting with the chairperson at eleven-thirty this morning." I buttered my toast.

"Oh...I need the car this morning too. I have an interview in town. Where's yours?" He gazed at me over the rim of his coffee cup.

I told him the address.

"You're kidding. That's where I'm heading too."

"What time?"

"Eleven."

It had to be a coincidence. "Who with?"

"Christina Reed."

"Me too." I laughed. "She heads the women's committee that Bianca and I met yesterday at the club. Why are you meeting with her?"

"I'd originally scheduled an interview with her to find out more about Tiffany and her work with charities. Now I can use it to dig up something for my investigative articles too."

"Now that you mention it..." I reiterated Ida's comments and what I'd overheard Val and Stacy say in the washroom. "It makes me even more curious about the real Tiffany."

He paused in thought. "Want to sit in on my meeting this morning? I'll introduce you as my editor."

"I don't think so. I'm already wearing too many hats. Ghostwriter, newsletter writer, Bianca's project assistant—"

"So?"

"Forget it. We'll drive in together. I'll wait in the reception area while you meet with her. My meeting with her shouldn't take more than a few minutes. You can drop me off at the shop later on your way to the *Herald*."

Christina Reed did a double take when she saw me sitting in the reception area of her office half an hour before my scheduled appointment. "Hi, Megan, you're early," she said to me. "I hope you don't mind waiting while I meet with this young man first." She gestured to Michael who had just introduced himself to her.

"Not if Michael doesn't mind making me wait," I said, laughing.

"She's usually not this rude." Michael chuckled, then explained our relationship.

"Oh, isn't that a lovely surprise," Christina said, smiling. "Well, Megan, we can't have you sitting here. If Michael doesn't mind, you can join us. After all, what we're going to discuss will end up in the

Herald for everyone to read, won't it?" She looked at Michael.

"That's the general idea," he said.

Christina's office was painted steel blue. The color emphasized the dozen or so large black-and-white illustrations of historic sites hanging on the walls. Not a surprising choice of décor for someone who was a staff member of Greater Portland Landmarks—a fact I picked up from the sign on the exterior door to her office. Her desk looked as if it had been salvaged from days gone by, its ornate carvings a contrast to the sleek suede armchairs Michael and I were sitting in. Thick books and binders lined a shelf behind her desk.

"So that we're clear about this interview beforehand, I'd like to approve your article before it goes to publication," Christina said to Michael.

"No problem," Michael said. "I'll send you a preliminary copy by email."

"Good." Christina sat back and adjusted the cowl neckline of her pink sweater. "Now what would you like to know?"

He leaned slightly forward. "Tell me about Tiffany Gray and her work with charities."

"I'm afraid I didn't get to know Tiffany as well as I would have liked to. I sit on several committees and spread myself thin trying to meet my responsibilities to each of them. However, what I did appreciate about her was the passion she put into her work. It's something I can relate to." She smiled. "We initially accepted her on the committee as a favor to her husband. Ironically, she proved to be extremely hardworking."

"Other people haven't been as flattering," Michael said, driving the discussion forward.

Christina laughed. "I'll tell you, I've seen enough backstabbing in my days to last a lifetime. If there's one thing I won't tolerate, it's jealousy. Women can be especially cruel in that respect." She gave me a discerning glance. I knew she was referring to the incident at the committee meeting when she'd stopped Val and Stacy from gossiping about Tiffany.

Michael pretended not to notice and went on. "Let's backtrack," he said. "Your committee accepted Tiffany as a favor to her husband.

Can you expand on that?"

"Since George is somewhat of a local celebrity, the women's committee didn't hesitate to accept a member of his family into our group. I'm fiercely loyal to George. He and I go back decades, actually. We went to university in England together. I thought he was a pretty good catch at the time. Unfortunately, he had other goals in mind." She paused. "Let me show you something interesting." She turned to lift a thick binder off the shelf behind her and opened it. "There's a lot to be said about the Gray family lineage. This is their coat of arms." She turned the binder around to show us a photo. It displayed the profile of a lion rearing up on its hind legs. It was painted against a red background coating a metal shield. The image included a knight's shiny helmet at the top.

"There must be a lot of history behind this crest," I said to her.

"Absolutely. The Gray name is of Viking origin. Early settlers took up residence in North America in the 1600s. Their ancestors in England had fought numerous battles and were associated with honor and royalty. The royalty part included a marriage between a Gray family member and a sister of Henry VIII. Now that's something to brag about, isn't it?" She laughed. "Over the generations, the Gray family gained respect in economic, military, and scientific arenas, and were successful in fields from art to zoology. All to say that I'm honored to sit on certain committees alongside George and his father Stanley." She returned the book to the shelf.

Michael steered the discussion back on track. "I recently published a tribute to Tiffany in the *Herald* that included your testimonial from the Women's Sponsorship Committee."

"I read it," Christina said. "Lovely article."

"Thanks. Can you tell me more about Tiffany's work with the charities? Any feedback from the events she handled?"

"As I said earlier, Tiffany's passion was reflected in the work she did and she did it to perfection. But there will always be critics, no matter what, and Tiffany was an easy target."

"In what way?"

"People were polite to her because she was George's wife. I know for a fact that his inner circle of acquaintances had never truly accepted her. I think Tiffany sensed it too and probably had her guard up. What amazed me is that she continued to take on fund-raising events, even when George's encouragement waned."

"What do you mean?"

"George was enthusiastic about attending charity galas with his wife at first—lovely media publicity and all." She paused. "Things changed quite abruptly this summer. They were seen less often together at dinner parties and the like."

"Any idea why?"

"Ever since I've known George, he was all about making money. When Tiffany entered the picture, she was all about giving it away. Not everyone warmed up to her generous outlook—maybe least of all George."

"Interesting. Can you explain?"

"He had to attend more fund-raising events than ever before, which can translate into quite a drain on time—especially when you're a busy entrepreneur like George. Months ago he told me how he had to stop escorting Tiffany to charity events because he didn't have enough time to take care of his own affairs. I empathized with him and wondered if Tiffany would be capable of drawing as many donors without George by her side."

"And?"

"She doubled her efforts and actually did better without him. Like I said earlier, it was all about the passion." Christina checked her watch. "I'm sorry, Michael, but that's all the time I have for you today. I look forward to seeing your write-up." She stood up.

"I appreciate it," Michael said as we both rose to our feet.

Christina glanced at me. "I haven't forgotten you, Megan." She reached for a manila envelope on her desk and handed it to me. "I've included the handwritten suggestions and emails I received from the women. You'll find some lovely ideas there. Good luck to you both."

On our walk back to the car, Michael said, "Can't deny that Christina is a strong supporter of the Gray family—George in particular."

"Her loyalty to him could explain why she's so protective of Tiffany," I said.

He shrugged. "Maybe she liked Tiffany."

"Hard to tell."

"I'm hoping my next interview will disclose more about Tiffany. I'm meeting with Ben Leblanc tomorrow morning. He's a services coordinator for an adult day shelter in town. He worked with Tiffany on a fund-raiser last spring. Want to come along?"

I was curious but didn't want to admit it. "I have to work on Bianca's newsletter."

"We could pop in to see him any time."

"What makes you think I'd want to go with you?"

"You said you wanted to know what the real Tiffany was like. Ben saw my article on Tiffany in the *Herald* and contacted me. He wants to talk to me about her. It sounds like the guy would offer honest feedback."

I was even more curious now. "Okay."

Michael checked his watch. "How about we grab a quick lunch somewhere?"

"Sure."

Michael found a parking spot on the street near Starbucks. While we were waiting for our tomato and mozzarella paninis, I opened the envelope Christina had given me. A large paperclip held a handful of notes and photos. I dropped the paperclip into my handbag and scanned the notes. Four suggestions were seasonal, so the timing was off. Two suggestions were useful and inspired me to come up with tangible ideas for the newsletter.

After Michael dropped me off at the shop, I was eager to discuss the newsletter ideas with Bianca, but she had other plans. She proposed we take a drive.

"We're going to George's warehouse," she said. "I want to give him this rubber tree plant to thank him for the Birchwood referral." She pointed to a three-foot plant that had a large red bow around a gold pot. "It's a surprise."

"How do you know he's at the warehouse?" I asked her.

"I called his office and they told me."

"I'm surprised they'd tell you over the phone."

"They know my voice by now."

"Why don't you have the plant delivered by Lee?" I would have preferred to work on the newsletter and done anything to weasel my way out of the trip.

"Because it shows more personal effort and gratitude if I deliver it myself."

I couldn't argue with that.

We left the city core and hit the I-295 northbound. Minutes later, we entered an industrial sector where the only thing separating large rectangular structures were asphalt laneways.

Bianca turned onto the sprawling grounds of Gray Climate Care. The white siding of the two enormous warehouse units gleamed like the underbellies of two giant orcas frolicking in the ocean. She parked in one of the dozen parallel spots reserved for visitors and retrieved the rubber plant from the back of her SUV. "It'll be perfect for George's lobby in the warehouse. It does well in lots of artificial light."

I opened one of the double doors to the entrance of the main building. Bianca carried her three-foot-high cargo into the lobby. The cracks in the terrazzo that paved the lobby floor indicated negligence on the owner's part. I figured that George's investment in his Falmouth mansion might explain why he'd chosen to ignore a few cracks in the floor here.

Off to the left was a receptionist's station, the top edge of a computer monitor visible over the wood counter. A woman wearing a headset greeted us.

"We're here to see George Gray," Bianca said.

"I'm sorry, you just missed him," the receptionist said. "He left to attend an urgent meeting."

"Oh," Bianca said, disappointment crossing her face. "Would you please make sure he gets this plant? I've included a note."

As we got back into the SUV, Bianca said to me, "So much for surprises."

Thursday morning, I set out with Michael for our meeting with Ben Leblanc. If anyone would have first-hand information about

Tiffany and her charitable endeavors, I supposed it would be Ben.

Michael parked the car downtown where a growing concentration of social services outlets were located, in addition to shelters for teens and adults. "One of my friends in Toronto works as a caseworker for a shelter," he said as we walked down the street. "He helps get the homeless off the street and into subsidized housing."

"I read that some homeless people prefer living on the street because it's the life they've come to know and trust," I said.

He nodded. "For others, a shelter is a refuge from troubles back home. It helps if drifters know their options. Certain day shelters offer free facilities where they can take a shower or use a phone."

"Basic things we take for granted in our own lives."

"Right. I went online and checked out the shelter Ben works for. Their food pantry feeds more than a hundred families each week. The soup kitchens in this town serve more than a thousand meals every day."

"It's a good thing cities have resource centers that offer this kind of help."

"They could always use more."

We came up to an unassuming red brick building and stepped inside. The lobby was a sunny yellow and smelled as if it had been recently painted. A leafy artificial plant filled a corner. I followed Michael to the back of the lobby and around the corner. The first door on the left was ajar. A sign on it read: Resource Center -- Coordinator.

Michael knocked on the door.

A man looked up from behind a computer. White hair, overweight, thick-framed black glasses.

"Ben? I'm Michael Elliott, the reporter."

Ben stood up. "Hey, Michael. Come on in."

Michael introduced me. "This is Megan, my writing associate."

I'd acquired yet another title.

"Sit down, please." Ben indicated two vinyl chairs across from him, then squeezed past us to shut the door. "I hope you didn't mind coming here. I like to meet people face-to-face and see who

I'm talking to." He sat back down. "I have to tell you again how much I enjoyed your tribute article on Tiffany Gray. You said earlier that you were writing another article about her."

"Yes," Michael said.

"Nice lady. I was sorry to hear about her death. The community could use more people like her." Piles of papers and folders covered his desk. He pushed them aside to make room for a cup of coffee that had probably grown cold.

"You mentioned you were at a fund-raising event with Tiffany last spring," Michael said.

Ben nodded. "The event was a pancake breakfast to raise money for the food pantry and for building repairs to the shelter."

"Did you get to talk to Tiffany the day of the event?"

"Oh, yes."

"What type of person would you say she was?"

"Down-to-earth—not like other hoity-toity types, you know what I mean?"

"Did she pop in for a photo op that day?"

"No way." Ben chuckled. "Did she ever surprise me."

"How?" Michael leaned forward.

"I never expect fundraisers to show up for the event itself. If they do, that's cool. It's the hands-on thing that amazed me about Tiffany."

"I'm not following you."

"I didn't recognize her at first without the makeup, hair done up, and fancy clothes, even though I'm pretty good with faces. But there she was, in jeans and a ponytail and no makeup, preparing the plates in the kitchen as if she'd done it all her life. Even stayed till the end to help clean up."

"Did anyone else recognize her?" I asked Ben.

He chuckled again. "I doubt it—especially after she'd introduced herself by another name."

"What name was that?" I asked.

He rubbed his chin. "I forget. It was a common name—not snooty like Tiffany. After I recognized her, she asked me not to tell anyone."

"Why not?"

"At first I thought she didn't want her high-flying friends to find out she was dishing out food at a fundraiser. She surprised me again when she said it was because she enjoyed doing something useful as part of a group for a change. Didn't know what she meant by that. Still don't. Now that she's gone, I think people deserve to know what a decent person she was. I thought you could use this event in your article." He gave Michael a knowing look.

"You can count on it," Michael said. "Do you want to see the preliminary write-up of my article?"

"No need to. You're good to go with it."

After our meeting, we were no further ahead. Ben had succeeded in adding yet another layer of complexity to a woman whose life was turning out to be as mysterious as her death.

CHAPTER 7

"It's a matter of divide and conquer." Michael stood by the stove and punctuated his words with a wave of the spatula. "The way I see it, I need to divide my investigative reporting into three separate topics: Tiffany's fund-raising events and connections, her family and household staff, and her final autopsy results. Everything else stems from these areas."

"Sounds logical to me," I said after he'd asked my opinion Friday morning. "How are those scrambled eggs coming along?"

"Ready to go." He scooped the eggs into our plates and continued to describe his plan of attack. "So far, I've got the fund-raising topic covered. More tributes, plus the interviews with Christina from the women's committee and Ben at the shelter, served that purpose. Want to look my article over later?" He set the plates on the kitchen table.

"Sure."

"My second article in the series depends on getting an interview with George Gray. I don't know why he hasn't returned my calls."

"I can't help you there, but these eggs are fantastic. Hurry up and eat yours, or they'll disappear before you know it." I winked at him.

"You wouldn't dare."

"Try me."

He took a few bites. "Mmm...yeah, these are good." More bites. "Oh...meant to tell you...I need the car today. I'm meeting the guys from the *Herald* for drinks and dinner later." He finished his plate.

"I'll drive you to Bianca's Gardens at noon or whenever you're ready to go."

After breakfast, I reviewed the first of Michael's investigative articles on Tiffany that included his interviews with Christina and Ben. Christina signed it off minutes after he sent it to her for approval. I spent the rest of the morning working on the suggestions for the newsletter that I'd received from the women's committee.

I was eager to run my ideas by Bianca, so Michael dropped me off at the shop at eleven-thirty—half an hour early.

I peeked into Bianca's office. "Can I see you for a minute?"

"Sure." She waved me in.

I shut the door and pulled up a chair. "I have several concepts for the monthly newsletter."

"Super." She watched as I produced the notes I'd jotted on my canary yellow notepad.

"To start with, I think an article on How to keep your Flowers Fresh would be popular. You can include care instructions for a different flower or plant in each issue. Start with A and go to Z. What do you think?"

"Sounds good."

"You could also include photos of seasonal floral designs with an offer of discount coupons—"

Bianca's phone buzzed. "Excuse me." She hit the intercom button. "Yes?"

"George Gray is here to see you," Joyce's voice came through.

Bianca glanced through the partially open blinds. "I'll be right down." She hung up. "Come with me, Megan. I'd like you to meet him."

I followed Bianca down the stairs to the main floor. I was curious about George but didn't want to seem too obvious about it.

Two men were standing at the front counter. Bianca introduced me to George Gray—early fifties, hair clipped just so, perfect teeth that represented a small investment in the dental trade, not to mention a slim physique honed by a personal trainer.

"Pleased to meet you," George said with a slight British accent. He smiled at me, then glanced at Bianca. "Beauty obviously runs in your family."

Bianca laughed, then introduced me to George's assistant, Tyler Wilson, a young man with short hair highlighted blonde at the tips. At that moment, I recalled where I'd first seen Tyler. He was the man standing next to George in the photo I'd taken near the entrance to The Birchwood Club.

I'd planned on making myself scarce right after Bianca introduced me, but it didn't work out that way. She kept me rooted to the spot when she mentioned my relationship to Michael and his tribute to Tiffany that ran in Tuesday's *Herald*.

"The article reflected a sincere respect for Tiffany," George said. "Truly a wonderful piece." His eyes lit up. The rest of his face showed no emotion and increased the likelihood he'd had Botox injections across his forehead and around his eyes and mouth. His gaze held mine. "I'd like to thank Michael personally for his kindness. Would you have him contact me?"

I wondered why he hadn't returned Michael's calls and was about to mention it. But the awestruck look on Bianca's face prompted me to smile and say, "I'll ask him to get in touch with you." I excused myself and walked toward a table of potted geraniums.

With a moisture meter in hand, I pretended to check the soil for watering requirements while I studied George more closely. From the tailored lines of his expensive suit and French cuffs down to the polished black leather shoes, he exuded style. His charm was characteristic of a more privileged class where the best of everything was available at the snap of a finger.

"What kind of flower arrangements would you like for the funeral mass?" Bianca was asking him.

"I haven't given it much thought," he said.

"If you need more time—"

"I prefer to get the formalities out of the way as soon as possible." The stunned look on Bianca's face caused him to elaborate. "It'll provide closure and a time for grieving privately. You can understand."

"Oh...of course."

His eyes flitted around the shop, as if he were trying to decide what he wanted.

"May I make a suggestion?" Bianca asked him.

George swung his gaze back to her. "Certainly."

"How about a wreath of soft pastels? We could include hydrangeas, Casa Blanca lilies, snapdragons—"

"Whatever you think is best." He dug a slip of paper out of his suit pocket. "The mass will be held Monday at St. Andrew's Church. I'll need three wreaths for the hearses, six baskets for delivery to the church, a casket flower spray..." He droned on as if he were placing a take-out order at a fast food outlet.

"Anything in particular for the basket arrangements?"

"I'll leave the choice up to you. Your expertise in these matters far exceeds mine."

"You're being too modest, George," Bianca said. "Your selections have always been excellent."

"Thank you." He smiled. "I can't compete with Victor, though. When it comes to financial matters, your husband's advice is commendable. In fact, I'm scheduled to meet with him after I'm done here regarding some legal papers. Oh...thank you for personally dropping off the rubber plant. I'm sorry I wasn't at the warehouse to greet you. I had to rush off to a business meeting at the last minute."

"You're welcome, George. I can't thank you enough for the referral to the Women's Sponsorship Committee. It'll be an honor to work on a project that Tiffany initiated."

"Speaking of Tiffany, there is one other matter I wanted to mention." He drew in a breath. "The usual delivery of roses arrived today. Quite disturbing."

Bianca's face paled. "Oh, no. I'm so sorry, George. I was certain we'd canceled that standing order." She threw a cursory glance over her shoulder at Doreen who was entering a sales transaction on the POS for a customer. "I'll make sure it doesn't happen again. I'll credit your account too."

"I apologize if I appear to be paranoid. Ever since my wife's unexpected death, I don't trust anyone these days—not even my closest associates."

Tyler darted a glance in George's direction and looked uncomfortable, but he remained silent.

Bianca leaned forward. "George, I think you should know that the police recently questioned Victor and me about Tiffany."

He straightened up. "What? That's ludicrous."

"We thought so too. The interrogation at the station was an experience I hope we never have to go through again."

He glanced around, lowered his voice. "I truly regret any inconvenience it might have caused you and Victor. I'll have a word with the lead investigator. There's clearly been a misunderstanding."

"A misunderstanding?"

"What I mean is..." He ran a hand over his tie. "I'm concerned about the way they're handling the investigation. Shoddy at best. I don't want to bother you with such mundane details." He waved the topic away, then checked his watch and glanced outside.

Bianca took the hint. She turned and walked over to the POS system where Doreen had just completed a transaction. "I think our computer is acting up again," she said to Doreen, who looked on as she processed George's new order. "I discovered another mistake."

With her back to him, Bianca couldn't see the way George was staring at her. But I could. From my vantage point behind a group of tall potted ferns, I noticed how he kept his eyes fixed on her. What sort of man ogled another woman days after his wife had died?

Bianca placed the order sheet before George. "Sign here, please." She offered him a pen.

He signed the form, then put his hand on hers, lingering for a second longer than good manners would dictate. "Thank you so much, Bianca."

I waited until George and Tyler had left, then stepped out from behind the ferns and walked up to Bianca. I checked the floor to make sure no customers were close by. Doreen was still standing near the POS, her back to us. "Does George always leave it up to you to choose his floral arrangements?"

"No, he's usually much more involved with this sort of thing. He's quite the expert in flora, you know. He studied botany at the university level." She shrugged. "The strain of the investigation must be getting to him."

Behind us, Doreen groaned. She turned around. Her face was crimson. "I have to go to—" She covered her mouth and rushed off toward the back of the floor.

Bianca stared after her. "I hope whatever she has isn't catching." She went over to the POS. "I definitely remember canceling that standing order to Tiffany. How on earth did it get processed this week?" She hit several keys and a screen opened up. "Oh, no. The records show Henry made the delivery."

"Who put the order through?"

She hit a few more keys. "That's odd. It doesn't say. The space is blank. I'll have to ask Doreen about it. Maybe she remembers what happened."

"Hadn't you canceled that order yourself?"

"I thought I did, but it's still active. Look." She pointed to a line on the screen. "I must have messed up the transaction. I'll get it right this time." She pressed the delete key. "There. It's gone for good." She glanced around. "The other girls are probably busy filling orders in the workroom. Would you mind checking on Doreen?"

"Sure."

I figured Doreen might not have made it in time to the second floor washroom, so I checked the workroom first. Gail and Joyce were working on baskets. No sign of Doreen.

I headed upstairs.

The door to the washroom was open, but no one was there. The sound of muffled voices emanated from the kitchen at the far end of the floor. I was about to call out Doreen's name when I heard her throaty whisper. "I could feel his eyes on me. I was sure I was going to barf. I thought I'd never make it to the can. Damn lucky the urge passed by the time I got there."

The hairs on the back of my neck bristled. Were they talking about George Gray?

"The clock is ticking, Lee," Doreen said. "You have to pay your gambling debt by month end."

"Don't sweat it. They know I'm good for it."

"But you haven't collected the friggin' money yet."

Lee emitted a low guttural laugh. "He knows he owes me. He'll come round."

"How can you be so sure?"

"Tell you tonight. Have to get back to work." A chair scraped. Lee's boots thumped across the linoleum.

I rushed downstairs, rounded the edge of the divider, and flew into the workroom. No one was there. I picked up pieces of stems strewn across the table, anticipating that Lee would pass by at any moment on his way out to the back.

He did.

He met my gaze with an icy stare, and I knew right away that he'd seen me upstairs. And worse. He knew I'd overheard their conversation.

At break time, I left the shop to grab a coffee at Starbucks. I sat down on a park bench across the street and called Michael. I figured I'd tell him the good news first. "I met George Gray today when he came into the shop." I smiled, knowing the thrill I had in store for him.

"Is that right?"

"Yes. When Bianca mentioned your connection to me and that you wrote the tribute article to Tiffany in the *Herald*, he said it was a wonderful piece."

"You're kidding. He said that?"

"Yes. And better. He wants you to call him."

A pause. "You're kidding."

"Nope. He wants to thank you personally."

"That is so terrific. Thanks, Megan. I'll call him right now. Oh… don't forget. I'm meeting the guys from the *Herald* tonight. See you later." He hung up before I could tell him about the second conversation I'd overheard between Doreen and Lee.

I returned to the shop to find Bianca and Doreen at the front counter, staring at the screen on the POS.

"Any idea how that order got processed?" Bianca pointed to a transaction.

"I haven't a clue," Doreen said, shaking her head.

"Henry delivered the roses. He knew Tiffany was dead. He should have known better than to drop them off."

"Don't blame Henry," Doreen said. "He probably thought the flowers were meant for someone else in the house."

"The name of the recipient is usually on the delivery slip."

"Maybe it wasn't. The entire entry could have been a glitch in the system."

Bianca shrugged. "Maybe you're right. Let's forget it. I've deleted the standing order anyway, so I'm sure we won't see a repetition of this problem." I was walking by the counter when Bianca turned and noticed me. "Megan, you're back. Do you want to continue our discussion about the newsletter?"

"Sure," I said, eager for the opportunity to finally showcase my ideas.

We went upstairs to her office. I was determined to mention the conversation I'd overheard between Doreen and Lee, but Bianca began to talk about the newsletter before we'd even sat down.

She launched into the items for the newsletter that I'd proposed earlier. We decided to start things off this month with an article on A for African Violet, an easy-to-grow houseplant with lavender, purple, pink, or white flowers and fuzzy leaves. Bianca would supply the photos, and I'd write up the care instructions with Sarah's help. The newsletter would include a discount coupon for a limited time period toward the purchase of seasonal items available at the shop.

"I'd like to release this first newsletter to coincide with a Halloween costume party I want to hold at the shop for my customers," Bianca said to me. "Any suggestions for an article we can add to it?"

"How about a piece on superstitions?"

"Super," she said. "I think we've covered everything."

Her phone rang and she took the call. It sounded like business, so I left.

The afternoon was hectic at the shop with customers buying fall flowers and accessories. After closing time at five, I was serving the last customer at the checkout counter when I noticed Henry trudge in from the back after his final delivery run. He looked around as if he were searching for someone, then walked into the workroom.

Within seconds, his voice boomed across the shop. "You made me look like a fool." Moments of silence passed, then Henry shouted, "You did it on purpose. You made me deliver the roses so I looked bad." Again, there was no reply.

I glanced up at Bianca's office window. She was sitting at her desk, unaware of Henry's outbursts. I was certain the rest of the staff had left for the day. Was Henry talking to himself?

My uneasiness was outdone by the consternation in my customer's eyes. I smiled and handed her a receipt for the bouquet of flowers she'd purchased, then escorted her out the door and locked it behind her.

I tiptoed over to the workroom and stopped inches before the dividing wall to hear Doreen's hushed, yet rasping, voice. "I did no such thing. You're losing it, Henry."

I peeked around the corner and was met with Doreen's backside. She was wearing her coat, and her purse was slung over her right shoulder. Henry was facing her, but her large frame blocked him from my view. All I could see were his fists clenched at his side.

"If—if you were my daughter, I—I would—" Henry's voice cracked.

"What would you do, Henry? Tell me. Would you torch my house down?" Doreen laughed.

I walked in. "What's going on here?"

Doreen turned to face me. "Oh...Megan." She let out a nervous giggle. "Henry and I were teasing each other. Right, Henry?" She looked back at him.

Henry nodded. "I have to go clean up in back." He scurried past us.

"Poor Henry," Doreen said, shaking her head. "Some days he just can't take a joke." She dug out a set of keys from her purse. "Well, that's it for me. See ya."

On the drive home, I told Bianca about the bizarre exchange between Henry and Doreen.

"Doreen can be a little rough around the edges," Bianca said.

"Well..."

"Don't get me wrong. I don't always excuse Doreen's behavior, though it helps if you understand where she's coming from. When she was four years old, her father skipped town. Money was tight, so her mother gave Doreen and her younger sister up for adoption. The girls were adopted by different families in Augusta and lost touch with each other. When Doreen was old enough, she tried to find her sister but couldn't. You know how tight-lipped some adoption agencies can be."

"What about her biological parents? Was she able to find out anything about them?"

"Not that I know of. She doesn't talk about it like she used to. I think she's given up. She thinks of the staff as her family now. That's why she's comfortable joking and mouthing off to them. She knows they'll take it and still be there for her."

The image of a fist-clenching Henry came back to mind. "I don't think Henry took it too well."

"Funny, I've never seen him get angry with her before. The irony is that Doreen is usually so protective of him."

I didn't know what to believe anymore.

It was almost eleven o'clock. Everyone else in the house had gone to bed when Michael tiptoed in from a night out with his newspaper buddies.

"Getting a chance to speak with George Gray was the best thing I could have hoped for. Thank you. Thank you. Thank you." He planted kisses all over my face.

"Okay, I get it. You're grateful." I slid out of his grasp and hopped onto the bed. I clasped my arms around my knees, felt the soft cotton pajamas against my skin. "Tell me exactly what happened. Don't leave anything out."

A dim nightlight lit the short passageway that led to the

ensuite bathroom, but I could still see Michael as he slipped out of his clothes and placed them on the armchair. He lay down on the bed next to me in his boxers and stretched his legs out.

"I called George right away," Michael said. "He thanked me for writing the tribute to Tiffany and said he had a proposition for me. He suspects Tiffany was murdered. He said he'd reward me financially if I discovered anything in my investigation that could confirm it."

"What about the police? The last time I checked, they were handling her investigation."

"He doesn't trust them."

I had a flashback of George ogling Bianca. "Maybe his marriage wasn't all that great, and he's worried the police will consider him a prime suspect."

"Why would you say that?"

"There are rumors that Tiffany might have had a fling or two, but I have a feeling George wasn't faithful either."

He stared at me. "I think I know where this is coming from. Not every man cheats on his wife."

"Maybe George does."

"Even if you're right, you can't launch a personal vendetta against every disloyal husband."

"Why not? It's good therapy for me."

He let out a deep breath. "Okay. Let's say in due course we find out George cheated on Tiffany. Until then, do me a favor."

"What?"

"Don't jump to conclusions about him without proof."

"My opinion is based on personal observation."

"I need specifics."

It was hard to put it into words. "It's the way he looks at other women."

Michael grinned. "I wasn't aware it was a crime. Give me specifics."

I heard footsteps in the hallway outside our bedroom door and put a finger to Michael's lips. Bianca would sometimes go to the kitchen to get a glass of water or make herself a hot chocolate if she had a hard time falling asleep. I brought my voice down to a whisper. "It's about how George acted toward Bianca at the shop—all flirty and touchy-feely. You know what I mean."

"You think he's having an affair with your cousin?" Michael whispered back.

"Of course not." I sighed in exasperation. "Let's drop it. We're getting off track. What did you say to George?"

"I told him that my job as investigative reporter for the *Herald* is a full-time responsibility. That I'm bound by a code of ethics to seek the truth and report on it."

"So you refused to help him."

"Not exactly."

"You're not serious. Wouldn't accepting payment from George be a conflict of interest? With the *Herald*, I mean."

"I'm not planning on sharing *any* information with George. And I'm definitely not accepting money from him. I'm in it for the story. You of all people should know that, Megan."

Michael loved his job, no doubt about it. Anyone else might have found it difficult to turn his back on wealthy family roots, yet he'd done it years ago. Although he'd inherited a small fortune from his late grandmother, he'd refused to touch a penny of it and preferred to use our joint income to pay the bills instead.

Michael went on. "The upshot of my talk with George is that he accepted my request for an interview. It's set for Saturday afternoon."

"That's good news."

"You bet. Keeping in touch with him and the people in his inner circle could lead to a break in the case. That's how I can help George—nothing more—and I told him so. The interview also gives me a chance to cover the story from his perspective. It'll come in handy for my second investigative article."

"Did George say why he approached you in the first place? There are other journalists in town who'd give anything to get an interview with him."

"I'm an outsider. He thinks I can give the public an unbiased approach to the case and protect his reputation in the process."

"You think he'll open up to you?"

He grinned. "He told me I'd have access to the autopsy results, his home computer—"

"His home computer?"

"After the police are finished with it. Why?"

More footsteps in the hallway outside our bedroom. Probably Bianca on her way back from the kitchen.

I waited, then whispered, "I overheard Doreen and Lee in the kitchen again. They were whispering about extorting more money from a man. This time I'm sure they were talking about George."

"What makes you think that?" Michael asked.

"Doreen felt sick to her stomach right after George left the shop. When I went looking for her, I overheard her telling Lee that she had felt his eyes—George's eyes—on her. She'd been standing at the POS the whole time Bianca was serving him at the other end of the counter."

"Anything else?"

"Yes. Lee knows I overheard their conversation. He was practically on my heels when I was rushing down the stairs. He gave me the creepiest look."

"You're going to have to be more careful, Megan." He paused. "You were saying...about George's computer?"

"The information stored on it might prove that Doreen and Lee are blackmailing him."

"We'll find a way to get our hands on it. One more thing. I thought you might want to take on your interviewer role again."

"What do you have in mind?"

"Come with me when I interview George Gray."

"I can't go with you," I said, keeping my voice low. "He saw me at the shop. He knows I'm not a reporter."

"No problem."

"Why not?"

"I told him that in our real lives, I'm a crime writer and you're a freelance ghostwriter."

"True, but it has nothing to do with investigating Tiffany's death."

Michael paused. "Well...I told him something else too."

I sighed. "What?"

"That we sometimes work together as an investigative team."

"You didn't."

"Yep. So are we still on?"

"Are you kidding? I wouldn't miss it for the world."

CHAPTER 8

We'd barely finished breakfast Saturday morning when the doorbell rang.

Victor rose to his feet. "Are you expecting a delivery?" he asked Bianca.

"No," she said.

Victor went to open the front door.

There was a mumbling of voices before the front door closed, then footsteps echoed in the hallway.

Victor entered the kitchen followed by a man I immediately recognized.

"This is Detective Flanagan," Victor introduced him. "Detective, you've already met my wife. These are our houseguests." He introduced Michael and me.

Flanagan shook our hands. He looked different dressed in a sports jacket and jeans. It suggested a relaxed acceptance about life in general, which I supposed came in handy as a smokescreen to get nervous suspects talking. On the flip side, a solid six-foot-four frame might present a deterrent to felons contemplating an escape while in his custody. "Megan, yes, I remember seeing you at the flower shop. Michael, I read your tribute to Tiffany Gray in the *Herald*. I liked it a lot."

"Thanks," Michael said. "They've asked me to do a series of investigative articles about her death too."

"You're not planning to upstage the police department, are you?" Deep circles under the detective's eyes marked decades on the job and gave him a stern look, but his expression softened when he smiled.

"I couldn't begin to compete with you guys," Michael said, smiling back.

The detective studied him. "I'm not too sure about that. Anything lined up yet?"

"I know George Gray is looking for answers."

"I don't doubt it." Flanagan kept his gaze on him. "If you happen to come across sensitive information you think the police should know about, give us a call."

"No problem," Michael said. "I have your number on my contact list."

"And we have yours."

"So Detective, what brings you to our home?" Bianca's gaze was uneasy.

The detective gave Victor a side-glance.

"Detective Flanagan just informed me my office was ransacked last night," Victor said.

"Oh, my God, no," Bianca said, putting a hand to her mouth.

"The door was kicked in," Flanagan said. "The security guard discovered the break-in when he started his morning shift." He looked at Victor. "We'll need you to go to the office and see if anything's missing."

"I don't get it," Bianca said. "Why would anyone want to rob Victor? Everyone in town knows him."

"We believe the robber was looking for something specific," Flanagan said, then turned to Victor. "That's why we need you to inspect the premises."

"If it's okay with you," Victor said to the detective, "I'd like Michael to come along."

Flanagan nodded. "Okay."

After the men had left, Bianca said to me, "Poor Victor. What more can happen? Thank goodness I don't have to go to the shop today. It's such a relief to know that Doreen can take care of things when I'm not there. Do you and Michael have any plans for today?"

"Michael is interviewing George Gray this afternoon," I said.

"He asked me to go along." The confused expression on her face prompted me to add, "To take notes...make sure the facts in his investigative articles are accurate."

"Oh...of course." She nodded slowly, maybe not quite convinced.

I walked over to the sink. "I'll take care of the dishes, then I'll go clean up the bedroom and change my clothes."

"Okay." She glanced at Alex playing with his Lego cars on the floor nearby. He was making little engine noises. "Let's go upstairs, Alex. Mommy needs you to help put away the toys in the toy box, then I'll give you a bath."

"Okay, Mommy." Alex got up and took her hand.

She winked at me and whispered, "Toy is the magic word."

We'd barely had time to get through our routines before Victor and Michael returned.

Bianca was the first to rush down the stairs after they'd walked in. "So? How was it?"

"For one thing, the guy sure took his damn time going through the place," Victor said, hanging his and Michael's jackets in the front closet. "I won't be able to tell what's missing until everything is put back in order."

"That bad?" Bianca asked him.

Victor nodded. "He practically went through every damn file in the cabinets."

"To cover his tracks," Michael said. "The police dusted for fingerprints, but the robber probably wore gloves."

"You want me to help you put things back in order?" Bianca asked Victor.

"Sure, but it will take all day."

"I'll get Alex ready. We'll bring him with us."

As Michael drove further north from Bianca's house, the number of houses we spotted decreased in proportion to the increasing density of woods bordering the road. We were entering an area of Falmouth where real estate homes were priced in the millions. And George Gray's mansion was among them. Other than offering a glimpse of a home obscured by trees from time to time, the single-lane road we were following offered zilch in the way of sightseeing.

At a sign that read "Gray Residence" in an elegant script, Michael turned onto a private path. It led to tall iron gates barring the entrance to George's property. After Michael cleared our arrival through the intercom system, the double gates swung open. We drove through and followed a paved road that curved upward through dense shrubs. Aside from the tips of white eaves that reflected the sunlight, George's residence was hidden from prying eyes—as was the rest of his estate. From this angle, it was impossible to judge how expansive his property was, but we'd soon find out.

A circular driveway of interlocking stone led to the house. Michael parked the car in one of the available spaces to the left of the property and stepped out. I grabbed my slim portfolio and joined him.

I gazed up at the three-story gray stone mansion. Narrow black bars were welded on the exterior of the windows. The curtains were drawn in every window, probably as a matter of security or privacy. I doubted it was a sign that George was in mourning.

We climbed twelve stone steps leading to a front porch large enough to hold a dinner party for twenty. The front doors were double, made of a frosty decorative glass, and trimmed with wrought iron. They could probably ward off a break-in with a bulldozer. The same glass panels bordered both sides of the doors. I noticed a tiny camera mounted overhead and held back the urge to peer through the glass.

Michael rang the bell. A pleasant chime echoed inside—something from *The Sound of Music*.

A figure walked by one of the panels and the front door opened. "Hi, Megan. I remember you from the shop. Hi, Michael. Please come in." Tyler motioned us into the foyer, then closed the door behind us with a firm push. "I'm Tyler Wilson, George's personal trainer." He shook hands with Michael.

The foyer was bright—too bright to have lighting as its source.

I glanced upward to discover a sunroof in a raised ceiling.

"Cool, eh?" Tyler said to me, smiling.

"Sure is." I smiled back and discreetly observed him. He wore a fitted T-shirt and tight workout pants. I figured he might have been on his way to the gym when we arrived. Tanned and muscular, he had biceps on his arms the size of my thighs. I placed him in his mid-thirties. If rumors about Tiffany's affairs were true, I could see why she might have had his name at the top of her list.

"George will be down soon," Tyler said. "Please make yourselves comfortable in the living room." He gestured to the right of the foyer, then disappeared behind a circular staircase that spiraled upward.

I was about to move on when a familiar item in the foyer caused me to linger there. I recognized it from one of the photos Michael had spread out on Bianca's kitchen table. The sight of the still empty vase on a pillar sent chills up and down my spine.

I caught up with Michael in the living room. What stood out in my immediate line of sight was a grouping of four modern white leather armchairs decorated with nail head trim. I'd seen similar furniture in the windows of exclusive stores and trade magazines. Not for the average buyer on a budget. As they say, if you need to know the price, you can't afford the merchandise.

Almost everything else in the room was dark. The wood floor was a dark brown—probably stained oak, judging from the grain. A deep red oriental rug covered the center of the floor, but the furniture hid most of it from view. A black marble mantle and matching borders encased a fireplace in the back wall. A painting of Tiffany in a white dress and George in a black tux hung above it. I assumed they'd posed for it soon after they were married or after one of their black-tie events.

The room looked full, yet something was missing. There were no plants or flowers anywhere. George clearly hadn't replaced the ones the police had seized for analysis but had chosen to leave the empty vases standing here—as he had in the foyer.

While Michael inspected a collection of books in the twin bookcases along the right-hand wall, I continued my tour. Vintage model airplanes, boats, and cars on coffee tables and bookshelves told me George was a collector of memorabilia, although another interest competed for equal time: photography.

Framed pictures crammed the entire wall on the left and were hung so close that there was little space between them. I counted about ten rows by ten—at least one hundred pictures. The mementos draped the wall like chronological glimpses of one's life frozen in real time. At the top were photos of George as a child through to his university graduation. Several rows down were shots of George with his parents and grandparents—judging from their resemblance to one another. The bottom rows boasted photos of famous sports figures and entertainment celebrities standing next to George and later, next to George and Tiffany. Whether it was a black tie or no tie event, everybody smiled and looked happy. Then again, even synthetic smiles can thwart the camera's eye.

Of notable exclusion were photos of Tiffany with George's parents. I wondered if they'd chosen not to be photographed with her or whether someone had removed any pictures of the threesome on purpose.

Michael came up to me. "Anything interesting?"

"Talk about capturing the moment," I whispered. "It's a collage of the rich and the famous according to George Gray."

"Could have fooled me." He squinted at them. "I thought they were shots from auditions for toothpaste commercials."

"Very funny." I poked him in the arm.

Footsteps approached and our critique of the photo compilation came to an end. We turned to see George walk in. His purple cashmere polo shirt and beige corduroys were a far cry from the tailored business suit and French cuffs he was wearing when he dropped by Bianca's shop. Although his attire projected comfort, his hair had been gelled into obedience.

"Hello, you two. How are you?" George smiled and shook our hands with a firm grip, as if we were good friends he hadn't seen in a while.

"Thanks for meeting with us, George," Michael said.

"My pleasure." George took a seat in one of the white armchairs and motioned for us to sit down. "What would you like to know?"

He cast an expectant look at Michael.

"As I mentioned earlier," Michael said, "I'd like to write about Tiffany's fundraising work, her daily schedule of activities… Sort of a human perspective that celebrates her life."

"A human perspective." Interest gleamed in George's eyes. "I like it. Where do we begin?"

I opened my portfolio and reached for my pen. I hadn't a clue where Michael was heading, but I sensed the interview would be an interesting one. I wrote the date on my canary yellow notepad and prepared to take notes.

"I'd like to get a general feel for the activities of that last Friday," Michael said. "Tell me what you were doing the day Tiffany passed away."

George grew pensive, tapped his fingers on the armchair as if he had to recall a memory from a distant era rather than one that had happened days ago. "I spent most of the day in meetings with representatives of the Maine Port Authority. My cold storage facilities have aroused international interest lately. In view of the scope of the potential demand, I'm now considering expanding my operations." He lifted his chin with pride.

Michael brought the discussion back on track. "Did you speak with Tiffany that day?"

George nodded. "I called her in the afternoon."

"What did you talk about?"

"She was organizing a gala event and was having problems with the invitations. She was concerned they wouldn't be printed on time. She'd been talking to the people at the printing company all morning. She was quite upset. My wife strove for perfection in everything she did and expected it in others as well."

"Did she mention if she'd spoken to anyone else that day?"

George smiled. "Tiffany spent hours on the phone every day. She spoke with decorators, event planners, and many other people regarding upcoming events."

"Did she leave the house that Friday?"

"Odd that you should mention it. It was one of those rare days when she stayed home. Like I said, she was trying to sort out a problem with the printing company."

"Did she mention if anyone had come to the house that day? Friends? Repair personnel? Courier service?"

He looked away. "Not that I recall."

I jogged his memory. "I think Tiffany received roses from Bianca's Gardens that Friday."

George sat upright. "You're absolutely correct." He blinked as if he were embarrassed he'd forgotten such a vital fact, but he recovered in the next instant. "I suppose one can forget things when under duress." He turned to Michael. "To answer your question, Bianca's Gardens delivered an order of long-stemmed roses that last Friday as they did every week. I remember now. Tiffany told me the roses had arrived moments before I called her. She said they were gorgeous. In fact, she was about to tend to them and put them in a vase. It was the last time I spoke with her." He looked down.

There was a deafening pause before Michael asked, "Were any other deliveries of flowers made to your home that day?"

"I can't say for sure," George said. "Tiffany insisted on having fresh flowers in every room. Deliveries arrived almost daily."

"Who handled the deliveries after they arrived?"

"Only Tiffany. No one else was allowed to touch the flowers— not even me. She trimmed them and arranged them in vases. She even took care of the watering requirements."

"I noticed there weren't any flowers in the vases in the foyer and living room," I said.

"The police confiscated all the flowers from our home the day Tiffany died," George said. "They thought she might have had an allergic reaction to one of them. They've since confirmed it wasn't the cause of her death." Suspicion flickered in his eyes. "Why all the questions about flowers?"

Michael leaned forward and joined his hands. His voice took on a somber tone. "George, I don't want my articles to be seen as another exploitation of the Gray family name. As I said earlier, I want to give them a personal touch. I'd like to describe your wife's death as the loss of a caring individual. Charities and flowers— things she cared deeply about. You see where I'm going with this?"

George relaxed. "Of course."

Michael sat back and resumed his questioning. "During the short time you knew Tiffany, how would you best describe her?"

"She was a beautiful, kindhearted person."

"Do you mind my asking how you two met?"

George sighed. "Tiffany came into my life completely unexpected, like a breath of fresh air. We were judges at a local beauty contest. Aside from the fact she'd been a former beauty pageant queen, I was quite taken with her charm and sociability. I didn't know it then, but she would become a valuable commodity."

Commodity? Is that how he categorized his wife? I bit my tongue.

"Can you elaborate on that?" Michael asked, keeping his cool.

"Oh, don't misunderstand me. I'm not implying that Tiffany was a trophy wife." George's tone was defensive. "On the contrary, she became the means by which we, the Gray family, enjoyed countless opportunities for recognition in the community."

We, the Gray family?

"You're referring to her commitment to charity work, right?"

"Of course. Tiffany loved to campaign for the underdog. She thrived on organizing events to help the less fortunate. You could say her fundraising was a testament to her compassionate goals. I know you're quite familiar with that aspect of her life by now." He smiled at Michael.

Every word George said was true, yet Tiffany's generous nature continued to baffle me. It contradicted the negative comments I'd heard about her from Bianca's staff and the women's committee. It was one thing for a small-town girl to bask in the limelight of beauty pageants and rub elbows with the rich and famous, quite another to devote her days to raising money for the underprivileged. That she'd inspired the Gray family to dig deeper into their pockets to do the same was an achievement in itself. Maybe there was far more depth behind Tiffany's superficial façade than most people realized.

George stared at the floor. "There's something about my wife that not many people know."

I held my breath, expecting him to confirm the rumors we'd heard about Tiffany's flings with other men.

He looked at me. "Did you know she'd go to flower shops—including Bianca's Gardens, of course—and personally order the flower arrangements for every single event she organized?"

"I didn't know that," I said. "She must have had an extensive knowledge of flowers."

"She did. She learned everything she could about flowers. Her passion gave her life a sense of purpose she'd never had before."

"How's that?" Michael asked.

George crossed his legs. "Off the record—and I'll sue you if you print this," he said, giving him an astute look, "Tiffany couldn't have children."

"I'm sorry to hear that," I said and meant it.

He dismissed my compassion with a wave of his hand. "No need to feel sorry. She lived a short but full life."

His glib response made me wonder whether he had preferred their marriage that way—childless.

Michael took advantage of the awkward pause to change the subject. "You have quite a collection of mementos." He gestured toward the wall of photos.

George glanced at them. "Yes. Superb memories."

"The photo of you in a cap and gown," I said, indicating it. "Where was it taken?"

An expression of pride crossed George's face. "At the University of Cambridge in England."

I was curious. Bianca had mentioned George was an expert in flora, but I asked anyway. "What kind of studies did you pursue there?"

"I studied Plant Sciences at first, then switched to the Arts and dabbled in theater. It was more in line with my preferences."

I held my gaze on the photos. "Are Tiffany's relatives in any of those shots?"

"No. Tiffany wasn't exactly close to her family."

"Bad blood?" Michael threw in.

George ignored the question, kept his expression blank. "I've given you a solid base for your investigative research into my wife's death. Who knows? You might even get to the bottom of her unexplained demise before the authorities do, considering their slipshod ways."

His comment triggered a memory. "George, when you came to the shop to order flowers for Tiffany's funeral, Bianca told you the police had interrogated her."

"Yes, I was quite bowled over by it," he said, his words a contrast to the emotionless look on his face. "Are they still pestering her?"

"I don't think so," I said. "You mentioned you'd have a word with the lead investigator. Something about a misunderstanding..." I let my voice trail off on purpose, hoping he'd fill in the blanks.

George's expression remained passive. "My desire was—and still is—to assist the police by guiding their investigation in the right direction. However, even the wheels of authority can steer off course at times." He looked at Michael. "Your impartiality is the reason I granted you this interview and made you privy to certain information. I truly hope your investigative skills will help to explain this tragic event."

"Then I'll need to interview your household staff," Michael said.

"It's pointless. They weren't here that afternoon."

"Where were they?"

"The maid has Fridays off. The cook went grocery shopping. Tyler drove into town to pick out new sports clothing for me. Aside from playing golf, I work out at the gym most days, so I need lots of T-shirts and shorts."

"Convenient, wasn't it?"

"What do you mean?"

"No one was around to help Tiffany."

"It wouldn't have made the slightest difference. The ME said she died within seconds."

"I'd like to speak with your staff anyway. Their viewpoints will lend a personal touch to my investigative articles."

George nodded. "Ah, yes, the human perspective. Fine. I'll make the arrangements. In the meantime, you have my permission to look through the autopsy report and other documents concerning

Tiffany's death. I've set these out for you in her private room upstairs." He paused. "Oh...you'll find a computer there too. I don't think there's anything on it except email babble between Tiffany and her luncheon friends. I've never used it. I have my own." He made a move to get up.

"One last question, please," Michael said to him.

George leaned back. "Fine, but make it quick."

"There's talk that Tiffany might not have been loyal to you."

George shifted in his chair. "That's bullshit."

"Not according to my sources."

"Who are your sources?"

"I'm not at liberty to say. Confidentiality agreement."

George's gaze hardened. "Be forewarned. You are not to publish any information without my consent. If you do, I'll sue you and the paper. Do we have an agreement?"

"Yes," Michael said.

"Run the articles by me first for approval. Clear?"

"No problem."

George stood up. "You must excuse me now. Tyler is waiting for me to change into my gym clothes. He'll show you the way upstairs."

Michael and I rose to our feet. We turned to see Tyler in the doorway. How long he'd been standing there was anyone's guess.

"Thanks for coming over." George shook our hands. As he hurried past Tyler, he said to him, "I'll be ready in fifteen."

Tyler smiled at Michael and me. "I'll walk you guys up to the third floor. This way, please." A set of keys jingled in his hand as he led us toward the circular staircase.

I scanned the foyer looking for George but he'd vanished—probably through one of the four open archways cut into the cream-colored walls.

Tyler led the way up the winding staircase. I averted my eyes from his rippling thigh muscles and focused on the steps instead. I didn't have to count them. I knew from the pull in my calf muscles that there were a lot more steps between the floors in this house than in other homes with standard eight-foot ceilings.

At one point, Michael passed me by and engaged Tyler in a

bit of male chitchat about exercise. "I haven't had much time to go jogging since we arrived, but I jog every day back home. Do a little biking too."

"Oh, you'd love it here," Tyler said. "Upscale communities like Falmouth offer biking, jogging, and cross-country skiing—sometimes in their own backyards." He laughed. "It's a waterfront community, so there's access to sandy beaches, rocky shores..."

The men continued their chat and trotted along like a pair of gazelles. They completed the steep climb thirty seconds before me. I took a deep breath to avoid panting as I met up with them.

The third-floor hallway could have doubled as a bowling lane. The hardwood floor was a shade lighter than that in the main living room but dark nonetheless. The saving grace was that a runner in a red, gold, and brown floral print stretched over it, adding a touch of warmth.

As we walked along, I counted six closed doors—three on either side of the hallway. Tyler stopped in front of the third door on the left, sorted through his set of keys, and pulled one out. He unlocked the door and swung it open.

The room measured about twenty feet by twenty feet and was painted sky blue, including the ceiling, which was dotted with appliqués of white clouds. Opposite the doorway, white lace curtains along a tall window were parted to reveal a green landscape beyond. Under the window, a giant teddy bear and four pillows in a blue and white motif sat atop a white loveseat. A fluffy shag rug lay on the floor in front of it. Further to the right was a white wood desk with a computer on it. A floral watercolor in pastel shades hung above it and looked as if a child had painted it. I made a mental note to take a closer look at it later.

Considering the brief but flamboyant lifestyle Tiffany had led as George's wife, the furnishings in her private room would have led anyone to believe it belonged to a ten-year-old girl. My guess was that she wanted to create a little fantasy retreat for herself away from the hectic agenda of social events. Or maybe she had a desire to hang on to her childhood for some unknown reason.

On a white bamboo table closer at hand, documents were laid

out for our perusal as George had promised.

"I'll come get you in about an hour," Tyler said, jiggling the keys in his hand.

I wondered if he meant he'd lock us in the room until then.

I must have had a strange look on my face because he added, "Is that enough time for you guys?"

"No problem," Michael said. He waited until the sound of Tyler's keys disappeared down the hallway, then whispered to me, "I think George is starting to feel pressure from the police. Funny how he expects me to save his ass."

"He avoided answering questions about Tiffany's family," I said. "He's hiding something."

He nodded. "Too bad he cut short our meeting. I had lots more to ask him."

"Do you have enough information for your articles?"

"Are you kidding?" He grinned. "This get-together was the bait for my whole fishing expedition. Lucky for me, you mentioned the delivery of roses and moved things along."

"At least we found out Tiffany was alone in the house when she died."

"Right. Question is: Was it intentional or accidental?" He walked over to Tiffany's desk and turned on the computer, staking his claim to probe for any potential evidence there.

I reached for the documents on the bamboo table and leafed through them. The ME's report and the preliminary autopsy report on Tiffany indicated what we already knew about the time and manner of death. The section where the cause of death should have been entered was filled in as Unknown. No matter. We'd soon know the answer. I glanced at the signature at the bottom. Dr. Trudy Sayer had signed the report.

I glanced around the room. A five-tiered bookcase in the left corner held an assortment of paperbacks. I crossed the floor to browse through them, hoping Tiffany's taste in books might shed more light on her true personality.

The provocative titles and book covers displaying half-clothed couples told me she liked romance novels. Small wonder. Although

George was respectable and rich, I wondered why any woman would be attracted to a man almost twice her age, let alone want to have sex with him. Then again, maybe Tiffany didn't have sex with George. Maybe it was a business arrangement of sorts. Maybe she'd found what she needed between the pages of romance novels—not to mention between the sheets with younger, more alluring men.

I suddenly felt sorry for George. What if I'd misjudged him? I seemed to be doing a lot of that these days. If it were true that Tiffany had cheated on him, I could easily empathize with the way he might be feeling—betrayed, rejected, abandoned. Since he'd dabbled in drama at university, maybe he'd learned how to hide his true feelings.

The pendulum swung the other way when I recalled that George was still a murder suspect in my books. That notion immediately canceled any compassion I'd felt for him moments earlier.

I walked up to Michael. "Find anything?"

"A bunch of emails that date back several months. Chatter like George said."

"About what?"

"All sorts of girly stuff...new diets to try...the latest fashions..."

"What about the names in her contact list?"

He tapped a few keys. "I found about a dozen email contacts. I compared them to the ones on emails she received. All email addresses are accounted for except Augbabe. There are no messages on file from this sender. No personal info in Tiffany's contact list on Augbabe either."

"Sounds secretive. It could be one of her lovers."

Michael reached for a pen and paper. "I'll jot down the email address and check it out on my computer later. Anything in the documents on the table back there?"

"Nothing we don't already know. Are we done here?"

"No. I want to run a check of the directory. Files might have been copied before they were deleted." He entered a command and a window opened up to display a column of entries. "See these entries?" He pointed to file names on the screen that were time-stamped. They were dated the same week Tiffany died.

"So?"

"They were probably copied onto a portable flash drive. I'll keep on searching in case something else pops up."

Sometimes I wished I were more like Michael. His snooping into other people's private lives didn't bother him at all. I'd once asked him how he could remain so detached from the situation. He'd said that it was an essential part of his quest for the truth and his personal fight for justice. What could I say?

I stood next to him and hoped his enthusiasm would rub off on me, but I got bored when nothing surfaced after five minutes. Then I remembered the painting.

I looked up and scanned the artwork for a name or initials. There were none. I reached over Michael's head and took hold of the canvas. Lucky for me, it was hanging on one nail, which made it easier to take down.

"Find something?" Michael asked.

"Not yet." I turned the canvas over. It had a faint address stamp at the bottom edge. "I can't make out the name of the store this canvas came from. All I can see is part of the town name. Augusta. Hmm...Doreen Dale used to live in Augusta."

He shrugged. "Doesn't mean anything."

"I guess not." I hung the painting on the wall, then stood back to make sure it was straight. I adjusted it a little.

Michael continued to scan computer records. Feeling restless, I decided to do a bit of perusing of my own.

I strolled out into the hallway and glanced around to see if I could spot any surveillance cameras. There weren't any. One by one, I tried the doorknob to each of the closed rooms, but they wouldn't budge. Who would lock all the rooms in their house?

As I was trying the last one, Tyler turned the corner at the landing. "Looking for something?"

"Uh...yes," I mumbled, surprised that the jingling of keys hadn't alerted me to his arrival. He'd obviously ditched them. "The washroom."

"Around the corner on your right. I'll go check on Michael now. We can all go back down together afterward." He winked at me.

From the moment I opened the door to the bright and spacious bathroom, I knew that Tiffany hadn't shared it with anyone else. The blue-and-white paisley draperies, matching shower curtains, and crystal candelabra were in line with the decorative choices in her private room. A beveled mirror framed in ornate silver hung over a blue granite-topped sink. The storage space under the sink held several rolls of toilet paper. Most women would have adorned their counter top with perfume bottles or other toiletries, but there weren't any. No vase filled with fresh flowers either, like the ones I'd noticed in the crime photos Michael had shown me. Even the shower stall and Roman tub contained no soap or shampoo or wash puffs. Tiffany's personal items had been completely removed from here.

I went back to her private room. Michael had finished his research and was chatting with Tyler, telling him how he hadn't found anything worthwhile on the computer.

"You're covering all the bases," Tyler said. "It's what George wants." He escorted us downstairs, no doubt to ensure our speedy and direct exit. I wasn't surprised when he loitered on the terrace until we drove away.

The ride down the slope and through the open gates seemed faster than the trip up. Maybe it had to do with my relief at having survived our first meeting with George and not having been banned from the house.

"Too bad I couldn't get into the other rooms," I said to Michael after I'd described my unexpected encounter with Tyler in the hallway.

"Don't worry," he said. "We still have to interview Tyler, the cook, and whoever else works there. Oh...and George's parents made our short list too."

George's parents? I could hardly wait.

The Gray family name was also on Victor's lips that evening after we'd gathered around the kitchen table. "George Gray's last will and testament was stolen," he said.

"As if we needed more bad luck connected to George," Bianca said, her shoulders sagging. "We managed to put the files in order.

At least Victor's office is operational again."

"The thief knew exactly what he wanted," Victor said. "It doesn't look as if anything else is missing."

"It had to be someone who knew you had a copy of George's revised will and broke in to get it," Michael said. "The question is why."

I remembered how Victor had once said that he wouldn't want to be in George's shoes after he saw his revised will. "The burglar might be affected financially—good or bad—from what was specified in the revised will. Right?"

Victor nodded. "Right."

"It had to be someone desperate," Michael said.

"Right again," Victor said.

"Do you have any idea who?" Bianca asked him.

"No. All I can say is that things look worse for George now than ever."

CHAPTER 9

Tiffany Gray's funeral mass was scheduled for Monday morning at St. Andrew's Church. Doreen had arrived at the shop at seven o'clock to process the deliveries and help Lee load them onto the truck, then she'd closed up the shop and left for a doctor's appointment. Bianca had insisted on making an early appearance at the church to ensure the flower arrangements were all right. She asked me to open up the shop in case Doreen wouldn't make it back for nine o'clock. I'd meet Bianca at the church later.

It started to rain as I stepped inside Bianca's Gardens. I shut the door behind me, making sure to lock it. The sweet, heady fragrance of jasmine in nearby containers drifted my way. I took a deep breath. Umm...so relaxing. I looked around and surveyed the foliage in its various shapes and species. All that greenery had a calming effect on me. I felt at one with nature—albeit the indoor variety.

I glanced at my watch. Eight-forty. With twenty minutes to spare until opening time, I sat on a stool at the checkout counter. Michael and I had stopped to pick up coffee and toasted bagels with cream cheese before he dropped me off, so I had lots of time to enjoy my breakfast.

The shop was quiet, except for the cooler humming at the back of the store and the rain hitting the windows. The flicker of a tiny yellow light on the computer jolted my memory. I'd promised Bianca I'd check the day's deliveries.

I abandoned my half-eaten bagel and turned on the POS.

It made a purring sound and the screen lit up. I pressed a key to display the Main Menu, then clicked on Delivery to see what was on the agenda for the day.

The system prompted me for a password. I entered the one I shared with Bianca and Doreen. A window opened up to reveal the deliveries made to St. Andrew's Church this morning. I accessed George Gray's customer account to compare the delivery information. To my surprise, there was an extra entry in George's account. An order of roses to Tiffany Gray was scheduled for delivery in several days. How was that possible? I'd seen Bianca delete that standing order myself.

I didn't want to fiddle with the data, so I made a mental note to tell Bianca about it later.

I stared at the screen, wondering if I should look for other potential tampering. Like the infamous delivery Mrs. Spencer claimed she'd never received—the one Henry swore he'd delivered. I'd never been alone in the shop before, so it might well be my last chance to verify information without attracting attention.

I chose the Customer option from the Main Menu and entered the name Spencer. Three names popped up—two of them male, the other female. I chose the latter. A delivery came up for Mrs. Martha Spencer in October. I noted that Sarah had prepared the flower arrangement, Doreen had entered it into the Delivery schedule, and Henry had made the delivery.

So why did Mrs. Spencer say she'd never received the flowers?

I clicked open the Delivery page and searched for her name. It was there but the address was different. I knew that the customer's billing address was automatically copied to the Delivery page unless the customer gave instructions to make the delivery elsewhere. This wasn't the case with Mrs. Spencer's order. Someone had gone into the system and manually changed the delivery address. Since Bianca, Doreen, and now I shared that responsibility, it was clear which one of us had fudged the information. I was determined to make it right for Henry's sake.

A pounding knock at the front door startled me. I turned to see Doreen holding an umbrella in one hand and pointing to her watch with the other. I checked my watch. It was five minutes after nine.

I hurried over to open the door. "Sorry. I guess my watch is slow."

"Lucky there weren't any customers," Doreen said, unsmiling. "It's pouring rain and I'm holding an umbrella. Otherwise, I would have fished in my purse for my own keys." She huffed past me, trailing a wet umbrella.

My eyes darted to the POS. I panicked and hoped she wouldn't notice Mrs. Spencer's name on the screen. What if she did? Would she suspect that I was checking up on her? What if she'd watched me from outside before knocking at the door? Could she see the information on the screen from that distance? Lee must have told her I'd overheard their conversation upstairs on Friday. No doubt she was keeping a close eye on me.

Adrenaline pumped inside me as she plodded past the front counter. She had her back to me, so I couldn't tell if she'd glanced at the screen or not. As she climbed the stairs, I pretended to arrange the pots of mums on a nearby table but kept an eye on her. When she finally disappeared from sight, I rushed to the computer and closed the multiple windows I'd opened. The last one blinked shut and relief spread over me, swiftly replaced by a feeling that I was being watched. I stole a peak at the window in Bianca's office. I could have sworn I saw the blinds move ever so slightly. Was Doreen watching me?

The thought of being alone with her put me on edge. When she went out back to load other deliveries, I eased up somewhat. We managed to avoid crossing paths until Sarah arrived at nine-thirty.

I was standing at the counter when Bianca phoned. "How's it going?" she asked.

"Uh...fine." I wanted to tell her about the tinkering I'd discovered on the POS but then figured it was better if she saw it for herself.

"Is everything okay? You sound distracted."

"It's a little busy," I said, taking note of two people checking out the potted plants nearby.

"The mass begins in an hour and the church is already packed. You leaving soon?"

"Yes, Michael is picking me up in half an hour."

The moment I stepped inside Saint Andrew's Church, my eyes were drawn upward. Radiant light shone from behind arch-shaped beams in a high-domed ceiling. White arches and pillars bordered the side aisles of the church. The sun gleamed through vibrant stained glass windows depicting biblical scenes and reflected slivers of color onto surfaces. Polished wood pews that could accommodate a thousand parishioners were filled to capacity, resulting in standing room only at the back of the church. The place buzzed like a school auditorium before the announcement of an important event.

Pallbearers had already carried Tiffany's casket into the church and centered it at the front. The trace of incense was overshadowed by the aroma emanating from the elaborate wreaths and baskets of flowers positioned near the altar and the front pews. Adding to the fusion of fragrances in the air were women's perfume and men's cologne.

I noticed Bianca standing off to the left at the back of the church. She was speaking with an older woman. As I approached, I heard Bianca say, "No, I didn't know. That's awful."

I touched her arm. "Hi."

"Hi, Megan." She turned to say goodbye to the older woman, then whispered to me, "The woman I was talking to told me that Father Paul Griffith—he's the parish priest here at St. Andrew's—passed away yesterday. He was about to say mass when he collapsed. Can you imagine?" Her eyes went wide.

"That's too bad. How old was he?"

"About fifty. Poor man." She shook her head. "The woman said another priest will say the mass for Tiffany here today." She looked past me. "Where's Michael?"

"He dropped me off and went to park the car. The flower arrangements look fantastic."

"I know. The girls worked so hard on them. Doreen went to the shop this morning to finish up. I don't know what I'd do without her." Bianca gazed past me. She smiled and waved at someone.

I turned to see Christina and Ida from the women's committee sitting in a pew at the back. They smiled at me. I smiled back.

"Victor is sitting somewhere in that section on the right," Bianca said, pointing with her chin. "When we first got here, I ran into customers and started to chat. You know how it is."

I felt a hand on my arm and turned to see Michael. "Hi. You made it."

"Had to park the car blocks away," he said. "Even the mayor and some local celebs are here." He acknowledged Bianca with a nod and a smile.

Music streamed through the air. Not the usual mournful sounds that an organ emits but live music nevertheless. It was coming from the front of the church. I strained to see between the heads of people standing in front of me.

Michael leaned over and said, "It's a live quartet."

The foursome played their rendition of Enya's "Only Time." Several women pulled out facial tissues and wiped their eyes. After the music stopped, a priest walked up to the pulpit and said a homily in memory of Tiffany. He spoke about her generous contribution to the community and how she had accomplished so much in such a short time. His words triggered more wiping and sniffling from the congregation.

When the priest took his position at the altar and began the mass, somber organ music emanated from the mezzanine above us. It boomed and seemed to bounce off the domed ceiling and fall back down again.

During a lull in the music, when all we could hear was the priest chanting, Michael whispered in my ear. "Do you think you can meet me for lunch tomorrow?"

"What's the occasion?" I whispered back.

"I thought you might like to meet Dr. Trudy Sayer, the medical examiner."

I recognized the name from the preliminary autopsy report that George had made available to us. "Won't she wonder what I'm doing there?"

"Not if I pass you off as my research assistant."

Why not? One more phantom label to add to my repertoire. "What's the meeting about?"

"Autopsy results." He gave me *the look.*

"Oh…right. By the way, the parish priest of this church died yesterday. Father Paul Griffith."

"So?"

"He collapsed here right before Sunday mass. Could be a heart attack. No one knows for sure."

The woman standing in front of me turned to look at me. She put a finger to her lips and frowned.

I felt as if I were back in grade school again. I was so humiliated.

I stole a glance at Bianca. She smiled, then started to laugh and put a hand over her mouth. Luckily for her, the organ music started up again and drowned out her giggles.

The service lasted another half hour, after which the slow exodus of family and friends proceeded down the aisle, accompanied by the quartet's instrumental rendering of Bocelli and Brightman's "Time to Say Goodbye."

I wanted to catch a glimpse of the Gray family members as they went by, but I wasn't tall enough. I could only see the tops of their heads as they followed the pallbearers and Tiffany's casket out the front door.

CHAPTER 10

Michael smiled as he steered the car along Middle Street the next morning. "Sure helps to know people like George. How else would I be meeting Dr. Trudy Sayer for lunch?"

"You can thank me for that."

"How can I ever repay you?" His smile widened.

"I'll think of something." I returned his smile and laughed. I'd decided to drive into town with Michael this morning, making it easier to meet him for lunch but complicating my schedule at the shop again. Bianca didn't seem distressed by my unpredictable timetable, which was a good thing. "Tell me more about Dr. Sayer."

"She works in a private crime lab and helps out local government resources. Not much more to tell. You already know she doesn't have the final results from Tiffany's autopsy yet. Could take a while."

I knew that much from dealing with Tom's death. Performing an autopsy was one thing. Completing the final report on the findings was another. The whole process could take days, if not weeks.

Michael grew pensive. "I keep thinking about the similarities between Tiffany and Gladys's deaths. I have a gut feeling there's a connection there."

"I don't like where this is heading. Please don't mention Bianca's shop."

Michael's phone rang. He glanced at the screen. "It's Drew." He swung the car into an empty parking space and returned the call. "Hi, Drew. What's up?" A pause. "You're kidding. They did?" He stared at me. "Okay, I will. Thanks." He ended the call. "Guess what? Liz at forensics told Drew that a preliminary autopsy on Father Paul Griffith showed an anomaly in his lungs."

"What? How is that possible? I know we've been talking about flowers, but what if we're wrong? What if there's a strange virus going around?"

Michael pulled out of his parking spot. "I can always ask Dr. Sayer."

"What do you mean?"

He grinned. "You're gonna love this one."

"What? What? Tell me."

"Drew said Dr. Sayer oversaw the team who performed the preliminary autopsies on all three victims."

"Ha! Admit it. You love the challenge."

He chuckled.

"How are you going to work this little miracle, Michael?"

"You'll see."

Bianca had seen me walk into the shop and wasted no time in asking me to join her upstairs. She smiled at me from across her desk. "How would you like to be my official Halloween party organizer?"

I wasn't keen on it but couldn't admit it without hurting her feelings. "Well...I don't know. Michael is going to wrap up his investigative articles soon. We'll be heading back to Montreal."

"Oh." Disappointment flashed across her face. "I was counting on you to visit until the end of the month."

I hated to let her down. "I'll talk to Michael. Maybe I can convince him to stay a bit longer."

Bianca's face brightened. "Super." She turned to her computer screen and placed her fingers on the keyboard. "The first thing we need to do is print out a customer list. I expect at least fifty people— maybe a hundred—will show up. We need to send out invitations, hire caterers and decorators..."

I remembered the episode with Doreen yesterday morning

and glanced at the floor near the window. There were no air vents beneath the window. My gut feeling had been right. Doreen had been watching me through the blinds. "Bianca, before we get into the Halloween details, I need to talk to you about something important."

She pulled her gaze away from the screen. "Go ahead."

I described my discovery of the computer data concerning Mrs. Spencer. "I think someone changed the delivery address on purpose so Henry would deliver it to the wrong place."

"Let me check the files." She tapped several keys.

I walked around the desk and looked over her shoulder as she retrieved Mrs. Spencer's customer file and compared it with the information on the Delivery screen.

"I don't see anything wrong," she said. "The address is the same in both files. I guess Henry is still at fault on this one."

I peered at the screen. "It can't be. Doreen must have changed the address back to the correct one."

She frowned. "Doreen? I admit she's had her moments, but she's a very efficient employee. She saved me more than a few dollars when she located orders that had been entered incorrectly in the POS last Christmas and Mother's Day—our busiest days of the year. That girl can zoom in on the tiniest error, no matter where it is in the system."

I went on to explain the next oddity I'd discovered—that the standing order of roses for Tiffany Gray was still in the system.

"Impossible. I deleted it the last time George was in here. You were there." Bianca accessed the relative files. "Just as I thought. It's not in the system."

"What?" I stared at the screen. The entry was gone.

It proved one thing: Doreen had noticed the information on the POS screen when she'd walked in Monday morning. She'd waited until I'd left the shop to perform damage control and cover her tracks. "Doreen changed those entries after I saw them." I sat back down.

Bianca raised an eyebrow in my direction. "You realize what you're implying?" She paused. "Our eyes can play tricks on us.

Maybe you thought—"

"I know what I saw. Both times."

She shook her head. "Unless you can prove Doreen is tampering with the computer, she's in the clear in my books."

This wasn't going according to plan. Too bad I hadn't printed out a hard copy of the information I'd viewed earlier. "You keep records, don't you?"

"Financial ones for accounting purposes only."

I was doomed. Then I remembered the conversations I'd overheard between Doreen and Lee about the money. I told Bianca.

She shrugged. "I knew Doreen and Lee had a load of debts when I hired them."

"But it sounds as if they're threatening someone."

"It's also possible that a relative or friend owes them money and they're angry about it."

I couldn't argue with her logic. Lee had indeed said that someone owed him. And yet...

"Now...back to the party." Bianca turned her attention to the computer screen. "I'll print off a customer list so we can get started with the Halloween party invitations. I think the costume party idea is going to be a hit with my customers. Megan, don't forget about the article on superstitions for the newsletter. This is so exciting." She looked more cheerful than I could ever pretend to feel at the moment.

When I went back downstairs, Doreen was at the counter serving a customer and didn't look my way. Joyce was helping Sarah with a new shipment of roses in the workroom. No one noticed me, so I slipped out back.

Henry was sweeping out the loading area and stopped when he saw me. "Is something wrong?"

"No, Henry. I have a bit of free time. I thought I'd come and talk to you for a while." I smiled at him.

"Oh." He shifted his gaze to the floor.

"How do you like working here?"

His face lit up. "I love it. This is a great job. Bianca's the finest kind of boss I ever had." He looked at me. "Do you like it here?"

SANDRA NIKOLAI

"It's different from what I usually do, but yes, I like it." I leaned against a stack of wood crates and watched him push the broom with slow, easy strokes along the cement floor. Sunshine filtering through the narrow windows in the garage door caught the dust as it hung in the air over his head. "What do you like best about your job, Henry?"

He stopped sweeping and smiled. "I like to see the happy faces of customers when I make the deliveries. It makes me feel good inside."

"You're right. I never thought about that. It must feel especially nice when the delivery is a surprise."

"Yes. Like the time I delivered the flowers to Mrs. Spencer. She was real happy." He shrugged. "They said I made a mistake."

"Do you think you made a mistake?"

"Doreen said so, but I know I didn't. I delivered the flowers to the right address. I checked the delivery slip twice like I always do. It's wicked confusin', it is."

"Was Lee with you that day?"

"Yes. Lee drives the van." Henry began to slowly guide the broom across the floor again.

"Do you and Lee get along well?"

"Kind of."

"Does he ever get angry with you?"

"Sometimes."

"Why?"

"'Cause I don't do what I'm supposed to."

"Everybody makes mistakes, Henry."

"You can't trust too many people these days. Sometimes not even your own family."

"Do you have family?"

He hesitated. "I used to. A wife and two daughters."

"What happened?"

He shook his head. "I—I don't want to talk about it. It makes me sad."

A grunt sounded from the doorway. I turned my head to see Lee standing in the doorway. "We got deliveries," he said to Henry,

108

then stared at me, his eyes narrowing.

I met his hard gaze. The hairs stood up on the back of my neck. I wondered how much of our conversation he'd overheard.

The sun broke through the clouds as I set out to meet Michael for lunch. I reached the waterfront and took a deep breath of fresh air. The briny scent seemed to revitalize my senses, and I couldn't get enough of it.

Up ahead was DiMillo's On the Water. True to its name, the floating restaurant was located in a boat on the waterfront in the Old Port area. I'd checked it out on the Internet earlier and discovered the DiMillo family had purchased the boat in 1980 and opened the restaurant in 1982. The restaurant rises and falls with the tides twice each day and is one of the largest of its kind in the country.

I entered the restaurant and walked up to the reception desk.

A woman with dark curly hair greeted me. Large dangling earrings, classy red cardigan, lots of mascara. "Hello. A table for you today?" She smiled.

"I'm meeting someone," I said. "Reservations are under the name Elliott."

She tapped a few buttons on the electronic monitor. "Yes. This way please."

I followed her along a carpeted floor and glanced around. The restaurant was decorated with nautical artifacts like handcrafted boats, old lanterns, and even a deep-sea diver's suit—items you'd find at auctions. Best of all, it offered an incredible view of the water from every table.

Michael and Dr. Trudy Sayer had already arrived.

Michael stood up and shook my hand. "Thanks for coming, Megan."

"Thanks for asking me," I said, playing along.

He introduced me to the petite, thirty-something woman whose appearance said bones no matter where I looked: prominent cheekbones, a pronounced chin, and long thin fingers.

"Nice to meet you, Dr. Sayer," I said, extending my hand. What I got in return was something lifeless, clammy, and cold. A dead fish came to mind.

"Trudy will do," she said to me, turning to smile at Michael.

Sweet. I wondered why he wanted to include me in this cozy get-together in the first place.

We took our seats.

"Trudy is one of the country's foremost experts in poisons," Michael said to me.

How apropos, I thought.

Trudy held her gaze on him. "I read your investigative article on Tiffany Gray this morning in the *Herald*. The charitable institutions she supported offered quite the personal perspective about her work. I enjoyed it."

"Thanks," he said.

"I understand you're writing two more articles in the series?"

"That's right." He paused. "Trudy, maybe you could give Megan a summary of your recent findings on the Tiffany Gray autopsy."

She gave me a quick once-over. "Of course."

Was it my imagination or did she eye me with a complete lack of interest?

"To be honest," she said, "this autopsy has been a revelation of sorts for my team. I'll sum it up by saying that we completed a preliminary examination to establish the possible cause of death. Of course, we performed a thorough analysis afterward." She intertwined the palms of her hands together as if in prayer. "We began by looking for specific symptoms."

"Like what?" Michael prompted her.

"Signs of vomiting, convulsions, skin lesions, inflammation, damage to internal organs—that sort of thing," she said in a casual way, instantly canceling any desire I had of ordering an entrée.

"Did you discover any of these symptoms?"

"Not even close—except for the anomaly in the subject's lungs, which you and I discussed earlier."

If I hadn't known otherwise, the lingering smile she gave Michael suggested there was more than a business connection between them. I held back a strong urge to cough. Michael had suggested we keep the truth about our relationship from Trudy to give the impression we were business partners of sorts. I had agreed. Now I wondered if it had been such a good idea.

"Given that the anomaly was a symptom we didn't easily recognize," Trudy was saying, "I changed the focus of my team's efforts to a more suitable course of action."

She had the conviction of a general leading a team into battle. I studied her white knuckles. They protruded like miniature mountain tips above craggy cliffs. I was in the process of imagining those bony hands dissecting a cadaver when a waiter popped up to take our orders.

Michael and I ordered the fried seafood sampler. Trudy followed suit, if only to agree with Michael.

"Where was I?" she asked herself after the waiter had left. She paused to smooth out an imaginary fold in the white tablecloth, then rested one hand over the other as if she were harboring a priceless gem underneath. "Oh yes, the focus of our analysis." She gave Michael another inane smile and kept her gaze on him.

He nodded politely.

"After we discounted other types of poisons, such as industrial, medical, and the like, we turned our attention to plant poisons." Trudy raised a forefinger. "I want to point out something here. In most cases, death from plant poison is extremely rare. Regardless, in addition to performing tests on all the flowers and plants seized at the scene, we performed the obligatory tests on plant poisons. They revealed that none of the plant poisons we tested were responsible for the anomaly in the subject's lungs."

"What about your findings from the Gladys Lindstrom and Father Paul Griffith autopsies?" Michael asked her.

A flush tinted Trudy's cheeks. She gave me a side-glance, then said to him in a low voice, "I told you it was confidential information. I could lose my job if—"

"Journalistic privilege. No one else has to know but us." He included me with a wave of his hand.

She hesitated. "Well...as long as I can rely on your complete discretion." Another furtive glance in my direction. I was beginning to feel like a criminal.

"You have our word as journalists," Michael said. "Right, Megan?"

"Right," I said, my fingers crossed under the table.

Trudy nodded. "Fine."

Michael went on. "Do you think the anomaly in Tiffany's lungs is similar to that in the lungs of the other two victims?"

"Not similar," Trudy said. "Identical. A comparison of test results confirmed it."

"I don't get it," he said. "If you ran tests for every feasible poison in existence, what else is there?" He shot her a dubious look.

"The purpose of the autopsies was to assure the authorities that we had explored all known potential causes of death by poison, which we did to the tee, based on the forensics evidence provided and our professional knowledge of the matter," she said with a hint of annoyance, as if he'd questioned her judgment.

"No offence intended, Trudy. I'm well aware of your expert qualifications in the field." He smiled.

She returned a shy smile. "Then you can understand why this case is so important to my career. I was going to keep it a secret but..." Another side-glance in my direction. "I hope to publish a paper about these autopsies and win a Medical Examiner award. It would be helpful if I could garner extra merit along the way." Her eyes searched his.

Michael shrugged. "Sorry, Trudy. I don't have enough facts to write up an article and give you due recognition for it. You'll have to meet me half-way."

She glanced down, settled her hands in her lap. "Fine. I can tell you what our theories are. However, if they're made public before they're proven, the repercussions could put my team and me in a precarious situation."

"I promise I'll wait for your go-ahead."

She nodded, took a deep breath. "Based on our findings, we believe the police investigation into Tiffany Gray's death has the potential to become a criminal one."

"That's a strong statement coming from someone who can't even prove the cause of death," Michael said, working his strategy as an interviewer.

Trudy straightened up. "Our findings support the irrefutable conclusion we've reached so far."

"Which is...?"

She scanned the room as if she were about to make a statement that would change the course of events around the world. "The tests conducted on the subjects do not indicate any physical symptoms associated with poisons that are derived from flora originating in this country."

"Am I hearing you correctly?" Michael asked. "It comes from a foreign country?"

"Yes and no. To be precise, the flora is not grown in America—at least, not legally. However, with a bit of research, we might be able to find a source."

"Where would you begin?" I asked her.

She blinked at me as if she were surprised I could speak, then switched her gaze to Michael. "I have contacts through my memberships in international associations. They offer a wealth of information on poisonous flora."

Okay, so I was invisible.

"What's the next step?" Michael asked, leaning closer to her.

She batted her eyelids and smiled, no doubt mistaking his body language as a personal interest in her. "I've sent emails to my peers abroad. As soon as I hear from them, you'll be the first to know."

"Have you notified the police about your findings to date?"

"Not yet. I'd like to gather as much information as possible before I send them a final report."

Michael gazed at her and smiled. "Would you do me a big favor, Trudy?"

"That depends." Her hand went to her hair in a nervous gesture.

"Hold off on sending that report. Don't tell the police about the existence of the poisonous flora unless they raise the topic."

Maybe it was the confident timbre of his voice. Or maybe Trudy wanted to believe that Michael was interested in her. Whatever the reason, she said, "The authorities haven't yet voiced a suspicion that the deaths of the three victims are connected. Perhaps they haven't considered poisonous flora as a common denominator. As long as I haven't concluded my findings, I won't be sending them a report. So I'll grant you that favor." She smiled at him.

The waiter arrived with our plates.

Conversation through lunch was pleasant enough, even if Trudy probed Michael about his personal life and continued to ignore my presence. As usual, Michael was the ultimate diplomat. He answered her questions in vague terms, managed to change the topic often, and pulled me into the conversation whenever he could.

After coffee was served, Trudy glanced at her watch and said she had to rush off to a VIP meeting. She asked Michael if she could drop him off somewhere, pouted when he declined, then thanked him for lunch and left.

I waited until the top of her head disappeared down the stairs. "What can I say, Michael? She's perfect for you." I smiled and batted my eyelids at him.

He chuckled. "Sometimes ya gotta do what ya gotta do."

"Including bribing the medical examiner with a delicious lunch on a floating restaurant and suggestive body language?"

"I'll do anything to get to the bare bones of the matter."

"Oh, and funny too." I poked him in the arm. "You owe me another favor for this one."

"Even if my reasons for lunch were personal as well as professional?" He reached for my hand and squeezed it.

"Admit it. You asked me here to protect you from her."

"Could be. She did seem disappointed after you joined us, wouldn't you say?" A chuckle accentuated the twinkle in his eyes.

After he'd settled the tab, Michael walked me back to the flower shop. Our meeting with Trudy had propelled the investigation into a whole new area and triggered an avalanche of questions in my mind. I was about to ask him something when his phone rang.

He spoke briefly, then ended the call. "Remember the flowers the police seized from George's house?" he asked me.

"Yes."

"Liz at forensics confirmed what Trudy had told us. The plants and flowers were purchased locally and weren't poisonous. Forensics even checked the garbage bags at the Gray residence and found nothing lethal."

"Which means the local florists are off the hook."

Michael shook his head. "Not yet."

"Why not?"

"If Trudy is right, one of them might be secretly cultivating poisonous flora."

"Which you suspect made its way into George's house somehow?"

"You got it."

"So why didn't forensics find the least hint of poison there?"

"I don't know. Maybe the killer had the assistance of a local florist."

I held back from mentioning Bianca's Gardens. "You realize you're including anyone who works in a flower shop, don't you? It translates into dozens of potential suspects."

Michael shrugged. "We can't limit ourselves, Megan. The police have no leads."

"How can you be so sure Tiffany came in contact with the poison through a flower shop to begin with?"

"It's based on a gut feeling. I have to go with it."

"Well, my gut feeling tells me we should keep a close tab on George."

"You're overlooking something."

"What?"

"The common denominator. It's going to be damn hard to link George to the other two deaths."

Michael was right—again. "So what do you have in mind?"

"Plan A."

"What's Plan A?"

"Research. A mountain of it." He eyed me. "You're the only person I can trust to do it."

"What am I supposed to research?"

We came to a stop in front of Bianca's Gardens.

He glanced at his watch. "You'll be late for work. We'll talk about it later."

"Bianca isn't fussy about my schedule. Tell me now."

"No. Later." He leaned over and kissed me, then hurried away, leaving me to speculate what complications Plan A might possibly involve.

CHAPTER 11

It took me a while to realize a phone was ringing somewhere in the house. I glanced at the clock on the bedside table. It was almost four in the morning. Voices murmured in the hallway. There was a rush of footsteps and a knock at our bedroom door.

Michael opened the door a crack. "What's up?" he whispered.

"The police called," Victor said, his voice low. "There's been a fire at the shop. I'm on my way there now."

"I'll go with you. Give me a sec. I'll throw some clothes on."

"I'll wait for you downstairs."

Michael shut the door. He turned on the bedside lamp and grabbed his jeans and T-shirt.

I stepped out of bed and reached for my clothes.

"I think you should stay here with Bianca," he said.

"Okay, but promise you'll keep in touch."

"I will."

After Michael had gone downstairs, I opened the bedroom door and peeked around. No sign of Bianca or Alex. I tiptoed to the landing near the top of the steps and listened in the darkness.

"Of all things—a fire," Victor said, opening the closet door in the hallway. "What next? I have to ask myself if someone's trying to drive Bianca and me out of business. Do you think there's a connection?"

"The fire at the shop might not have anything to do with your office break-in," Michael said. "The important thing is that you and your family are safe."

I heard the jingle of keys. The front door closed behind them. "Megan."

I jumped and spun around to see a figure standing in the shadows. "Bianca. You almost gave me a heart attack."

"Sorry." She walked up to me. "I checked in on Alex. I thought I'd heard him stir, but he was sound asleep. Victor told you about the fire at the shop?" Her voice quivered.

"Yes. Michael went with him." I didn't think she'd overheard the conversation between the two men, so I didn't say anything about it. It would put her more on edge.

"I'm so stressed out. I wanted to go with Victor, but he insisted I stay here with Alex. I can't sleep. I'm going downstairs to make a cup of hot chocolate. Want some?"

"Sure."

The porcelain tiles on the kitchen floor felt cold under my bare feet. I curled up in a chair and tucked my legs under me.

Bianca poured milk into a container and placed it in the microwave. "Victor didn't want me to go with him. I can't blame him for trying to keep me out of harm's way. With all that's been going on lately, it's a wonder I can hold it together and take care of Alex." She looked like a big kid herself in fluffy white slippers and pink pajamas adorned with polar bears. "First a break-in. Now a fire. I bet you didn't expect this much action on your first visit here, did you?"

Add three dead bodies with identical lung anomalies, I held back from saying.

The microwave beeped. Bianca filled our mugs with hot milk. She dropped two tablespoons of chocolate powder into each cup and stirred. "You still like chocolate as much as you did when you were a kid, don't you?"

"More. Old habits die hard."

She smiled and placed a cup of the hot liquid before me. "I still love gummy bears. When I was pregnant with Alex, I couldn't get enough of them. Now I buy two bags every week." She sat down. "We haven't had much time for girl talk since you arrived." Her wedding ring caught the light and reminded me of the one I no longer wore.

"What do you mean?"

"You know, about you and Michael." She eyed me, waiting. When I remained silent, she went on. "Aunt Lucia and Aunt Elena think you rushed into another relationship too soon after Tom's death. They probably expected you to wear black for three years, those old nags. Mama told them to mind their own business." She giggled.

Bianca was referring to two elderly aunts on our mothers' side of the family who lived in New York City. Their gossip might have hurt my feelings in the past, but when I considered the pain my two-timing husband had caused me, I felt I owed no one an explanation for my lifestyle choices. "They don't know the whole story anyway."

"They don't need to. Mum's the word. Pinkie swear." She smiled.

Her words brought back memories of secrets we'd shared as children growing up in Montreal. There was no one on earth I trusted more than Bianca. For this reason alone, I'd reached out to her after Tom's murder investigation. I told her about Michael and how he'd stayed by my side, even after the police had fingered us as prime suspects.

"I wish I could have been there for you, Megan, but Alex was so young and I couldn't—"

"Forget it. It was all over before I knew it. What mattered to me was that you kept in touch."

She nodded, grew quiet. She had avoided talking about the fire until now. I wasn't surprised when seconds later her eyes welled up. "Oh, Megan, what am I going to do if my shop is destroyed? What about my staff? They'll be out of work. I can't let that happen to them."

"Wait until Victor calls. It might not be as bad as you think, Bianca."

"I hope not." She sniffed. "I've worked so hard to set up a business I could be proud of. How could this be happening?"

The phone rang, jolting us both to our feet.

Bianca answered. It was Victor. "Yes…about a thousand dollars. Oh, no…okay. See you later. Love you too." She hung up. "I kept a thousand dollars in cash in a metal chest in my office drawer. Victor said someone broke the lock and stole the money."

"What about the damage from the fire?"

"Victor said it wasn't too bad. My office suffered the worst of it."

"Your office?"

She nodded. "He thinks the fire might have started there. He called our insurance company. They're going to examine the shop and arrange for cleanup and repairs."

"Any other damage?"

"The back door was broken into. That's how the arsonist got in. The police nabbed a man running down the alley and brought him to the station for questioning."

"Do they know who he is?"

"Not yet."

An hour later, Victor and Michael stood in the foyer looking like a pair of burnt fuses. Their appearance told me the fire might have been worse than Victor had let on. Dust coated their hair, aging them by twenty years. They looked as if they'd swept out a chimney headfirst. Their shoes and their clothes were filthy and emitted the acrid scent of smoke. They'd probably never be worn again.

At first glimpse, I didn't know whether to laugh or cry. Bianca in her fluffy slippers and polar bear pajamas and me in my blue pajamas decked with tiny white sheep must have looked as absurd to the men as the two of them looked to us.

Bianca took the edge off when she shook a finger at them and said, "Neither one of you is walking into this house until you take off all your clothes."

By the time everyone had showered and dressed, and Bianca had prepared a pot of coffee, the police called with more news.

The suspected arsonist in custody now had a name: Henry Glover.

CHAPTER 12

"Henry is the last person on earth who would have set fire to my shop," Bianca said, clearing the table Wednesday morning before we'd even finished our coffee. "Megan, you know what Henry is like. He wouldn't hurt a fly."

"I agree with you," I said. "I can't believe he did it."

"We discussed this last night—or rather, very early this morning," Victor said, standing up. "We don't have all the facts yet, so we don't want to judge rashly."

Bianca stacked the dishes in the sink and glanced over her shoulder at Victor. "Don't forget to put a thicker jacket on Alex this morning. It's getting colder. And pack an extra piece of cheese in his lunchbox. He needs the calcium. He's a growing boy." She turned on the tap, then turned it off. "I almost forgot. Alex isn't going to day care today. He's going to Sarah's instead."

Michael raised an eyebrow in my direction.

I figured adrenalin must have been fueling Bianca. Like the rest of us, she hadn't had much sleep last night.

Victor walked over and put his hands on her shoulders. "Relax, Bianca. It's seven in the morning. At this rate, you'll never make it to the end of the day."

She ran a soapy washcloth over a serving tray. "I want to get to the shop before the cleaning crew arrives. I need to see for myself how bad the damage is."

"I told you. It's not that bad. I'll finish up here and leave Alex at Sarah's on my way to the office. Okay?"

She dropped the cloth in the sink and wiped her hands on a paper towel. "I'm so lucky to have you, Victor." She gave him a hug and kissed him on the cheek. "Let's go get ready, Megan."

An hour later, Bianca and I were standing in the alley behind the shop. A telltale trace of soot stretched from a broken window on the second floor of Bianca's shop across the white clapboard to the neighboring building. The back door had been kicked in last night after the perpetrator had used an ax to initiate the process. Michael had helped Victor board the door up with makeshift wood panels they'd retrieved from the loading dock.

"Oh, my God. It looks like an abandoned building." Bianca's eyes welled up.

"Maybe it's not as bad as it looks." My feeble attempt at playing down the situation. "Bianca, no matter what, you'll manage. Remember how hard you worked serving tables in the evening and on weekends to help pay for your college tuition?"

She nodded. "I thought I'd never make it, but I did."

"And how you studied till the middle of the night and got up early the next morning to attend classes?"

"Yes. And even after I married Victor and could afford to stay home, I worked long hours to set up Bianca's Gardens."

"Not to mention ran a household and raised Alex at the same time."

"And that too." Bianca smiled. "You're right. I didn't fight my way through all of those things to give up now. I guess there's only one way to find out how bad it is. Walk in the front door." She dug out her keys and headed out of the alley.

I almost had to run to keep up with her.

She unlocked the front door to the shop and swung it open. The scent of the flora couldn't disguise the pungent odor of smoke that hit us. "Whew!" she waved a hand in front of her face. "Good thing I gave the staff the day off. Imagine working in this stench." The Closed sign flapped against the door as she shut it behind us. She locked the door and dropped the keys into her purse.

I looked around. "Nothing much was damaged down here, except those plants." I pointed to two wide ferns in overturned pots near the foot of the staircase. "They must have been in the path of the firefighters."

"Let's go see upstairs," she said, leading the way.

Dirty footprints on the stairs extended to the second floor. They probably belonged to the firefighters, or maybe Victor or Michael or even Henry.

Bianca opened the first door on the left and peeked into the stockroom. "Okay in here."

It was a different story when she checked her office. The filing cabinets lay on their sides like wounded soldiers in battle, red file folders spilling out of the drawers. Where wall-to-wall carpet had once provided softness underfoot, a black hole in the center of the floor marked the spot where the fire had started and held black remnants of whatever might have fueled it. Grimy residue speckled the rest of the carpet, and our feet made squishy noises with each step we took. Smoke stains had tainted the cream-colored walls, white stucco ceiling, and vinyl blinds.

A sudden breeze from somewhere caused cinders to spiral upward in the air like feathers and glide back to the floor.

Bianca's complexion paled. "What a horrible mess."

"A coat of fresh paint will help," I said.

"How about charcoal gray?" She let out a nervous laugh, but the sadness in her eyes negated the humor. "Wait till the staff finds out the police have Henry in custody."

"You didn't tell them?"

She shook her head. "It's better if I tell them in person later."

Bianca's attitude didn't surprise me. Her protective shield had already encircled Alex earlier this morning. Fearing that something bad might happen to him next, she'd refused to drop him off at day care. Since Victor had meetings with clients all day, and Michael was rushing to meet deadlines, she had to compromise. She'd asked Sarah to babysit Alex.

I studied the patch of burnt carpet. "Sure is a strange place to start a fire. It would have caused much more damage if it had been set downstairs."

"The fire marshal said we were lucky someone called it in sooner rather than later."

"Who was the Good Samaritan?"

"I don't know. If I ever find out, I'll give him a fat reward." She looked at the carpet. "We have a remnant in storage that could cover this hole. I'll have it repaired this week."

My eyes followed the trail of dirt and muddy footprints out of the office, down the corridor, and into the bathroom. I walked over to check it out and noticed the window in the bathroom was broken. I realized it was the same one I'd seen from the alley earlier.

Bianca joined me and stared at the window. "How on earth—? We'll get it replaced."

We moved on to the kitchen. File folders were piled on the table and counter. Some of the folders had slid over and overlapped bordering ones like so many giant decks of shuffled cards suspended in motion. Michael and Victor told us they'd transported them here from the office after the firefighters had left. Their efforts had salvaged most of the documents from damage, though exposure to water had curled paper edges and flames had burned others.

Bianca pushed aside a pile of files on the table to make place for her purse. She began sifting through the folders. "I hope my backup CDs are in here. There should be six of them—one for each working day of the last week."

I remembered my own reasons for wanting to find them. I glanced at the table and noticed a CD peeking out from under folders. I reached for it. "I found Tuesday." I handed it to Bianca.

"Super. It's yesterday's CD." She took it from me. "I won't have to reconstruct any information. Thank goodness, it's all here."

Not exactly. Doreen's as-yet-unproven handiwork wasn't on the CD that Bianca was now placing in her purse. Two original bits of information—the change in the delivery address for Mrs. Spencer's flowers and the reinstated standing order of flowers to Tiffany—were on Saturday's CD. I had to find it if I wanted to prove Doreen had tampered with the data.

I lifted the file folders, one by one, and tilted them to see if another CD would slip out. "The other CDs should be here somewhere."

"Forget it, Megan. It's okay. It's the most recent one that counts and I have it."

I ignored her and increased my efforts to search in other places. "Maybe Victor took them."

"If he did, he'd have told me." She sighed. "Okay, Megan. What's wrong?"

I had to say it. "I think the arsonist destroyed the other CDs or stole them."

"Why would anyone want to do that?"

"There was specific information in those files that he didn't want anyone else to see."

"Like what? How many glass vases we sold last week?" She let out a nervous laugh.

"I'm serious. If someone wanted to cause serious damage to the shop, why would they bother to break in and set fire to your office? Why not torch the whole place?"

Bianca shrugged. "Maybe it was a warning—like the robbery in Victor's office."

"A warning for what?"

"I don't know."

I tried a different tactic. "Don't you find it odd that the arsonist spared the main floor? As if he cared too much for the flowers and plants to destroy them?"

"It can't be Henry. He wouldn't do this to me."

She was right. Henry Glover didn't have the physical aptitude to carry out a disaster like this, let alone dream it up in the first place.

Then why did the police catch him running away in the alley behind the shop late last night?

Before I could say another word, the front door buzzer rang. The cleaning crew had arrived.

We watched in amazement as the four-person team proceeded to assess the damage and divide the tasks among themselves. They cleared out the debris and scrubbed the smoke residue off the walls and ceiling in Bianca's office. They mopped up the dirt on the floors and stairs, and deodorized the air to neutralize smoke odors. In spite of their speed and efficiency, I was convinced the acrid stench of burnt carpet and plastic had found permanent residence in my nose.

Bianca and I spent the day organizing the documents and files. We stored them in cardboard boxes, marking every box with enough details so that we could easily transfer the files into new cabinets later. After we'd finished, we wiped the kitchen counter and table.

When Bianca went downstairs to check orders on the POS and call up customers who had deliveries scheduled today, I rummaged through more files. I didn't find any more CDs. The fact that someone might have stolen or destroyed them infuriated me to no end, but I had to let it go. There was nothing I could do about it right now.

I paid close attention to the staff as they arrived Thursday morning—in particular, Doreen and Lee. Call me biased, but I didn't want to miss a movement, a glance, or a word that might be construed as being out of place. I couldn't begin to explain why I suspected Doreen and Lee had had a hand in the shop fire. If the Good Samaritan hadn't reported it in time and the shop had burned down, they would have been looking for a new job today like the rest of the staff. Maybe my suspicions about them were wrong. Maybe I was just looking for someone to blame.

As expected, questions from the staff gushed forth as soon as they entered the shop:

How did it happen?

Was there much damage?

Was it arson?

Do the police have any suspects?

Bianca held off saying anything until she'd taken a seat at the front counter and gathered everyone around her. Everyone except Lee and Doreen, that is. For whatever reason, they chose to remain a little off to the side. No matter. From where I stood, they were in my direct field of vision.

Bianca told them what she knew so far—that the damage was minimal and business at the shop would continue as usual. She added that the police didn't know how the fire started, but an investigation was underway.

"Where's Henry?" Doreen asked, glancing around.

"The police are questioning him about the fire," Bianca said.

"Why?" Joyce asked.

Bianca tensed up. "They found him running away in the back alley after the fire started."

Doreen gasped. "Oh, my God. Not Henry. He'd never set fire to the shop. He loves it here." She exchanged concerned looks with Joyce and Gail.

"That poor man had no life until he started working here," Joyce said, her eyes teary. "I don't know much about him except that he's been trying to find his wife and two daughters for years. He told me how much he was looking forward to the Halloween party." She pulled out a tissue and blew her nose.

"Henry loves working here," Sarah said. "I can't believe he'd do this."

Gail joined in. "Henry's an okay kind of guy. I think the police made a huge mistake in arresting him."

"They haven't arrested him," Bianca corrected her. "They don't know for sure if he had anything to do with the fire or not."

"If they caught him running away from the scene, what chance does he have?" Doreen asked, searching her co-workers' faces for support.

"Doreen's right," Joyce said, adjusting her bifocals. "Henry doesn't have much money. He wouldn't be able to afford a good lawyer."

"He'd never ask any of us for help either," Gail said.

I caught Lee staring at me. Was that a smirk on his face?

Bianca went on. "Let's not assume anything yet. Henry's presence in the alley could be considered circumstantial. Right, Megan?" She turned to me with an expectant look.

"That's right," I said, adding a semblance of say-so to my

voice. "As far as the police are concerned, any one of us might be considered a suspect."

Responses of "Not me" and "I'd never do that" spilled from the women's mouths.

I stole another peek at Lee. The smirk was gone. In its place was an icy stare that chilled the blood in my veins.

CHAPTER 13

Michael asked me to meet him at Gilbert's Chowder House for lunch on Thursday. Though I welcomed his invitation, our date was a business meeting. Trudy would be joining us.

I walked up to Michael's table and was surprised when he stood up and greeted me with a kiss. I pulled back. "Be careful. What if Trudy sees us?" My eyes flitted to the front entrance.

"Don't worry," he said as we both sat down. "She's not coming. She can't make it."

"Why not? Wait. Don't tell me. She couldn't tear herself away from her cadavers." I batted my eyelashes at him.

He smiled. "She had to attend an important meeting. She sent me an email this morning, but I didn't want to cancel lunch with you." His eyes lingered on mine.

I felt butterflies taking flight in the lower part of my anatomy and smiled back. "What about the research she was supposed to do for you?"

"It's done."

"And?"

"I called Drew and asked him to join us. As soon as he gets here, I'll brief you both on it."

"Oh…it's a business lunch with your boss. I shouldn't be here." I made a move to get up.

He touched my hand. "No. Stay. It's not a big deal." He glanced toward the front door. "Here he comes now."

"Hi, Megan, nice to see you again," Drew said. "Michael, I

rushed over as soon as you said you were treating me to lunch." He laughed, then sat down and placed his smartphone on the table.

"I know you two have business to discuss," I said to Drew. "I hope I'm not in the way."

"If anyone's in the way, it's me," Drew said, smiling at me. "Michael knows the routine. We don't use names."

A waitress came by to take our orders. We all chose the clam chowder. Michael and Drew added an order of fried shrimp with French fries. I opted for a crabmeat roll.

With the preliminaries out of the way, Drew went straight to the point. "So Michael, what has our source told you?"

Michael leaned forward. "She hinted at an exotic area that could yield a certain type of poison."

"Where is it?"

"Her associate in Southeast Asia cited a rare ancient plant that grows there. The tiny seed, not the actual plant, is poisonous. The scientific community has done limited research on it because of the high risk involved in handling the seeds."

"Does the plant have a name?"

"It's commonly known as Black Whispers. Here's a picture she sent me." He reached for his phone and tapped the screen to pull up a photo.

The flower had a thick stem topped with overlapping black petals around a yellow center. If I hadn't known better, I'd have mistaken it for an oversized Gerbera daisy.

Drew asked, "Who would take a chance on importing lethal plants into the country?"

Michael shrugged. "Maybe it wasn't imported. It was implied the plants could have been cultivated here."

"Interesting."

"Either way, there's a catch."

"What's that?"

"The seeds have to be submersed in water or stored in a freezer while in transit."

"Why?"

"Air activates the reproduction cycle. That's when the seeds can explode—with dire consequences to humans. A researcher in Bolivia accidentally died while handling a single seed."

Drew grimaced. "How the devil would our victim have come into contact with it?"

"All I know is that its vapor is airborne and kills within seconds. Just like that." Michael snapped his fingers.

His search had produced yet another similarity to Tom's death. The seed vapor had killed Tiffany instantly. Cyanide had killed Tom within moments of exposure to it too. I shivered involuntarily.

"You okay?" Michael peered at me.

"I'm fine." I smiled.

Drew laced his fingers and leaned in. "Okay. Here's what we know so far. We have a woman with an anomaly in her lungs who might have been killed by an airborne poison from a seed."

"Let me take it a step further." Eagerness spread across Michael's face. "Suppose we buy the source's findings that all three victims died from the same cause. The common link is the assumption they were all exposed to a seed from Black Whispers."

"Seeds that could have originated from the same source. Locally?"

"As yet to be proven, but highly likely."

"Like flower shops. Right?"

"Right."

I tensed up.

"There can't be too many in the area." Drew paused in thought. "I know of Bianca's Gardens in town. They're fairly popular. Have you checked it out?"

I gave Michael a subtle kick under the table.

"I'm looking into several outlets right now," he said.

"Good." Drew nodded. "How's that second article in your series coming along?"

"Working through interviews with the victim's family and household staff. Waiting for more facts for the third and last article covering the source of the victim's death."

Drew's eyes lit up. "I just thought of something. Since Jeff is still away on assignment, how about extending your investigation by branching out into the other two deaths? Present all three deaths as separate incidents linked by common factors. Go from there as details come in."

Our plates arrived. I couldn't have been more relieved when the conversation turned to popular tourist attractions, shops, and leisure activities. I kept hoping the topic of flower shops wouldn't come up again—specifically, Bianca's Gardens. It didn't.

Before we'd ordered coffee, Drew answered a phone call, then excused himself, saying he had to hurry back to the office to take care of something. He thanked Michael and left.

"This case is sprouting wings," Michael said to me. "Who'd have predicted that one mysterious death would develop into an international search for a poisonous seed?"

"So how do we find the source? It's not as if the lifestyles of a rich socialite, a homeless person, and a priest have much in common."

"That's why we need to focus on Plan A."

"You never told me what Plan A was besides research."

"Like Drew said, we launch our own investigation into local florists. There has to be a connection somewhere." He briefly glanced away. "Don't take this the wrong way, Megan, but I think we should tackle Bianca's shop first."

"You've got to be kidding." I sat rigid in my seat.

"I'm not pointing a finger at anyone. Logic says we have to act on the fact that George and Tiffany ordered flowers regularly there."

Seconds of uneasy silence followed.

"I understand we're talking about family," Michael said in a calm voice. "I'm asking you to trust me. I'd never do anything to hurt them—or you."

I crossed my arms. "George bought flora from other florists too."

"I realize that. Until we discover otherwise, Bianca's Gardens is the best place to start."

His comment stirred a vague recollection. I knew it had to do with Bianca's Gardens, but what was it?

Michael's voice snapped me out of my reverie. "You saw

the pictures of George's house. Almost every room had flower arrangements. And in the alley, Gladys was—"

"Holding a bunch of wildflowers—no connection there, though. And yes, St. Andrew's Church usually has baskets of flowers around the altar." It triggered a thought. "What about the flowers that were in the church on Sunday—the day Father Griffith collapsed? Did forensics check them?"

"Trudy said they found no trace of poison in any of the flowers seized at the scene."

I remembered what I wanted to ask him. "Did the flowers they seized from the church that Sunday come from Bianca's Gardens?"

"I don't know."

"There you go. It proves my point. Why even consider Bianca's shop as the source?"

Michael shrugged. "I agree it's not much to go on, but flowers are common to each victim's surroundings. We need to follow this lead until something better comes up."

It was hard to ignore the look of determination in his eyes. It reminded me how he'd stood by me when the police had suspected us of murdering Tom and how he'd risked his life to catch the real killer. If I had to place my trust in anyone, it would be Michael. In fact, I'd bet my future on it.

"Okay," I said. "What do you want me to do?"

"I'd like you to get the personal information on the staff at Bianca's Gardens without arousing suspicion. Can you do that?"

"I have access to the computer. Maybe it contains their personal files."

"Do you think you can get the information on Henry Glover first and call me? I'd like to see what kind of guy is a suspected arsonist."

"Okay."

"I'll ask Dan Cummings to dig up background checks on Henry and the rest of the staff."

I wasn't surprised when he mentioned Dan Cummings, his old college friend and top-notch criminal lawyer. Dan had legal teams in major cities across Canada and easy access to legal information through associates around the world. I'd first met him when the police were investigating Tom's death. He'd offered us indispensible legal advice and remained a vital part of our lives ever since.

Michael grew silent, thinking. "In the meantime, we still need to interview George Gray's family and the household staff so I can complete the second article in my series. Depends on how soon I can get the interviews scheduled."

"What about the extended article Drew wants?"

"No problem. We'll interview the staff at St. Andrew's Church. We'll go back to see Ben at the adult shelter in case Gladys might have visited there. I'll contact others to get things rolling."

"Hold on a sec, Michael. Are we going to have enough time to do all this before we leave town?"

"We can extend our trip another week—if that's okay with you."

"I have nothing else planned."

"To think that my byline will appear in articles covering Portland's most infamous investigations. Where can I get better publicity than that?" He smiled.

I smiled back, but in truth I was more concerned about his safety than his byline. Unexplained death had entered our lives again, threatening the delicate relationship we'd begun to build together. His coverage for the newspaper, though a notable achievement in his career, might hurl him into more danger yet.

The fire had thrown my work schedule off balance, so I was putting in a full day at the shop today. I returned after lunch to find Joyce standing at the checkout counter.

"Two men in suits are upstairs with Bianca," she whispered to me, an anxious look on her face. "I think it has something to do with the fire."

"How long have they been here?"

"Maybe ten minutes." She bent over to pick up a gift basket. "I have to bring this out back. The others are helping Lee load deliveries onto the truck. Can you cover for me here?"

"Sure." I placed my handbag in a cabinet under the counter. "Is Lee making the deliveries alone?"

"He has no choice." She heaved a sigh. "With Henry away, Bianca wants to keep things moving as smoothly as possible."

I waited until Joyce had sauntered off. I wanted to find out if I could access the employee files from the POS. Maybe the system interfaced with Bianca's office computer upstairs.

Minutes into my search, I stumbled on a directory of files I hadn't noticed before: STAFF. I clicked on it. A window opened to request a password. I took a chance and entered the same one Bianca had given me to access other restricted files. It worked. A list of staff names appeared. I clicked on Henry's file. I looked around. I was alone. I grabbed a memo pad and scribbled the information down. I tucked the sheet in my jacket pocket.

Out of the corner of my eye, I detected movement at the back of the floor. Doreen and Lee were standing at the entrance to the workroom. I couldn't make out what Doreen was saying because she was whispering. Her face was flushed and she was gesturing wildly at him. Her demeanor contrasted with Lee's firm stance inside his thick-soled boots, arms by his side, hands forming fists as he stared at her. It almost looked as if he was about to punch her out. In the next instant, he turned and stomped out the back.

Doreen gazed in my direction. I pretended I hadn't witnessed her confrontation with Lee. In case she'd decide to head my way, I cut short my covert search and closed the open windows on the screen. I tapped buttons on the POS to open up the Delivery menu. Since Bianca had re-scheduled deliveries due to the fire, today's timetable was a heavy one—too heavy for Lee to handle alone. I almost felt sorry for him, but it passed when I recalled the vile looks he'd given me lately.

I reached for a stray glass vase on the counter that needed a price sticker.

Doreen walked up to me. "Men," she said. "Sometimes you can't do anything with them, and sometimes you can't do anything without them." She let out a deep-bellied laugh. "Do you and Michael have tiffs sometimes?"

I was so taken aback by her question that I almost dropped the vase. I placed it on the counter. "We're not married, so it's different between us. You know what I mean."

"Yeah," she said. "The good old days."

I looked at the screen. "Do you think Lee can handle all these deliveries today? With Henry gone—"

"Lee can handle it."

The door chimes announced the arrival of a customer.

I turned around to see George Gray walk in. Dressed in a dark blue suit with a red silk tie and matching breast pocket handkerchief, he looked as if he'd just come from a photo shoot for *GQ*. Accompanying him was Tyler in a white polo shirt and a plaid sports jacket that strained across his chest.

George glanced around the shop, then approached the counter. "Hello, Megan. I'm looking for Bianca." A faint odor of after-shave— lemon-scented—hung in the air between us.

"She's in a meeting right now," I said. "Can I help you?"

"I purchased a large plant." He pulled out a slip of paper from the inside pocket of his jacket and showed it to me. "It's scheduled for delivery to a business associate today. I thought I would pick it up and have Tyler deliver it personally instead."

Tyler gave me a quick smile. "Hi, Megan, how are you doing? If you need help carrying the plant to the front counter, please let me know. I wouldn't want you to hurt yourself." His gaze swept over me.

I felt a slight blush. I looked behind me, expecting to see Doreen, but she was nowhere in sight. How she'd managed to vanish so quickly was beyond me. I noticed Gail with a customer at the other end of the floor. "I'll go check on it. Excuse me." I headed to the back, hoping to catch Lee before he drove off with the deliveries.

Coughing sounds coming from the workroom drew me there first. I peeked inside. Doreen was bent over one of the sinks, vomiting.

Joyce was by her side, rubbing her back. She noticed me and said, "Doreen's not feeling too well. Must be the flu or something."

"George Gray is here asking about an order," I said.

Doreen coughed, then reached for a paper towel and wiped her mouth. Without looking at me, she said, "The truck's gone." She stooped back over the sink.

Could she be pregnant?

I returned to the front counter. "I'm sorry, George. The truck already left with the orders."

"That's fine. I took a chance. Please give my regards to Bianca." He gave me a nod and left with Tyler.

I looked around. Gail was still busy with the customer. I could hear Doreen and Joyce chatting in the workroom. It was probably the only chance I'd get to call Michael.

I took my phone out of my handbag and rushed upstairs. Bianca's door was closed. I slipped into the washroom and called Michael. I gave him the information I'd obtained on Henry from Bianca's computer files.

Minutes after I'd returned to the front counter, two men toting briefcases came downstairs. They wound their way around the potted plants and walked out the door.

Bianca came down soon afterward and made a beeline for me. "At least that part's over."

"Police?" I asked.

"No. Insurance people. I told them what I knew about the fire and sent them to see Victor. He handles the paperwork for the shop." She looked around. "Where's everyone else?"

I brought her up to date, including Doreen's condition and George's visit.

She whispered, "I'm glad I was busy upstairs. I didn't feel much like talking to George anyway. As for Doreen..." She smiled. "It sounds like morning sickness to me. Good news."

"Here's more good news. Michael and I will be staying in town at least another week. The *Herald* extended his assignments."

"Super." She glanced around and whispered, "Now for the bad news. The police called me earlier. They told me Henry gave up without a fight."

"Gave up? What do you mean?"

"He confessed to setting the fire here."

CHAPTER 14

The news about Henry Glover put a damper on the conversation around the dinner table Thursday evening. Bianca had a hard time dealing with his admission of guilt and vented her thoughts at every turn. Luckily, Michael's delicious beef ravioli, a green leaf salad, and a bottle of *Chianti* helped to alleviate the somber mood.

"I heard that other florists have already hired extra delivery staff through to Thanksgiving and into the New Year," Bianca said. "It's going to take me forever to find someone to replace Henry." She sighed. "I don't know what possessed him to say he torched my shop."

"The police have yet to confirm it," Victor said.

"Maybe he was depressed," Bianca said, looking at him. "I should have spoken with him more often at the shop. I feel as if I've let him down." She drank some wine.

"The man might have personal problems," Victor said. "Don't go blaming yourself now." He paused. "Getting back to your delivery problem, there are lots of people looking to make extra money for the holidays. It's early yet."

"It's not early." Bianca stared at him. "I have to advertise the position and interview the applicants." She groaned. "Frankly, I don't have the time."

"Maybe I can help," Michael said.

"You know someone who might be interested?" Bianca asked him.

"Yes. Me."

I almost dropped my fork.

"You can't be serious." Bianca's hopeful smile betrayed her words.

"Why not? I'm a good driver. I know my way around the city." He shrugged. "I'm great with people too."

"I don't doubt it." She grew serious. "You'd work a few hours a day. It can't interfere with your job at the newspaper." She wagged a forefinger at him.

"No problem."

"Can you start on Monday?"

"Sure."

"Then the job is yours." Bianca laughed. "That was the easiest interview I ever had to do. Cheers." She lifted her glass of wine.

"Me too." Michael chuckled, lifted his glass. "Cheers."

What a smooth operator...

"Making any progress on your investigative articles?" Victor asked him.

Michael nodded. "Drew asked me to extend my investigation to include the deaths of Gladys glad rags and Father Paul Griffith."

"Oh?" Victor took a sip of wine. "The *Herald* never did say what Gladys or Father Griffith had died from, did it? Are there any similarities in the three deaths?"

"A couple," Michael said, not revealing more.

"As long as the police don't come to interrogate me about their deaths," Bianca said.

"Why would you say that?" Victor asked her.

"With my luck these days, you never know," she said. "Ever since Tiffany's death was linked to my shop, I've worried that my business will suffer. After the fire this week, I can't afford any more bad news."

The phone rang, cutting into the moment.

Victor stood up. "I'll get it. I'm expecting a call from the locksmith." He answered the phone. "Yes. Of course. We'll be here." He hung up. "That was Detective Flanagan. He's coming over. I think he has news about the theft at my office." He returned to his seat.

"Good news, I hope," Bianca said, sipping her wine.

"We'll know soon enough," Victor said.

We'd just finished dinner when the doorbell rang.

Victor answered the door and led Detective Flanagan into the hallway. "We can talk in my home office."

"Do you have a larger room?" Flanagan asked. "I'd like to include everyone here in the conversation." He gestured toward the kitchen where the rest of us were sitting.

"Oh...of course." Victor ushered us into the living room. He offered the detective a seat in one of the two Italian provincial armchairs and sat down in the other. Bianca, Michael, and I settled on the couch opposite them.

"Detective, you said on the phone that you had information you wanted to discuss," Victor said. "Is it about the robbery at my office?"

"I'm here on a different matter tonight." The detective switched his gaze to Bianca. "I've been assigned to the case covering the fire at your shop. I have a recording of the caller who phoned it in. It originated from an untraceable number, so it offers no leads. The voice is disguised, but I thought you might be able to help me out."

He retrieved a smartphone from his jacket and tapped buttons on the screen to play the recorded message.

"Please send the fire trucks to Bianca's Gardens. There's a fire on the second floor. Please hurry!"

The words came across in clipped bites, as if they'd been computer-generated or the caller had used a special apparatus to mask his voice. I'd heard similar recordings before. The tone made it difficult to tell if the caller was male or female. I didn't detect any lisps or accents or any background noises.

Flanagan said, "I'll play it one more time." After we'd listened to it again, he put away his phone and asked, "Do any of you notice something that might help us identify this person?"

"He's polite," I said. "He said please twice."

"He didn't give the street address," Michael said. "He assumed the fire department knew where the shop was. I'll bet he's familiar with the place himself."

"It could be a customer," Bianca said.

"Or a member of the staff," I said. "Maybe Henry himself."

My suggestion drew a puzzled look from Bianca.

"I've requested a voice print analysis of this call," Flanagan said. "I'll let you know if we get conclusive results. Thanks for your help." He stood up. "Oh...one more thing. The timing of the fire interests me. So soon after the robbery at your office, Victor."

"Do you think there's a connection between the two incidents?" Victor asked him.

"It's a theory we're considering."

Bianca frowned. "I don't understand why. The only things missing from my shop are cash and CDs containing bookkeeping information from days ago. I have the latest CD—the most important one. The others aren't important."

"The perpetrator didn't think so," Flanagan said.

"I can't believe Henry set fire to the shop and stole my cash."

"It's an educated guess. Henry might have had help in setting the fire."

"What makes you think that?"

"He didn't have any CDs or cash on him when we found him wandering in the alley. We suspect he passed the load to an accomplice."

Bianca shook her head. "Well, I'm sorry. I don't see it. Henry is a good person. I don't believe he's capable of breaking the law in any way whatsoever."

"I interviewed Henry. Chances are he's a lackey following orders. Whatever his reasons are for admitting to breaking the law, we don't know. I'm asking that you all remain vigilant. If it turns out that he does have an accomplice, it means the perpetrator is still at large."

After the detective had left, Victor poured the rest of the *Chianti* into our glasses. We sat around the kitchen table, sipping our wine and rehashing events in the light of Flanagan's visit.

"Why wouldn't the Good Samaritan identify himself?" Bianca said about the anonymous caller. "What he did was commendable."

"He didn't want to get involved," Victor said. "You know how it is."

"Maybe he had another reason for hiding his identity," Michael said.

"Like what?' Bianca asked.

"You might know him."

"Michael's right," I said. "You're not going to like this, Bianca. I'm almost certain Henry made that call."

Her eyes widened. "You honestly believe that?"

I nodded. "You said it yourself. He's a good man. If someone forced him to set fire to the shop, maybe he felt guilty about it and wanted to make amends."

"You know, I can almost picture him doing something like that." She blinked hard. "What a nightmare this week is turning out to be." She looked at Victor. "And now the detective thinks there's a connection between the theft in your office and the fire at the shop. This is about George Gray, isn't it?"

He reached over and put a hand on her shoulder. "The important thing is that the police are on top of things." His weary eyes rested on Michael and me. "I'm sorry you two got caught up in our personal troubles."

"Not a problem," Michael said. "I wish we could do more to help." He finished the last of his wine, then stood up. "You'll have to excuse me. I need to get some sleep and save my energy. Next week, I'm starting a new job for this female slave driver—"

"Oh, you rascal," Bianca gave him a light slap on the hand. "I should hang you by the ears until you beg for mercy." She pretended to reach for his ears.

Michael laughed and raised his arms in mock fear. "Megan, help me."

"No way," I said. "You got yourself into this one."

"Scoot, both of you," Bianca said, waving us away. "Victor and I will do the dishes tonight."

With the evening ending on an upbeat note, Michael and I said good night and retired to our room.

Behind closed doors, I asked him, "Why on earth did you offer to go work for Bianca?"

"Because I do my best work in the lion's den."

I folded my arms. "So you put yourself up as bait?"

"We agreed that Bianca's shop was the first stop on our hit list of retailers, didn't we?"

"Yes."

"Well then?"

I shook my head.

"What?"

"Don't you think the staff is going to ask why you're working there? You're a writer, not a deliveryman. What if they suspect something?"

He shrugged. "I'll tell them I offered to give Bianca a hand. After all, we're practically family. Relatives help one another through tough times. Right?"

He had a point. "Okay, but be careful. The last time you jumped into a situation like this, it almost cost you your life—and mine."

"Don't worry. I'll make sure I have a foolproof getaway plan." He slipped his arms around me. "And if I need to, I'll call in the troops."

He'd already won my confidence in his ability to think on his feet. Yet my instincts told me we were about to try our hand at an extremely dangerous game of blind man's bluff.

CHAPTER 15

At nine o'clock Friday morning, the new three-inch steel door to the back of the shop still hadn't been mounted. The repairmen had shut off their drills and stood by as Lee transported deliveries out that same exit to the delivery van parked in the back alley.

It hadn't been Lee's choice. The loading dock was filled with incoming inventory that the staff had yet to uncrate and verify. There was no extra space there for Lee to park the truck and load the deliveries.

"Sorry, guys," Bianca said to the two men decked out in grease-stained jeans and work shirts. "Five more minutes, I promise."

Five minutes stretched to ten, then fifteen. The repairmen kept looking at their watches and muttering to each other.

"Don't worry about the extra time," Bianca said to them. "I'll cover it."

"Ma'am, it's not about the money," the heftier worker said. "We got a tight schedule to follow. Hitches like this give the company a bad rap." He took a step back as Lee slipped by with a sizeable fern. "My boss ain't gonna like it if we're late for the next job."

"A few more minutes, please?" Bianca pleaded. "How about I get you guys some coffee?"

All the while, I'd been standing at the front counter, trying to download the employee profiles off the computer without Bianca noticing. I couldn't slip upstairs to use her computer either—I had customer service duty this morning for a couple of hours. It meant I had to serve customers and process orders on the POS.

Out of the corner of my eye, I saw Bianca turn to face me. I'd have bet anything she was going to ask me to run over to Starbucks.

And she did.

I grabbed my handbag and set out on my errand. Laden with two *grande* coffees, I rushed back to the shop as fast as I could before the clock struck ten. The rest of the staff would arrive to begin their shift then.

I handed out the coffee cups and re-claimed my position at the front counter. It was nine forty-five. I had fifteen minutes to carry out my furtive deed.

I glanced at the back. Bianca was chatting with the repairmen as they sipped their coffee. It was now or never.

I moved over to the POS and opened up the STAFF information file. The first one I accessed was Gail's. I saved it to the flash drive Michael had given me. I managed to load more files before I heard Bianca's footsteps approaching. I recalled a customer's name and accessed it in the Customer file.

Bianca came over and peered at the screen. "Can I help you with anything?"

"Oh...I was looking for the name of a fancy flower arrangement we sent to a customer last week," I said, gesturing toward the screen. "I thought it started with a B and wanted to include it in next month's newsletter. You know, the next topic in our A to Z articles?"

Bianca nodded. "Try begonia. How's the article on superstitions coming?"

I'd hardly worked on it. "I need to check out a couple more things."

"Okay." She glanced away as Lee whizzed by with two baskets of flower arrangements.

Nine fifty-five. I was still taking notes for my article—or pretending to be. Bianca hovered around the counter, making tidy. The repairmen continued to sip their oversized cups of coffee.

Nine fifty-eight. Lee declared he'd loaded the last delivery into the truck. Bianca hurried over to give him final instructions. With determination outweighing relief, I rushed to download the last two profiles to my flash drive.

The repairmen chucked their empty coffee cups in the garbage bin in the alley and the drilling resumed.

At ten sharp, I still hadn't completed my task. I'd downloaded all the employee profiles except for one—Doreen Dale. Wouldn't you know it?

I watched as Doreen, Gail, and Sarah walked in. Bianca introduced me to Kathy LeBreton, the part-time employee who'd returned to work this morning after a two-week course.

If I thought I had a battle on my hands before, the arrival of extra bodies did not bode well for the completion of my secret mission. What's more, customers soon began trickling in, looking for bargains among the marked-down Halloween items.

But all was not lost. Two customers needed service: one at the back near the cooler, the other near the side window in the hanging baskets section. Gail and Sarah tended to them, while Doreen and Kathy went into the workroom.

The repairmen had finished mounting the steel door. They ensured the fit was good and rushed out to their next job. To my delight, Bianca announced she was going to the bank and left.

Good. Now all I had to do was retrieve Doreen's information.

My heart stopped when I saw her emerge from the workroom. She'd put on a pair of mud boots and was strolling toward the back, probably to unload supplies.

I hit the computer key to bring up the last profile—hers.

Then the unthinkable happened. The computer screen froze. It had happened a couple of times before, either when too many transactions were being processed or too many windows were open at once. Neither was the case here.

I heard Doreen's footsteps thumping toward me. I held my breath, hoping she'd detour to another part of the floor.

She didn't. She was heading straight for the front counter.

I clicked on the tiny x to close the window that displayed her profile. Nothing happened. I clicked again. Still nothing.

On impulse, I dragged the customer window I'd opened earlier so that it would cover Doreen's profile. Oh, no. Part of Doreen's file was still exposed. I stood my ground in front of the POS and prayed she wouldn't glance at the screen.

She came up to me and looked around. "Have you seen my red box cutters? I think I left them here somewhere."

I recalled having seen a pair in a drawer earlier. I opened the drawer and handed the box cutters to her.

"Thanks."

I turned back to the POS and hoped she'd walk away.

She didn't. "What are you working on?"

"Stuff for Bianca," I said, feeling the blood rush to my face.

"What stuff?"

My heart pounded so hard I thought my chest would burst. "A flower arrangement...for an article I'm writing." I envisioned wrapping my arms around the monitor to block her view. Instead I leaned forward into the screen.

I couldn't have predicted her reaction. "Oh, is it a surprise? I won't tell." She laughed.

I could feel her body heat, smell her breath as she moved in closer and peeked over my shoulder.

Her staff file closed a split-second before her eyes could take it in.

"Oh, that's one of our fall specials," she said, reading the item name from the customer file. "Yeah, it's a popular one. It has orange gerberas, mums, and huckleberry. Pretty." She waved the box cutters in the air and thumped away.

I watched until she disappeared from sight. I checked around to make sure no one else was within snooping distance, then I re-opened Doreen's employee file and hit Save for the final time.

I tucked the flash drive into my jacket. I had it all, including the date of birth, social security number, and address for each of Bianca's employees.

All I had to do now was print out copies for Michael.

I caught Gail's attention and pointed upstairs to indicate I had to go to the washroom. She nodded and I took off, clipboard in hand.

I passed Bianca's office and picked up a lingering odor of smoke. I wondered if the scent from the fire would ever disappear. Her new office furniture was expected to arrive today. The smell of new wood and leather would help. In the interim, she was making the best of her makeshift workplace in the kitchen.

With minutes to spare—maybe less—before Bianca returned, I sat down at the kitchen table, turned on the PC, and popped in the flash drive. I hit a couple of buttons and the printer started to hum.

It took forever for the employee profiles to print out. One...by...one. Ever...so...slowly.

I held my breath at the sound of footsteps climbing the stairs. They stopped and a door shut. Probably the washroom door. Was it Bianca? Doreen?

I had two more profiles to print. They slid out of the printer just as the washroom door opened.

Footsteps coming my way.

I shut off the PC, snatched the flash drive, and slipped it into my pocket. I grabbed the stack of profiles.

Doreen's head popped around the corner. "Do you know where Bianca is?" Her eyes zoomed in on the papers in my hand.

"She's out. Should be back soon." I tucked the papers into the clipboard and met her stare. "Do you need help with anything?"

She shook her head. "Nah, it can wait."

I exhaled a sigh of relief as she walked away and headed downstairs.

Did I feel guilty?

No doubt about it. I felt as if I'd robbed a bank. An image of the police dragging me off to jail sped through my mind, and I began to have second thoughts. If only I'd obtained Bianca's consent from the start, things would have gone so much easier.

On the other hand, Michael was right. The less Bianca and Victor knew, the better off they were. Sure, my ethics had been challenged, but we might be one step closer to solving Tiffany's death. Mission accomplished.

Bianca whizzed in moments later—in time to receive the delivery of her new office furniture. The desk was a dark oak and had more surface space than the old one. The scent of the brown leather sofa and two matching armchairs hid any lingering odor from the fire. The steel filing cabinets were sleeker and larger.

The makeover boosted Bianca's spirits, helping her to forget the disturbing event that had taken place here.

Later that morning, the rest of the girls handled the incoming inventory out back while Doreen and I took over customer service duty on the floor. Among the first customers to walk in was an elderly couple.

"Wayne, look at this scarecrow. Isn't he the cutest thing?" A gray-haired woman nudged a man standing by her side, a bored look on his face. "Well?"

"I see it, Ingrid, but I don't think it's for sale," Wayne said with a hint of impatience. "There's no price tag on it. Can we go now?"

"Nonsense, dear. Let's ask the clerk how much it is." Ingrid approached Doreen and asked her.

"I'm sorry, ma'am, it's not for sale," Doreen said. "We use it for decorative purposes only."

"Surely you can make an exception," Ingrid said. The warm smile she gave Doreen would have melted the North Pole.

"Well...give me a moment," Doreen said. "I'll go ask my boss." She went upstairs and returned a minute later. "Okay, I can sell it to you, but you can't tell anyone else you bought it here. We don't make a habit of selling our displays."

"Oh, we won't tell a soul," Ingrid said, giving Wayne a little nudge.

"Course not," Wayne said.

Doreen lifted the scarecrow off the stand. "Would you like it gift-boxed? It's free."

"What a wonderful idea," Ingrid said. "Yes, please."

"I'll bring it to the wrapping section and meet you folks at the front counter in a little bit." Doreen heaved the scarecrow off its stand and carried it to the workroom.

The exemplary customer service Doreen had shown the elderly couple impressed me. What if Bianca was right? What if I'd exaggerated my suspicions about Doreen's behavior?

The phone rang and I answered. Bianca wanted to see me upstairs.

My palms felt moist. Had she found out about the employee

information I'd printed out? Had Doreen told her she'd seen me hanging around her computer earlier?

I walked into Bianca's office and sat in the armchair across from her desk. "What's up?"

She picked up a sheet of paper and shook her head.

I braced myself. Had I blown Plan A wide open?

"I've been reviewing our guest list for the Halloween party," she said, glancing at the paper. "I can't fit everyone in the shop if they all show up. I decided I'd mail out the invitations today anyway. I'll hire the decorators and place an order with the caterers too." She put aside the list. "It's not the only reason I wanted to talk to you."

Uh-oh.

She sat back in her chair. "Do you remember how Detective Flanagan said they'd run the anonymous phone call through some tests?"

"Yes."

"He just phoned me. The police didn't need to identify the caller because he came forward." Her brow puckered. "You were right. It was Henry."

"Oh, no."

Tears welled in her eyes. "Why would Henry want to destroy my shop? Did I do something to make him hate me?"

"He doesn't hate you. He couldn't hate anyone."

"He set the fire and then called the fire department to report it. Tell me, has the world gone mad?"

I saw her point. It was bad enough there were real perpetrators in our midst. We didn't need people like Henry pretending to be one of them. "Bianca, you know what the real Henry is like. There has to be more to this fire than we realize. The truth will come out, sooner or later."

I met Michael for lunch in Tommy's Park. The maple trees that had formed a protective barrier against the sun on warmer days were bare. Gusts of wind scattered foliage across a pedestrian path and into the street. I raised the collar of my wool jacket and wished

I'd worn a heavier sweater underneath.

I'd have accepted Michael's invitation to go to a restaurant instead, but I only had half an hour for lunch and didn't want to take advantage of Bianca. Though she hadn't said anything when I'd returned twenty minutes late after lunch with Michael and Trudy the other day, I did notice her checking her watch—albeit something she did every time staff returned from lunch.

I sat down on the bench next to Michael, gave him a quick kiss, then handed him the printouts of the employee profiles from Bianca's Gardens. "I feel like a thief."

"You shouldn't. You're doing it for an honorable cause." He leafed through them, then tucked them into his leather jacket.

"I can't help feeling guilty."

"This might help." He dug into his satchel and offered me a panini from Starbucks. "Ham and Swiss cheese."

"Thanks."

He pulled out a silver container and two mugs. "I bought enough coffee at Starbucks to fill this thermos." He poured some into the mugs, gave me one, and set the other down between us on the bench. "I brought some of these along too." He handed me a bag of chocolate almonds.

"Now you're talking." I stuffed it into my handbag.

"My buddy Dan came through for me," Michael said, unwrapping his panini. "I have news about Henry Glover."

"What did he say?"

"That Henry served time for a criminal offense twenty years ago."

"What? It has to be a mistake." I took a bite of my panini.

"No mistake. Dan got this through his legal network. Bona fide info."

"What was the crime?"

"Arson. He set fire to a house."

"You're kidding, right?"

Michael shook his head. "Nope."

"How much time did he spend in jail?"

"One year. He was released early due to good behavior."

"Small wonder. Where did it happen?"

"In a town called Lansing. No other details." He sipped his coffee.

"Bianca told me Henry had had some sort of nervous breakdown in the past. Maybe it's connected to his prison term. Where's Lansing?"

"About fifty miles from Augusta. Didn't you tell me Doreen Dale had lived in Augusta?"

"Yes, with her adoptive parents. What else did you find?" I drank some coffee.

"Employers that Henry worked for. Nothing much there. A hardware store…several courier services. He spent most of his life collecting social assistance. The question remains: Why would he set fire to Bianca's shop?"

"Not so fast. I'm still at the part about the fire in Lansing… something I overheard Doreen say to Henry in the workroom when she thought no one else was around. Oh, I remember now. She was taunting him and asking if he'd torch her house down. Maybe she knows about Henry's past felony."

Michael shook his head. "It's a long shot. That kind of information is hard to come by unless you have the right contacts. Must be a coincidence." He poured more coffee into our cups.

"Why is it that the more answers we get, the more complicated the situation becomes?"

"We'll get back on track. You'll see."

His comment did nothing to reassure me. I was on a mission and nothing could stop me. "Something else bothers me. Why would Henry burn—or steal—the shop's backup CDs? What would he have to gain from doing that?"

"Beats me." He took more bites of his panini.

"Oh…Detective Flanagan called Bianca this morning. You'll never guess who the Good Samaritan was on that recording he played for us."

"In that case, I give up."

"Henry Glover."

"That's plain crazy." Michael stared into the distance.

"Another thing. What if Detective Flanagan is right? What if there's a connection between the fire at the shop and the theft in Victor's office?"

"Like what?"

"George Gray."

"I think you have a case of *gray matter* on the brain." He chuckled.

"Cute." I poked him in the arm. "Come on, Michael. Be serious."

"Okay. I'll admit the targets—Bianca and Victor—and the timing of the two incidents could be more than a coincidence. What I don't see is a connection between the crimes. It might simply be that a crime was committed for a different reason in each place. Maybe even by different people. With the info you gave me, Dan can get me the dirt on everyone else who works for Bianca. It's a good start."

I couldn't argue with the logic behind Michael's perspective. Moreover, I trusted his instincts. He had that going for him in aces. It was my own frustration that gnawed away at me more than anything else…a road I'd traveled not too long ago.

"Speaking of Gray," Michael said, "I finally got an interview with George's parents tomorrow. Want to come along?"

"Sure." A burst of wind swept over us. I glanced upwards. Menacing clouds floated across a clear sky. Strange. The morning forecast had called for a sunny day. Proof that even calculated events don't always turn out the way we expect.

"I have to go." Michael stood up. "I have a meeting with the staff at the newspaper." He gathered the wrappings and threw them in a bin nearby. Then he packed the thermos and mugs into his satchel.

"I have to head back to the shop too," I said, getting up. I took out a pair of leather gloves I'd tucked in my pockets and pulled them on. "Thanks for lunch. See you later." I started to walk away.

"Hey," he called out.

I turned around. "Did I forget something?" My hand went to my handbag.

"Yes." He strode over and kissed me.

I felt the warmth of his lips on mine and the strength of his arms around me. Every time he kissed me, he made it all the more difficult to leave. "See you tonight," I said, kissing him again before I pulled away.

I opened the door to Bianca's Gardens and caught a whiff of cinnamon. Six chunky candles in glass hurricanes flickered on a nearby table, revealing the source of the comforting aroma.

The delight of the moment was obliterated by a whiny voice at the counter. It belonged to an older woman whom I recognized as Ingrid from her visit to the shop this morning.

"My name is Ingrid Vanderwyk. I insist on seeing the manager." Her wrinkly hands trembled.

"I'm sorry, Mrs. Vanderwyk. The manager isn't here right now." Kathy glanced my way.

I walked up to them. "Can I help?"

"Mrs. Vanderwyk said we delivered a scarecrow to her home this morning," Kathy said. "She wants to return it but doesn't have the bill. I don't think she bought it here because we don't sell scarecrows to—"

"And I told you, young lady, I bought it here," Mrs. Vanderwyk retorted, then gazed at me. "It wasn't you either." She looked around. "I don't know her name. I remember she was blonde and on the plump side."

"You're right," I said. "You bought the scarecrow from us. I saw you here earlier."

Mrs. Vanderwyk's face lit up. "Well, finally, someone remembers me."

"Was there a problem with the scarecrow?" I asked her.

"I'll say. It was filled with hay, not straw, and had maggots."

"Maggots?"

"Darn right. Dozens of them. They swarmed all over my kitchen floor as soon as we opened the box. It was horrifying. My husband gathered every last one. He's waiting outside in the car." She motioned toward a dark blue sedan parked on the street, the box from Bianca's Gardens propped up in the back seat and sticking out the side window.

I weighed the possibility the maggots might have been inside the scarecrow at the time of purchase versus the likelihood they'd originated in Mrs. Vanderwyk's home.

As if she'd read my mind, she said, "We thought the scarecrow was made of straw. We got scammed. You won't find any of those creepy crawlers in straw. Only in hay because it's damp and moisture breeds insects."

I doubted the woman was lying. I made a mental note to check the other items in the shop later. Who knew what might be lurking inside them?

"I'm sorry, Mrs. Vanderwyk," I said. "What can we do to help?"

"If it's not too much trouble, I'd like a refund, please."

"Of course," I said. "And you don't have the bill, right?"

"The clerk never gave me one."

I turned to Kathy. "Where's Doreen?"

"Gone out for lunch."

I turned back to the customer. "How much did you pay for the scarecrow?"

"Fifty dollars plus tax in cash."

I rang up the entry on the computer and handed her the cash. "I'll have someone bring in the box. In the meantime, please sign this receipt as proof that you've received a refund."

She signed the paper, then smiled at me. "Thank goodness there are honest people left in this world. Bless you, dear." She walked out the door.

"Where's Lee?" I asked Kathy.

"Out on a delivery run. Everyone else is on lunch break."

I hurried out after Ingrid.

Her husband stepped out of the car and helped me to retrieve the box from the back seat. It had heavy-duty duct tape around the edges—probably to keep the maggots inside. I winced as I envisioned the creatures squirming through the scarecrow's stuffing.

The box wasn't too heavy, though I hated carrying it so close to my face. Since there wasn't a garbage bin large enough to hold it on the street, I had no choice but to walk through the shop and dump it in the large bin out back in the alley.

Kathy held the front door open for me.

I hurried into the shop and laid the box on the floor. I looked down at my jacket. A maggot clung to the lapel. "Damn." I brushed it off with my hand. It landed on the floor.

"Eeeugh!" Kathy was staring at me. "Gross! Two of those yucky things are stuck in your hair." Her face contorted and she backed away.

"Oh, for heaven's sake." I bent forward and flapped a hand through my hair, trying to shake the maggots loose. They didn't fall out. I straightened up.

Kathy didn't budge. Her face remained contorted and she let out another "Eeeugh!"

Panic seized me as I imagined the maggots wiggling their way over my collar and onto my neck. "Go get some plastic gloves. Hurry!"

She raced off to the workroom and returned wearing the gloves. She stood a safe distance from me and reached out to pluck two dead maggots from my hair.

At least I thought they were dead. They fell to the floor and wriggled and twisted.

Kathy jumped back. "Eeeugh! They're alive!"

I raised a foot and put them out of their misery, praying I hadn't disturbed the balance of nature in any way that might result in a karmic boomerang. I picked up the boxed scarecrow, raced out back with it, and dumped it in the garbage bin in the alley. I retraced my steps, checking the floor to make sure I hadn't dropped any maggots along the way. I took off my jacket and checked it. No maggots.

"Do you see any more in my hair?" I asked Kathy who remained a safe three-foot distance away.

Dread lingered in her eyes as she circled and examined me. She shook her head. "No."

I swept up the maggots I'd crushed earlier and disposed of them in a garbage pail. I grabbed my handbag and dashed upstairs to the washroom to check my hair in the mirror. I stared at my reflection. A tiny maggot was squirming above my right eyebrow!

I yanked it off and tossed it into the toilet. Good thing someone had left the seat up.

I scrubbed my hands with soap and warm water for twenty seconds—the rule of the land. I still felt dirty and wished I could take a shower. I took out a hairbrush and vigorously passed it through my hair to make sure no other maggots were hiding there. After the last pass, I glanced at my brush. No maggots. I applied the age-old practice of mind over matter and went back downstairs.

Kathy was spraying the counter with disinfectant. She looked up as I approached, her eyes scanning my hair and clothes. "Are you okay?"

"Yes, now I am," I said. "Did this ever happen here before?"

"Not that I know of. Weird, isn't it?"

I nodded, consciously gazing at the floor around my feet in case more maggots might emerge.

"Hey, I read your boyfriend's article on Tiffany. I thought it was pretty cool the way he talked about what she did for charities."

"Thanks, I'll let him know. Did you ever have Tiffany as a customer?"

"A couple of times," she said, tearing off a paper towel from a roll beneath the counter.

"The girls told me her husband used to send her roses every week."

Kathy nodded. "He had a standing order with us."

"Did you know we sent out an order of roses to his wife after she died?"

She gaped at me. "We did?"

"By mistake. Her husband came in to complain about it."

A wry smile spread across her face. "I'm sure glad it wasn't me." She glanced around and whispered, "Doreen always manages to get herself into trouble, one way or another."

"What do you mean?"

"Everyone knows only Bianca and Doreen have the authority to prepare and send out standing orders. And I know it wasn't

Bianca." She gave me a pointed look before turning away to serve a customer.

When Joyce returned from lunch, Kathy repeated the story of my ferocious battle with the maggots. "You should have seen them," she said, shuddering as she described how she'd picked a couple of maggots out of my hair. When Sarah and Gail walked in minutes later, she started all over again, keeping the small crowd of listeners grimacing and doubled up in laughter. By her fourth recount, this time to Bianca, the tale had become quite convoluted, as had the number of insects, which Kathy now described as "a dozen maggots crawling all over Megan's head and body."

Needless to say, Bianca didn't find the tale amusing and hushed the girls into silence when customers started to stare at them. "Okay. Everyone back to work. No more talk about you-know-what things."

All the while, I'd kept a fair distance away, inwardly chuckling along with them as I inspected items that might contain stowaway maggots. I knew Bianca would want assurance that the shop was clear of anything that didn't belong there. I remembered how Mrs. Vanderwyck had said the scarecrow was made of hay and not straw. Like me, Bianca was a city girl. I doubted she knew the difference either.

I spotted a handful of foot-high scarecrows on a nearby shelf and reached for the first one.

Bianca walked up to me. "Oh, you don't have to check those. They're made of one hundred percent cotton. I bought them from a local crafts shop in town." She unbuttoned a scarecrow's shirt to show me, then put it back on the shelf.

"The maggots are a real mystery to me," I said. "I can't imagine how they got inside the large scarecrow."

"Well, we don't know everything about the couple who bought it. It's possible their home isn't the cleanest, you know." She raised an eyebrow. "Thank goodness I bought the scarecrow from a reputable source."

"In town?"

She lowered her voice. "I bought it from Doreen."

"Doreen?" I couldn't hide my surprise.

"She needed the extra money. I help her out from time to time by buying her homemade creations."

"Oh."

Bianca blinked. "Come to think of it, who sold the display scarecrow anyway?"

"I thought you knew."

"Knew what?"

I looked around for Doreen but didn't see her on the floor. "Didn't Doreen get your okay to sell it?"

She frowned. "Of course not."

The front door opened. Doreen and Lee were returning from lunch.

"Doreen, can I see you for a minute, please?" Bianca waved her over.

Doreen sauntered toward us. Lee wandered off toward the back.

Bianca didn't mince words. "Doreen, I don't recall you asking my permission to sell the large scarecrow."

"Well...I didn't," she said, her face flushing. "I was going to, but your office door was closed. I didn't want to disturb you. I came back down and told the sweet old woman it was okay. I knew you'd have done the same thing in my place. I hope you're not angry with me for having sold it. I can always make you another one." She put on an apologetic expression.

"No, I'm not angry with you," Bianca said, mellowing. "I'm angry because the customer returned it—along with a bunch of maggots."

"Maggots?" Doreen's jaw dropped. "Maybe they came from the customer's home."

"I've considered it," Bianca said. "Anyway, it's over and done with. We refunded the customer. You can go back to work." She waited until Doreen was out of earshot, then whispered to me, "What is going on here? It's as if my shop is being tested for every disaster known to humankind. Are Victor and I targets of *Mal Occhio*?"

Mal Occhio, or the evil eye. An ancient Italian belief that someone's envious thoughts—usually those of a person you might consider a friend—is causing you bad luck. Though I viewed the long-standing tradition as a superstition, I couldn't deny that a lot of bad things had happened in this town lately.

And something told me it wasn't over yet.

CHAPTER 16

Michael's attempts to contact Augbabe ran into a dead end when he discovered the email account was closed. It only added to the secrecy surrounding Tiffany and to our frustration with trying to find a connection to her family or friends.

I hoped we'd have better luck with Stanley and Josephine Gray on Saturday.

The experience was like déjà vu as Michael announced our arrival through the intercom system at the entrance to the senior Gray's estate. A male voice asked him to wait until the iron gates had fully parted before driving through. When they did, Michael drove onto a paved road bordered with dense fir trees. It was only after a curve in the road that the mansion came into view.

History had it that Stanley Gray's ten-bedroom Victorian mansion had been in the family for generations. The 1890s stone house was nested on twenty groomed acres of prime riverfront land that alone was worth millions. Unlike George's home, it wasn't hidden behind a dense brush atop elevated land but was out in the open for everyone to see—albeit a mile beyond the twelve-foot-high wrought iron fence at the front of the property. Like George's house, a high-tech security system provided added protection.

I counted three floors of gray stone offset by white shutters and trim. It was evident that George's home was modeled on this historic structure with one visible difference so far. Clusters of red mums, purple asters, yellow daisy-like flowers, and miniature evergreens enhanced a rock garden that stretched across the front of the house and around both corners.

"Wow," I said. "Talk about huge."

"Yeah," Michael said, easing the car onto a parking lot of interlocking stones large enough to hold half a dozen cars. "Kind of reminds me of my parents' home."

I wouldn't know. I'd never met his parents. I only knew what Michael had told me—that he'd attended private schools and vacationed in Europe most of his adolescent years. He'd lived the life of privilege until he turned his back on it and became an investigative reporter. His career choice did more to alienate his parents than the miles between them ever could, but over time, they grew to accept his journalism awards as tributes to his success in the field. Had he spoken to them lately? I wouldn't know that either.

We walked under a sheltered portico of timber beams and stopped before a pair of ornate wood doors. Michael rang the bell.

A maid opened the door wide and invited us into the foyer, then excused herself and vanished around a corner to let our hosts know we'd arrived.

Unlike George's sunlit foyer, the charcoal gray ceramic tiles on the floor and dark oak panels on the walls gave the entrance a more rustic feel. On the wall facing us and impossible to miss was the Gray family Coat of Arms.

"Looks exactly like the one we saw in Christina Reed's office," I whispered to Michael.

I was contemplating whether the Gray sense of honor had been transferred down through the generations when Josephine and Stanley Gray entered the foyer. At first glance, I could tell that George had inherited his commanding presence and impeccable grooming habits from both parents.

Josephine Gray was slim without being bony and stood almost six feet tall in flats. Her straight back and broad shoulders projected confidence and good breeding. Her hair was dyed a silvery gray and cut in the shorter version popular with women in her age group, which I pegged to be around seventy-five. Her complexion glowed and wasn't pasty like the faces I'd seen on other seniors. She wore beige pants and a blue silk blouse that was rolled up at the cuffs. I attributed her obvious good health, as well as her appearance, to a life of leisure and regular visits to beauty spas.

Stanley Gray was as tall as his wife and though his waistline was fleshy, he hid it well beneath a long-sleeved shirt that he wore loosely over a pair of chinos. He had a thick head of hair that he'd allowed to go white and piercing blue eyes that seemed to size you up in a second. Like George, he had a slight British accent. Combined with a baritone voice, it gave him an authoritative air. I could envision him in a dark suit sitting at a high-level business meeting flanked by peers in stylish clothes and manicured nails.

After we'd exchanged formalities and settled in the living room, Michael began the interview. "Did either of you see or speak with Tiffany the day she died?"

"I didn't," Josephine said.

"No," Stanley said. "She rarely called here. George calls us about once a week. He keeps me up-to-date on company matters."

Michael went on. "How did you find out about Tiffany's death?"

"From George," Stanley said. "He called me that Friday afternoon. I'd just returned from a business meeting in town. Josie was at the country club with friends."

"Stanley told me about it when I walked in minutes later," Josephine said. "It broke our hearts to see George suffer like that." She glanced over at Stanley who was sitting next to her in a matching bulky armchair and gazing at the floor. When he didn't react to her statement, she went on. "He seems to be getting over it, thank goodness."

"Of course he is," Stanley said, frowning. "The man has a business to run, for Pete's sake." He let his arm fall with a thud against his armchair, then addressed Michael. "I assume you're looking for more substantial information from us than the current state of our son's emotional condition."

His comeback was swift and direct, but Michael wasn't fazed. "Tell me about Tiffany," he said, keeping his eyes on the older couple. "How would you describe your relationship with her?"

"Polite at best," Josephine said.

Stanley waved a hand in the air as if to dismiss his wife's

comment. "We didn't see much of the girl," he said. "She and George traveled a lot. Attended public events."

Michael nodded, waited.

"Tiffany was a beautiful girl by all standards," Josephine said, forcing a smile, "but her sparkle was limited to the exterior. To be blunt, she wasn't what one would call cultured."

"Come on now, Josie." Stanley glanced at her. "You know very well what that poor girl was up against. She didn't have a chance with you and your circle of chatty—"

"Save yourself the trouble, Stanley." Josephine stopped him with a stare that warned of harder times ahead. She switched her gaze to me, her expression softening. "It's not that I disliked Tiffany, but you know how cruel some women can be at times."

I gave her a polite nod, then jumped in to take advantage of our woman-to-woman moment. "What about Tiffany's charity work? The recognition she received from the community must have earned her ample respect."

"I suppose so." Josephine shrugged. "However, I've often wondered what the real reason was behind her charitable endeavors."

"What do you mean?"

She pursed her lips. "That girl would have done anything to flaunt her pictures across the tabloids."

Stanley shot her a look. "Now, Josie, let's not forget how instrumental she was in putting our family name on a number of monuments in this town...building a new wing to the hospital... raising funds for charities. We have to acknowledge that much."

"Regardless, she didn't fit into our social circle and never would have." Josephine's manner was stiff. "Not in a thousand years."

"Is it safe to assume you didn't approve of George's marriage?" I asked her.

She raised an eyebrow. "For good reason. Tiffany was dirt poor. No notable family roots to speak of. She didn't fit into our practice of marrying into a proper family, if you know what I mean."

Stanley sighed. "We have to give the girl some credit, Josie. She did have a brief reign as a small-town beauty queen. It takes a certain knowledge of etiquette in the public arena to carry out that function."

Josephine rolled her eyes. "Rich men will always be suckers for beautiful women."

"You sound angry," I said to her.

"Angry?" She let out a strained laugh. "Not at all. Frustrated, perhaps. I don't know why George had such a hard time finding a suitable spouse. He dated the finest young women through his university years. They were proper and came from respectable families."

Stanley tried to change the subject. "Years after George graduated, he decided to focus on the family business and that was fine with us."

"Yes...the business," Josephine echoed. "Which meant that George put off getting married for years, then went off and married the likes of... Well, it was just beyond me." She shook her head.

I wondered about her growing annoyance. How could a mother hold so much animosity against her son for not having married a *proper* woman?

"We can say all we want about the matter," Stanley said. "In the end, George chose Tiffany. Even if we weren't one hundred percent behind the marriage, it was obvious he was in love with the girl."

"Love? The only reason he married her was to get us off his back." Josephine crossed her arms.

Stanley gave her a side-glance. "We never pressured him."

"Don't get me started, Stanley." She switched her gaze to Michael and me. "You're looking for the truth? Well, I'll give it to you. Our son married Tiffany to royally piss us off. That's what he did."

A grin crept up on Stanley's lips. "That's news to me."

Michael ignored their banter. "Would you say they had a happy marriage?"

Stanley's expression went as blank as an unplugged monitor.

"I would imagine you'd already asked George that question," Josephine said.

"I'd like an impartial viewpoint," Michael said.

"From us?" She grinned. "You can't be serious."

Michael leaned forward. "I'll give it to you straight. There were rumors that Tiffany was seeing other men."

"Hogwash." Josephine waved the notion away. "People spread lies about our family all the time. Pure jealousy, that's all it is."

She said it with such conviction that I wondered if she hadn't heard rumors about Tiffany through her social circle of gossips and was prepared for Michael's question. Or maybe she'd had a one-on-one conversation with George after our visit with him to make certain their statements wouldn't conflict.

Stanley cleared his throat. "For the record, I don't want any of this conversation to appear in print except for what pertains to the theme of your articles. Ignore the rest."

I understood the rationale behind his request. Despite her opinion of Tiffany, Josephine was quite protective of her son—as was Stanley in his own silent way. It was evident neither of them was willing to reveal information that might jeopardize George's reputation or the family's good name.

Michael nodded. "As I mentioned earlier, I'd like to play up the humanitarian aspect of Tiffany's life." He paused. "There are rumors that her charitable work might have rubbed some people the wrong way. Do you know anyone who might have wanted to see her dead?"

His question prompted wide-eyed looks from the Grays.

"I didn't know the police had turned this into a murder investigation," Stanley said, frowning.

"They haven't," Michael said. "Since the cause of Tiffany's death is still unknown, I'm keeping an open mind. I'm going to pursue all avenues until I get the answers I'm looking for."

"In that case," Stanley said, "you've got your work cut out for you."

"That was an exercise in futility," I said to Michael as we drove off the Gray property and onto the main road.

"I expected it," he said. "People with that much money tend to keep their private lives out of public view. Especially when murder is involved."

"So you agree with me. You think they're protecting George too."

"Not for the reasons you think." He kept his eyes on the road.

"Okay. Spill the beans."

"Not yet."

"Why not?"

"I need more proof."

"For what?"

Michael didn't answer.

I stared at him. "You don't trust me."

"It's not that."

"What is it then?"

The muscles along his jaw twitched. As far as he was concerned, it was the end of the topic.

Undaunted, I tried a different approach. "Dealing with the likes of Josephine must have put a strain on George's marriage. How can a mother be so candid about hating her son's wife? Do you think she had anything to do with—"

"Tiffany's death? No way. She's all talk. Let's face it, when you believe that money should only marry into money..." Michael shrugged.

"It didn't stop George," I said. "I guess he didn't agree with his mother's philosophy. In a way, I admire him for it, though I think the rumor about Tiffany being a gold-digger might be true."

"It's the same old story. When you come from nothing, you make sure you never go back there. Tiffany definitely took care of number one."

"It works both ways. I'm sure George considered her a great catch for someone his age."

"Money buys anything."

Even murder.

CHAPTER 17

Despite Henry's criminal record, I wanted to believe it wasn't in his nature to compromise his job and his future. I was convinced he'd lied to the police about setting the fire, and I intended to find out why.

"No way," Michael said when I mentioned I was looking forward to visiting Henry in prison Sunday morning. "You're not tagging along."

"Why not?"

"If Henry sees you, he'll clam up about the fire."

"On the contrary. He'd feel more at ease if he sees me. A familiar face can open doors. Besides, Henry likes me."

He studied me for a long moment. "Okay."

Earlier that morning, we'd researched the Cumberland County Jail on the Internet. Home to more than five hundred inmates classified as minimum, medium, and maximum offenders, it was a modern facility equipped with high-tech video surveillance. Visitors had to abide by strict regulations, which meant leaving personal belongings such as jackets, hats, purses, watches, body jewelry (with the exception of a wedding ring), and even gum outside the secure area of the facility.

The body jewelry part gave me pause. I'd heard of metal body piercings causing problems with airport security personnel who used hand-held wands. The metal often triggered alarms during a scan and sometimes prompted removal. I was glad I'd never attached anything to my body other than a small tattoo.

So why did the jail disallow body piercings or body jewelry?

I discovered there was the possibility these body garnishes could change hands and be used as tools. I thought back to *Prison Break*, the popular TV series about two brothers orchestrating a jail escape and using small tools from other interested prisoners to do so.

The purse thing bothered me more. I hated to part with my personal papers and credit cards. They represented my lifeline, my proof of identity. I finally conceded, reasoning that I couldn't pick a better person than a brawny Correctional Officer to watch over my purse.

Tables and thick plexiglass windows separated prisoners from guests in the visiting quarters. The mood was restrained and offered a semblance of hope as those from the outside reached out to those on the inside, and vice versa.

I almost gasped when I saw Henry. The strain of imprisonment had begun to show in the way his eyes shifted around the room, as if he were wary of anything that moved. He was paler than usual and wore a plaster on his right temple.

"Hello, Henry," I said, smiling. "Do you remember me?"

He blinked. "Of course, I do, Megan." He switched his gaze to Michael.

"This is Michael, my boyfriend," I said.

"Oh, yeah...the reporter," Henry said, his brow furrowing. "I'm not supposed to talk to anyone about what happened. My lawyer said—"

"That's okay, Henry," I said. "We're not here to talk about the fire."

"You're not?"

"No. We want to ask you questions about other stuff."

"Like what?" Henry asked, shifting in his chair.

I went into ad lib mode. "Like what happened to your forehead?"

"Oh." He touched the plaster. "I tripped." He glanced down.

I went on. "Henry, do you remember the day Doreen was joking with you in the workroom and I walked in?"

Henry gave me a guarded look. "Sort of."

"Doreen was teasing you. Right?"

"I don't want to say anything bad about Doreen." He peeked at Michael before lowering his eyes again.

"That's okay, Henry. I don't expect you to. Can you tell me why you were angry with Doreen?"

Henry straightened up and met my gaze. "Doreen said I made mistakes with some deliveries. But it wasn't my fault. I told her so."

"She didn't believe you, did she?"

"No." He slumped in his chair.

"Why not?"

He shrugged. "I don't know." He removed his eyeglasses, rubbed his eyes, then said something that sounded like "trust her" under his breath.

"What was that, Henry?"

He hesitated. "I don't get much rest here." He adjusted his eyeglasses.

Michael picked up the conversation. "Henry, can I tell you a secret?"

Henry's eyes narrowed. "About what?"

"About the fire at Bianca's."

"I'm not supposed to talk—" Henry began.

"I know, Henry," Michael said. "You don't have to say a word. Listen to what I have to say. Okay?"

Henry nodded.

"Megan and I know that you didn't set fire to Bianca's office."

Henry's face revealed surprise, then confusion and suspicion. He made a move to get up.

"Wait, Henry, please," I said, placing a hand on the glass between us.

He settled back in his chair. The wary glance he gave Michael told me we had to use a different tactic if we wanted to maintain his trust in us.

Michael stood up. "Excuse me. I need to make a call." He turned away from Henry and whispered to me, "I'll wait for you in the lobby."

Henry watched Michael walk away. "Is he mad at me?"

"No." In fact, I didn't know whether Michael had to make a call or not, but it didn't matter. Henry was placated. I tried another approach. "Henry, you and I have talked before. I know how much you love working at the shop with Bianca, Joyce, Sarah, and the others. Right?" I omitted Doreen's name on purpose.

"Oh, yes." Henry smiled. "Bianca is the finest kind of boss. She's gives everyone a fair chance." His face became downcast. "I feel bad. It's not her fault that..." His voice trailed off.

"That what?"

"It's not her fault that bad things are happening."

My heart raced. Was he referring to the fire or something else? "I know what you mean. First, there was the fire and then the maggots."

"Maggots?" His eyes went wide.

I told him about the sale of the scarecrow to the elderly couple. In an offhand way, I mentioned that Doreen had handled the transaction.

At the mention of her name this time, Henry bristled. "Doreen is trouble. She steals little things. She needs to be taught a lesson."

"What little things?"

He didn't answer.

I took the opportunity to revisit a previous topic. "That's what you were trying to tell her in the workroom, weren't you, Henry?"

"Yes."

I glanced at my watch. I only had a minute of visiting time left. I had to speed things along. "I think Bianca would punish Doreen if she knew she was up to no good."

Henry didn't blink an eye.

I pushed forward. "Sometimes Bianca doesn't see what her staff is doing. She needs helpers, like you and me, to be her eyes and ears."

Henry's mouth tightened, then relaxed, then tightened again. He leaned forward and whispered, "If I tell you something, do you promise not to tell?"

"Cross my heart," I said, making an x over my heart.

"I didn't do it, Megan. I didn't set the fire in Bianca's shop."

"Do you know who did?"

"I can't say." He looked down.

"You can't or you won't?"

He shook his head, said nothing, kept his eyes cast downward.

Only seconds remained of our visiting time. "Someone set you up, didn't they? They forced you to set the fire at the shop. Right?"

Henry sat there, not making eye contact, not moving a muscle.

"What do they have on you, Henry? Is it something about your past?"

His head jerked up. I saw panic in his eyes.

I searched for one last frantic reason to get him to confide in me. "Henry, how are you going to find your family if you're locked up in jail?"

He opened his mouth as if to say something, but a guard tapped him on the shoulder. "Time's up."

Without even saying good-bye, Henry stood up and walked away, leaving me with more unanswered questions.

CHAPTER 18

I caught up to Michael in the visitors' lobby of the prison. "Damn it."

"What's the matter?"

"Henry admitted he lied about setting the fire at Bianca's shop. If I'd only had a bit more time with him, he would have opened up and told me more. Let's go." I led the way out the door to the parking lot.

Michael fell into stride with me. "Did he say who did it?"

"No."

"Anything else?"

I told him what Henry had said about Doreen. "I'd overheard them arguing at the shop, so the only part that's new to me is that she steals little things."

Michael unlocked the car doors with a double click of his key. "Don't be so hard on yourself. Henry likes you. He'll be glad to see you again." He slid into the driver's seat.

I got in beside him. "Probably. I don't think he gets many visitors. Which reminds me. He got all gloomy when I mentioned his family."

"What about his family?"

"From what I heard at the shop, he's been trying to track down his wife and two daughters for years. I feel sorry for him."

"Yeah, he seems like a decent sort of guy."

"All the more reason for wanting to help him. I wish I could do something."

Michael paused. "There might be a way."

"How?"

"We'll have to do some digging."

"Where would we start?"

"The jail in Lansing where he served time. It's about an hour's drive north of Portland. We can go there now if you like."

"Sure."

"How about taking the scenic route? It'll be less monotonous."

"Okay." I remembered something else. "Did you actually phone someone back there?"

He nodded. "We have an appointment with Father Healy at St. Andrew's Church later this afternoon."

The welcoming sign at the entrance to Lansing read "Population of five thousand." After driving around, we noticed that the town core stretched ten blocks in any direction and included more churches than schools and restaurants combined. We drove by a grocery store—the only one in town—two dry cleaners, a hospital, and a medical clinic, but no jail.

We circled the area three times before Michael agreed to ask a pedestrian for directions. Only then did we learn the jail no longer existed. Ironically, the lot where it had once stood now boasted a fire station. Two red fire trucks were parked out front.

A man wearing a white T-shirt with Lansing Fire Department printed in black letters on the back of it was polishing one of the trucks. He straightened up as we approached. "Hi. What can I do for you?"

"We're trying to find someone who lived here twenty years ago," Michael said.

"You should talk to Leo Sneed, our volunteer firefighter. He's lived here all his life. Knows everyone in town. Come on in." He gestured for us to follow him.

In what was the most immaculate kitchen I'd ever seen, the firefighter invited us to sit down at the table. He went off in search of Leo through a side door.

"I can't believe this place is so clean," I whispered to Michael.

He grinned. "Neat freaks. These guys should open up a cleaning service on the side."

Leo walked in. "Hello, folks." A middle-aged man in a red checked shirt, a wide belt buckle, and jeans introduced himself with a handshake that left my hand numb for a few seconds. "I heard you're lookin' for someone." He pulled out a chair and flipped it around, then sat down and used the back as a resting place for his arms. "How can I help you?"

"We came looking for the jail," Michael said.

Leo's smile intensified the wrinkles around his eyes. "They took it down fifteen years ago. The court's been sending offenders to Augusta ever since." He paused. "Are you private investigators or somethin'?"

"No," Michael said. "We're looking for a mother and her two daughters. They lived in Lansing twenty years ago. We're doing this as a favor for a friend—Henry Glover."

Leo jerked upright. "Henry? You're joshin' me, right?"

"No," Michael said.

"Holy critters, I thought Henry was as good as dead." Leo ran a hand through thick gray hair combed back like Elvis Presley's. "I can't believe he's still kickin' around."

"Why's that?"

"Well...after the fire..." He hesitated, searched our faces, seemed to be unsure as to whether or not he should continue.

"We know Henry spent time in jail here because of the fire," I said. "He's been trying to find his family and we want to help him."

Leo frowned. "After all these years, that fire's still a puzzle to me."

"Why?"

"I'd have to start at the beginnin' of the story to tell you that," he said, as if he were apologizing for backtracking through time.

"We're in no hurry," Michael said.

He nodded. "Sally—that's Henry's wife—she threw him out of the house one night. A squabble over money, if I recall. Henry had nowhere to go, so he stayed at my place. Slept like a log. Next thing we know, Sally's gone with their two girls, their house is burned down, and Henry gets arrested. I swore under oath that he hadn't left my place all night, but the court didn't believe me—especially after Henry's testimony." He shook his head. "I still wonder to this day why he said he'd set the fire to the house when everyone knew he hadn't."

I glanced at Michael but he kept his eyes on Leo.

Leo went on. "Anyhow, Henry left town soon as he got out of jail. Couldn't stand people pointin' at him on the street. Told me he felt guiltier than when he'd been inside. I hadn't heard a peep about him till you folks showed up."

"Do you have any idea where his family is?" I asked him.

"None. My wife Alice was pretty close to Sally and the girls. She sobbed for days on end after the fire. We went to visit Henry in jail twice a month. Didn't help much, though. I heard he never got over the shock of it all. Had some kind of a breakdown."

"Did Henry's family contact him while he was in jail?" Michael asked him.

"Not that I know of. Henry always kept pretty much to himself."

I refused to believe we'd hit a dead end. "Do you have any idea where Sally and the girls live now?"

"Sally's dead. Liver complications. Happened many years back. The folks at the hospital called my wife to let her know. They had Alice's name as reference in case of emergency."

"And the two daughters?"

"They were adopted." He paused for a second, then his eyes lit up. "Wait. There's a letter. Yep, my wife got a letter one day from the older girl. I believe she sent it to the school where my wife used to teach. Hang on. I'll call Alice for you." He headed across the room to a wall-mounted phone and keyed in a number. "Hi Alice, it's me. Hon, you recall a while back, you got a letter at school from one of the Glover girls? You still have it?"

There was a short pause.

"Yep, I know it was a long time ago but... Fifteen years?" He let out a low whistle. "Yep, I'll wait." Leo looked our way and said, "She's gone to get the letter. Won't be long now. She knows exactly where it is."

I could feel my heart pounding against my chest. Our lead had turned out better than I'd expected. I glanced at Michael. His eyes reflected the same enthusiasm.

Alice returned to the phone.

"Un-huh...yep...hold on." Leo reached for a pen and a pad of paper on the counter. He jotted the information, then thanked his wife and hung up. "Here's the return address that was on the letter." He handed the sheet to Michael. "It might help put you folks on the right track."

"Thanks." Michael glanced at the note, folded it, and slipped it into his jacket pocket. "It's a wonder your wife kept that letter for so long."

"Alice has a good heart," Leo said, smiling. "She likes to hang onto mementos. Makes her feel like she's still in touch with the people she cares about. She said that letter came in a real pretty Christmas card. I'd forgotten about it until she reminded me. Her memory's way better than mine." He chuckled. "Anything else I can do for you folks?"

"No, thanks," Michael said as we stood up. "We're good."

"Sure hope things work out for Henry," Leo said. "Say hi to him for me."

As we drove away from the fire station, I asked Michael, "How about sharing that address Leo gave us?" I held out my hand.

"Hang on a sec." He pulled into an empty parking space a block down and turned off the ignition. "I held off showing it to you until now. You'll understand when you see the address." He handed me the slip of paper. It read:

Mr. and Mrs. Gary Dale, 278 Valley Drive, Augusta, Maine

"Dale? That's Doreen's family name. Her adoptive family, that is. Do you suppose that—"

"Henry is her father." Michael grinned. "Plain crazy, isn't it?"

"I wonder if Doreen knows."

"Or Henry."

"Talk about a coincidence."

"I'm not sure where this is going. There's only one way to find out." Michael turned on the ignition.

"You mean now?"

He checked his watch. "We have time. Augusta is about an hour from here. We can grab a bite on the way. Okay?"

"Okay."

I sat back and collected my thoughts based on what Henry had told me. He said he knew who had set fire to Bianca's shop, but he wouldn't tell me.

Could Doreen have set the fire at the shop? If so, was Henry protecting his daughter by taking the blame for her? According to Leo, Henry had done it once before.

Then again, if Doreen knew that Henry was her father, would she deliberately stand by and let him go to jail for a crime he didn't commit? Or did she want to avenge something that she perceived to be a wrongdoing decades ago?

As always, I ended up with more questions than answers.

Out of chaos comes order, I reminded myself, and prepared for more bombshells to land in my lap.

CHAPTER 19

Michael nodded toward the house across the street from where we'd parked. "That's the place."

There was nothing notable about the two-story home with white clapboard and green awnings. A trimmed hedge and pots of pink mums on the porch added to the appearance of a modest but inviting abode.

My eyes strayed down the street. There were no mothers pushing baby strollers and no children playing. Several houses down, two elderly women stood chatting on the sidewalk. The lofty oak trees on both sides of the street confirmed that this was an established neighborhood. I tried to imagine Doreen growing up here.

We stepped out of the car and walked over to the house. Michael rang the doorbell.

A silver-haired woman in a pink jogging outfit opened the inside door but left the outer screen door closed. "Yes?" Cautious blue eyes peered at us.

Michael introduced us as acquaintances of Leo and Alice. "Leo gave us your address and said you might be able to help us find someone we're looking for."

At the mention of familiar names, the woman's expression relaxed. She smiled and said, "Please come in." She unlocked the screen door and pushed it open. "I'm Eleanor Dale. My husband stepped out to run errands. He should be back soon."

She led us into the living room. Like the outside of the home, it reflected simplicity and neatness. A loveseat in a floral pattern and a set of armchairs sat on beige wall-to-wall carpet. A pen and a white coffee mug lay next to a crossword puzzle book on the coffee table.

Eleanor smiled. "My, my, this is certainly a surprise. It's been ages since Gary and I saw Alice and Leo Sneed. Strangers don't drop in too often looking for people. Are you trying to find someone here in Augusta?"

"We'd like to help a friend locate his two daughters," Michael said. "His name is Henry Glover. He got separated from his children about twenty years ago. His wife died when the girls were kids."

"That's unfortunate, but I don't recognize the name Glover," Eleanor said. "What makes you think I know him?"

I went out on a limb. "We believe that you and your husband might have adopted one of the girls. Her name is Doreen."

Eleanor's face stiffened. "I haven't seen or heard from Doreen in months." She gave us a wary look. "Is she in trouble again?"

"We wouldn't know," Michael said. "We're trying to determine if this is Henry's daughter."

Eleanor stood up and reached for a framed photo on a corner table. "This was the last picture taken of Doreen before she moved out years ago." She handed it to Michael, who gave it a cursory look before passing it to me.

The resemblance to Doreen was evident—the short blonde hair, the wide toothy grin. She was plump but had put on another fifty pounds since then. I smiled and handed the photo back to Eleanor.

She returned the picture to its original place and sat down. "Gary and I adopted Doreen when she was a young child. We were living in Lansing at the time. The guardians at the orphanage there told us how their biological mother had given Doreen and her sister Jennie up for adoption. I assumed it was for financial reasons. Unfortunately, we couldn't afford to adopt both girls."

At least Doreen hadn't lied about that part. "Do you know what happened to Jennie?" I asked Eleanor.

"I think she was adopted by another family in Lansing months later. She was tall and slim and had long blonde curls. Not at all like Doreen. The girls attended the same school and continued to see each other at birthday parties for about a year until we moved to Augusta. Jennie's family moved away that same year too. They didn't leave a forwarding address, though. Of course, Doreen was devastated, completely devastated." She let out a sigh. "We went through a number of turbulent years because Doreen missed her sister so much. We tried to make her happy, but nothing seemed to work. She wasn't good at hiding her pain either." Her eyes brimmed with tears. "I hate to admit that Gary and I were relieved the day she announced she was leaving home." She reached into her pocket for a tissue. "Forgive me."

It sounded like a typical relationship between a teenage daughter and her mother. I felt Eleanor's grief and wanted to tell not to worry, that Doreen was alive and well in Portland, but Michael and I had agreed we wouldn't mention it.

Eleanor dabbed at her eyes and took in a deep breath. "Mind you, we do keep in touch." She smiled. "From time to time, she sends me an email. The last one I received was on Mother's Day in May. It was quite kind. I keep it close at hand." She picked up the puzzle book and pulled out a folded sheet of paper. She handed it to me. "You can read it. I don't mind sharing it."

I unfolded it. It read:

"Dear Mom, Portland is beautiful this time of the year. The flowers and trees are gorgeous. Wish you could visit, but Lee and I just moved into a new place and we don't have much furniture. Maybe in the fall when we're settled in. Happy Mother's Day."

I happened to glance at the top of the page. I couldn't believe my eyes. The sender was Augbabe. I hid my surprise with a smile. "Very nice," I said to Eleanor. I passed the letter to Michael along with a subtle glance to suggest he study it closely.

Eleanor said, "If I understand correctly, Doreen's real father has now resurfaced and he's looking for his daughters."

"Right," I said.

"That's quite peculiar."

"Excuse me?"

"Oh, not that he's looking for his daughters. Rather that the orphanage told us nothing about Doreen's biological parents. I assumed she and her sister were orphans." She paused. "I still remember the nightmares Doreen used to have when we first brought her home from the adoption agency. She would scream out, asking her mother to stop the fire, over and over in her sleep. I can't remember exactly when the bad dreams stopped. I was so grateful when they did."

The lock in the front door clicked.

A man of medium build walked in. "Hello there," he said, setting a bag of groceries down on the floor.

Eleanor introduced us to her husband Gary and gave him the gist of our conversation.

"She sure was a handful, Doreen was," Gary said with a shake of his head. "Losing contact with her sister didn't help. Too bad Jennie's adoptive parents didn't bother to keep in touch with us."

"Would you happen to know the family name of Jennie's adoptive parents?" I asked them.

Gary's brow furrowed. "It was an odd name—kind of sounded like a cat or bird."

"It started with the letter *p*," Eleanor said. "Like penguin or pelican—"

"The letter *p*..." Gary scratched the back of his head.

"Persimmon," Eleanor said. "That's the name. It's a fruit. Not at all in the cat or bird family." She smiled at her husband.

"There you go." Gary chuckled, then said, "Strange that so many folks have come here from Portland recently."

Michael looked as surprised as I felt. "What do you mean?"

"It could be a fluke but..." Gary turned to Eleanor. "Do you remember one afternoon when some fancy-pansy investigator dropped in from Portland, looking for information about Doreen's sister?"

Eleanor shook her head. "No, I don't remember. Are you sure I was home?"

"Come to think of it, you'd gone to a bake sale or charitable event at the church." He looked back at us. "This stranger—I never did get his name—rings the bell. I open the door." He chuckled. "He had the stiffest expression I ever saw on—"

"Now, Gary." Eleanor's voice was quiet but firm.

"It's true. Besides, you weren't here, so you didn't see him."

She shrugged.

Gary continued. "As I was saying, if I hadn't seen him standing on my doorstep all by himself, I'd have thought he was a life-sized puppet. Something was sure pulling his strings tight." He laughed—a deep-bellied laugh that was oddly similar to Doreen's and as infectious.

Eleanor tried to hold back the giggles but failed.

Michael and I chuckled along with them.

"My, my," Eleanor said, catching her breath. "I haven't laughed this hard in a while."

"As I was saying," Gary went on, "the fellow told me Doreen had hired him to find her sister. I didn't buy it for a second."

"Why not?" Michael asked.

"For starters, I didn't trust the guy's attitude, the way he seemed to be looking down his nose at me. I figured, heck, if Doreen wants help in finding her sister, she can give us a call. Right, Eleanor?"

"It would have been the decent thing to do," Eleanor said with a nod.

"What did you do about the guy at the door?" Michael asked Gary.

Gary shrugged. "I dealt with the situation as best I could. I said 'no thanks' and told the jerk to get lost."

As we drove off, I said to Michael, "Do you believe it? Doreen is Augbabe. Why would she be writing to Tiffany? She hated the woman. Do you think she sent Tiffany hate mail?"

"Which question do you want me to answer first?" Michael smiled as he kept his eyes on the road ahead.

"This one: Why does George Gray keep popping up everywhere

we go?"

"It's simple. He's following the same trail we are. He must have tapped into Tiffany's email and retrieved the Dales' address from Augbabe before the files were deleted. My question is why?"

I gave it some thought. "Maybe I'm wrong. Maybe Doreen didn't send Tiffany hate mail. Maybe she asked George and Tiffany for help in finding her sister. The Grays have a lot of contacts—not to mention the funds it would involve in tracking down Doreen's sister."

"Could be, but why would George pass himself off as an investigator? He could have hired someone else—even me—to do the groundwork for him. The whole thing feels out of whack to me."

"Everyone at the shop knows Doreen is looking for her sister. If she asked George for help, why didn't she tell anyone about it?"

"Maybe she doesn't want them to know."

"Why not?"

Michael shrugged. "Beats me. It's only a theory."

"We should ask George about it."

"No, not yet."

I saw a flicker of light in his eyes and a grin creeping up on his lips—signs that he was thinking through a new strategy. "Okay, spit it out. What's going on inside that head of yours?"

"You said Doreen and Lee could be blackmailing George."

"So?"

"The question is why."

"We've been through this before," I said. "I think George hired them to poison Tiffany. Now he has to pay them money to keep his dirty little secret buried."

"I disagree. I think Doreen and Lee are trying to blackmail George for another reason. They might think they have something on him, but it's only about getting their hands on his money."

"Believe whatever you want about George, but he isn't as innocent as you think."

"The guy isn't a murderer. At least not in my mind."

Michael's hunches had often proved accurate, but he wasn't the only one with gut feelings. I had them too. Regardless, I didn't want to keep on arguing for the sake of arguing. It wasn't worth the effort. "I need to rehash another theory out loud."

"I'm listening."

"Let's say George visited the Dales because he was helping Doreen. If so, why would she blackmail him? It doesn't make sense."

"We don't know what George's intentions were. If Doreen is blackmailing him, maybe he visited the Dales as a pretext to try to dig up dirt on her."

The situation seemed a lot more complicated in my mind. "I'm not sure about that. In fact, I'm not sure about anything anymore."

"What do you mean?"

"The unresolved questions about Tiffany's death. The weird things that have been happening since we got here. All the lies and contradictions—"

"What lies?"

I felt a lump in my throat.

"Don't shut me out, Megan." He pulled over to the side of the road and turned off the engine. "This is about Tom, isn't it? All those unanswered questions about his murder. Right?" He put a hand on my shoulder.

How was it that he could read me better than anyone else?

I swallowed hard to keep control. I wished I could let go of the guilt that had lingered inside me since Tom's death, but I couldn't. Not yet. And I wasn't ready to admit it to Michael either. "No, it's about how Doreen bullied Henry and set him up to look like an incompetent employee. How she screwed up Bianca's computer entries and got away with it. How maggots mysteriously ended up in a customer's purchase—"

"Maggots?"

I recapped the episode, including Kathy's unchecked storytelling about my fearless ordeal with the yucky life forms. "As if that wasn't bad enough, I had to endure everyone's dumb jokes all day long."

Michael tried not to laugh but didn't succeed. "Sorry, Megan." He was still chuckling as he started up the engine. Every so often, he stifled a laugh and covered it up by pretending to cough.

I rode the rest of the way home without saying another word to him.

By the time we reached Portland, it was three o'clock and my neck was stiff. Small wonder. I'd dozed off during the last half hour of the trip with my head against the window. All I wanted to do was go home, take a hot bath, and relax.

I gazed up at the sky. Threatening clouds had gathered. A downpour was imminent.

"How about going for a bite to eat?" Michael asked. "We can make it to the pizza place down the street before the storm breaks. I can park in the lot over there." He indicated one coming up on the right. "What do you say?"

I often wondered how Michael's cravings for food could be so spontaneous. "Okay," I said, my alternate plans for the rest of the day evaporating.

He'd eased the car into a parking space when his phone rang. He answered and had a short conversation, then hung up. "It was Ben Leblanc from the adult day shelter. I'd put in a call to him about Gladys. He wants to see me. It's not far. We could walk over." The eager expression in his eyes told me he'd decided his all-dressed pizza could wait a while longer.

We found the door to Ben's office door ajar like the last time. Michael knocked. "Hi, Ben."

"Come on in, guys." Ben waved us in.

"Working on Sunday?" Michael said to him.

"I put in extra hours here and there. Can't keep up with the paperwork otherwise."

"You said you had information about Gladys," Michael said as we took our seats.

"Sure do. I'd known Gladys for decades. Almost everyone in the city knew her. She was a creature of habit. Handy when you need to track down a person."

"Right," Michael said. "So what have you got?"

Ben grabbed a stack of papers in his "To do" bin and flipped through them. "Something that should help you piece together the last day of Gladys's life. I know I put the info close by...ah, here it is." He pulled out a lined sheet of paper, the sort that goes into a three-ring binder. "Gladys would drop into the shelter twice a week to bathe. The last time she used the facilities was the Friday evening before she died. Here's where the info gets sketchy." He paused to study his notes. "A street friend of Gladys remembers meeting her along Middle Street around nine-thirty that night. She said Gladys was on her way to do some shopping."

"Shopping?" I asked.

"That's what street people call going through other people's garbage," Ben said in a hushed tone of voice, as if it were inside information. "They wait until nightfall because most businesses are closed then. It's also safer to go shopping when it's dark."

"Did her friend say exactly where she went shopping?" Michael asked.

"She wasn't sure. She thinks it was either the alley off Exchange Street or the next one over. She said that's where they have the best stuff. She walked with Gladys about a block or so before they split up."

"Did anyone else see Gladys that night?" Michael asked.

Ben shrugged. "Don't know. That's all I got."

A wall of heavy rain greeted us as we stepped outdoors. Damn. I'd forgotten to grab the umbrella.

We waited ten minutes, expecting it to subside, but it didn't. To my dismay, Michael suggested we make a run for it.

It didn't take long before water was dripping down my face. I could only imagine to what extent my curly hair had mushroomed. Walking into a restaurant looking as if I'd taken a shower with my clothes on was not on my agenda. I hoped Michael's appetite for pizza had fizzled.

"You were right," I said to him after we got inside the car, the smell of our wet clothing filling the small space. "Gladys went shopping in the alley behind Bianca's store." I reached for the box of facial tissues on the back seat and handed some to Michael.

He wiped his face. "The two plastic tubes...the red ribbon.

Items they found in her handbag. The pieces are starting to fit. She must have made contact with the poison seconds before she died."

For lack of a better place, I discarded our used tissues in the narrow section of the passenger door. "Poor woman. When I think about how Doreen and Lee had poked fun at her death—"

"What are you talking about?"

I repeated the conversation I'd overheard between Doreen and Lee upstairs at the shop about how an "old hag" had gone shopping. "I'd already told you about it, but I didn't make the connection until now. When I heard them talking about money and extortion and how they were going to con someone, I knew they were talking about George and focused on that."

We sat in silence for a while, staring out the windows at the pouring rain.

"If the poison took effect within seconds, why was Gladys's body found yards away from the shop?" I asked Michael.

"Someone must have moved her."

"Why would anyone want to do that?"

"To deflect attention from the original location. Gladys must have picked the poisonous flowers out of the waste bin behind Bianca's Gardens moments before she collapsed. It's the only logical assumption."

My guard was up. I wanted to believe that nothing more than a bizarre twist of fate had caused Gladys's death, that it had been regrettable but not deliberate. "If poisonous flowers ended up in a garbage bin in the alley, it doesn't necessarily mean they came from Bianca's shop. A stranger could have walked by and dumped them into the bin."

"It's a long shot."

I gave it more thought. "Something's still not right."

"Like what?"

"Whoever moved Gladys would have been affected by the poisonous vapors, wouldn't they?"

"Maybe not. If the poison vaporized within seconds, it would explain why she was exposed to it and no one else."

"Why move the body? I mean—if she died there—"

"Megan." He gave me *the look*—the same one I'd given him when I was trying to get a point across.

"What?"

"I know you don't want to hear this, but the trail keeps leading us back to Bianca's Gardens. It's the only florist shop in the area."

His tenacity was beginning to irritate me. "Bianca didn't do it."

"Then we'll have to eliminate her and every other innocent party at the shop, one by one. That's where you come in."

"Me?"

"Do you think you can find out if any flowers were thrown out the day Gladys died?"

"Are you serious? The girls throw out large bins of clippings and damaged flowers every day."

He shook his head. "That's not what I meant. Maybe there was a mistake with a customer order—the wrong color flower or whatever—and they had to ditch the order. There could be a record of it."

"Fine. I'll check it out."

"Don't do anything to arouse suspicion. We don't want to add our bodies to the growing list."

"The only ones I have to be careful about are Doreen and Lee."

"How did Bianca ever manage to hire those two losers anyway?"

"She has a soft spot for the underdogs of this world, so don't ever say a word against either one of them in front of her," I said. "Trust me on this one."

"No problem."

I ventured further. "I wouldn't be surprised if Doreen set fire to the shop and put the blame on Henry. Like her mother might have done years ago." There it was—an outlet for my pent-up venting.

Michael raised a finger. "Hold on. We have no proof Doreen was involved with the fire."

"Not yet but I'm working on it. I'll get Henry to break his silence at my next visit."

"Maybe Doreen and Henry don't even know they're related," he reminded me. "Tread lightly."

He was right. "You're so special." I planted a kiss on his cheek.

"What's that for?"

"For being the most generous, considerate, and loving person I know."

"Is there more where that came from?" His blue eyes twinkled.

"Maybe." I smiled at him, then checked my watch. "Let's go. We only have ten minutes to reach St. Andrew's Church."

CHAPTER 20

Rows of candles in red glass holders cast a warm glow in the vestibule of St. Andrew's Church. Father Healy, the temporary vicar assigned to the church, met Michael and me at the scheduled time and was now guiding us toward the altar. He wore a black clergy shirt with a white Roman tab and black trousers. His wispy white hair and a chipped front tooth added an impish air to him. The sound of coins or something metal jingled in the air about us. I assumed it came from a set of keys he carried in his trouser pocket.

"This is my favorite time of day," Father Healy said, casting a glimpse at the empty pews. "At this hour, I often have the Good Lord all to myself." His chuckle was light and merry, as if he'd dared to entertain a selfish thought about his relationship with God.

We came to a stop not far from the altar.

"Right there—that's where the Good Lord came and took him away," he said, pointing to an area on the marbled tile where Father Griffith had collapsed last Sunday. His gaze remained fixed on the spot such that I half-expected to see the late priest's body materialize there at any moment.

"So you were here the day Father Griffith collapsed," I said to him.

"Sadly, no." Father Healy shook his head and sighed but kept his gaze on the vacant spot.

Michael grimaced at me over the priest's head in a way that said, "Let's get on with it."

I scowled back at him.

Father Healy clasped his hands together. "Perhaps we ought to sit down and begin the interview now. Please follow me."

The tinkling in his pocket increased as he led the way out through a side exit. He whisked us across a reception area, where four wooden chairs were lined up against a wall. Long-stemmed roses, dark and drooping, looked abandoned in a vase on a corner table. He opened another door and we entered a narrow corridor. The scent of freshly waxed parquet surprised me. I didn't think anyone waxed their floors anymore. Then again, the church looked as if it had been built in the fifties.

He stopped in front of a door with a gold plaque affixed to it that read "Father Paul Griffith." He pulled out a set of keys from his pocket. "This is my temporary office." He opened the door and flipped the light switch on, then ushered us in.

The décor spoke of frugality befitting a hermit. A simple wood table, a bookcase that contained five rows of faded books, and three buffed up wood chairs almost filled the entire space in the room. Judging from the scent of wax, the parquet in this room had also been recently polished. The only item that hinted of comfort was an electric heater on the floor beneath a window, but it wasn't plugged in.

"Please sit down." Father Healy gestured to the empty chairs, then took a seat behind the desk. He propped his arms up and joined his hands. Although the top of the table cut off my view of him from his mid-chest down, I could see his legs dangling in the air. An image of the proverbial Humpty-Dumpty sitting on a wall came to mind, and I smiled in spite of myself.

Father Healy smiled back at me, then looked at Michael. "Michael. Now there's a strong Christian name if you ask me. An archangel's name, in fact. You know that from your catechism lessons as a young boy, don't you?" He smiled at him, no doubt expecting an affirmative reply.

"Actually, it's the first I hear of it." Michael gave him a sheepish grin. "I'm afraid I wasn't much of a student of religion back then."

"Oh." A frown flitted across the priest's brow.

"Though I am a fervent believer in the Golden Rule," Michael said in an attempt to reclaim his good standing.

"Do unto others as you would have them do unto you." Father Healy nodded, then moved on to the topic at hand. "You mentioned you were working on an investigative article for the local paper. How can I be of service to you?" Eagerness reappeared in his eyes.

"I don't mean any disrespect, Father. I was hoping to interview other members of the clergy or staff who were present the day Father Griffith collapsed."

"Unfortunately, the only other resident staff member here is Mrs. Assunta Canto, our cook and housekeeper. Would you like to interview her now?"

"Yes, if it's possible," Michael said.

The phone was barely within the priest's reach. He picked up a pencil and hit the intercom button. He paged Mrs. Canto, then whispered to us, "She's never too far away. She'll be here soon."

Assunta Canto. The name sounded Italian. Years before I'd chosen a career as a ghostwriter, I'd worked for a big city bank. I became acquainted with the names of customers from diverse ethnic backgrounds and often discovered the origin of their names from the customers themselves.

Moments later, there was a light rap at the door.

"Come in, Mrs. Canto," the priest called out.

As far as what a live-in cook and housekeeper of a church would look like, she was precisely what I'd expected. Of average height with ample bosom that matched equally ample hips, Mrs. Canto slowly closed the door behind her. Her smile radiated through the room, as did the scent of something divine that emanated from her hands or from the apron she wore. On a second whiff, I concluded it was roast chicken.

"Yes, Father Healy, what can I do for you?" Mrs. Canto asked in an accent that supported my assumption she was Italian.

"Mrs. Canto, please come meet these young reporters, Michael and Megan. They'd like to ask you some questions about the late Father Griffith."

Mrs. Canto hesitated, her expression shifting from expectation to uncertainty.

"It's all right, Mrs. Canto," Father Healy said. "This won't take long. Come join us."

She did as she was told and sat in the chair next to mine. She smoothed out her apron, then smiled at me.

"Mrs. Canto has been working here for more than ten years," the priest said by way of introduction. "Father Griffith's death has distressed her immensely, as it has the other parishioners. Please go on with your questioning, Michael."

Michael leaned forward and addressed Mrs. Canto. "Can you tell me about Father Griffith's activities preceding the Sunday service on the day he died?"

Mrs. Canto glanced at her hands—strong broad hands that looked as if they'd kneaded countless loaves of bread in their time. "Father Griffith went for an early morning walk. When he returned, I made him breakfast. I prepared toast with orange marmalade and coffee." She sounded sure of herself and had probably repeated the same details to the police often enough.

"What did Father Griffith do next?"

"He went to get ready for Sunday mass."

"Did he receive any visitors that morning?"

"No." She paused. "Excuse me. It wasn't a visitor. It was someone who dropped off a delivery."

"A delivery?"

Mrs. Canto nodded. "Yes. A woman left a box of flowers for Father Griffith. The box was tied with a beautiful red ribbon."

"What kind of flowers were they?" Michael continued to probe.

"Oh, my goodness." Her eyes went wide and she laughed softly. "They were the most beautiful red roses I ever saw. A dozen of them."

"Did you put the roses in a vase?"

She nodded. "Yes."

"Can you explain in detail how you tended to the roses?"

"The usual way," Mrs. Canto said. "I filled a vase with water and put it on the table. I removed the tubes from the stems and put the roses in the vase. Except the last one."

"Why's that?"

"The doorbell rang."

"What did you do then?"

"I took the empty box and went to answer the door. The garbage bin was on my way. When I went back to finish, someone had put the last rose in the vase."

"Who?"

Mrs. Canto shrugged. "It must have been Father Griffith."

"Are those the same flowers that are on the corner table in the reception area?" I asked her.

"Yes. I had no time to throw them out. The police were here asking questions, taking pictures… No time to even change the water in the vase." She looked down and shook her head in shame, as if she'd committed an unspeakable act of negligence.

I sensed Michael's excitement as we headed for the finish line. Or maybe it was my own heart beating like a set of drums.

"Mrs. Canto, do you remember the name of the delivery service that dropped off the flowers?" I asked.

"No, no, it was not a delivery service," she said, waving a finger in the air. "It was a young woman—a parishioner. I'm sorry. I don't know her name."

"Can you describe her?" I asked.

"No, I'm sorry. It was too fast."

Not another dead end.

All of a sudden, Mrs. Canto's face lit up. "Wait. I remember now." Her eyes darted to Father Healy.

"Go on, Mrs. Canto," the priest said.

"It isn't a nice thing to say. May God forgive me, but I remember thinking what strange eyes this woman had."

"What do you mean?" I asked her.

"One was blue and the other was brown."

Our meeting ended soon afterward. As Mrs. Canto escorted us out, Michael took the opportunity to ask her for a favor.

On the short trek back to the car, Michael said to me, "It always pays to ask nicely." He smiled.

"I've heard of reporters bribing their sources to get to the truth," I said as I opened the passenger door and got in, "but I have to admit you've outdone yourself this time."

"She was going to ditch them anyway. All I did was offer her money for a new vase and flowers." He grinned and handed me the vase containing Father Griffith's withered red roses, including its original supply of water, the whole lot wrapped in layers upon layers of plastic foil.

CHAPTER 21

By six o'clock Monday morning and before any member of the Hobbs family had come down for breakfast, Michael had called Trudy twice.

His initial attempt at convincing her to analyze Father Griffith's roses had proved unsuccessful. She confided that police investigators had asked her for background information regarding poisonous flora in relation to the Tiffany Gray investigation. As a result, she was obliged to hand over the information she'd collected so far on Black Whispers. She didn't want to jeopardize the investigation by giving Michael preferential treatment over law enforcement officials.

Her refusal didn't discourage Michael. He took a few minutes to ponder his next strategy, then called her back. Judging from his side of the conversation, he pleaded with her to the point of embarrassment. My embarrassment, that is. He vowed he'd never bother her again if she granted him this one favor. He went as far as to promise her exceptional newspaper coverage when the case broke.

It worked. He delivered the flowers directly to her at six-thirty in the morning.

"I think I've dealt my last ace," he said to me after he'd returned home. "Trudy thinks it's too risky to do favors for outsiders from now on. Law enforcement boundaries." He poured more of the strong Colombian brew into our cups.

I took a sip and mulled over this latest development. More than anything, I wanted to reassure Michael that things would work out, yet I was battling my own frustrations. "We should have visited St. Andrew's Church sooner."

I didn't have to worry about Michael's reaction. Being an optimist at heart has its advantages when one is confronted with bleak circumstances. "We couldn't have known," he said. "The cops didn't know either. They seized the flowers from the Gray household, not the water in the vases. Even an expert like Trudy didn't think of analyzing the water for microscopic traces of the seed. It wasn't a viable alternative in anyone's mind until now." He put the pot back in the coffee maker and sat down.

"The evidence is only beginning to tell the story. We need more time to find the other pieces to the puzzle."

"Don't worry. Trudy has the church flowers and the original water Mrs. Canto put in the vase. This evidence isn't valid in a court of law, so the cops can't use it, but we can. I'm counting on Trudy's analysis to determine the next step in my investigation." He sat down. "We also need to find out how poisonous flowers ended up in the garbage bin in the alley. That's another missing link."

"Right...another missing link. All we have so far are pieces of information that don't fit. I suppose adding one more to the pile won't hurt."

Our discussion ended as the sound of Victor's footsteps made their way down the stairs and across the hall. "Good morning," he greeted us, flinging the jacket of his business suit over the back of a chair. "You two are up early." He reached for a cup in the cabinet over the counter.

"Investigating three unexplained deaths at once is a real juggling act," Michael said.

"I expect it is." Victor filled his cup with coffee, then dropped a cube of sugar into it and stirred. "However, I doubt you'd want to switch places with me this morning. I'm meeting with Stanley Gray." In response to our silence, he said, "I thought so."

"Dealing with his son is enough for me right now," Michael said, "but I'd give anything to be a fly on the wall at your meeting."

Victor grew quiet. He stirred his coffee again, which told me that he had more on his mind than the Gray family. He looked at us. "This Henry Glover thing. It's ripping Bianca apart. She can get quite depressed when someone she cares about gets into trouble. She's having a hard time accepting he set fire to the shop."

"I'm with Bianca," I said. "I think Henry's been set up."

"The police are convinced they have their man," Victor said.

"The police are wrong."

"You know the staff at the shop quite well by now, don't you?"

"Some of them better than others." I felt Michael's eyes on me and held back from mentioning specifics. "Why?"

Victor took a sip of coffee, then said in a low voice, "I don't want Bianca to hear this. I've tried to appease her fears, but I suspect there might be an ongoing conspiracy to run her out of business."

"You think the fire was part of it?" I asked him.

"Absolutely." Victor's brow tightened up as he joined us at the table. "What other reason is there to deliberately set fire to a place? Whether Henry was responsible or not, I'm glad he had the courage to call it in before the shop burnt to the ground." He shook his head. "I'd often told Bianca that she was too trusting of the people she hired. I'd insisted on background checks, but she was in a hurry to get the shop up and running and overlooked that aspect."

"Are you saying you suspect one of the staff set the fire?" I asked, wondering if Doreen's name might surface.

"I'm not sure." Victor took a sip of coffee. "After the fire, I asked a friend of mine—a private investigator—to check out Lee Chen. He was the last employee Bianca hired. The rest of the staff had worked at the shop for months by then and without any incidents."

"What did your PI dig up?" Michael asked.

"That Lee served jail time years ago for possession of drugs and burglary," Victor said.

"Does Bianca know this?" I asked him.

"She does now but she dismisses it. She believes that Doreen would never have encouraged her to hire Lee if he weren't okay. Bianca says she's had no complaints about his work so far."

"Did you check out anyone else?" Michael asked him.

Victor shook his head. "I wanted to verify Doreen's background, seeing as she's married to Lee. However, Bianca wouldn't hear of it."

Michael continued to probe. "Where did Lee serve time?"

"The name escapes me. I have it in my notes at the office. I'll call you after my meeting with Stanley Gray and let you know."

"No problem," Michael said. "You can reach me at my private number or at the shop this afternoon."

Victor smiled. "That's right. You're helping Bianca with the deliveries." His expression turned serious. "Can you do me a favor?"

"Name it."

"Watch your back."

Bianca had given the staff a heads-up about Michael temporarily joining their ranks as a part-time delivery person. She greeted him with a hug when he arrived at noon on Monday. "Michael, welcome to our home away from home. Come and meet my staff."

She made the rounds and introduced him to Joyce, Gail, and Sarah.

"Pleased to meet you, Michael," Joyce said, smiling. "I'm looking forward to reading more of your articles in the *Herald*."

"Hey, Michael," Gail said, shaking his hand. "If I can help you with anything, give me a shout." When Michael wasn't looking, she raised a thumb and winked at me.

"Hi, Michael," Sarah said. "Now I can tell my friends I met a real author." She blushed.

Michael's good looks and relaxed nature put everyone at ease—with two visible exceptions.

Doreen nodded in Michael's direction and said "hi." Even though she managed a quick smile, she went back to her task at the POS without so much as another word and printed off a copy of the delivery schedule. As for Lee, he added a grunt to his nod, which could be considered an effort.

As Doreen handed Lee his afternoon delivery route, she gave me a wary glance. I pretended not to notice. I could only imagine what she was thinking. I didn't blame her for having doubts about Michael's sudden addition to the staff to give Lee a hand with the deliveries. The whole town knew Michael was an investigative reporter working on three unexplained local deaths, so Doreen might have suspected he had other motives for working at the shop. Then again, maybe that notion existed only in my mind.

The bottom line was that Doreen had Bianca's wholehearted trust, but she didn't have mine and she knew it. She also knew that I was watching her. She'd observe me from time to time when she thought I wasn't looking. I played her cat-and-mouse game, but my guard was up—constantly.

Funny thing about guilt. It makes you act in ways you normally wouldn't. The way I saw it, Doreen was guilty. What's worse, she knew that I knew. My instincts told me she'd covered up the computer glitches, forced Henry to take the blame for the fire at the shop, and was in the process of extorting money from George. Heaven only knew what other outrageous feats she could lay claim to. The only drawback was that I couldn't prove any of it. Not yet, anyway.

In the meantime, I decided I'd implement a different approach to throw her off. I'd make her feel as if she were no longer under my microscopic view. I'd pretend to ignore her. It would drive her beyond the edge of her comfort zone into the realm of carelessness.

And I'd be waiting.

Ironically, fate lent a hand when Bianca assigned Doreen and me to handle an early afternoon rush of clients keen on taking advantage of the "fire" sale. Bianca had decided to offer certain products at reduced prices because she'd detected a slight acrid smell in them. When I wasn't busy serving customers, I helped Doreen process sales transactions for her customers and wrap their purchases. She thanked me, her expression revealing a modicum of awe, if not bewilderment, about my supportive gestures.

After things had calmed down, Doreen stayed at the front counter and I retreated to the workroom. I wanted to see how the other girls were doing with last-minute arrangements for a cancer fundraising banquet tonight. A new committee in town that had been referred to Bianca's Gardens had called at noon to place a rush order. Bianca had put three girls to work on it to make sure the flowers would be delivered on time.

"Aren't these roses beautiful?" Gail held a bouquet of pink roses in her arms to show me. She smiled and gazed at it as if she were coddling a baby. "This one's for the centerpiece at the fundraiser tonight. I love roses, especially the pink shades." She carefully placed the bouquet on the worktable.

"They're gorgeous," I said.

"Joyce and Sarah are working on the other two arrangements. Pink flowers too, but their arrangements are larger than mine."

Joyce peered at me over her eyeglasses. "If the customer calls, we'll be done in about an hour." She gazed at Sarah. "You doing okay?"

"Yes, I'll be done by then too." Sarah smiled and went back to work.

"Want to give me a hand with these plastic bins?" Gail asked me.

"Sure."

We each took hold of a bin filled with leftover clippings from the day's work and carried it out back to the alley.

"I can't believe how much garbage a flower shop produces," I said.

"We only use the good stuff," Gail said. "It kills me when a customer calls up to complain about wilting flowers, and it turns out to be a simple problem—like they forgot to change the water."

I took the cue. "Maybe that's what happened to the flowers Tiffany Gray returned."

Gail's brow furrowed. "I doubt that was the problem."

"How do you know?"

"The box hadn't been opened. It was dented when she brought it in—like she'd thrown it around or something. The way she slapped it silly against the counter, the roses inside couldn't have been in terrific shape." She grimaced.

"Did anyone open the box and look inside?"

"I don't know. You might want to ask Sarah. She was at the cash."

"What happened to the flowers?"

"I saw Doreen walk out the back door with the box in her hands later. I'm sure she dumped the whole works in one of these outdoor bins."

After we'd emptied the trash, we carried the bins back to the workroom.

"Gail, can you handle an order for a dozen boxed red roses?" Joyce asked her. "Doreen left the customer info there." She gestured to an order slip on the table.

Gail reached into a drawer and came out empty-handed. "Funny. I could have sworn I put new bags of tubes in here yesterday morning. We couldn't possibly have gone through a thousand of those thingamabobs." When no one answered, she went off in search of a new bag.

I went upstairs to the washroom to gather my thoughts and recap my findings so far. I'd succeeded in tracing the path of the roses Tiffany had brought back to the shop a week before her death. I went a step further and contemplated what might have occurred after Doreen had tossed the roses into the outdoor bin in the alley.

I imagined how Gladys glad rags might have checked out the trash bin and reached in to grasp the elegant box wrapped in a single red bow. The ribbon was no doubt a treasure for someone unaccustomed to finding such items during her nighttime shopping trips, so she'd tucked it into her handbag. I assumed she'd taken the lid off the box of flowers, and when she did, she removed two plastic tubes from the stems of the roses, maybe to take the roses themselves. That released the fatal poison in one or both of them. Logic told me she'd dropped both tubes into her handbag—that's where they were found—before she collapsed to the ground. Like Michael had suggested, someone could have carried her away from the shop, positioned her on her back, and placed wildflowers in her hands.

I shuddered at the possibility that my cousin's shop had been used as a conduit that resulted in an innocent victim's death. It made me even more determined to bring justice to Gladys's memory and she'd help me do it. Even dead people can speak the truth.

I couldn't wait to share my theory with Michael.

The pace at the shop slowed down to a crawl by mid-afternoon. While the girls cleaned up in the workroom, I sat on a stool at the counter and made my share of customer appreciation calls. There were ten. The first two customers weren't available, so I took notes to call them back later. Three out of the group were polite and said they'd definitely refer us to their friends and family. Four customers said they loved the choices at Bianca's Gardens and would shop here again. Only one customer was disappointed in the service because the delivery had arrived earlier than expected. Go figure.

I'd completed my calls when the phone rang. It was Victor. "Hello, Megan. Is Michael around?"

"No. He's out making deliveries. Do you want him to call you when he gets back?"

"I'm about to go into a meeting. Can I give you the information?"

"Sure."

"I have the name of the town where Lee served time in jail years ago."

I grabbed a pen and paper. "Go ahead."

"It's Lansing."

Michael folded his arms and leaned back against the kitchen counter. He'd finished his delivery run with Lee minutes earlier and met me upstairs. "You're sure Victor said Lansing? Do you realize what this means?" His blue eyes sparkled. "Lee knew Henry from jail."

"Not so loud," I whispered. "Someone might hear you."

"I'll bet they got chummy during their jail time together. When destiny connected them again at Bianca's Gardens, Lee saw a scapegoat in Henry. Maybe he threatened to tell Bianca about Henry's prison record."

"You don't know Bianca. She gives everyone a second chance."

"Humor me. If Lee threatened to tell on him, Henry probably thought he had no choice but to go along with their plans." He paused. "Next question. Does Doreen know Henry is her father?"

"Maybe she does, and she's taking it out on him for having

abandoned her as a child."

He shrugged. "All she had to do was confront him about his paternity."

"I can't begin to understand what goes on in her mind." I took a step back and glanced down the corridor. "We have to make this quick. Someone might come upstairs. Did you find out anything more from Lee on your delivery run?"

He shook his head. "It's like prying open a mummy's tomb. One thing I did notice. He has a tattoo of a flower on his lower back. I saw it when he bent over to pick up a plant."

"Lots of people have tattoos of flowers. I have one."

"So I've noticed." He grinned. "Anyway, his tattoo was black. So black, it almost glowed in the dark."

"What are you getting at?"

"I'm almost sure it's Black Whispers."

"Oh, my God." There was something else I had to tell Michael…

"We have the perfect setup. A former jailbird who deals in deadly flora and the unsuspecting owner of a flower shop."

"Don't forget the competent manipulator in Doreen." I expected a comeback about my merciless fixation with the girl, but Michael said nothing. "Oh…I wanted to tell you. I have a theory about how the poison got into the roses."

"I'm listening."

"I think we can trace Gladys's death to the long-stemmed roses that Tiffany brought back to the shop a week before she died." I was explaining the link to the red ribbon and plastic tubes found in Gladys's handbag when I thought I heard footsteps. I glanced down the corridor but saw no one. I walked up to Michael and whispered in his ear. "Inside the plastic tube at the tip of the—" I stopped. I could have sworn I heard a noise again. It came from the other end of the corridor and sounded like a creak on the stair.

Michael heard it too. He put a finger to his lips. In a normal voice, he said, "I'm going to grab a coffee at the corner. Want me to bring you something?"

"Yes, please. A large mocha coffee."

"You got it."

Michael walked down the corridor and checked inside the stockroom, the bathroom, and Bianca's office. He shook his head to indicate the rooms were empty, then he went downstairs.

I couldn't help wondering how much of our conversation someone else had overheard.

CHAPTER 22

Our timing couldn't have been better. Interviewing the household staff at George's mansion was a crucial factor in Michael's investigation of Tiffany's death. He accepted George's invitation to meet with them Tuesday afternoon. Bianca had no problem with Michael's absence at the shop—the delivery schedule was light today.

With my work schedule at the shop still up in the air, Bianca asked me to go in Tuesday morning instead of the afternoon. She had to bring Alex to the dentist and wanted me to log the responses to the Halloween party invitations. The timetable worked for me, so I agreed.

I shut the door to Bianca's office and sat at her computer. I recorded the names of the fifty guests who had replied by email. I added the names of guests who had replied by phone or dropped by to hand in the RSVP in person.

I had lots of time left to develop my article on superstitions for the newsletter. I searched the Internet and came up with a short list of amusing items, old and new:

1. If you catch a falling leaf on the first day of autumn, you will not catch a cold all winter.

2. Two people breaking a wishbone is said to lead to good luck for the person with the larger piece.

3. You should never turn a loaf of bread upside down after a slice has been cut from it.

4. Never take a broom along when you move. Throw it out and buy a new one.

5. Find a penny, pick it up. All day long, you'll have good luck.

6. Opening an umbrella indoors is supposed to bring bad luck.

7. It's unlucky to walk under a ladder.

8. A cricket in the house brings good luck.

9. It's bad luck to let milk boil over.

10. It's good luck to find a four-leaf clover.

I sent the piece to Bianca by email so she could take a look at it. With only final touches remaining, the October newsletter would be ready for distribution by Halloween.

I opened the door to Bianca's office. Low voices floated my way from the kitchen. I kept the door slightly ajar and listened.

"That bastard is gonna get us fired," Lee said.

"She'd never put us out on the street," Doreen said.

"Ya think? He said he'd stop sending business here if she didn't get rid of us."

"Oh." A pause.

"Take care of it. I gotta go load deliveries."

I quietly shut the door.

Michael picked me up at the shop after lunch and we set out for George's Falmouth mansion.

I didn't waste time telling him about the conversation I'd overheard between Doreen and Lee in the kitchen. "I can't believe George Gray would threaten Bianca like that. If anything, she would have told Victor—or even me."

"Something's off with Doreen and Lee. We'll have to keep our eyes open." Michael maneuvered a curve in the road through the dense wood. "I can't wait to interview George's staff. I think our interview with his parents triggered his invitation today sooner than I expected."

"He's taking a chance, seeing as the interviews with his staff might not work in his favor," I said.

"It's all about showing interest in the case. Oh…I didn't tell you. George approved the write-up covering my interview with him."

"Did he have a choice? You're writing an investigative series about his wife's death. He has to show he's cooperating with the media."

"True." Michael nodded. "Public interest makes it difficult to ignore the unexplained death of a beautiful and charitable young woman. People feel they have a right to know what happened to her."

"I don't blame them."

We arrived at our destination and went through the same checkpoint routine. George wasn't home, which suited our purposes. We hoped that the household staff would divulge more information in his absence.

First up was Tyler Wilson, thirty-five, former gymnastics coach turned personal trainer, valet, and lackey for George Gray. He insisted on meeting with us in his apartment on the second floor. I understood why as soon as he ushered us in. His open-concept, one-room habitat covered more square footage than a small gymnasium. To say that it was a typical man cave would be an understatement.

Impossible to miss, gym equipment that included a treadmill, two exercise bicycles, and a bench press with weights were positioned in the middle of the room. A steel worktable along the right-hand wall was topped with sports accessories, including an assortment of lighter weights, skipping ropes, a stack of hula-hoops in florescent colors, at least six pairs of leather gloves, and other gym gear I couldn't begin to identify. A flat-screen TV on the wall above the table could be viewed from any location within a twenty-foot radius. On either side of it were two oversized posters of Christian Bale in costume from his Batman movies. Along the rest of this wall and the one meeting it at the far end, mirrors stretched from floor to ceiling and gave the appearance the floor space was twice its actual size.

I watched as Michael perused Tyler's collection of muscle-building apparatus with a look of awe similar to that on a kid's face on Christmas Day. I could have predicted he'd start a conversation with Tyler about their respective workout routines in the next moment.

While they chatted, I glanced around.

To either create drama or to ensure privacy or both, light-blocking curtains spanned the width and height of most of the wall facing the TV. I figured they hid patio doors leading to an outside deck.

Along the left wall perpendicular to the curtains was a u-shaped sofa in black leather with a glass table centered in front of it.

Beyond the sofa and tucked into the left corner of the apartment was a granite bar and four chrome stools topped with black leather seats. No glasses or liquor bottles were visible, so I assumed Tyler stored them under the counter. A laptop, three remote controls, and a set of keys lay on the counter.

I was wondering about the remote controls when Tyler walked over and picked one up. "Michael, if you think that's something, take a load of this," he said, clicking it.

The curtains parted to reveal sliding doors that led to a wood deck. Not your everyday wood deck either. Patio furniture included a table for twelve, a sun umbrella that could have doubled as a satellite dish, and a stainless steel barbecue the size of a small boat. I had the impression we were at a home and garden show. Beyond the terrace was a dense forest that surrounded the Gray mansion like a protective shield.

As Michael and I gaped in awe, Tyler chuckled. "I always get that reaction. Please, have a seat. We should get started with the interview."

The three of us settled on the u-shaped sofa. Michael and I shared one section. Tyler sat facing us.

Michael began his interview with an inconspicuous question. "How long have you been working for George?"

"Three years," Tyler said. "He discovered me, so to speak, in a local fitness center. He asked me if I wanted a job here as his personal trainer, food and board included. I jumped at the chance.

Who wouldn't?" He grinned.

"How would you describe your current relationship with George?"

Tyler blinked. "We're talking work relationship here, right?"

"Yes."

"We're good. Very good, in fact. George loves to work out."

"How was your relationship with Tiffany?"

He looked confused. "As her personal trainer, you mean?"

"Yes."

"Oh, she didn't need me. She was in excellent shape." He smiled and stretched an arm over the back of the couch, his beefy biceps indicative of the hours he spent on his own exercise routine.

"Would you say that George and Tiffany were happily married?" I asked Tyler.

His gaze switched to me. "As married couples go." He shrugged. "Personally, I think relationships between unmarried people are lots more exciting." His eyes remained riveted on me and he smiled—a slow, enticing smile that said more than words ever could.

Was he coming on to me? I felt my cheeks get warm.

Michael interrupted the moment. "Anything out of the ordinary happen the day Tiffany died? Anyone come over unannounced?"

Tyler glanced away, thinking. "No visitors that I recall. It was the usual routine. I had breakfast...worked out a bit. Then I had to run out and buy George new exercise wear after lunch."

"You had to?"

"Hey, that's what I'm paid for." Tyler grinned. "George got a call at the office from his favorite clothing store in town. They'd received a shipment of designer exercise outfits. He wanted me to pick up a dozen outfits in his size before they sold out. You know how it is." His hand did a little wavy motion in the air before it returned to its former resting spot on the sofa.

Michael went on. "What time did you get back home?"

"A couple hours later. I met some friends for coffee in town. I was having a blah day. They put me in a good mood." His chuckle implied something naughty.

"Did you get back home before Tiffany collapsed?"

Tyler looked down. "She was long gone by then."

"What kind of mood was she in that day?"

He stared at Michael. "I don't know. I'm not psychic."

Had we hit a nerve?

Michael stayed cool, didn't break eye contact. "You live here. You must have run into her once in a while."

Tyler clenched his jaw. "Fine. You want it straight? Tiffany was in her usual bitchy mood, okay?" He punctuated his statement with another flick of the wrist. "Going around the house, fussing over the flowers and plants like they were her pets. That's all she ever cared about. She ignored problems the cook had with last-minute dinner plans for twenty guests. She complained when I played music too loud during my workouts. All that bitch did was complain, complain, complain."

The interview was gaining momentum. I felt the excitement as Michael leaned slightly forward, his hands extended in a gesture of frankness. "I'll get right to the point. There's talk that Tiffany might have been seeing other men. Can you attest to that?"

"Even if I could, what the hell does it have to do with her death?"

"There's a theory circulating that she might have been murdered."

He eyed Michael with skepticism. "You can't be serious."

"It's a theory, but I'd like to follow up on any leads—rumors or otherwise."

Tyler glanced around the room, seemed to be weighing the consequences of his response. "I'll tell you this much," he said, his gaze intense. "She was screwing anything in pants."

"What makes you so sure?"

His eyes darkened. "Because I was one of them."

An awkward silence followed.

"How long did your relationship last?"

Tyler shrugged. "Not long. We got it on three or four times. Then she got involved with someone else."

"Do you have a name?"

"No, but she spent hours chatting online. Research, she said. I didn't believe her."

"Do you have proof she was seeing another man?"

"Personally, no. I heard about her afternoon orgies through a reliable source. Like what she was really doing when she was supposed to be at an afternoon tea party or art gallery exhibit." He raised a well-plucked eyebrow.

"Do you have any proof?"

"Take my word for it. The woman was a slut."

"Sounds as if you had a grudge against her for dumping you."

Tyler's eyes narrowed. "What are you implying?"

"I'm not implying anything." Michael pressed on. "Did George ever find out about Tiffany's affairs?"

"Are you kidding? He wore blinders the whole time." Another wave of the hand. "Even if he'd found out, he wouldn't have left her."

"Why not?" I asked, expecting that he'd say George would never want to pay alimony.

Tyler kept his gaze steady. "It was a marriage of convenience."

"In what way?"

"She was his trophy wife. George loves to collect beautiful things."

Michael joined in. "Why should we believe you?"

Tyler huffed and tapped his fingers on the sofa in a sign of exasperation. "Look, George and I are tight. He confides certain things in me."

"Like what?"

"It's personal."

"Secrets cause problems. What are you hiding?"

Tyler stiffened. "You really want to know what their marriage was like? Here's the inside scoop. Tiffany wanted everything—men, money, power, fame, you name it. She didn't give a damn about George. She was using him and his connections. If you ask me, the day that bitch dropped dead, she did us all a favor."

Tyler accompanied us downstairs to the main floor of the Gray mansion. He chatted along the way, telling us how Mrs. Shana

Nolan prepared every meal in the house, ensured the pantry shelves were well stocked, and supervised the table arrangements. Her popularity as a chef at a five-star hotel in downtown Portland where George had often dined had prompted him to hire her years ago. I didn't ask, but it was safe to assume George didn't dine there anymore. Tyler warned us not to let Mrs. Nolan's appearance fool us. She was a "tough old broad" of Irish heritage who didn't hesitate to verbalize her thoughts and feelings.

We walked through one of the archways and along a corridor that led to the kitchen and to Mrs. Nolan. As soon as Tyler had made the introductions, he excused himself and left for an appointment at the hair salon. I entertained the notion that his hair stylist could well be the source of his gossip about Tiffany. From personal experience at the salons I frequented, I knew that some customers treated their hair stylists as confidants. They disclosed information that they wouldn't dare tell their family or close friends, believing that their secrets were secure for the price of a haircut. It didn't matter whether the details that customers shared were true or not. Interesting tidbits were worth repeating.

As far as cooks went, Mrs. Nolan wasn't the type of person I expected to see managing a kitchen the size of a drive-through car wash. She was petite and round, had a reddish complexion, and looked every bit the frazzled cook with wisps of white hair protruding every which way from under a hair net. While the white cook's jacket was standard wear, I wondered if the black fishnet stockings and ballet flats she wore were about making a statement of sorts. I'd soon find out.

I'd suggested to Michael that I share the interview questions with him. I pointed out there was something about a conversation between two women that extracted juicy tittle-tattle. When he agreed without hesitation, I was surprised. Did he agree because he believed I could do it, or did he agree because he thought I was a gossip?

Mrs. Nolan studied me and smiled. "With a name like Megan and that lovely auburn hair, surely ya got some of the green in ya, have ya not?" she said in a distinctive Irish brogue.

"On my father's side," I said.

"Thought so." She nodded, then focused on Michael. "You're a fine thing." She gave him a coy smile. "I'm afraid ya caught me at a bad time. I'm preparing a beef stew and can't risk running off schedule. Sit yourselves down. I'll be done shortly." She headed for the stove.

Michael and I slid onto stools along the island in the center of the kitchen. Like the rest of the counters, the island was topped with black-and-white marbled granite. Four whole potatoes and bowls of chopped onions, celery, turnips, and carrots awaited Mrs. Nolan's attention. Sunlight poured in from tall windows on the left and shone on a row of aluminum and copper-based pots and pans hanging overhead. Facing us, white cupboards shared space with a stove and fridge and stretched to the ceiling. Knowing that it required a short stepladder to reach the top shelves, I looked around and noticed one tucked in a corner.

We waited while Mrs. Nolan sautéed beef chunks in a large pot. She returned to the island to claim the bowls of chopped vegetables. After she'd emptied the contents into the pot and stirred, she added water and spices. She stirred again and reduced the heat to a low boil.

The aroma was making my mouth water. I looked over at Michael who smiled and passed a hand over his stomach.

Mrs. Nolan joined us at the island. "I'm ready now. Fire away." She picked up a potato peeler and began to peel a spud so rapidly that I had a hard time focusing on her movements.

"Tell me about the kind of working relationship you have with George," I asked Mrs. Nolan.

"My relationship with Mr. Gray is grand." She kept her eyes on her work.

And distant, judging from her use of the formal "Mr. Gray." I went on. "What about Tiffany?"

She shrugged. "Grand."

"I heard she was difficult at times."

She picked up another potato and began to peel it. "Experience has taught me to do my job and keep my mouth shut about matters that don't concern me, so I did."

Good. Things were starting to heat up. "Did you ever overhear George and Tiffany arguing?"

"It's a natural occurrence between married couples." She glanced at me. "A smooth relationship is a pipe dream, if ya ask me."

Was this the attitude Tyler had warned us about? Or were my questions rubbing her the wrong way? I tried a different approach. "I understand that Tiffany took care of all the flowers she received."

"Oh, that she did. And heaven help anyone who interfered. Mrs. Gray was particular about her flowers, she was. She tended to them all by herself, which was fine by me. I had—and still have—plenty of chores to take care of."

"Did you ever resent the demands Tiffany placed on you?" Michael asked her.

She eyed him as if she were sizing up the freshness of fruit for a dessert salad. "If I say so, will ya keep it confidential? I don't want to lose my job."

He nodded. "You have my word as a journalist."

Mrs. Nolan frowned. "I don't like talking bad about the dead. I don't like surprises either. Truth be told, especially the sort Mrs. Gray used to spring on me. She often called at the last minute to say she was arriving with guests for lunch. Ridiculous, it was, to cause me such stress. It made me curse the day she was born, that one, but I meant her no harm."

"Were any of her guests men?" I asked.

"Would ya want a spectacle?" She gave me a wide-eyed stare. "They were well-to-do women chums she fussed over so they'd support her charities."

I was disappointed. I'd expected her to come up with something more scandalous.

She picked up the last of the potatoes and made short work of it. "Sorry," she said. "I must tend to these purdies." She placed the potatoes in a bowl, rinsed them in the sink, and returned to the island with them.

"Mrs. Nolan, can you describe your schedule the day Tiffany died?" Michael asked.

"The usual." She grabbed a cutting board, placed a potato on it, and began to chop it up. "After I'd served breakfast, I made a list of things I needed for the week. I sat down with Mrs. Gray and added items she requested to the list. Later I prepared lunch for her. She had a toasted chicken and lettuce sandwich on whole wheat bread. At two o'clock, I left to go do the messages in town. When I returned, an ambulance and police cars were parked in front of the house. The police wouldn't let me in, but it was far better that way."

"Why?"

"They found Mrs. Gray over there." She gestured with a nod of her head to the floor behind her. "Lucky I didn't see her. That image would have stayed in my mind for all eternity."

Michael probed further. "Do you know what she was doing in the kitchen?"

"Probably tending to flowers. That's all she does in here."

"What kind of flowers?"

"It must have been the roses. They delivered a box of them every Friday." She held the last potato firmly in place and began to chop it.

I didn't know how to broach the next subject, so I dove in. "We heard talk that Tiffany might have been having an affair."

"That's a crock of—" The knife came down hard and she gasped. Blood dripped from her finger. She rushed to the sink and ran cold water on it.

"Are you okay?" Michael jumped to his feet.

"Just a nick," she said over her shoulder. She opened a side drawer on her left, retrieved a plaster, and wrapped it around her finger. She hurried back and checked the potatoes. "No blood on the purdies, thank goodness. I'll rinse them again to be sure." Once done, she dumped them into the pot. She reached for a bottle of red wine and poured two cups into the mix. Without so much as a glance our way, she walked back to the island to fetch the knife and cutting board and disposed of them in the sink. She returned to wipe the counter with a soapy dishcloth, then moved back to the stove to stir the stew.

I wondered if her back-and-forth trips between the stove and the island were meant to waste time. Granted, we'd infringed upon her schedule, but my instincts told me she was holding something back.

"Would ya like some wine?" she asked us, removing a glass from the cupboard by the stove and filling it. "A wee bit helps to bring down the blood pressure."

"No thanks," I answered for both of us, feeling my pressure rising as she took a couple of sips. "Mrs. Nolan, please, we're investigating a potential murder case here. If you can help us—"

She gaped at me. "Sweet Mary, Mother of Jesus. Do the police think Mrs. Gray was murdered?" She put her glass down.

I nodded. "We think she might have died under mysterious circumstances."

"Give me a moment." She adjusted the temperature knob on the stove and returned to her spot at the island. "What exactly do ya want to know?" Her expression grew somber.

I spoke in a low voice. "We heard that Tiffany might have had a fling with Tyler."

She pointed a thumb toward the ceiling. "That half-polluted excuse for a man?" She laughed.

"Polluted?"

"He drinks a fair bit. If anything happened between them, it'd have been a miracle." She laughed again.

"Because he drinks?"

"No." She leaned forward and whispered, "Because he prefers men." She winked.

I was speechless. Her statement made me question Tyler's credibility. I decided to put his other disclosures to the test. "There are rumors that Tiffany might have had affairs with other men too."

"Utter nonsense." Her eyes turned dreamy. "Ya know, I did some theater in my younger days. Acting, singing, dancing on the stage in front of a live audience... Bloody thrilling days, they were." She smiled at me.

I smiled back. Now I understood where her passion for black stockings and ballet shoes came from, but what was she trying to say?

"I was quite the ingénue back then—truly naïve." She giggled. "I've seen peculiar carryings-on in my time, scandalous shenanigans even, so I'm capable of distinguishing a reckless woman from a loyal one."

"What are you getting at, Mrs. Nolan?"

She looked at me. "Mrs. Gray could never have had an affair."

"Why not?"

"She was much too transparent." She shrugged. "Moreover, I can't imagine what would possess her to seek out other men when she was married to such a fine gentleman like Mr. Gray. She was mad about him, she was."

She'd rendered me speechless for the second time in the last five minutes. Her testimony about Tiffany refuted Tyler's, but I had good reason to believe her instead. Unlike Tyler, there was no pretense of mental processes going on. Mrs. Nolan was as candid in answering my questions as she'd been in putting together a beef stew without a cookbook.

On the other hand, her familiarity with the stage could make it easier to distort the truth and present it with conviction.

Maybe our next interviewee would shed more light on the real Tiffany Gray.

Housekeeper Lori Jenkins was a petite brunette with a shy smile and a penchant for Beatles music. At any rate, that's what was playing on her laptop when Mrs. Nolan accompanied Michael and me to her living quarters.

Steps from the kitchen, Lori's apartment was a fraction the size of Tyler's and had patio doors that looked out onto the same landscape but at ground level. The place was neat and clean and had none of the knick-knacks or stuffed animals that other twenty-year-olds kept in their bedrooms or college dorms. A café table and two chairs, a hideaway couch, a crowded bookcase, and a TV on a stand took up most of the floor space. Off to the left was a fridge. A microwave on the counter next to it told me that she either ate store-bought meals or warmed up her share from Mrs. Nolan's menu of the day.

Lori's appearance was as neat as her apartment. She wore blue-tinted glasses with thin black frames and her hair was tied back in a ponytail. Her blue housekeeping dress was freshly pressed, and as she sat down, she held the hem at the back so she wouldn't crease it. Her slim legs looked lost in white running shoes weighed down by thick soles. Considering the mileage she had to cover in this house, I couldn't think of a better shoe for the task.

Michael and I shared the couch while Lori pulled up one of the kitchen chairs and placed it adjacent to us. During our initial chitchat, she told us how she'd considered herself lucky to get the job as live-in maid at the Gray mansion last year. Although she hadn't had much work experience, let alone as a maid, she'd needed the job to support her mother and two younger siblings. To her surprise, Tiffany had chosen her from among a dozen candidates.

"I was so nervous when I first started working here, but Tiffany—I mean—Mrs. Gray was wonderful," she said, smiling. "When you work for someone like that, you try to do more than what's asked, and that's what I did. I'm still surprised she hired me. I'll always be grateful for the opportunity."

"Will you be leaving or staying on here?" I asked her.

"I don't know," Lori said, gazing at the floor. "Maybe I should start looking for another job." At first I thought she was asking our advice on the matter, but then she addressed Michael. "Mrs. Nolan told me you were writing an article about Mrs. Gray's death. What would you like to know?"

"Tell me about your routine that Friday she died," Michael said.

"I was off work. I did my laundry and cleaned up my apartment."

"All day?"

She shook her head. "I went shopping in the afternoon."

"Was anyone else in the house when you left?"

"Mrs. Gray was the only one I saw."

"What was she doing?"

"She had placed a white vase on the kitchen counter. She was waiting for a delivery of roses to arrive." She blinked. "It was the last time I saw her alive."

"When did you get back?"

"Around three o'clock."

"Was anyone else in the house?"

Lori shrugged. "I don't know. I came in through the back entrance. That's where employees park their cars." She hesitated. "I saw Tyler out back as I drove up."

"What was he doing there?" Michael asked.

"I think he'd gone shopping because he was holding bags, and the trunk of his car was open."

"So you both walked into the house together?"

"No, I didn't wait for him. I went straight to my apartment."

"When did you find out about Tiffany's death?"

"When Mr. Gray came home. He found his wife in the kitchen and pounded on my door, yelling like a wounded animal."

"What did you do?"

"I followed him back to the kitchen. That's when I saw Mrs. Gray on the floor. I asked what had happened and he said she'd fainted. When she didn't come to after a minute or so, he called 911." Tears welled up in her eyes. She pulled out a tissue from her pocket. "I'm sorry. I still have a hard time believing she's gone." She dabbed at her eyes.

"Do you remember seeing any flowers in the kitchen?" Michael asked.

"Oh...I'd forgotten about the roses." Lori paused. "No. I guess Mrs. Gray must have taken care of them while I was out."

I stepped in. "Sounds like you two were close friends."

"We were." Her expression brightened. "She was like an older sister to me. She'd often knock at my door late at night. She'd bring me leftover cupcakes or biscuits from her fancy lunches with the rich women she invited here. We'd watch TV or chat for a bit."

"What did you talk about?"

"Her charity work...clothes...movies...that kind of stuff." She smiled.

"You confided in each other about personal things?"

"Sometimes."

"Like what?"

Lori looked away. "I promised I'd never tell anyone."

I took a chance. "It's okay. We have access to Tiffany's personal computer and her personal stuff."

"Oh." She gaped at me. "Her email too?"

I nodded. "We know she was communicating with someone regarding her family tree." Not an outright lie, and it might help us get the answers we needed.

She relaxed a little. "Mrs. Gray was trying to contact her relatives. She always had lots of people around her, but I think what she missed the most was her family. She told me there'd been a falling out lately...that she was trying to smooth things over."

"Did she mention any names?"

"No. Whenever she spoke about them, she never called them by name." She smiled. "She loved children. She would have given anything to have babies but couldn't. Physically, I mean."

At least I knew that much was true. I took a breath. It was now or never. "Did she ever mention she was seeing another man?"

Lori scowled at me. "Of course not."

"We heard she might have had a fling with Tyler."

She caught her breath. "Who told you that?"

"Tyler."

Her hand flew to her mouth. "Oh, my God. I'm not saying another word."

Michael leaned forward and clasped his hands. "Please, Lori. We need your help. We can't serve justice otherwise."

"Justice? What do you mean?" Fear filtered through her voice.

"There's a possibility that Tiffany might have been murdered. That's why we're here."

"Oh, no. Oh, my God, no." She folded her arms—a bad sign.

"Lori, listen to me," I said, keeping my voice soft. "Do you know anyone who would want Tiffany out of the way or wish her harm?"

She shook her head. "I don't want to get into any trouble."

"You won't. Whatever you tell us stays within these four walls." I waited.

Her eyes flitted around the room. She was probably debating whether or not she should trust us. She stared at my handbag. "Do you have a recorder hidden in there?"

"No, I don't." I opened it up to show her. "See?"

She nodded and let her hands slide to her lap.

I drew her back into the conversation. "Did Tiffany ever say how unhappy she was about her marriage to George?"

She stared at me. "Yes. How did you know?"

I shrugged, said nothing.

"Mrs. Gray cried a lot during our last visits. She said she wanted to leave but she needed money. She was looking for a way to provide for herself without help from anyone—especially Mr. Gray."

"Did she say why she wanted to leave him?"

"Yes, but I'll do better than tell you. I'll show you." She stood up. "Come with me."

Michael and I waited in the hallway outside Lori's apartment while she tiptoed to the kitchen to check on Mrs. Nolan. It seemed the older woman had a habit of dozing off once in a while.

Lori hurried back to us. "She's asleep at the table. There's an empty bottle of wine in front of her. We have a good hour before she wakes up. Come this way."

I cringed as we followed her upstairs. If anything, the recurring pain in my calves from my previous excursion up these steps was an incentive to start an exercise program.

We reached the third floor and followed Lori to a door at the far end of the hallway. She pulled out a small set of keys and unlocked it, then opened it wide. "This used to be Tiffany's bedroom."

I noticed she'd reverted to the more familiar name. "Tiffany's bedroom? Didn't she share a bedroom with George?"

"Not since the summer," Lori said. "Mr. Gray still occupies their joint bedroom. It's the next room over."

The first thing I noticed was the size of Tiffany's bedroom— slightly larger than Tyler's apartment. If size were based on personal status in this house, I'd have given anything to see the size of the bedroom she'd once shared with George.

The second thing I noticed was the four-poster queen size bed. The silver posts had been treated to appear antique and were capped with ornate finials that looked like crowns. The white silk brocade bedspread and mounds of white pillows contrasted against the backdrop of a fresco depicting a deep blue sky with white clouds. In keeping with the "girly" furnishings of Tiffany's private room down the hall, touches of blue and white dotted the room: the blue polka dot pillows on a white loveseat, the blue paisley vase in the corner next to it, the white linen shades bordered by silk damask curtains with a blue-on-blue floral print... Since it all flowed quite well, I assumed that an interior decorator had had a say in the décor and that Tiffany had tried to copy a similar theme in her private room. Another similarity between both rooms was that there were no photos of Tiffany or George or anyone else.

I turned to Lori. "What did you want to show us?"

She shut the door behind us and locked it. "Come over here." She walked over to the window and parted the curtains. "I wanted to show you the fountain."

Michael and I took turns peering out at a running fountain in the midst of a pond surrounded by a rock garden.

"What about it?" I looked at Lori who was standing next to me. I caught a side view of her eyes behind her glasses. One was brown and the other was blue. I hid my surprise.

"The fountain is a point of reference," she said, meeting my gaze.

"For what?"

"I'll show you." She crossed the room to another door and opened it.

Michael and I followed her into a walk-in closet that measured about fifteen feet by fifteen feet. Cubicles of shoes ran along the entire left wall. I did the math and counted at least two hundred pairs of dress shoes and sandals. Cubicles along the back wall displayed jewelry, scarves, and hats. Another cubicle held cameras, a pair of binoculars, and cell phones. On the right, glittery gowns, bejeweled jackets, short skirts, long tops, and sportswear of all colors hung neatly and were grouped according to occasion.

"Isn't it fabulous?" Lori smiled in a way that said she felt privileged to have access to such a private part of Tiffany's life. She went over to a top shelf and retrieved a floppy straw hat with a print scarf tied around the base. She ran a finger along the scarf and pulled out a USB flash drive. "This is one of the secrets Tiffany told me about. I hid it here."

"Weren't you afraid someone might find it?" I asked.

"Not anymore."

"What do you mean?"

"Days before Tiffany died, she went to a fund-raising event. She was gone most of the day. I was cleaning up on this floor and noticed the door to this room was slightly open. I peeked in. Mr. Gray and Tyler were going through it like madmen, undoing the bed covers and combing through everything in the closet. They didn't see me. I checked later and they'd put the room back in order. That's when I knew it would be safe to hide the flash drive in here again." She held it out to Michael. "You can have a look at it if you want."

He took it. "What's on it?"

"You'll see. Return it to me after you're done."

"Can't we load it onto your computer?"

She looked down. "Well...I'd rather you didn't."

I wondered about her hesitation but wrote it off to the fact we might have overstayed our welcome.

Michael didn't seem to have a problem. He slipped the flash drive into his jacket pocket. "I'll get it back to you ASAP."

Something still nagged at me. "Lori, why did you hide the flash drive here? Why not keep it in your apartment?"

"Someone's been going through my things," she said. "I think it's Tyler. I was afraid he'd find it."

"Why would you think it was Tyler?"

"He's the only other person besides Mr. Gray who has a full set of keys to this house. I wanted to have the lock to my apartment changed so I could have my own key. Tyler said I couldn't for security reasons."

I still thought the whole rummaging scenario was weird. "Why would you think he'd be searching for this particular flash drive anyway?"

Lori glanced away. "You'll see why later."

As we left Tiffany's room, I seized the moment to follow up

on another topic. "Lori, I was wondering about an order of flowers that was delivered here a week after Tiffany died."

"Oh, those would be the ones Mr. Gray told me to throw away."

"Why did he want to throw them away?"

"He didn't want any flowers in the house after Tiffany died. Painful memories, he said. He told me not to bother opening the box, just to throw them out." She shook her head. "I would have kept them for myself, but I was afraid Tyler would find out and make trouble for me. I felt bad about throwing out such beautiful roses."

"How did you know they were roses? Did you open the box?"

"No. I knew Mr. Gray sent Tiffany roses every Friday afternoon from Bianca's Gardens."

"What did you do with the roses?"

"I couldn't throw them away, so I donated them to the church."

I knew the answer but had to ask. "Which church?"

"St. Andrew's."

CHAPTER 23

A vague premise had been struggling to emerge from my subconscious during the short drive back from George's house. Absolute dread swept over me as it surfaced. "I got it! The roses Lori gave to the church were meant to kill George."

"What?" Michael unlocked the door to Bianca's house and we stepped inside.

My pulse picked up speed. "It's about the standing order for Tiffany. We were led to believe it was a clerical error...that the roses were delivered by mistake to her house a week after she died. But it wasn't a mistake. Someone's trying to kill George."

Michael frowned. "So now you're saying George is a victim as well as a suspect?"

What had once been a mishmash of scenarios was starting to fall into place. "I know it sounds absurd. Let me explain."

"Go for it."

I followed Michael into Victor's den. "A week after Tiffany died, George came to the shop to see Bianca. He told her he'd received a delivery that Friday—the usual standing order of roses for Tiffany. It was a mistake and should never have been sent out. Those were the same roses Lori gave to St. Andrew's Church. I'm sure they were poisoned."

"How can you be sure?"

"Doreen had something to do with that delivery. I can't prove it because Bianca's CDs were stolen or destroyed in the fire, and the transaction is on one of them. If my theory holds, Doreen is out to get George."

"We've discussed this theory before, Megan. What motive would Doreen have for killing George? If she's trying to blackmail him, she might need to keep him alive and breathing."

He was right. "Damn it. We keep going around in circles."

"In the meantime, let's take a look at the flash drive Lori gave us."

The moment Michael loaded the flash drive onto his computer, we understood why Lori had shown discomfort about viewing it in our presence. We also understood why Tyler had searched Lori's apartment. In fact, we understood a lot more than we needed to.

Taken with a zoom lens, photos of George and Tyler left little to the imagination. Scene after scene showed them running naked around the water fountain behind the Gray mansion.

From her private bedroom, Tiffany would have had a clear view of the escapade that took place that sunny summer afternoon. Anyone who happened to glance out a window facing the back of the mansion might have witnessed it too. I assumed that's what Mrs. Nolan meant when she said she kept her mouth shut about matters that didn't concern her.

I put myself in Tiffany's shoes and tried to imagine what might have been going through her mind when she snapped those shots. It was one thing to discover that your husband was having an affair, quite another to find out it was with another man.

My guess was that she'd arrived home from a luncheon or other event earlier than expected and discovered the two men's tryst by accident. Judging from their laughing faces and playful splashes in the photos, they might have attracted her attention with the noise they were making. She probably glanced through the curtains and spotted them. Maybe she wasn't quite certain who they were at first, those two men chasing each other around the pond, grabbing at each other in suggestive ways. Maybe she didn't want to know. Good sense guided her to pick up a pair of binoculars or use the zoom lens on her camera. It would have set straight any doubts she might have had about their identities.

The first pictures were blurred, probably because her hands

were unsteady. By the time she'd snapped the sixth photo, the pictures were sharper and more revealing. It must have taken a lot of determination to continue taking shots despite what she was witnessing through the lens, yet she persisted and took dozens of them.

I imagined how it might have played out if Tiffany had confronted George later. How had he explained his behavior? He couldn't have denied it, especially if she'd shown him the photos. Then again, maybe she hadn't shown him the photos. Maybe she'd kept them to herself—at least for a while. If it were true that she had no means of supporting herself, she might have decided to hide the photos, delay her threat, and live a marriage of deception until she could find a way out. If she truly loved George, she might have tried to save their marriage in spite of what she'd seen. Would she have asked if the incident had been a one-time spree brought on by a bout of mid-life crisis? Would she have probed further and asked if his relationship with Tyler was serious? His reply would have determined her next course of action.

On the other hand, maybe Tiffany had decided to end their marriage there and then, perhaps suggesting they divorce on friendly terms, but George had refused. Confronted with defeat, she'd threatened to use the photos as proof of his infidelity so she could get a divorce on grounds of adultery. George might have considered the humiliation that such a scandal would attract, not to mention the amount of alimony he'd have to pay out. In his straight-faced manner, he might have called her bluff, reminding her how she'd have to relinquish her lavish lifestyle if she chose to leave him.

Whether or not Tiffany had shown George the actual photos or mentioned she had them locked away is anyone's guess. At least she'd managed to keep a copy in a safe place. I imagined how George might have worried she'd ruin his reputation in the next moment. Maybe he had Tyler spread rumors about her indiscretions with him and other men. Tyler might have searched through Tiffany's computer files for the photos, but she'd already transferred them to the flash drive. Failing to find them, the two men searched her private bedroom as Lori said but came out empty-handed. Somehow they'd found out about Tiffany's secret visits to Lori's apartment, so they extended their search there. With no luck in finding the photos and fearing the worst, George panicked and made arrangements to get rid of his "problem."

"It's plain crazy," Michael said after I'd shared my potential theories with him.

"Which part?" I said, stretching my legs on the couch in Victor's den.

"For starters, we have no proof George was involved in Tiffany's death." He stood up from the desk and walked toward me.

"He was unfaithful."

He shrugged. "How does having an affair make someone a murderer?"

"Tiffany could have ruined George's reputation—and his life—just like that." I snapped my fingers. "He wouldn't have given her the chance to do it."

Michael glanced away, a tiny muscle pulsing along his jaw. He looked back at me. "Admit it. Seeing George behind bars would make this a win-win situation for you."

"Not true."

He stared at me. "Then work with me, not against me."

"I can see that helping you with this case was a mistake." I stood up and started to walk away.

"Megan, please." He put his hands on my shoulders and spoke softly. "I'm asking you to play fair. George isn't a punching bag for your pent-up feelings about Tom."

My eyes stung with pain. I felt the tears well up and fought them back. Maybe Michael was right. Maybe I was experiencing a hatred I hadn't yet resolved—a hatred that didn't belong here at all but one that had lingered from my life with Tom.

"It must be tough," I said, keeping my eyes downcast.

"What?"

"Being right all the time."

Michael held me close and whispered, "That was a low blow on my part. I'm sorry."

"No, I'm the one who's sorry."

"I don't want us to argue. We'll keep George in the picture if you want." He kissed me on the lips.

"Don't agree with me just because—"

"I'm not." He kissed me again.

My knees felt weak. Butterflies fluttered in my stomach. I was losing control. "If we keep this up, we won't get anything done."

His eyes twinkled. "We have the house all to ourselves for another hour."

"Well...if you put it that way."

Later that night, Michael and I looked over the information we'd accumulated on the three Portland deaths. We marked an index card for every piece of evidence we'd discovered and for each suspect and victim. Sitting side by side on the bedroom floor and framed by a semi-circle of index cards and crime scene photos, we reviewed the elements.

Michael kept his voice low so Bianca and Victor couldn't hear us. "Three murder victims linked by a common clue: flowers. The source of Tiffany's death: a fatal poisonous seed from Black Whispers." He picked up the card marked Black Whispers. "Our most important clue."

I picked up the cards marked George, Doreen, and Lee. "Our likely perpetrators."

Michael was still holding the card marked Black Whispers. "By the way, I sent Trudy an email earlier. I pressured her about getting the results from the analysis of Father Griffith's roses."

"That's asking a lot, isn't it? You dropped off the flowers forty-eight hours ago."

"She has contacts in forensic botany analysis. They'll get it done ASAP."

I scanned the cards. "Speaking of flowers, you can add a card for plastic tubes to the group. I don't see one here."

He scribbled Tubes on a blank index card. "Done."

I glanced at the card marked Bianca's Gardens. "We need

nothing short of a miracle to resolve this whole mess. Bianca is holding a Halloween costume party at the shop Friday evening. So far, almost everyone is going to show up."

There was a knock at our bedroom door.

Michael and I froze—but only for a second.

I scrambled to my feet.

Michael gathered the cards into a pile and placed them on the night table.

I opened the door a crack. It was Bianca.

"Hi," she said, giving me a shy smile. "I saw your light on. Could I offer you and Michael a cup of hot chocolate? I'm going downstairs to the kitchen."

"No, thanks, we're going to turn in soon," I said.

Michael was at my side. "Yeah, thanks anyway, Bianca."

"Okay, I'll see you in the morning," she said, then walked away.

I closed the door. "Do you think she heard us?" I whispered.

He shook his head.

Michael's phone rang and I jumped. He took the call. "Oh, hi, Trudy. No problem. I was up... Yes, I understand... Thanks. Good night." He turned to me with a dazed look on his face. "This is one for the books. Trudy received the forensic analysis of Father Griffith's flowers. The water in the vase contained microscopic bits of the Black Whispers seed." His brow puckered. "George would have been dead by now if he'd kept the roses for himself."

"I hope Lori never finds out the flowers she donated to St. Andrew's killed Father Griffith."

"Lucky for Mrs. Canto that she hadn't taken the tube off that last rose."

"But so unlucky for Father Griffith."

Michael paused in thought. "The bits of seed Trudy mentioned earlier. She didn't find a thing when she analyzed the flowers and plants seized from the Gray residence after Tiffany's death."

"The police didn't seize the vases containing the water. They left them in George's house."

"Doesn't matter. There was moisture on the stems or plant roots. Enough for seed bits to stick to them."

My thoughts went off on a tangent. "Maybe they forgot to bring some flowers in for analysis."

"Not a chance. Craig told me they were methodical."

"I have another theory, but you won't like it."

"Go for it."

"George ditched the poisonous flowers before the police arrived."

He shook his head. "No way. Why would he risk exposure?"

"The vapors would have dispersed by the time he walked into the house. He would have known how to protect himself with gloves and a breathing mask. He wouldn't have removed the plastic tubes from the rest of the stems, and he would have discarded the roses. He could have gotten rid of them before he knocked on Lori's door."

Michael studied me with increased interest. "Possible but hard to prove."

I had an idea. "Do you have Craig's photos? The ones taken right after Tiffany died?"

He reached for an envelope on the dresser and handed it to me.

I sat on the bed and flipped through the photos until I found what I was looking for. "Check out the foyer in this shot. Does anything strike you as odd?"

"An empty white vase. What about it?"

I spread out the other photos on the bed. "The shots taken right after her death showed flowers in each of these rooms." I spread out the photos on the floor to show him. "So why not in the foyer? After Tiffany collapsed, George threw out the roses and put the empty vase back there to avoid suspicion."

A grin spread across Michael's face. "It's a long shot. If George deliberately threw away the evidence and made sure no one would find it—"

"We have all the more reason to suspect him."

"And I've been a complete fool."

"If anything, you've been my inspiration." I leaned over and kissed him on the cheek.

"Thanks, but we're not done yet." He reached for the stack of index cards. "What's that expression about biting the hand that feeds you?"

"Whose hand are you referring to?"

"George's. He might be an unsuspecting target of his own undoing."

"How?"

"Let's say Doreen and Lee are involved in Tiffany's murder and are blackmailing him, but George refuses to pay up. He probably knows they're out to get him. That's why he asked Lori to throw out the roses that arrived from Bianca's Gardens a week after Tiffany died."

I was relieved that Michael was beginning to see George through my eyes, yet something nagged at me. "We've said it before. Why would they want to kill George? No George, no money." I yawned. I couldn't think straight anymore.

"Try revenge." Michael gathered the photos. "Let's call it a night. Oh...one more thing. Trudy is sending her research data to the police in twenty-four hours. They'll know as much as we do by then. It means we have to go to Plan B next." His eyes lit up in the same way they did every time he anticipated a new and exciting venture.

"Which is?"

"Getting inside Doreen and Lee's place."

"Oh, no. You're not getting me to break into their house."

"We've gone over every possible scenario we can think of. What we need is solid evidence."

"Michael, be reasonable. It could land us in jail."

A look of desperation crossed his face. "We're running out of time. We have to make a move tomorrow night. Those two scumbags will disappear as soon as George points a finger at them."

He was right—again. "I'll hate myself for this later. Okay, I'll do it. On one condition."

"What's that?"

"If I spot a single maggot, I'm out of there."

CHAPTER 24

With Kathy's return to the shop, Bianca had a full staff and decided I could come in whenever it suited me from now on. I wanted to discuss the newsletter article on superstitions with her, so I drove into town with Michael Wednesday morning.

I reached Bianca's office as she slammed the receiver down. "What's up?" I asked her.

She waved me in. "More bad news."

I shut the door behind me and sat down opposite her.

Her face was etched in worry lines. "The police seized George's documents from Victor's office."

"Did they say why?"

She shook her head. "They didn't have to. They had a search warrant. Victor had said it would happen. Who knows what the fallout will be once the word gets around. He could lose clients...or his entire business." Her face paled.

"The police could be looking for a lead in Tiffany's death."

"That's what Victor said. I have a hard time believing they'd find it in George's investment portfolio." She grimaced.

Her favorite client might be paying out blackmail money to Doreen and Lee, but I couldn't share that theory with her until I could prove it.

Bianca reached for a sheet on the desk. "We received thirty new replies to the Halloween invitations from customers who dropped by or left word with my girls by phone. How many had you counted the other day?"

"Fifty-five. So that's eighty-five so far. Pretty good."

She nodded.

"Did you have a chance to read my article on superstitions?"

"Yes, I did. It's fine." She glanced at her watch. "I'm sorry if I seem distracted. I promised Victor I'd meet him for lunch. He's so worried about what happened. Can you replace Doreen at the checkout counter when she goes for lunch?"

Thrown into the lion's den again. I dreaded sharing the same space with that girl. The memory of those squiggly critters still sent chills down my spine, and I'd be checking the floor whenever she was around. Knowing what heinous acts she was capable of carrying out threw me into a cold sweat. Try as I might, I couldn't think of a convenient excuse at the moment. "Sure," I said to Bianca.

"You can work in my office until then." She paused. "Oh, I almost forgot. You know how Doreen has been feeling under the weather lately? Well, the girls agree with me. She could be pregnant. Isn't that super?"

"Yeah...super."

Bianca grabbed her purse and left.

I spent the rest of the morning putting the finishing touches to the newsletter for Bianca's Gardens, including my article "A for African Violet" and its care instructions. I had enjoyed the change of pace, but I was eager to wrap up my visit and head back to Montreal. I missed my cozy condo and the view of Mount Royal from my living room window. I missed shopping at the busy downtown malls. I especially missed ghostwriting Michael's crime novels and other projects that Bradford Publishing sent my way.

As I promised Bianca, I went downstairs at noon. Doreen was wishing a customer a good day as she handed her a plant in the shop's trademark green bag. An image of maggots swirling at the bottom of it flashed through my mind. I blanked it out.

Doreen turned to face me. "Bianca said you're replacing me for lunch."

"That's right." I put my handbag in a cabinet.

"Good. I'm so hungry. I'm going to get Lee to bring me to the pizzeria down the street. I have this insatiable craving for pepperoni." She smiled as if we'd always been the best of friends, then sauntered toward the back of the shop.

I waited until she disappeared from view. I stepped up to the POS and clicked the Deliveries option on the screen. The schedule wasn't a busy one, which was lucky for Lee since he was working alone today.

Michael had to complete his second investigative article covering the interviews with George and his household staff, and George's parents. He was also working on the third article in the series, which would reveal the cause of Tiffany's death. An extended article linking all three mysterious deaths in Portland would be his grand finale.

The stillness in the shop distracted me. I looked around. I was alone on the floor. Since Doreen and Lee hadn't walked by the counter yet, I assumed they'd left for lunch by the back door. Gail had probably left for lunch too. I'd seen Joyce in the workroom earlier.

To ensure that no more poisonous roses would be shipped from Bianca's Gardens, I decided I'd verify the deliveries every day. I went through the items now, one by one. I stared in disbelief when I noticed a delivery scheduled for the Gray Climate Care offices across the street.

With a healthy dose of paranoia now integrated into my routine, I clicked on the customer file, then clicked on Special Instructions. I expected to find the name of a staff member, someone to whom George might be sending flowers to mark a birthday or other special occasion, but I found nothing. A rapid glance at the Products to be Delivered line caused my heart to skip a beat. It was an order for a dozen long-stemmed roses. I checked to see who had prepared the order. It was Bianca.

A red flag went up. Frantic, I scanned the floor. Joyce had since reappeared and was busy watering the plants at the far side of the floor. Gail was still at lunch. Bianca wasn't due back for at least another hour.

I took note of the phone number displayed on the screen and called Climate Care. When the receptionist answered, I told her I was calling to confirm a delivery of flowers to their office today. She put me on hold while she verified it.

Having learned my lesson, I hit the Print Screen button on the keyboard and printed off a copy of the information. To make double sure, I pulled a blank CD from a supply in a drawer and slid it into the POS slot. I saved the Deliveries section of the program, hoping I wouldn't mess up. I grabbed the sheet as it slid out of the printer, folded it, and tucked it and the CD into my jacket pocket. I closed the open windows on the screen and returned to the Main Menu.

Another woman from Climate Care came on the line—someone from purchasing. She confirmed that no deliveries were expected from our shop until Monday next week. Three pots of mums were on order for delivery that day.

I thanked her and hung up. What the hell was going on? I began to imagine the worst. I took a deep breath and focused. I picked up the phone and called Michael at home.

No answer.

I called his number at the *Herald*.

No answer.

No answer at his private number either.

My pulse was racing. I thought about rushing across the street, but I couldn't leave Joyce alone in the shop. Bianca insisted on having two employees on the floor at all times. I was about to defy her standards when an opportunity for action presented itself. Gail returned early from lunch and agreed to replace me at the checkout counter.

I took my handbag and hurried across the street to the Gray building. While I crossed the lobby to the elevators, I tried to reach Michael at the *Herald* again.

On the second ring, he answered.

"Thank goodness," I said. "Where were you?"

"In a meeting. What's up?"

"The shop delivered more roses to George. I don't have time to explain. Can you meet me in the lobby of his office building in five minutes?"

"Yes but—"

"And bring the car over," I added before hanging up.

I stepped into the elevator with eight other people. We stood facing the stainless steel doors like so many sardines crammed in a metal tin. I remembered the leather gloves in my pocket and slipped them on, then did some deep breathing to calm my nerves as the elevator ascended. It seemed to take forever to reach the fourth floor.

The doors finally opened and I got out. I turned left and opened a glass door that led to the reception area of Climate Care. Sitting on top of the receptionist's desk was a rectangular box. A red ribbon was wrapped around it, topped off with a red bow in the center.

My pulse quickened. I was positive it was the order of long-stemmed roses that Doreen had sent. I approached the receptionist, a woman in her early thirties with blonde hair that fell in waves to her shoulders. A Tiffany lookalike.

I introduced myself as Megan from Bianca's Gardens.

"Oh, I spoke with a woman there minutes ago," the young woman said, her dark lipstick enhancing a flawless porcelain complexion.

"You spoke with me," I said.

"Oh." Her lips formed a perfect red circle. "Well, the driver dropped these flowers off a minute ago. It must be a mistake because we didn't order them."

"Yes, I know. When I realized the error, I decided to come over and get them. I'm so sorry for the mix-up."

"I tried to tell the driver. He said that he couldn't possibly take the order back to the shop. Anyway, it's not a big deal. Mr. Gray is out of town today."

I wondered about her comment. On a whim, I glanced at the gift card on the front of the box. It read: *To George Gray with thanks. Bianca.*

"Please tell Mrs. Hobbs that we appreciate the gesture," the receptionist said in a soft voice. "Ever since Mr. Gray's wife died, he refuses delivery of any flowers sent to him personally."

I mumbled another apology and walked away, the box tucked under my arm. I stepped into the elevator and tried to make sense of it all. One thing I knew for certain: I had thwarted Doreen and Lee's plans to kill George Gray and whoever else might have been standing near him.

The box felt heavy in my arms. I shifted it a little, trying not to hit any of the passengers standing next to me. It still felt heavy. Did it contain more than roses? My imagination explored other possibilities. I envisioned a multitude of mucky maggots meandering their way among the soft red petals. As if that weren't gruesome enough, I realized that, should I happen to drop the box and spill its contents, the vapors of Black Whispers might do me in—along with everyone else in the elevator.

I could feel the sweat gathering along my forehead and upper lip. I held my breath, praying I wouldn't inhale any of the poison inside the box. In desperation, I tore my gaze from the potential catastrophe in my arms to the indicators that signaled what floor the elevator was on. Only the third? What was taking so long?

Getting stuck in small dark spaces was a phobia that originated from my childhood days. I'd locked myself in a cedar chest by accident once while playing a game of hide-and-go-seek in the attic. My mother had rescued me after my playmates had told her I'd vanished into thin air.

My claustrophobia was in full force now. I looked to my left, then to my right. People behind me. People in front of me. The elevator was filled to capacity. Like a recurring nightmare, the doors opened on almost every floor but no one got off. The doors kept opening and closing, opening and closing, until I thought I'd scream.

I didn't remember the rest of the ride down. When the elevator doors opened on the ground level, an invisible net seemed to pull me into the lobby with the others and force us to move as one. My legs felt stiff. I couldn't break away.

The crowd finally dispersed and cleared a path in front of me.

I saw Michael. His expression turned to one of unease the moment he spotted me. His stare dropped down to the oblong box in my arms. I could always tell when he gets worried. Tiny furrows form along his brow and his blue eyes lose their sparkle.

"I parked the car in the back," he said. "Let's use the side exit. It's less risky." His words spilled out slow and tranquil, like snowflakes falling from the sky on a windless day.

With his hand on my arm, he guided me out a door and into the parking lot. Even though I was putting one foot in front of the other, I had the sensation that I was floating and that my feet weren't touching the ground.

I suddenly became aware that we were sitting in the car. I was no longer clutching the box of flowers in my arms.

I panicked. "Where are the flowers?" I turned to look at the back seat. It was empty.

"They're in the trunk," Michael said.

"They're poisonous. We have to get out of here!" I reached for the door handle.

He grabbed my arm. "It's okay. The vials are still intact. I checked."

"You checked? Are you crazy? You could have been killed."

He studied me. "You're pale." He reached for a satchel on the back seat and pulled out a stainless steel flask. A pungent smell escaped when he uncapped it. "Here. Take a swig of this." He held it out to me.

I took a small gulp. Brandy burned its way down my throat. I coughed, returned the bottle to him. "Michael, this is so scary. I don't remember getting here. What happened?"

"I think you suffered an anxiety attack. Maybe a bout of temporary amnesia."

It explained a few things. As I began to relax, the recollection of recent activities filtered back. I filled in the gaps for Michael, including what I'd discovered from the receptionist.

"So you decided to save the day without me."

"I had no choice. Things were happening too fast."

"You're damn lucky you didn't run into Doreen or Lee in the lobby." His words were stern, yet his gaze was caring.

"Tell me about it. What are we going to do with the flowers?"

"I'm taking no chances. I'll hand them over to the attorney at the *Herald*. He can ask Trudy to forward them to forensics. If the roses turn out to be poisonous, they can tag them as evidence for our court date."

"They should check for fingerprints on the box, if only for documentation purposes. I'm sure they'll find those belonging to Doreen or Lee." I lifted my gloved hands.

"Right."

"It's getting risky," I said. "Maybe we should tell the police what we know."

"Not yet. Let's wait until we put Plan B into motion." He grinned. "Then we can work out a deal with George."

CHAPTER 25

"We're going to get caught if we hang around here any longer. What if Doreen and Lee come back early?" I held the pocket flashlight as steady as I could—difficult to do while shivering in the cold night air.

"Don't worry." Michael continued to work the lock pick. "Lee told me they go to a Wednesday evening double feature every week. He won't leave until he gets his money's worth."

I looked past the neglected hedge behind the trailer home. Moonlight shone on bales of hay dotting the farmland in an adjacent lot. It explained where Doreen might have acquired the stuffing for the scarecrow she'd sold to Mrs. Vanderwyk. If any part of the hay had held humidity, it would have been the perfect breeding ground for mold—and maggots.

"Hold the flashlight level, Megan. I need a few more seconds."

My mind flashed back to the photo of Black Whispers that Trudy had sent Michael. He'd since confirmed that it matched the tattoo on Lee's lower back and felt confident we'd find the flower or its seeds in the couple's trailer home. An antidote for Black Whispers would have made me feel much more secure right now, but try telling that to an investigative reporter determined to find evidence—no matter what the risks.

I wasn't too keen on endangering my life to prove he was right. Any reason to call it quits would have suited me fine. "Isn't it illegal to use a lock pick?"

He chuckled. "I won't tell if you don't."

"What if a neighbor sees us trying to break in?"

"Don't worry. The next house is miles away from here."

He was right. I'd seen nothing but trees and meadows along the narrow road we'd taken to get here. We'd parked the car on gravel behind the trailer and out of sight. Not a difficult feat since the trailer was partially hidden by clusters of tall shrubs.

There was a clicking noise.

"We're in," Michael said. He handed me the lock pick. "Can you take this please? I have gloves in my pocket and don't want to put it in there."

"Won't you need it later?"

"No."

I dropped it into my handbag and handed him the flashlight.

He took it and opened the back door.

A stale odor wafted our way—something putrid and past its expiration date. Fighting the urge to run back to the car, I covered my mouth with a gloved hand instead and followed Michael inside.

He shut the door behind us and shone the flashlight over two tattered sofas and a floor lamp. "We could do with a bit more light." As he walked over to the lamp, there was a rustling of paper under his feet. "What the hell—" He switched on the lamp.

The faint light revealed layers of newspapers covering the floor. The sheets looked as if they'd been glued down. From the sepia tinge on them, I figured they'd been in place for months, maybe longer. I supposed it was one way to recycle newspapers.

As my eyes became accustomed to the dimness, I noticed tufts of green stuff—like grass—scattered over the newspapers. Probably the remnants of the scarecrow Doreen had put together for Bianca's shop—the one with the maggots in it.

I shook off a yucky feeling and glanced around. I noticed a gigantic flat panel TV on the wall. "Not bad for someone who works two part-time jobs."

Michael followed my gaze to the TV. "Maybe I'm in the wrong business."

"Makes two of us."

Aside from the TV, a wood coffee table scratched beyond repair and a faded painting hanging lopsided on a wall didn't make the place any more hospitable. Since the trailer wasn't large enough to hold a bed, I assumed Doreen and Lee slept on the sofas.

Half a dozen cardboard boxes were stacked against a wall. I opened one of them. I reached in and pulled out a cutoff T-shirt. "Ugh. This smells like Lee." I threw it back in.

The trail of newspapers wove a path to the kitchen where Michael was standing. Even in the dim light, I could tell that the eating area was no larger than two bathtubs side by side. I noticed a light switch on the wall and flipped it on, but it didn't work.

I looked around. Hanging from the window frame above the sink was a potted plant with dried-up leaves. Moonlight glistened on a spider web that extended from the base of the pot to the top of the frame. Piles of dishes filled the sink and tiny counter space. On the floor next to the kitchen sink was a large garbage bag. It wasn't closed up with a fastener and probably accounted for the horrible smell in the place. Needless to say, I wasn't tempted to look inside it.

The side drawers beneath the counters drew me closer. I opened the top drawer. It was filled with plastic tubes—the same type Bianca used at the shop. "Well, this explains our shortage of inventory." I caught Michael's eye and pointed to the contents.

He nodded, then shone his flashlight on a mound of clothes in a corner. He pushed the clothes aside to reveal a white mini refrigerator. "Can you hold the flashlight for a sec?" I held it while he slipped on a pair of plastic gloves he'd tucked into his pockets earlier. He opened the refrigerator door.

I peered over his shoulder and did an inventory count. Six beer cans and a piece of pizza on a paper plate. "I guess they eat out a lot."

He opened the door to the freezer section and slammed it shut before I could see what was inside. "I spotted a glass jar of something black in there."

"Black Whispers!"

"Yes. They're in a deep freeze, so we're safe." He looked down the narrow corridor. "Let's go see what's back there. Pass me the flashlight, please." I handed it to him. He edged past me, took a few steps and stopped, shining the flashlight to the right of him. "The bathroom."

I peeked inside. The white sink and tub were smudged with black marks. The mirror above the sink was so grimy, it was a wonder anyone could see a reflection in it. The washed out linoleum curled in along the base of the walls to reveal deep cracks. Cracks that allowed the right of way to anything that might happen to slither in from outdoors.

I felt nauseous. I took a step backwards and heard a squishing sound under the weight of my suede hikers.

Michael heard it too. "Don't move."

"Are you kidding?"

"I'll check it out."

He bent down. "Raise your right foot a little." He aimed the flashlight at my foot, then gazed up at me and grinned.

"What is it?" In truth, I didn't want to know if my life depended on it.

He looked down again and chuckled.

"Tell me, damn it. Is it alive?" My voice had a tiny shriek to it.

"Not any more. Neither one of them."

"I'm going to throw up." I raced to the back door and flung it open. I rushed down the steps and bent over, preparing to empty my guts. The fresh air seemed to help and the feeling passed.

From the doorway, Michael asked, "Are you okay?"

I glanced over my shoulder at him. "I'm not going back in there."

"Okay. Wait for me here. I won't be long." He went back inside and shut the door.

I walked around the lot, rubbing my boots on patches of grass here and there. As I neared the corner, a glimmer of light caught my eye. I peered through a bush and was surprised to see a gray sedan parked across the road. A man was sitting in the front seat, but I couldn't tell if he was looking in my direction or staring ahead.

I hurried back inside. I left the door open to counteract the stench inside. "Michael, I think we're under police surveillance." I told him about the sedan. "What if they arrest us?"

"Did anyone see you?"

"I don't think so. I was standing behind a bush and it's dark out."

"Then don't worry." He finished wrapping an object in newspaper.

"What's in there?"

"Trust me, you don't want to know." From inside his jacket, he produced a clear plastic bag. He slid the newspaper and its contents into the bag and sealed it shut.

My heart was pounding. "Please don't tell me you took the Black Whispers from the freezer."

"I didn't take the Black Whispers from the freezer."

"For heaven's sake, Michael, what's in there?"

The edges of his mouth curled up in a smile and his eyes twinkled, as if he'd done something very, very bad. "It's not what you think. I found a couple of CDs." He tucked the package inside his jacket.

"CDs? As in music CDs?"

"No, as in information storage CDs."

"The ones that disappeared from Bianca's shop?"

"We'll find out soon enough."

"Doreen's not dumb. She'll realize the CDs are missing."

"In this mess? I doubt it." He walked over to the lamp and switched if off. "Let's go. We're done here."

While Michael locked the back door on his way out, I peeked around the corner through the bushes. The sedan was still parked across the street. All of a sudden, the driver started the engine and drove off.

"That's lucky," I said to Michael as he came up to me. "He left."

"It was probably the police casing the place. He took off when he saw the lights go out."

"Maybe he thought we were Doreen and Lee. After all, we were in their house."

"Could be. Let's go."

Michael looked both ways before edging the car onto the road. "The coast is clear. No undercover cops around."

"Do you think George finally told them about his two blackmailers?"

"If so, we just ran out of time."

Later that night, Michael brought his laptop into the privacy of our bedroom so he could check the CDs he'd taken from Doreen's trailer. A first glance confirmed they were from Bianca's Gardens. The name of the shop appeared at the top of every page in the files. Details included customer names, addresses, phone numbers, purchase records, and delivery schedules. Of particular interest was the information Doreen had tried to cover up, such as the delivery to Mrs. Spencer and the one to George's house a week after Tiffany died.

"Why would Doreen want to hang on to these CDs? It's proof that she altered the shop records." I looked at Michael.

"Trophies," he said. "Some criminals like to collect memories of their deeds from crime scenes."

"Too bad we can't tell Bianca."

"We can't take the chance. If she accuses Doreen of theft, she'll bolt. We need to make sure she doesn't leave town before we reel in a bigger fish."

"So we're all set for tomorrow night?"

"You bet."

Michael and I realized our plan wasn't perfect. If we were going to succeed, it had to be a team effort. The success of our ruse depended on the ability of other players to carry out their roles with credibility. If they couldn't pull it off, we didn't stand a chance at nabbing the killers.

With Jeff back at the *Herald* from his out-of-town assignment, it only took a few calls on Thursday to set things in motion and get everyone on board. We agreed to meet in the evening to finalize the plan.

At seven o'clock, Michael and I met up with Jeff at a coffee shop north of town. He introduced us to Craig and Liz, the two people who had played a pivotal role in providing evidence linked to

Tiffany's death.

"You don't have to worry about trusting these two," Jeff said, indicating Craig and Liz. "Craig and I have known each other for years. He takes fantastic shots of crime scenes, but his true passion is working as a lighting assistant in the theater." He chuckled.

"More like the other way around," Craig said, smiling, his black shirt and pants adding an air of professionalism to his reputation.

Jeff went on. "And Liz, well, she's my girlfriend. She deals with dead people, so she doesn't talk much." He turned to smile at her. "When she's not busy in the lab, she works as a makeup artist, making people beautiful—like her."

Liz smiled and tilted her head in his direction, accentuating the red highlights in her hair. "Jeff thinks my work in forensics is boring. I keep telling him that dead people often speak louder than living ones do."

"Don't I know it," Jeff said to us. "I just came back from covering a kidnapping and murder court case in Augusta. The offender had taken pains to cover his tracks, but forensics managed to find traces of his DNA on the victim. Case closed."

Our chat changed direction when Michael stepped in and reviewed the agenda for the evening. "If everyone is okay with this, let's hit the road."

We arrived in full photo fashion at the Gray mansion at eight o'clock. Jeff had borrowed the van from the *Herald* to add credibility to our visit. Liz guarded her metal cosmetic box as if it contained precious cargo. Craig toted a camera around his neck.

It took a while to set things up but the team was organized. Everyone pitched in to move aside pieces of furniture in George's living room—the same room that Michael and I had sat in days ago. The men transported video equipment, lights, and other apparatus into the house. Craig set up the electrical and ran tests to make sure everything was functioning properly. Liz placed her makeup on a table by George's armchair and opened it up. I sat with pen and clipboard in hand, pretending to go over a list of questions for the interview.

All the while, Tyler stood surveying the operation, his biceps at the ready in case anyone wandered off to other areas of the house. I kept wondering how he could have lied so easily about sleeping with Tiffany. I figured George must be paying him well in exchange for his loyalty.

Jeff broke my concentration. "Okay, we're ready. Stand by, everyone."

Tyler left us to go get George. I began to have doubts about beating a pro like George at his own game. After all, wasn't this the same man who might have murdered his wife and managed to evade police scrutiny so far? The same man who had thwarted Doreen and Lee's efforts to poison him? The same man who made us believe he was an innocent victim?

My pulse accelerated. My palms grew sweaty. My throat tightened up. Michael noticed my nervousness and strolled over. He put his hands on my shoulders, then whispered in my ear, "It's going to work without a hitch. Pretend you're in a play."

And what a play it was going to be—with George cast in the leading role.

Ten more minutes went by before George made his grand entrance with Tyler steps behind him.

"Good evening, everyone." George lingered in the doorway, posing in a brown cardigan, corduroy pants, and tan loafers, then walked toward our little group as if he had something important to say. "Michael, if this photo shoot hadn't been for such a good cause, I'd never have consented to it. I'm an extremely busy man, you know." His eyes flitted over the equipment and the crew's attentive faces. "However, your offer to pose for a calendar of Portland's most prominent entrepreneurs made it impossible to refuse." He smiled at us, his ease in front of cameras only surpassed by his egotism.

"The Sisters of Silent Hope will appreciate the financial support this shoot generates," Michael said to him, keeping a straight face.

Jeff stepped into the act. "Excuse me, George. We need to do makeup and test the lighting. Would you like to take a seat here, please?" He indicated the armchair.

After Liz had applied makeup to George's face and neck, and Craig had adjusted the lighting, we were ready to initiate the next phase of our plan.

On cue, Liz began to complain about the drabness of the setting. "I don't know, Craig. I think the background needs color—something red." She glanced around the room.

"No way," Craig said. "It would distract from the subject."

Their arguments were more convincing than I could have anticipated. Liz pointed out the benefits of adding color, while Craig kept looking through the eye of the camera, claiming the set was fine the way it was.

A nod from Michael was my cue to cut in and do my share.

"Wait," I said. "I have a solution." I reached into a dark plastic bag I'd conveniently placed close at hand. "I told the staff at Bianca's Gardens that we were doing a photo shoot with you, George. One of the girls handed me this box of long-stemmed roses and said to make sure to give it to you." I pulled out a rectangular gift box. A red ribbon was wrapped around it. "You don't have to move. I'll open the box for you." I began to untie the red bow.

George bolted upright. "No, don't open it." He jumped to his feet and extended his palms outward.

"Why not?" I asked George. "Red roses are exactly what we need."

"Yes, they would be perfect," Liz said.

"No. You don't know what you're doing." George's eyes opened wide with fear.

Tyler rushed toward me but stopped when I removed the lid from the box. I took out one of the red roses. "What's the big deal, George? It's only a rose." I extended it toward him.

George backed away and stepped over wiring, almost tripping as he rushed out of the room.

"Don't any of you dare move." Tyler pointed a finger at us, then hurried out after George.

"Did you get it all?" Michael whispered to Craig.

"Every last bit," Craig said.

"Good. Keep the camera rolling."

Tyler returned moments later. "I'm afraid Mr. Gray won't be able to complete the session tonight. He's had a bit of a shock. With his wife's recent passing and—"

"Give me a break, Tyler," Michael said in a firm voice. "A deal is a deal. You go tell George to come and finish the shoot right now unless he wants to risk a lawsuit."

Tyler stared at him. "What?"

"You heard me. Tell George to come here. Now."

We held our collective breaths.

Tyler hesitated for a moment, then left the room.

Before long, we heard voices in the foyer. Tyler walked in with George.

"You're sure you're okay to do this?" Tyler peered at him.

"Yes, yes, I'm fine." George waved him away. "My apologies, Michael. Please, let's finish the shoot." He moved to the chair he'd occupied before and sat down.

"There's no photo shoot, George," Michael said. "We're going to have a serious discussion instead."

Tyler shifted his weight, but George's raised hand rooted him to the spot. "A discussion? About what?"

"About how your wife was poisoned," Michael said.

George nodded. "The police informed me this morning."

"Come clean, George. You knew long before then."

"Not at all." His expression remained deadpan. "The tests they performed on the flowers and plants they seized from my home had come up negative."

"Including the roses your wife received that Friday she died?" I asked him.

"I would assume so."

I called his bluff. "George, the same people are trying to poison you and you know it. That's why you ran out of here when you saw the roses."

"I already told you. The police warned me about the poison. Wouldn't you have done the same thing?"

Michael and I held back from disclosing how we'd retrieved an order of long-stemmed roses from his office. We hadn't received the report from forensics on it yet.

George's eyes narrowed. "By the way, that was a spiteful trick you all played on me."

Michael ignored him. "You asked me to share what I learned about your wife's death and I did. Now I know who's responsible and so do you. I won't mention any names. You shouldn't either for obvious reasons."

George's eyes flitted over us. "Then send your crew away."

"They're sworn to secrecy." Michael glanced at Tyler. "What about him?"

"Tyler assists me with business and household matters," George said. "You can talk freely in front of him."

Tyler crossed his arms and smiled at us, a smug expression on his face.

There's nothing like having a silent witness. Good thing the camera was still recording.

"We know that certain people are trying to set you up for your wife's death," Michael said to George. "They're also blackmailing you, aren't they?"

I saw the color drain from George's face, even through the thick layers of makeup.

Tyler stepped closer. "George, you don't have to answer. I'll get rid of—"

George raised a hand. "It's okay, Tyler." He looked at Michael. "I'll tell you what happened. Those two leeches came begging for money weeks ago. They wanted ten grand." He shook his head. "When I refused, they threatened to reveal ugly details about Tiffany's past. At first I thought the whole thing was ludicrous. A couple of small-time losers trying to squeeze lunch money from..." He tightened his lips. "I didn't want any trouble. I especially didn't want to risk ruining my excellent family name and my business reputation. So I arranged for Tyler to give them the cash and keep them quiet."

Tyler clenched his fists. "I'd have taken care of them in my own way, but you refused."

George stared at him. "Violence isn't the answer to everything, Tyler." He focused on Michael. "Days after Tiffany died, they came back and demanded more money—lots more. They said they'd frame me for her murder if I didn't pay up."

"If you're innocent, they can't pin her murder on you," Michael said.

I held back from saying something nasty. I sensed that Michael was working his peculiar strategy—one that I'd learned to respect even though it clashed with my logic.

George shook his head. "It doesn't matter if I'm innocent. Look what they did to Tiffany. They're ruthless. If I don't hand over the money, do you think they'll go away? They'll hunt me down and kill me."

I marveled at how easily George could twist the facts so that he appeared to be the victim and not the perpetrator behind Tiffany's murder. He was prepared for whatever we'd thrown his way so far. But we were one step ahead of him and the best was yet to come.

"Did you tell the police about your blackmailers?" I asked George.

He waved a hand in the air. "I tried to steer the investigators in the right direction. And what did those fools do? They brought in the wrong people for questioning."

"Bianca and Victor went through hell because of you," I said, finding a release for the resentment I harbored against him.

Compassion filled his eyes. "I truly regret that incident. They're both fine people. It's hard to trust anyone these days. People are after my money at every turn. I've had to revise my will faster than the ink dries."

Tyler's jaw tightened up and he briefly glanced away.

"Let's back up here," Michael said. "Why haven't you told the police about your blackmailers."

"I couldn't."

"Why not?"

"I had no proof."

"It didn't stop you from going to Augusta to try to find it."

George blinked. He was no doubt puzzled about how we'd managed to track his steps to the Dales' house and maybe even more confused about what Michael was insinuating. "I was trying to get to the truth. A lot of good it did me. Those bloodsuckers came back for more."

"In that case, you won't mind helping us."

"How?"

"By handing them over to the police."

George eased himself out of the chair. I thought he was going to ask us to leave, but then he said, "You weaseled your way into my home with this charade of an interview. You're obviously quite capable of delving into people's lives without their knowledge. Why would you need my help?"

"For starters, I don't see how you're going get out of this mess without us," Michael said.

"What more can I do? I told you I have no proof."

"That's the difference between you and me, George. I have evidence that links those scumbags to Tiffany's death."

"You do? What kind of evidence?"

"Sorry." Michael shrugged. "That's part of our deal. If you agree to help us, I'll make sure you're on the scene when the police arrest them."

The look of relief on George's face was unmistakable this time. "Fine. I'll do whatever it takes."

CHAPTER 26

"What am I going to do with these girls this morning? All they have on their minds is the Halloween party." Bianca nodded toward Gail, Doreen, and Joyce who were watering the plants. They were chatting about the event and emitting excited squeals from time to time.

"Can you blame them? Half the town is going to show up here tonight." I helped Bianca place white pumpkin shells containing orange roses, Gerbera daisies, sunflowers, and berries on a nearby table. They were the centerpieces for the pedestal tables the caterers would supply later.

She sighed. "There's so much to do. The decorators and caterers are coming this afternoon. I have to make sure things are set up properly. There are always last-minute details to take care of. Outstanding orders have to be prepared for pick-up and—"

"Relax. It's only nine-thirty. We'll get it done. Focus on tonight. It's going to be the event of the year."

The sound of approaching sirens diverted my attention. I gazed out the window as an ambulance came to a stop in front of the office building down the street. Two attendants unloaded a stretcher from the back of the vehicle and wheeled it into the building.

"I hope it's not serious," Joyce said. She walked over to the window to get a better look.

Gail came up behind her. "When an ambulance drives up, it's usually serious. I hope it's not someone we know."

I kept an eye on Doreen. She joined the two girls in surveying the scene. She didn't say a word, but the expression on her face was almost cheerful.

"Look," Joyce said, pointing. "People are gathering in front of the building."

"Bianca, is it okay if I go check it out?" Gail asked.

"You have exactly one minute." Bianca raised a forefinger in the air.

Gail rushed out and sprinted across the street, disappearing into the crowd. Bianca and I joined the others by the window.

Moments later, the attendants wheeled someone out and loaded him into the ambulance.

"Oh, darn, we can't see who it is," Joyce said. "Too many people."

The crowd began to disperse. Gail resurfaced and raced across the street toward the store.

"Here comes Gail," Doreen said. "Maybe she knows."

The door swung open and Gail rushed in, a troubled expression on her face. "Hey, guys, you won't believe this." She paused to catch her breath. "The man they took away on the stretcher? It was George Gray."

Bianca grew pale. "Are you sure?"

"I couldn't see him—too many people," Gail said. "I overheard some women talking. I think they worked for George. One of them said he collapsed minutes before a boardroom meeting. The other woman said she called the ambulance. I think she was his secretary. She was crying and said the attendants couldn't revive George."

"They say that when a couple is truly in love," Joyce said, "the death of one spouse brings on the death of the other. Poor George must have died from a broken heart."

"I don't know about that," Doreen said, a smirk crossing her face. "He might have heart problems, but I doubt it had anything to do with Tiffany. How could he have loved someone who was such a bitch?"

"That's a cruel thing to say," Bianca said, frowning at her.

"Sometimes the truth hurts." Doreen raised her chin.

Bianca kept her eyes on Doreen, and I could tell she was counting to ten. "We don't know for sure what happened to George," she said, infusing the usual dose of diplomacy into the conversation. "He could have had a stroke or a heart attack and survived it. Let's not jump to conclusions."

Doreen shrugged. "Whatever."

Before anyone else could add to the conversation, the chimes rang and a customer walked in. Joyce approached the young woman and asked if she could help her.

Doreen and Gail started to walk away, but Bianca called out to them. "Doreen, I'd like you to follow up on this week's purchases with customer appreciation calls when you're not busy. Gail, make sure today's orders are up to date and ready to go. Okay, girls?" They nodded and headed toward the counter. Bianca drew me aside and whispered, "I have to call Victor. He needs to know about George." She retreated upstairs to her office.

I had to make a call too. I waited a minute, then hurried upstairs to the washroom. I locked the door and pulled out my phone. I'd tucked it in my jacket pocket earlier. I hit the speed button for Michael's number at the *Herald*. When he answered, I whispered, "The ambulance just left."

"Okay. Stay tuned." He hung up.

I stopped by Bianca's office to see how she was doing.

She was crying and waved me in. "Close the door, Megan. I don't want the girls to see me like this." She threw away a tissue and reached for a fresh one. "I left a message for Victor to call the hospital and check on George's status." She dabbed at her eyes.

"But Bianca, Victor's not next-of-kin," I said. "They won't give him any information."

"He can try, can't he?" Her tone was abrupt. "Sorry, Megan. I can't believe what happened to George. He's such a wonderful man." She peered through the open blinds. "Oh, look. Kathy and Sarah walked in."

I watched as Doreen wandered up to them. It was obvious she was relaying the news about George to them. The blissful messenger of death. I winced as Kathy's eyes went wide and Sarah put a hand to her mouth.

"Those poor dears," Bianca said, her eyes brimming with fresh tears. "How am I supposed to throw a party when something like this happens?"

"Victor's coming to the party, right?" I asked, thinking he'd be here to comfort her.

"No. He's going to pick up Alex from day care later and stay home with him. He's not in a party mood these days." She looked at me. "What if George dies? Oh, my God. What's going to happen to Victor and me?"

"You said we shouldn't jump to conclusions...that George might be okay. He could be suffering from work-related stress. It's a known fact that corporate types devote their lives to their work."

Bianca dropped the tissues into a wastebasket. "You're right. For all we know, George could be okay. Let's go downstairs before I get emotional again. I have to keep busy."

Customers had begun to trickle in looking for last-minute gifts or seasonal items on sale. While Bianca checked the list of new orders she'd printed off the POS, I processed sales transactions at the counter. Joyce, Gail, and Kathy began to fill the orders for delivery in the workroom. Doreen and Sarah tended to the customers.

At one point, Joyce hurried over to Bianca and me, her face flushed. "I'm afraid I have bad news for you, dear," she said to Bianca. "A local radio station just reported that George Gray was dead."

Bianca began to cry as soon as the words registered. "Oh, my God, no." She reached for a tissue under the counter and wiped her eyes. "It can't be."

"I'm so sorry, dear," Joyce said. "I know you and your husband were close to George." Her eyes grew teary.

Bianca nodded. "Do the other girls know yet?"

Joyce shook her head. "Not everyone. Doreen and Sarah are serving customers."

"As soon as they're done, ask everyone to come to my office." She glanced at me. "I have to call Victor." She hurried upstairs.

I stayed at the front counter while the staff assembled for a meeting. I wished I could tell Bianca that things weren't what they appeared to be, but I was sworn to secrecy. In addition to secrecy, deception was an integral part of the ploy Michael and I had put together with the cooperation of the police and the media. It was vital in seeing our plans to completion. If all went well, we'd snare whoever was responsible for the recent murders in this town.

The girls returned to work fifteen minutes later, their eyes red and puffy. They went on with their tasks, though signs of any earlier enthusiasm had since vanished.

The exception was Doreen, who let out nervous giggles at anything a customer said, whether it was funny or sad. I wondered if her unstable behavior was a sign she was losing her mind. Maybe the guilty feelings she'd subdued until now were forcing their way out. If so, her timing was perfect.

Bianca left to run errands at noon, and I stepped out to pick up a coffee. On my return, Doreen was on the phone at the front counter. She had her back to me. I quietly opened the door, making the least amount of noise. When she didn't turn around, I assumed she was too engrossed in her conversation to pay attention to the sound of the door chimes.

"What do you mean, someone from our shop picked them up?" Doreen was saying. "That delivery was intended for Mr. Gray personally."

I froze.

"A mistake? She did?"

Damn it. Doreen was onto me. She'd made a customer appreciation call and found out I'd intercepted the delivery of roses to George's office.

Okay. Don't panic. On to the next round. If I could keep one step ahead of her, I might be able to beat her at the mind games she so loved to play.

I turned around and opened the door a bit, then shut it hard.

The noise drew Doreen's attention this time. She turned around, looking puzzled then surprised, but covered it up in the next moment. "Please accept our sympathies on your recent loss," she said, then hung up.

A fresh wave of paranoia kicked in. She was staring at me. I strolled by with as blank an expression I could muster and headed for the stairs. With each step I took, I felt her eyes burning into my back. A side-glance in her direction confirmed it. She turned and pretended to be busy on the POS.

Or maybe she was.

I rushed into Bianca's office. I sat down at the desk and accessed the Main Menu on the computer to check up on Doreen's latest maneuver. My fingers flew as I hit the buttons to open up the Deliveries window for Wednesday. The list of customers appeared. I scanned it once, twice to be sure. The delivery of roses to George's office had been deleted.

This cat-and-mouse game was Doreen's way of damaging my credibility. No matter. If she believed her vanishing computer entries would make me look like a liar in Bianca's eyes, she had a huge surprise coming her way. The CD in my handbag contained proof of her conniving handiwork, and I couldn't wait to make things right.

I peered downstairs through the parted blinds. Doreen was on the phone again. She had her back to me and was waving her free hand in the air in an animated conversation. I was positive she was alerting Lee about how I'd intervened in their plot to do away with George. No doubt they were as mystified about George's death as anyone else, wondering if their plan had succeeded in some bizarre twist of fate despite my meddling.

It didn't matter. I was a marked woman from this moment on.

Michael wanted to stay close to the action about to unfold, so he came in to help with deliveries at the shop. Before he began his afternoon shift, he went to console Bianca in her office.

When he came downstairs minutes later, he whispered to me, "I feel bad about lying to her. She'll never forgive me when she finds out the truth."

"Yes, she will," I whispered back. "Once she understands why."

"I'd better go out back and load the deliveries." He kissed me on the cheek and walked away.

I helped the girls carry last-minute orders to the back. It was two o'clock by the time Michael and Lee loaded the final one into the van. As Michael settled in the passenger seat, he winked at me, his way of reassuring me that everything was going to be okay.

Concern about Michael's safety hung in my mind, and I hoped that the afternoon would fly by. Luckily the customers I served were of the desperate variety—desperate to find a last-minute gift for a dinner party; desperate to buy a bouquet for a wedding anniversary; desperate to get the perfect flowers for that special first date... These buyers accepted my suggestions without hesitation. No wishy-washy indecision on their part about the color or cost of the gift. "Hurry up and wrap it" was their mantra.

I'd finished serving a customer when I caught a glimpse of Lee emerging from the back of the shop at the end of the delivery run. I expected to see Michael walk in behind him, but Lee was alone. He went up to Doreen and whispered in her ear. They shared a laugh before he strolled out the front door, not even glancing my way.

I figured Michael might have walked in earlier and I'd missed him. On the hunch that he might be washing up in the workroom, I went over there to check it out. No sign of him.

The loading area was next. Maybe he'd stayed behind to sweep away the debris there. He'd told me how lazy Lee was about cleaning up and how he'd taken it upon himself to do it. But Michael wasn't there either.

I opened the back door. Our Nissan was still parked in the alley, so he hadn't driven off to the *Herald* or anywhere else.

The second floor was my final option. Again, there was no sign of him anywhere.

The door to Bianca's office was open. She was sitting at her desk, gazing at the computer screen.

"Michael didn't come back with Lee," I said to her from the doorway. "Do you know where he is?"

She looked at me. "Did you check the loading area?"

"I checked everywhere. He's not in the shop."

"Did you ask Lee?"

"He left. I'll ask Doreen. Maybe she knows something."

I found Doreen in the workroom. She was wiping the table.

"Do you know where Michael is?" I asked, trying to control the panic building inside me.

She kept her eyes on her work. "Lee said Michael went home to get a clean shirt for the party."

"Oh...okay...thanks."

I walked away, convinced it was a lie. Michael had packed a change of clothes in the trunk of the car before leaving Bianca's house this morning. What's more, the car was still parked out back.

I checked my messages in case I'd missed his call. Nothing. I felt sick to my stomach. Something was terribly wrong. Michael wouldn't have detoured from our plan without telling me. Not in a zillion years.

I looked around. In the aftermath of a hectic afternoon, stuffed animals, miniature vases, and wicker baskets were in disarray on the tables and shelves. To ease my nerves, I set about putting things in order. It was short-lived.

The arrival of the decorating team did nothing but create more turmoil. Bianca's staff had to help move flowerpots, trees, and tables out of the way so the decorators could work their magic. Two decorators mounted ladders to suspend a black cobweb and occupying spider the size of anyone's worst nightmares over the center of the floor. They hung legions of skeletons, bats, and ghosts on the walls. A third decorator set up a dozen pedestal tables here and there under Bianca's direction and covered them with black linens. The finishing touch was the shop's signature white pumpkin centerpiece on each table.

We didn't have time to catch our collective breaths before the caterers walked in. Food servers placed trays of canapés on the workroom table. Bartenders brought in pop, beer, and the ingredients required for a huge bowl of punch.

After things settled down somewhat, I slipped away. In the confines of the washroom, I called Michael. There was no answer. I tried his office number at the *Herald*. When I got his voice message, I hung up. There was nothing left to do but wait and hope that he'd show up.

It was almost closing time when the last customer left the

shop. One by one, the staff had gone upstairs to change into their Halloween costumes. One by one, they now paraded back downstairs.

I liked Gail's cheerleader outfit and wished I'd thought of it first. A large white "G" sewn onto the front of a red sweater, a pleated white skirt, white bobby socks, a set of red-and-white pom-poms, and her hair in a ponytail took me back to my high school days.

Sarah's white bunny get-up was adorable—floppy ears and fluffy tail included.

The Mrs. Santa Claus outfit was appropriate for Joyce, considering she already had the required eyeglasses, gray hair, and plump figure.

Long-limbed Kathy in a French Maid uniform elicited friendly teasing from the others.

My appearance in a short white angel outfit, complete with hair sparkles and two-foot-high gossamer wings, also encouraged playful remarks.

"I didn't know angels were allowed to live in sin," Gail said, laughing.

I blamed Bianca. When she'd insisted she could rent one for almost nothing at a local party store, I'd left it up to her to choose my outfit. I inevitably had to supplement the delicate layers of fabric with a camisole and a pair of white tights. The white ballet flats were a given. I'd choose my own outfit the next time.

The last one to change into her costume was Doreen. We watched as she slowly made her way down in layers of cut-off skirts, strings of colored beads, and huge gold hoop earrings.

"Oh, Doreen," Joyce said. "You make a splendid gypsy."

Doreen smiled. "Thank you." She walked toward a display of day-old flowers and stuck one in her hair. "Now it's complete."

I checked my watch. It was five o'clock and still no sign of Michael. Or Lee.

Bianca hung a sign inside the door pane that read: *Private Party. By Invitation Only.* Decked out in a black cape, pointy wide-brimmed hat, and green face makeup, she joined me at the POS as I slipped a backup CD in place to copy the day's entries.

"Party time," Doreen and Gail echoed. They unrolled the blinds from the tops of the tall windows and let them cascade to the floor. The caterers placed trays of finger foods on the front counter over black linens. The bartender carried in a red cocktail punch and set up a temporary bar on the counter too.

Doreen clicked a button on a remote panel by the stairs. Halloween music blared through the speakers. She played with the dimmer until the low lighting gave the shop an eerie atmosphere.

Kathy and Sarah peeked through the blinds to see if any guests were approaching. I joined them, thinking I might catch a glimpse of Michael on his way back to the shop. Instead I noticed a gray sedan parked across the street. It was the same one I'd seen across the road from Doreen and Lee's trailer.

"It's now or never," Bianca said as she joined me.

"What's now or never?" I looked at her.

"The success of this party." She sighed. "It's too bad George won't be here to enjoy it."

"Whatever you do, don't cry. You'll ruin your green face."

She nodded and managed a smile. "I'll be fine."

The first guests entered the shop—Little Red Riding Hood and the Big Bad Wolf. Bianca walked over to welcome them. Soon Sarah, Gail, and Joyce were helping Bianca greet the incoming stream of partygoers wearing colorful disguises.

As the inward flow of patrons filled the standing-room-only space, uneasiness grew inside me. Where the hell was Michael? He should have been here by now to put the last phase of our plan in motion.

I maintained my stance near the stairs, a location that afforded a view of the people walking in. From time to time, I glanced at Doreen. She seemed comfortable enough, considering that Lee hadn't reappeared yet either. I surveyed her as she chatted with a customer dressed as a knight. As he drifted off, I approached her. "It's turning out to be a great party, isn't it?" I yelled over the boom of the music.

"Yes," she said. "Aren't the costumes marvelous?" She gazed at a group dressed up as the Addams Family.

I nodded. "By the way, where's Lee?"

"He'll be here soon." Her eyes displayed no emotion. "No sign of Michael yet?"

"No."

"Oh, they probably went out for a couple of beers together. You know how guys are when they get together." She laughed that hearty, rolling laugh of hers.

The hair on my arms rose up. *Michael hates beer.*

I pretended to buy into her feeble explanation, all the while searching for an excuse to get away. I got my chance when the next wave of guests headed our way and grabbed Doreen's attention. I slipped upstairs. If Michael was in danger, I had no choice. I had to break the code of silence.

Behind the closed door of Bianca's office, I retrieved my phone from the handbag I'd stored in her desk and called Jeff at the paper. To my surprise, he picked up.

"No, I don't know where Michael is," he said in response to my question. "I've been waiting for his call. We're all set to go at this end."

"I'm beginning to worry. It's not like Michael to be elusive."

There was an audible sigh at the other end of the line. "He might be in trouble."

My stomach felt queasy. "Has anyone seen him at the paper?"

"I'll call the newsroom. He might be there. Call me back in five."

In the meantime, I slid into a chair by the window and tugged on the slender cord to open up the blinds a crack. I hadn't turned on the light in the office, so I knew no one could see me. The view below was a cacophony of color and sound, with guests merging in lively costumes and bursts of loud conversation surging between blasts of music.

I scanned the floor, hoping Michael had slipped in while I was talking to Jeff. My eyes swept across the crowds, this time more slowly. Michael hadn't planned on wearing a Halloween costume, so I skipped over the ones in disguise.

He wasn't there.

I called Jeff back. He told me he'd reached several newsroom desks, but no one had seen or heard from Michael.

"Something's happened to him," I said. "I can feel it. When did you last hear from him?"

"A couple of hours ago," Jeff said.

"What did he say?"

"That he was on his last delivery run."

"That's all?"

"He said he had met the newspaper deadline and was looking forward to the Halloween party. He hoped they had some good beer on ice at the party."

"Good beer on ice? Are you sure that's what he said?"

"Word for word. Why?"

"It's a clue as to where Michael is. To begin with, he doesn't like beer. Second, I think he was trying to tell you that he's somewhere cold." Then it hit me. "I know where Michael is. We have to help him. He's in serious trouble."

CHAPTER 27

From my perch at the top of the stairs, I spotted Doreen chatting with Bianca on the left side of the floor. Doreen was gesturing wildly, lost in the frenzy of their conversation. I was glad for the diversion and hoped I'd get out the front door unseen.

I made my way downstairs, passing a ballerina in a pink tutu, a hefty cop wearing a convincing uniform, and a man in a doctor's white lab coat, a stethoscope hanging from his neck. At the foot of the stairs, a mosaic of shapes and colors formed a barrier between the exit point and me. I felt as if my angel wings had abruptly expanded and used my elbows to tuck them in, clasping my handbag in both hands. I squeezed around an elf, two fairies, and a pair of Ghostbusters without leaving behind any part of my angel wings. As I reached the door, a tall customer disguised as an ice cream cone walked in and held the door open for me. I stepped outside into the drizzle.

So far, so good. No one had seen me leave. No one, that is, except for the two figures in the gray sedan parked across the street. Although a mist covered the car windows, I could definitely make out two men sitting in the front seat.

I walked to the corner and hailed a taxi. It came to a jerky halt, which didn't surprise me. My angelic getup, with its glittery wings and layers of white chiffon flowing in the wind, would have stopped a bull in its tracks. I tucked my angel wings behind me, got into the back seat, and gave the driver the address.

Fifteen minutes later, I could see my destination from the

highway. The Gray Climate Care warehouse loomed in the distance, its white exterior panels lit up under the glow of security spotlights placed strategically around the premises.

We had driven off the highway onto a two-lane road when a van sped around the corner in front of us, its headlights blinding us as it slid into our lane.

"Holy crap!" The taxi driver veered the car to the right, barely missing the van. "Where the hell did that guy come from?"

As the van whizzed by us, gravel hit the windows like pellets from a BB gun. I looked out the back window. A street lamp shed enough light for me to read "Bianca's Gardens" on the rear door of the van. It had to be Lee.

The taxi driver studied me in the rearview mirror. "You sure you got the right address, Miss? This is a commercial district. And damn dangerous from the looks of it."

"It's okay," I said to the driver. "I'm meeting someone. Please take the next right."

The driver soon pulled onto the grounds of Climate Care. As we approached the front entrance, I saw Jeff's news van. He flashed his headlights twice as promised. I paid the driver his fare, tucked my wings, and got out.

As the taxi coasted away, Jeff stepped out of his van and smiled at me. "You're a vision from heaven."

I smiled back. "Have you been waiting long?"

"A few minutes."

"Did you happen to see a van drive away from here?"

"Tell me about it. The guy drove off like a maniac right after we got here. I couldn't see who was driving, but I think there were two people in the van. Our guest said he didn't see a thing from where he was sitting." He gestured toward the van, then opened the sliding door.

The seat was tilted back. All I saw of him was a pair of jeans and leather loafers. "Hi, George," I said. "What does it feel like to be resurrected from the dead?"

"I'll tell you once the evening is over," he said. "Could someone please tell me what we're doing here? I thought we were supposed to be at Bianca's Halloween party."

"Change of plans," Jeff said. "We had to make a pit stop here first." He waved him out. "Let's go."

"I'd rather wait here, if you don't mind," George said.

"Forget it," Jeff said. "We need you to get us inside this place."

George stayed put. "A private security company patrols here every evening. If I bump into the guard dressed like this, I'll be the laughing stock of the city."

"Think about where you'd be now if we hadn't staged that ambulance pickup," I said to him. "Maybe we should have left you to your own devices, battling off poisonous flowers and heaven knows what else. Good thing Jeff kept you safe."

"If you call staying in a sleazy motel room safe," George said, not budging. "Tyler must be frantic with worry by now. We should have let him in on our plan."

He was wearing me down. "We've been over this before, George. It's about secrecy. That's why we sent Craig and Liz home last night and excused Tyler while we discussed our plan in your soundproof den."

George said nothing.

"Don't you want to check your warehouse?" Jeff asked him. "That van we saw could have taken off with loads of stolen supplies tonight."

"My insurance will cover it."

"Not if you don't report it ASAP. I'm sure the security cameras on the grounds have already relayed the—"

"Fine." George stepped out of the van. His red-and-white striped T-shirt, matching cap, and black eyeglass frames stood out against the pasty makeup Liz had applied to his face earlier.

Jeff noticed my jaw drop. "It was tough to find a disguise we could throw together at the last minute."

I thought it was an excellent choice on Jeff's part, but I didn't say anything in front of George. At least "Waldo" would stand out in the crowd later on. Right now, we had more serious problems to contend with. "Let's go inside," I said. "We're wasting precious time."

George pulled a set of keys from his jeans and unlocked the front door to the building. We followed him inside where he walked up to the keypad on the wall and entered a security code to turn off the alarm system. After he'd unlocked a set of glass doors, we gained access to the lobby and followed him past the receptionist's station to a steel door at the rear. Once again, he entered a security code onto the keypad by the door.

"Does the code unlock the door and deactivate the alarm system too?" I asked George.

"Yes," he said.

Jeff pulled open the door and we followed George inside.

Florescent tubing overhead lit a concrete corridor that stretched the width of the building and seemed to go on forever in either direction. Built into the wall opposite us was a sizeable metal door identified by a large number 1 painted in black on it. Likewise, numbers 2 and 3 identified the metal doors built into the walls at the far left and right of us respectively.

I suddenly felt as if I'd fallen down the rabbit hole into Wonderland. "What's behind these three doors?" I asked George.

"Three separate warehouse units," he said. "One is cold storage space for clients. Another contains freezer and cooler inventory. The third is a truck bay."

"What about that one?" I pointed to a narrower door off to the side.

"That's the old basement elevator. No one uses it anymore."

"Which of these doors leads to Michael? Number 1, 2, or 3?"

George shrugged. "How would I know? I already told Jeff I had no part in whatever he thinks happened here."

"That has yet to be proven," Jeff said to him.

George's expression remained fixed. As a rule, I'm skeptical of people who don't show what they're feeling or don't say what they're thinking. They put up a protective wall so no one can see their true persona. George's makeup did contribute to his deadpan expression, but the thick black frames of his Waldo disguise made it even more difficult to figure out what was going through his head.

Even so, I refused to accept his excuse. "Lee gained access

to *your* building, so it's *your* problem. If something happened to Michael, I'll hold you criminally responsible."

"And I'll tell the police you kidnapped me and brought me here against my will," he said, raising his voice.

"Nice try, George," Jeff said. "Now give us your best guess. Where's Michael?"

"Maybe in here." George moved toward door number 1 and hit a switch on the wall. "The lights," he said, by way of explanation. He fumbled with his set of keys, trying one after another in the lock, but to no avail.

"Don't you know which key it is?" Jeff asked him.

"My foreman usually marks up the keys. This is a spare set. It hasn't been marked." He fingered several large keys. "It's one of these three keys, but I'm not sure which—"

"Hurry up and pick one," Jeff said.

George chose one and held it out to him.

Jeff tried the key. The lock gave and he pulled open the bulky door. A blast of cold damp air hit us. "You first," he said to George.

George didn't budge. "It's twenty below zero in the warehouse. I'll freeze to death."

"No, you won't." Jeff grabbed him by the arm and escorted him inside.

I was about to join them when a thought occurred to me. Still holding the door open, I asked, "George, can we open this door from the inside without a key?"

He turned to face me, and I noticed that his glasses had fogged up. He lifted them and looked at me. "Yes. There's an exit bar on the inside of every metal door in this complex."

I turned around. Sure enough, there it was. I let the door close behind me and followed them into a cold air vestibule.

Ice crystals had formed on the walls and floor, making our trek across the room treacherous. If Jeff hadn't been holding him by the arm, George would have landed on his backside on the wet and slippery floor. We proceeded through a strip door—transparent strips that act as an air flow barrier between the interior cold air of the warehouse and the exterior warm air. The strips fell back into place once we moved through them, but I wasn't prepared for what awaited us on the other side.

A blast of frigid air took my breath away as we entered a freezer warehouse the size of two hockey rinks. Bright lights shone overhead. Steel pallets of frozen food products were piled four levels high, except for the docking area at the rear where trucks loaded and unloaded the goods. Adding to the frostiness in the air was metal everywhere I looked: walls, ceiling, heavy-duty shelving...

I shuddered involuntarily. I couldn't help thinking that Michael could be hurt or tied up somewhere in this freezing warehouse. Otherwise, he would have made it to the door and walked out on his own.

On closer inspection, I noticed that the containers on the pallets held frozen meat, fish, and poultry products. Others held ice cream and an assortment of frozen dairy products. "There are so many nooks and crannies in here," I said. "Michael could be injured and stuck behind or between any of these racks."

"We'd better start looking," Jeff said.

"Oh no...not me," George said, shivering, his arms wrapped around his chest. "You're on your own from now on." He started to walk away.

"Wait." Jeff took off his jacket, revealing a thick sweater underneath. "Put this on. Please, George. We need your help."

Whether it was Jeff's pleading or the offer of instant warmth that convinced him, George did an about-face. "Fine." He slipped into the jacket.

"Is the area behind door number 2 as big as this one?" I asked George.

"No, it's half the size," he said.

"What's in there?"

"Freezers...cooling units..."

"Are they operational?"

"I don't know. My foreman handles those matters."

In addition to losing sensation in my fingers and toes, I was losing patience with George. I glared at him. "Take a wild guess."

He shrugged. "Some units might be operational for showcase

purposes."

"Michael could be freezing to death inside one of them." I was bordering on hysterics. I had to stay in control. I turned to Jeff. "There's only one way we can reach him in time. We'll have to split up. I'll go take a look behind door 2 while you and George start searching in here."

"Okay," Jeff said, handing me the set of keys. "Whoever finds Michael has to alert the others."

"I'll call you," I said.

He shook his head. "Those devices might not work with all the metal in this place. Come tell me in person if you find him." He pointed a finger at George. "Stay close. If you so much as think about running off, no one will ever be able to find Waldo again. You get my drift?"

I rushed out to try my luck with the keys. My wings flapping, I ran down the corridor to the far end until I reached door number 2. Remembering the interior lights, I found a switch on the exterior wall and flipped it on. I fingered the keys and chose the three largest ones. I got lucky with the second one and the door clicked open. I made sure there was an exit bar inside the door before I shut it behind me.

Similar to the first area, brightness flooded the premises. Like George had said, this second storage area was a lot smaller. It held dozens of freezers and coolers, but it wasn't as cold as the other one. Taking up three-quarters of the floor space were walk-in coolers of the sort Bianca used to store delicate flowers in her shop. There were ice cream freezers, beverage walk-in coolers, bakery showcases, and other refrigeration units. Stainless steel sink bowls, food pans, trolleys, racks, and other inventory items were displayed along the right-hand wall. I decided to start at the farthest point on the left and work my way back.

I called out Michael's name five or six times as I walked along, but all I heard was the humming of the florescent beams overhead. It didn't mean anything. Maybe he was gagged or drugged and unable to reply. I tried to block out the notion that the worst had happened to him.

My first target was a walk-in freezer—the type butchers use to store meat products in supermarkets. The door was ajar, which meant it wasn't operating. I looked inside anyway. It was empty.

I moved on to a chest freezer. I prayed Michael wouldn't be in there. I lifted the lid. It was empty and not operational.

I dashed past a row of upright storage freezers with glass doors. Empty. I peered into three stainless steel refrigerators. Empty.

Next up was another chest freezer. I lifted the lid. A blast of icy air hit me. As George had mentioned, certain freezers in the warehouse were operational and contained frozen food products to showcase them to clients. This one was filled to the top but that didn't stop me. I threw the products on the floor—George be damned—and emptied the freezer to the halfway mark until I was sure there wouldn't be room in there for a body.

I moved on to other freezers, repeating my routine, all the while hating myself for thinking that Michael might be inside one of these units. I stopped. What the hell was the matter with me? I should give him more credit than that. He'd have used brains if not brawn to protect himself if the situation had become desperate. This fact alone renewed my hope for a positive outcome.

But with each subsequent unit I verified, my optimism at finding Michael waned. I listened attentively as I raced from freezer to freezer, expecting to hear Jeff or George open the door and call out at any moment to say they'd found him. No such luck.

All hope vanished by the time I reached the last chest freezer. It had a padlock on it. I looked around for something to jam against it, then remembered the lock pick that Michael had given me after we'd broken into Doreen's trailer. I dug it out from the bottom of my handbag. It took a bit of maneuvering before the lock clicked open. I held my breath and flung open the door. It was empty except for a paper identifying the serial number and model number of the unit.

Where in this frozen hell was Michael?

My eyes scoured the floor. I'd covered every square foot of the place. I hoped Jeff had had more luck. I hurried out and turned off the lights, letting the door slam shut behind me.

I sprinted down the corridor, catching sight of the elevator doors as I whizzed by. I stopped. What if…

George had said no one used the old elevator anymore, but it didn't mean it wasn't functional. I pressed the button on the wall. It lit up. I could hear the elevator making its way upward.

The doors parted with a screech and I stepped inside. It measured about a foot wider and deeper than a standard residential elevator and had a familiar musty smell to it. Like Lee.

I pressed the button marked B. The doors closed with another screech, and the elevator groaned and rocked its way downward. The mechanism probably hadn't been greased in a while. I scanned the safety inspection document pasted on a wall. The last inspection had been performed ten years earlier. Small consolation.

The elevator came to a rough stop. I waited. Seconds passed and the doors didn't open. As much as I tried to talk myself out of it now, panic set in and a cold sweat came over me. I regretted I hadn't told Jeff about my plan to ride the elevator. Worse, I contemplated whether or not the air supply would dwindle before he'd figure out where I was and send the firefighters to rescue me.

Not too soon, the doors opened. I breathed a sigh of relief and dashed out, snagging one of my wings in the process. A tug on it produced a ripping sound. I glanced back over my shoulder to see a small piece of white fabric hanging from the edge of the elevator door. I didn't care. I was free.

The air was stuffy yet frigid. It reminded me of my grandma's unfinished basement in the winter. A thick layer of dust covered the concrete floor and felt slippery underfoot. A dim light bulb hung several feet above me, illuminating dust particles in the air. Above it were countless spider webs that had snagged flies and other insects. I moved away in case some of those creepy crawlies might fall on me. I checked the passageway on my right and left but couldn't see beyond twenty feet in either direction.

Ahead of me were two doors: a red one and a blue one. I used the hem of my angel costume to wipe away the cobwebs from the doorknob, then I opened the red door. I felt something scurry between my feet. I jumped. I turned to see a mouse run into the elevator and prayed it would be gone by the time I had to leave.

I strained into the darkness of the tiny room. Brooms, rags, and plastic containers littered the floor of what had once been a stockroom for cleaning products. From the amount of dust covering the items, I'd say no one had used them in years.

I moved on to the blue door and went through the same wiping routine, though this doorknob had less cobwebs on it. I tried the handle but it wouldn't budge. It was a push-button lock—the easiest to break into. I looked around. I needed something thin yet strong. Then I recalled the paperclip from Christina's notes that I'd thrown into my handbag. I found it, straightened it out, and inserted it into the lock. I wiggled it around. The lock gave.

I opened the door. This room was twice the size of the other and as filthy but so much colder. I peered into the shadows. Something shiny rested on the floor in front of me. I couldn't quite make out what it was. I stuck my head back out and searched for a light switch on both sides of the door. There weren't any. I was about to let go of the door to search for a light switch inside the room when I caught myself. I checked the inside of the door. There was no safety handle. This was the last room I'd want to get stuck in.

I took off my left shoe and wedged it under the door to prevent it from closing. The thought of putting my foot down on mouse feces or dead insects grossed me out, so I hopped over to the wall on the left and groped for a switch. I moved in a sweeping motion across the wall and up and down, through layers of spider webs and heaven knew what else. I did the same thing on the right-hand side. I was thoroughly disgusted and would have stopped searching if it hadn't been for the memory that Michael had once sacrificed so much for me.

But I couldn't find the damn switch.

I remembered my smartphone. I took it out of my handbag. The low light it emanated allowed me to see, albeit a short distance. I hopped forward and approached the shiny thing on the floor. I aimed the light at it. It was a hypodermic needle!

I kicked it away with my foot. It rolled off toward the wall on my right.

I aimed my phone and managed to shed a faint light on pieces of floorboard, wallboard, ceramic tile, and plastic garbage bags in the corner of the room. No sign of Michael. "Damn it. Where are you, Michael?"

I put my phone in my handbag and was about to leave when I heard a sound. I thought my imagination was playing tricks on me, but then I heard it again. My stomach churned. It was a low moan and came from the pile of debris in the corner.

I dropped my handbag and darted there with both feet on the ground. I yanked off the garbage bags, the pieces of floorboard and wallboard...

There, in a huddle, was Michael. He was gagged. His hands and feet were bound.

I pulled down the rag around his mouth and called out his name. He didn't answer. I held his wrist and checked for a pulse. It was faint. I took hold of his ankles and began to pull him toward the door. The dust on the floor provided a downy base, but I could only haul him inches with every heave. I thought about running off to get the others, but my instincts told me otherwise.

Was it getting darker in the room? I glanced over my shoulder and realized the door was slowly sliding to a close.

Fear shot through me. I gently released my hold on Michael and reached the door just before it shut. I wedged my shoe under it again, this time with a lot more force. I was certain the door wouldn't budge. I was equally certain I'd never wear these shoes again after tonight.

On my way back to Michael, my foot hit a small object on the floor. I knew it couldn't have been the needle—I'd kicked it away. I retrieved my phone and guided the light over the floor, moving side to side.

Then I saw it. A tube like the type Bianca's Gardens uses with its long-stemmed roses. Inside it was a tiny black seed in a bit of ice!

I clasped Michael's legs and heaved him out into the passageway in two seconds flat. I took a deep breath and hauled him several feet further. I snatched my handbag and shoe and slammed the door shut. I collapsed on the floor next to Michael, gasping for air, thankful that the temperature in the room had remained cold enough to prevent the ice from melting before I'd reached him.

I looked down at Michael. I needed something to cut through the plastic ties around his hands and feet. I headed for the storeroom. I kicked aside a mop and pail and rummaged through dirty utensils. I managed to find a pair of old scissors. They were tarnished but proved to be adequate for the job.

I sat next to Michael and cradled his head in my arms. His face was pale, but his lips still had a bit of color in them. I suspected he'd been drugged. Fear gripped me, fastening my stomach in knots. I couldn't bear to lose him—not so soon after Tom's death.

Tears streamed down my face. I bent over and kissed him on the lips. "Michael, please don't leave me." I wrapped my arms around him and rubbed his shoulders and neck. Then I rubbed his hands and legs.

He stirred and opened his eyes. "Megan?"

"Michael! Thank goodness, you're okay."

He winced. "Not quite." His hand went to his head. "Damn him."

"Who?"

He tried to sit up. "Lee."

"What happened?"

"We had a delivery here...a surprise birthday gift."

"Some surprise." I told him about Lee and the van from Bianca's Gardens that almost hit the taxi earlier.

"Something was off...I called Jeff...he read between the lines."

"For the record, I'm the one who figured out where you were."

He squinted as he focused on my costume. "How about that? An angel of love to the rescue." He smiled, then flinched in pain again. "Killer of a headache...feeling drowsy too."

"I saw a needle back there. I think you were drugged. How did you get into the building?"

"Lee had keys...the docking door at the rear. I followed him in... felt a stab in my arm...passed out."

"Lee must have dragged you into that room." I gestured toward the blue door.

"Not Lee. Big guy in a black cape...pointy ears."

"Yeah, right." He was still under the effects of the drug.

"A mega payoff...have to leave town now."

More gibberish. "Okay, Michael, you think you can make it to the elevator?" I reached for my handbag and stood up.

"No problem." He put a hand against the wall and rose to his feet but wavered.

I slid under his right arm, offering my shoulder for support, and guided him into the elevator.

"I'm starting to like this," he said, smiling.

We rode up to the ground floor. I helped him step out and propped him against the wall in the corridor. "I'll go tell Jeff and George that you're safe. I'll be right back. Don't move."

"Count on it." He rubbed his temples.

I noticed that all three metal doors in the corridor were shut. Rather than waste time trying the keys in the locks, I pounded my fists on each door and waited. There was no answer.

I rushed back to Michael. "They must have left the building. How are you doing?"

"The feeling's coming back in my legs, but this headache..." He frowned.

"Fresh air might do you good. Can you walk?"

"I'll have to."

I offered my shoulder for support. "Let's go."

A car from Safety Security Company was parked next to Jeff's van. A guard in a brown uniform stood conversing with Jeff and George. His eyes shifted to Michael and me, and he approached us. "What's going on here? A private Halloween party?"

George followed on his heels. "These people are my clients."

The guard shook his head in disbelief. "Let me see if I've got this right before I call the cops. We have the owner of a company who's disguised as Waldo trying to convince me that his clients all happened to be here tonight to look over some freezers. Including an angel." He glanced at me, then pointed to Jeff's van. "And we have the media covering the event too."

"If you don't believe us, it's your problem," Jeff said. He flung open the door of his van. "Everybody in. Last call."

I bounded into the passenger seat. George and Michael scrambled into the back. As Jeff hopped into the driver's side, the guard hurried to his car to radio for help.

I gripped the armrests as our van raced out of the lot.

While we sped toward town, Michael brought George and Jeff up to date on what had happened at the warehouse but left out the gibberish. The fresh air had helped clear his mind.

Minutes later, Jeff dropped us off in front of Bianca's Gardens. "I'll park the van and catch up with you guys soon."

I remembered the gray sedan and checked to see if it was still parked across the street. It wasn't, which disturbed me even more.

Michael looked at George. "You know what you have to do, right?"

George nodded. "Of course." He held a glass jar in his hands.

"Okay, let's go." Michael led us inside.

The Halloween costume party was in full swing. Spirited patrons had discarded their masks and were dancing to the booming beat of Halloween pop music. Trays of canapés had been moved to make room for two zealous female dancers in white boots and fringed "go-go" outfits from the 60s.

I scanned the crowd for a trace of Doreen or Lee. Michael spotted them first. He signaled their location on the right at the back of the floor.

As we'd planned, I moved to the left and went up the stairs. At the remote panel, I switched off the music and turned on the lights.

All movement below came to a halt and was followed by bursts of protests.

Doreen was the first to see Michael. She stared, not quite certain if it were Michael or not. Her face flushed red at the moment of recognition. Keeping her eyes on him, she nudged Lee hard, causing him to spill beer on his T-shirt.

Lee followed her gaze. His face stiffened as he caught sight of Michael standing several feet in front of him.

Bianca caught my eye, annoyance spreading across her face. She left her spot by the counter and edged her way past customers to where I was standing. "What's going on? Why did you stop the music? You're ruining my party."

"Please, Bianca, you have to trust me on this one," I said. "Just a few more seconds."

"Ladies and gentlemen," Michael said in a loud voice, then introduced himself. "I apologize for the intrusion."

A collective hush fell over the crowd.

Michael went on. "I'm here this evening to reveal those responsible for the recent murders in this city."

Expressions of surprise filled the air.

The front door opened and Jeff walked in, but there was no sign of the police yet. Every moment counted.

Michael stretched out his arm and pointed in Lee's direction. "Lee, good of you to show up. Considering you left me for dead in George Gray's warehouse."

Gasps from the crowd. People in Michael's line of sight moved out of the way, offering him a direct view of Lee.

Doreen's face was flushed. She clasped a hand over her mouth. I thought she was going to vomit.

Lee's fists were clenched and his eyes riveted into Michael, intensifying the odds he'd pounce on him at any moment. "You're drunk," he said, his lips contorting in a sneer. "You don't know what you're talking about."

"I have a surprise for you—no—two surprises." Michael stepped aside for the patron in the familiar red-and-white striped shirt to come forward.

George smiled as he held his precious cargo behind his back.

Doreen smiled back. "What kind of game is this, Michael? Do you want us to guess who your friend Waldo is?" She laughed loudly.

Others laughed along with her, probably thinking this sketch was part of the shop's Halloween festivities.

"Doreen, don't you recognize me?" George asked.

Doreen froze. Her expression went from disbelief to horror. "No, it can't be." She shook her head in denial. "You're supposed to be dead."

Lee's face knotted in confusion. He looked at Doreen. "Who is he?"

"George Gray," Doreen said, her voice trembling.

Lee's eyes went wide as the implication hit him.

The repetition of George's name rippled through the crowd.

I cast another glance at the front door, half expecting the police to barge in at any moment, but the door remained closed. I shifted my view across the room and noticed how two guests dressed in police uniforms were standing close to Michael. Lee was eyeing them too. I could tell he wasn't certain if they were the real thing or not because he kept looking around as if he expected more uniforms to surface.

A tall, broad-shouldered figure in a black cape and cowl with pointy ears was slowly making his way to where Michael was standing. Odd that I hadn't noticed him earlier.

George's raised voice drew my attention back to him. "As you can see, Doreen, I'm very much alive. By the way, I want to thank you for the lovely roses you sent me. In fact, I have a similar present for you and Lee. You can add it to your private collection." He extended a sizeable jar containing large black flowers toward them, including the imitation seeds we'd prepared for the occasion. He put a hand on the lid.

"No. Get away from me." Doreen edged back, with Lee following suit.

George took two steps toward them. "What's the matter? They were good enough for Tiffany, weren't they?"

Doreen stepped further back, bumping into guests in the process. "You wanted her dead," she said, screeching. "You planned the whole damn thing yourself. You wanted it to look like an accident."

"You murdered my wife." George's voice boomed across the floor. "Your own sister."

An audible gasp filled the room.

"You wanted that selfish bitch dead too," Doreen said. "You got greedy, George. You changed your will days before Tiffany died. You took everything away from her to make sure I didn't get a dime after she died."

"You murderers!" George twisted the lid off the jar and hurled

283

the contents into the air. Three black flowers landed on Doreen and Lee. They shrieked in horror, their cries resonating in the high-ceilinged room.

Batman lunged forward and aimed a gun at Lee. He fired a shot and missed. He aimed at Doreen. The two guests dressed as police officers jumped on the masked gunman and struggled to disarm him.

People scattered, screaming, tripping over one another in their panic to get out of the shop.

Except for Lee. He raced toward the back door.

Michael tore after him.

Jeff raced after them.

The front door burst open. "Police! Everybody get down!" A stream of uniformed officers stormed in, their weapons drawn.

Everyone hit the ground amid terrified screams.

Bianca grabbed my arm. Terror filled her eyes as she crouched down next to me on the stairs.

More officers streamed into the shop and slipped into strategic spots, securing the perimeter.

From my vantage point, I recognized Detective Flanagan. He spoke to the two police officers who were restraining Batman in a prone position on the floor. "Get the cuffs on Batman. Read him his rights. The woman too." He gestured toward Doreen who stood crying uncontrollably, grounded to the same spot as before.

Batman stood up. He was cuffed from behind and his cowl had been removed. It was Tyler!

George stepped in front of him. "I gave you the best part of my life and you threw it away. Damn you."

Another officer approached George. "Mr. Gray, we'll need a statement from you at the station. This way, please."

"I want to call my lawyer," George said before heading out the door.

Flanagan addressed the guests. "Listen up, everybody. Before you leave, give the officers your name and how we can reach you."

Grumbles merged with sighs of relief as the guests rose to their feet.

Loud voices broke through as two more police officers hauled Lee in from the back. Blood streamed down his forehead, but even handcuffs weren't enough to subdue him. He struggled all the way out the front door, kicking at the officers and shouting more obscenities than I'd ever imagined he had in his limited vocabulary.

A new wave of gasps escaped from patrons. Guests hunkered on the floor, no doubt persuaded that it was a safer position until the police had cleared the door with their cantankerous cargo.

My eyes darted to the back of the shop.

Jeff walked in, adjusting his jacket.

I waited.

When Michael didn't resurface, I rushed down the stairs and pushed my way through the crowd toward the back, only to collide with him.

He grabbed me and prevented us from toppling over. "Who are you chasing now?" His blue eyes twinkled.

"You." I flung my arms around his neck.

CHAPTER 28

Michael and I traveled to Portland several times over the following year to testify at court trials in connection with Tiffany Gray and Tyler Wilson. Warm spring days helped to alleviate the trauma surrounding the legal proceedings, but it was only after the final verdicts were announced that we experienced a sense of closure.

We returned to Portland in August to visit Bianca and her family. No one was better suited to join our celebratory dinner than Detective Flanagan.

"Detective, you must try some of these," Bianca said. "They're made from my grandmother's recipe." She scooped up a generous portion from a platter piled with zucchinis fried in egg batter and placed it on his dish.

"More wine?" Victor filled Flanagan's glass before he could reply.

"Thank you," Flanagan said, smiling. "This is better than Thanksgiving dinner."

"It's the least we could do to celebrate the success of Portland's most notorious court cases." Bianca smiled as she passed around another platter loaded with stuffed *calamari*.

Flanagan shrugged. "We were only doing our job. My team agrees we owe the honors to one heck of an investigative journalist." He gave Michael a discerning look.

"It couldn't have happened without your help." Michael smiled and took his share of the breaded veal cutlets making the rounds.

"Your investigative articles were the first tipoff. Of course, Dr. Sayer's findings helped us connect the poison to the roses. Since George was our prime suspect at the time, we focused our efforts on the people in his network."

"Including Victor and me—unfortunately," Bianca said, laughing.

Flanagan switched his gaze to her. "We got lucky when we checked your staff. Lee had a history of theft and drug-related charges. We kept an eye on him after the fire and Henry's arrest."

"Poor Henry. To think of what he had to endure." She shook her head.

"We knew he couldn't have broken down the back door of your shop by himself," Flanagan said. "Lee, on the other hand…" He shrugged.

"Victor had advised me to do background checks on my employees," Bianca said. "I didn't listen to him. Now I know better. I've hired new staff with spotless records. With two new accounts— the Women's Sponsorship Committee and the Birchwood Country Club—the shop is busier than ever. I trust Joyce and Gail to run things and put them in charge on alternate days. Now I have more time to spend with Alex." She hugged her son in the chair beside her.

"Speaking of trust," Michael said to the detective, "why didn't the police interfere with my investigation sooner?"

Flanagan dabbed his lips with his napkin. "We surveyed your comings and goings. We knew you were onto something. We were ready to act but couldn't make a move until Dr. Sayer confirmed that the last delivery of roses to George—the one you and Megan intercepted at his office—contained the same poison that killed his wife. Then you stepped in and handed us a perfect plan to nab the suspects. I don't know how we could have had our eyes and ears inside the shop without a Halloween costume party going on."

"What stunned me was Doreen's revelation that she'd been tracking Tiffany—or Jennie—for years," I said.

"Thanks to the Internet," Flanagan said, "Doreen followed Jennie's publicized debut as a child beauty pageant winner all the way to her success as a beauty queen years ago. She lost track of her until she discovered Jennie had changed her name to Mrs. Tiffany Gray."

Bianca picked up the conversation. "No wonder Doreen stopped talking about looking for her family. Who would have thought she'd plan her own sister's murder?"

Flanagan drew a deep breath. "Murder happens more often among family members than you can imagine—especially when huge amounts of money are involved." He took a sip of wine.

"Why didn't Doreen ask her sister for financial help?" Victor asked. "That's what family is all about."

"None of you were in court that day," Flanagan said. "According to Doreen's testimony, Tiffany refused to help her. She didn't want anyone to know about her past—including George."

"How did George find out?" Bianca asked.

"He had Tyler hack into Tiffany's computer after Doreen and Lee approached him for money. He read Tiffany's email and found out Doreen was her sister. He checked out Doreen's family roots himself. He was surprised his wife hadn't told him."

"It was rumored that Tiffany was planning to leave George and had no money of her own," I said, not revealing Lori as my source. "It could explain why she didn't offer to help her sister."

Flanagan shrugged. "George did testify that Tiffany was penniless and reliant on him financially. She wanted lots more money. She told him she had proof of his affair with Tyler—photos on a flash drive—and she threatened to expose him if he didn't give her a financial way out. George mentioned the threat to Tyler. We all know what happened to Tiffany next."

"To think that Henry's search for his daughters would end this way—one dead and the other in jail," Bianca said. "Did you know that Henry visits Doreen every weekend in jail? He's such a good man."

Flanagan nodded. "He put up a brave fight when he tried to stop Lee from setting the fire in your shop. Almost spilt his head open when Lee threw him across the bathroom floor."

"Doreen gave him such a hard time at work too. Poor Henry."

"She was trying to discredit him so he'd lose his job," I said. "With Henry out of the way, Lee could make the poisonous deliveries with no questions asked."

"Speaking of Henry...any news on the old fire in Augusta?" Michael asked Flanagan.

"Yes," Flanagan said. "We reviewed Henry's file and discovered the police investigation had loose ends. For one, Henry's alibi checked out. We also learned his wife made a claim against the fire insurance company right after their home burnt down. With Henry taking the rap for it in jail, she took the money, gave up the kids, and ran."

"I think Doreen blamed Henry for setting fire to their home when she was a child," I said.

"She probably believed what her mother told her," Flanagan said. "Hatred can build up for years before it explodes into revenge."

I recalled Eleanor Dale's account of Doreen's nightmares. "Is there a chance that Henry's wife set fire to their home?"

"We'll never know for sure." Flanagan shrugged. "By the way, Doreen contacted the Dales. She asked for their help in raising her baby while she's doing time."

"She needs all the support she can get," Bianca said. "It's a second chance for the Dales too. They must be thrilled." She smiled.

"I have good news of a different sort," Victor said. "George offered Henry a job as a landscaper on his property and a sizable pension when he retires." He smiled. "There's more. Stanley sent a couple of major accounts my way. He told me he wanted to make up for the losses my business incurred due to unforeseen events associated with his son. He said he and his wife enjoyed playing along with the media and the police while George pretended to be dead." He chuckled.

"After the trial ended, George came to see me at the shop," Bianca said. "He was so relieved that Doreen's testimony had cleared him." She looked at Michael. "He told me he donated a substantial sum to the homeless shelter in Gladys's honor and to St. Andrew's Church after he'd read your investigative article last year about the link among the three victims. He hoped it would make people forget about the sex scandal that Tiffany's flash drive exposed."

I glanced at Flanagan. "Detective, did Tyler say how he got rid of the roses that killed Tiffany?"

"Based on Lori's testimony, we suspect he put them in a bag and chucked them in one of the dumpsters on construction lots in the area. Long gone." He looked at Victor. "Another thing about Tyler. After we found the stolen copy of George's will tucked behind a Batman poster in his apartment, we knew we had your burglar. He testified that George had promised to divorce Tiffany and leave a large part of his inheritance to him—which George did. But George kept talking about changing his will. Tyler knew he had to get rid of him before George had the chance to revise it. That's when he asked Doreen and Lee to deliver a box of poisoned roses to George's office." He glanced at Michael and me. "After you staged George's death, Tyler assumed he was home free—and filthy rich."

"Greed brings out the worst in some people," Michael said.

"It was all about the money for Doreen too," I said. "She thought she deserved her sister's inheritance."

Flanagan nodded. "When Tyler told her that George had removed Tiffany from his will, she and her husband set out to blackmail George. Tyler incited their hatred toward George by feeding them lies about him."

"Doreen was gullible," I said. "Tyler masterminded Tiffany's death, but he led Doreen to believe he was acting on George's behalf. No wonder the sight of George at the shop made her ill."

"Tyler saw Lee and Doreen as a threat," Michael said. "He knew they could implicate him in Tiffany's murder. He offered them a hundred grand to leave town and went to the Halloween party to pay them off. He brought a gun in case the deal went sour but panicked when he saw George and me. His Batman disguise would have been a perfect cover if he'd made it out the door."

"Almost foolproof," Flanagan said. "He'd even covered his tracks by erasing the camera footage at George's warehouse. What he didn't count on was a police presence at the Halloween party. A bad assumption on his part."

"Well, thank goodness it's all in the past now." Bianca reached for her glass. "Here's to better days ahead."

Glasses clinked in celebration.

Michael smiled as I met his gaze. In time, recent bad memories would fade into nothing more than whispers in our minds.

Acknowledgements

This book would never have come together without the generous support of others. In particular, I'd like to thank Catherine Adams for a superb editing job and Carolyn Nikolai for a captivating cover design. Special thanks to Norma DiMaulo for providing her expertise in floral arrangements and the florist profession.

To authors Susan Russo Anderson, Gail M. Baugniet, and Michael J. McCann for reading an advanced copy of this book and offering timely testimonials.

A heartfelt appreciation to my husband John for his patience and understanding while I toiled on yet another manuscript involving murder and mayhem. And of course, to friends and family who cheered me on and encouraged me to fulfill my dreams.

To booksellers and readers for showing an interest in my work and making it all worthwhile.

About the Author

Sandra Nikolai is the author of the Megan Scott/Michael Elliott Mystery series. *False Impressions* and *Fatal Whispers* are the first two books in the series.

A graduate of McGill University in Montreal, Sandra worked in sales, finance, and high tech before devoting her days to writing. She has published a dozen short stories online and in print. Sandra is currently working on the third book in the series featuring ghostwriter Megan Scott and investigative reporter Michael Elliott. She lives with her husband near Ottawa, Canada.

To keep up to date with Sandra's latest books and events, visit sandranikolai.com

You can also become a fan on Goodreads or Facebook, or follow Sandra on Twitter: @sandranikolai

Made in the USA
Charleston, SC
04 November 2013